THE REHAB

BOOK ONE
OF
APOKALYPSE

MICHEL LOGUE-PROVOST

This is a work of fiction. All the characters and events portrayed in this book are either products of the author's imagination or are used fictitiously.

APOKALYPSE

THE REHAB

Printed by CreateSpace, an Amazon.com Company
Available from Amazon.com, CreateSpace.com and other retail outlets
Available on Kindle and other devices

ISBN: 978-0-9936597-0-6

This book is for you, Lugh, once you're old enough to say the F-word and get away with it.

CONTENTS

CITY OF INNERSTADT

WESTMORELAND
PRESIDENTIAL PARK

PRESIDENTIAL
PALACE

NORDERSTEDT
EXCHANGE

WEST POINT

NUREMBERG

WAREN

NORTH
BARRIOS

BARRIOS

SOUTH
BARRIOS

MINDEN

NO MAN'S
LAND

PADERBORN

SOUTH END
INDUSTRIAL

JANSSEN & JANSSEN
PHARMACEUTICALS
(ABANDONED COMPANY
HEADQUARTERS BUILDING)

DANGER

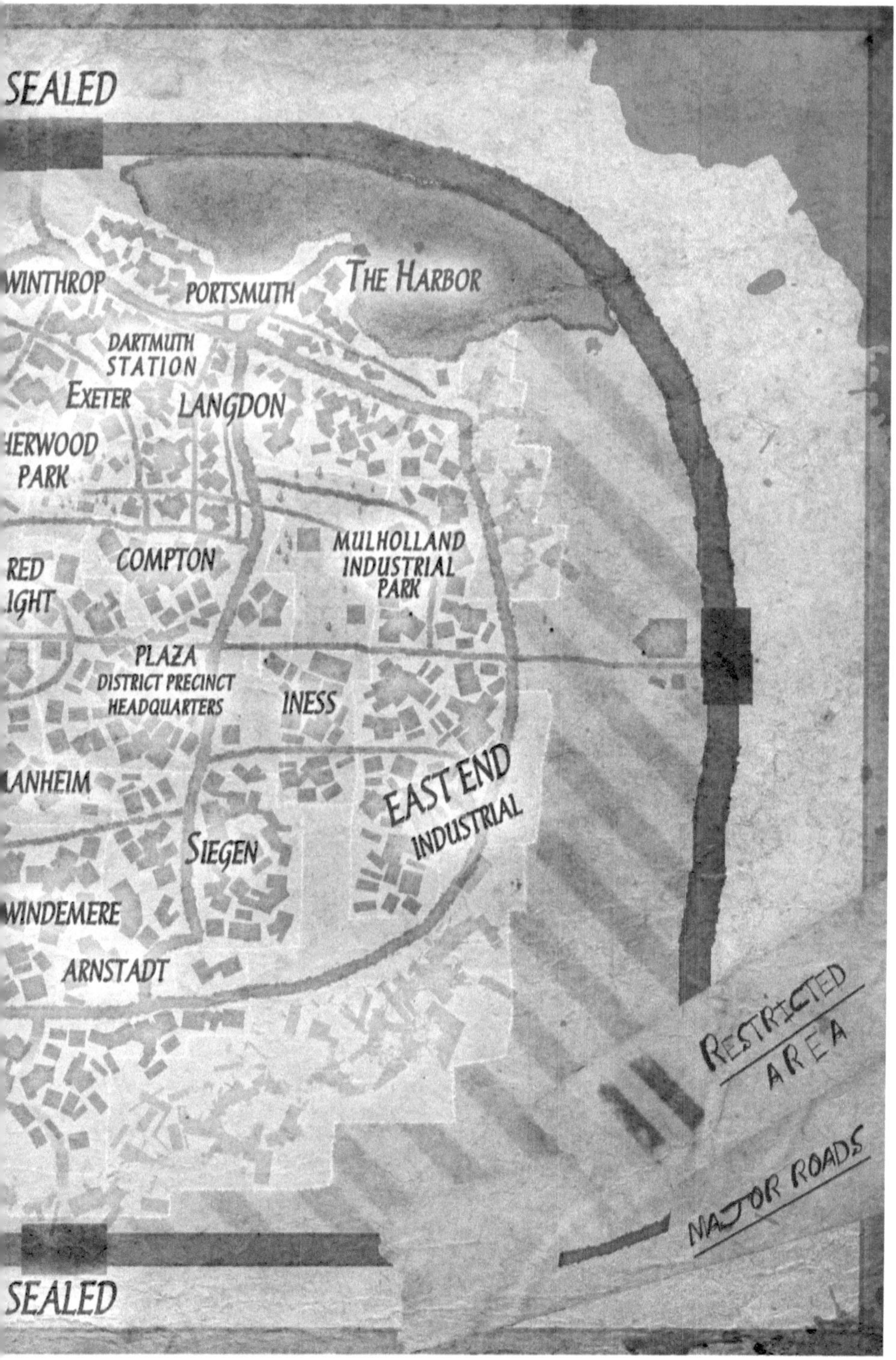

SEALED
WINTHROP
PORTSMUTH
THE HARBOR
DARTMUTH STATION
EXETER
LANGDON
HERWOOD PARK
MULHOLLAND INDUSTRIAL PARK
COMPTON
RED
IGHT
PLAZA DISTRICT PRECINCT HEADQUARTERS
INESS
ANHEIM
EAST END INDUSTRIAL
SIEGEN
WINDEMERE
ARNSTADT
RESTRICTED AREA
MAJOR ROADS
SEALED

CHAPTER
1

Danny Boy

A small boy sat propped up on one knee before his living room window, gazing blankly at the empty street three stories below. Blinking sleepily, he stifled a yawn, then rubbed at his eyes with his bunched-up hands and looked up.

High above the squalor of the streets, spanning as far as the eye could see, a dense veil of impenetrable smog loomed over the city, barring the sky and obscuring everything in its dark shadow. In the distance, the silhouettes of towering skyscrapers jutted thousands of feet into the sky, their peaks lost somewhere in the thick canopy of opaque clouds.

Sighing softly, the boy nestled his chin on his crossed arms and lowered his eyes again. He watched fixedly as thin wisps of white vapor floated up from storm drains lining the filthy street below. The curling tendrils swayed slowly and rose with the evening breeze, gradually dissipating a few feet above the old, cracked pavement.

The concerned frown that creased the child's round face contrasted oddly with his otherwise infantile features, giving him the appearance of one well beyond his years. "When's poppa getting home?" he complained, his contorted grimace shattering the brief illusion of maturity. He spun his head back toward the kitchen, where he could hear his mother preparing dinner, then glanced back out the window, blowing a wavy lock of blonde hair from his penetrating green eyes.

"He'll be here soon, Danny," his mother replied calmly, her voice barely audible over the clatter of pots and pans swooshing around in the kitchen sink. "Don't you go worrying yourself, love. I'm sure he hasn't forgotten."

Daniel sighed loudly and let his shoulders sag, obviously displeased with his mother's response.

"And stay away from that window," she added with an air of urgency. "It's dangerous out there!"

Daniel rolled his eyes exaggeratedly. *Only the rats will be out tonight,* he thought. *Or is it still day?* He never could tell, for all the sky's different shades of gray. His thoughts wandered to and fro like those of children sometimes did. *Mothers are so silly sometimes,* he mused, shaking his head. *The streets will be safe tonight with poppa out there, 'cause my poppa's the toughest poppa in all of Innerstadt. He doesn't take no nonsense from nobody! He'll get home soon. I just know he will!*

Ignoring his mother's edict, he continued watching the static scene below with renewed determination. The minutes seemed to drag on and on, but he persevered, carefully searching up and down the street for any sign of his father's arrival. Occasionally, an appetizing aroma wafted over from the kitchen and managed to distract him, if only for a moment. Barring the lone drunk that stumbled haphazardly across the way like a teetering marionette, the streets were all but dead.

Vigilance eventually gave way to doubt, and he wondered if his father would show up at all. His wavering faith rekindled as a beam of light flashed out from a side street at the end of the block. *Maybe that's him,* he speculated hopefully. He blinked and peered more intently as the light shone brighter, dully illuminating the gloomy street. It was growing stronger, closer. His heart began to race. Any moment now, his father would come zipping around that corner on his rusty old hoverbike. He just knew he would.

The urge to cheer that he felt building up inside was quelled the moment the light's true source—an imposing Mech Unit—slowly marched out into the street. It was so big and heavy that he could hear its footsteps, or at least he thought he could, now that he was listening for them. The top half of its rusty body pivoted roughly in his direction, routinely flashing its spotlights back and forth across the street. A few seconds later, it turned away and clanked off, continuing its patrol in another direction.

"Stupid, *dumb-head* robot," Daniel sputtered, furrowing his brow into angry-looking squiggles.

"Get away from that window, Danny," his mother called out, appearing out of nowhere to scoop him up in her arms. She carried him off so quickly that he didn't even have time to voice an objection. She set him down a few feet farther and strode back to the window, then paused momentarily to glare down at the Mech Unit. Her fists were clenched and pressed firmly to her hips. "I've already told you," she grated, then reached up and closed the curtains in one swift motion, "it's dangerous out there." She swiveled on her heels then and added, "Don't make me tell you again, mister," before striding back toward the kitchen and leaving a sulky little boy in her wake.

A loud and unexpected rapping at the front door drew their attention. "Oh Danny," his mother called out. "I think someone's here to see you!"

The excited child was there before she'd finished speaking. "It's him! It's him!" he squeaked, springing for the door.

A muffled voice came through from the other side. "Special delivery! Special delivery for a certain Danny MacBride. Mister MacBride? Hello? Maybe I've got the wrong address. I guess I'll just turn around and—"

Daniel yanked the door open and charged into his father's legs, nearly knocking the wind out of him. "Poppa!" he cried out with joy, hugging his legs fiercely. "Where have you been? You took *forever*! We thought you might never ever come back! We were waiting, and waiting, and waiting, but you—"

His father hoisted him up with one arm and ruffled his hair, putting a stop to his breathless jabbering. "Come now," the sturdy man said with a chuckle. "Settle down, Danny boy. Don't forget to breathe." He carried Daniel inside and wrapped his free arm around his wife. "I missed you, Elizabeth," he crooned, following up with an eager peck on her lips. It was a kiss that she gladly returned, though with a little less of his rugged ardor.

"Oh did you, now?" Elizabeth asked with mock skepticism.

"Terribly so. A man can only face so many cold and lonely nights before despair finally starts to set in."

"You were hardly gone a fortnight, you big ox!" Elizabeth exclaimed, sounding nonetheless delighted. "Honestly, Harrold, sometimes I wonder what you'd do without us." A giggle escaped her then, and she whispered back that she'd missed him too before pushing away, spots of crimson starting to bloom in her cheeks.

"Hardly a fortnight?" Harrold asked, feigning confusion. "I was sure I'd been away much longer. Six months? A year? Why, our little man here's grown at least an inch, if not two." He winked at Daniel, who cackled wildly like only a five-year-old or a complete madman could. "What smells so good?" he asked, his attention slipping momentarily. "You didn't make my favorite, did you?" He smiled wickedly then, and breathed in through his nose, clearly savoring the aroma permeating the kitchen.

Daniel nodded up at him vigorously. "Yup! It's marshed potatoes, pops." He tilted his head back exaggeratedly then, and breathed in deeply, in obvious imitation of his father. "Mmm. They're my favorite, too!"

Harrold's grin widened as he walked over to the kitchen table and set Daniel down on a sturdy wooden stool. "I'll wager they are, my boy. I'll wager they are. Yours and anyone who's tried them. But they have to come with a gravy volcano, am I right?"

Before long, they were seated around the table, discussing the events of the past weeks over steaming plates of potatoes and fried khesh. Daniel didn't like most fish, but khesh was an exception. It tasted salty all on its own, and salt was something they couldn't normally afford. According to his mother, not much was new at home, except for the tooth he'd lost a few nights back and the news that Madge Johnson and Berrett Every had lost their jobs at the packing plant. His father's brow had creased when he'd heard that, but it hadn't stopped him from shoveling more food into his mouth. *He eats like an alley wolf,* he thought with some amusement as he watched him clean his plate.

"Well that's a crying shame," Harrold finally said, getting up from the table to go fetch himself seconds. "Next time you see them... make sure they know we'll help them out however we can, yes? It just isn't right."

His mother merely nodded at that and answered, "Of course, dear. I already have."

When Harrold got back to his seat, he launched right into a detailed account of his latest adventures, and Daniel listened avidly to every word. According to his father, he and his crew had set out from Fort Mac two weeks ago to the day. It had been a resource gathering expedition just like any other, at first, but he'd gotten himself separated from the group for a time, and had seen some interesting things as he tried to find them again.

Daniel couldn't understand half of what he was going on about, and some of it sounded like fairy tales, but it didn't matter. He listened and watched with complete and utter adulation. *Everyone knows that the wastelands are dead,* he thought. *Everybody says so. Even on the news they say it all the time.* He thought it unlikely that his father had seen jackals, and even less likely that he'd seen actual *people* out there. *Walking around the desert without respirators or hazard suits; yeah right!* His father was no liar, though, and he wasn't about to interrupt him or question anything he said. Sometimes he lied when he told a joke, but this wasn't a joke, and he knew it. *My dad is a superhero,* he concluded, *like Gorlok the Barbarian or The Forlorn Kid.*

Harrold grunted laboriously and wiped a few crumbs of synthetic cheese from the corner of his mouth. "Well that was absolutely delicious, Liz. Thank you." He patted his full belly at that and grinned widely.

"I suppose you'll be going back for thirds, then?" Elizabeth stated more than asked. It wasn't really a question. Daniel could recognize teasing when he heard it.

"No, no, no!" Harrold protested, shaking his head from side to side as he pushed his empty plate away. "You want me to keel over, woman? Dinner was lovely. The food was great. But if I eat another bite, I'll explode all over the kitchen, and then you'll have a real mess to clean up."

Elizabeth laughed and pushed out from the table. "No dessert for you, then. I'm not cleaning anything else tonight. I'm pretty sure *you*'ll want some, though. Am I right, Danny?"

Daniel stopped chewing and looked up from his plate, bright eyed and apprehensive. "Dessert?" he asked after swallowing his food with an audible gulp.

"It's cherry pie," Elizabeth said, giving him more information than he'd asked for. "And it's made with *real* cherries. You'll have to get up and get it yourself if you want some, though. Go on."

Daniel gulped down a last mouthful of potatoes and hopped up from his stool. "Oh boy, cherry pie!" he exclaimed, bolting for the refrigerator. From the corner of his eye, he spied his mother nodding in his direction while staring at his father. *They think they're so sneaky,* he thought, *but I'm no fool!* He didn't know what was going on, but he knew that *something* was up.

Harrold winked at Elizabeth understandingly and waited for Daniel to come scrambling back to the table. When he was settled in with his new plate, he looked him over suspiciously. "Say... it wouldn't happen to be a certain young man's birthday today, would it?" He grinned wickedly then, turning aside to pull a small parcel from the worn leather jacket hanging from the back of his chair. "I wager you thought I'd forgotten. Am I right? Well, not only did I not forget," he added in a teasing manner, "but I also brought you a little something. Something from *out there*—from the wastelands. Picked it up on my last trip."

Daniel gaped openly at the package, his eyes wide with amazement. He could hardly contain himself. "What is it?" he asked, bubbling over with excitement.

Harrold tossed him the package, and chuckled heartily as Daniel set upon it, immediately starting to shred through its many layers of bound packing paper.

When he'd clawed his way to the center, Daniel stared at the black tome that lay within for what seemed like an eternity. The faded and cracked letters gilded across the front in gold leaf read "The Holy Bible", though he didn't understand what that meant. Beneath that, slightly smaller, were the words "Testaments New & Old". He wasn't sure what to make of it as it was written in strange characters, half of which he didn't even recognize. "What is it, Father?" he asked again, his voice no more than a whisper.

Harrold pushed up his sleeves and shrugged. "To be honest, I'm not quite sure, Danny boy. I do know that it's old, though. An Old World treasure, I guess you could say."

"How can you tell, pops?" Daniel asked, not entirely sold on the idea. The book didn't look *that* old, and treasure was usually much shinier, at least in the movies, it was. The letters on the front of it looked like gold, but that didn't really count, did it?

"You see those symbols, there?" Harrold asked, pointing to the lettering on the book's cover. He waited for Daniel to nod and then continued. "These symbols," he stated, tracing an imaginary line across the words with his finger, "these *letters*... they look like they might belong to one of the dead languages. Could be German or American, but I'm not really sure."

Daniel's eyes lit up at that, and his interest fueled Harrold's elaboration. "It could be from that language family, or for all we know, it could be the family's protolanguage—the one they all came from. Considering nothing's been written in either of those scripts for centuries, I'd wager this is pretty ancient, too. If you can learn to decipher the codes in this book, then maybe you can find out what it is. I'll even give you a hand with that, see if we can figure it out together."

"Ooh," Daniel cooed, mesmerized and at a loss for concrete words. "I like puzzles," he eventually added, snapping out of it. His father was good at them too, and he had a knack for bizarro languages. He was mainly just excited by the prospect of spending more time with him. "Where'd you find it?"

Harrold leaned forward then and looked around as though to ensure that no one was eavesdropping. "I found this when I was separated from the rest of the group, 'neath the rubble of an Old World building made all of stone. It was in a rusty box that broke pretty much to pieces when I pried it open. The quartermaster back at the camp told me that he'd seen one just like it, many years ago. He'd heard stories about the books, too. According to some," he whispered, leaning even closer, "they hold mysterious powers, and the Old Worlders used to worship them like... well... like some of the founder sects used to do in the under-city, with their sacred baubles and trinkets.

"He even claimed that the book was as old as what he called the 'Noachian times', but if you ask me, that part was probably just a load of malarkey. It looks like a reprint of some kind. Of something else that might have been common a very, very long time ago. It's quite rare now, though. Of that I'm sure." He paused for a few seconds then and donned a more serious air before continuing. "I'm entrusting this artifact to you, my son, in the hopes that you may someday unlock its secrets."

Daniel traced the tip of his tiny finger along the worn lettering, then down and across the unfamiliar cross. His gaping mouth was hanging wide open. He blinked out of his awed daze to find his parents smiling at him with warmth and adoration. At that precise moment in time, in that brief sliver of eternity, he felt like the luckiest little boy in the entire city.

But then the spasms started. He hated the spasms. He never knew when they were going to start, and once they had, there was nothing he could do to stop them. He jerked around in his chair and clutched at his head as a sharp pain rippled through his body and up his spine. When the wave reached his skull, everything flashed white. It felt like a thousand needles were stabbing into his brain at the same time. His eyes rolled into the top of his head and he started to foam at the mouth, but the pain soon receded, along with his body's uncontrollable shaking.

For a brief moment, he felt as though he'd left his body. He could see everything in the room. His mother was cradling him in her arms. His father had his hands on the table and was leaning in close. He could even see himself, just sitting there, motionless and with a blank expression in his eyes. The moment fled and the room darkened, and when he came to, he was both himself and his father. He saw what his father saw, with his father's eyes. He was both looking down at himself, and staring across the table at nothing. The dual perception hurt his head, wherever it really was. For a second, he had two minds, two sets of thoughts, two versions of worry and confusion. But then his consciousness ceased, leaving only his father's behind.

"Damnit," Harrold mouthed, pushing a damp lock of his son's hair from his eyes. The boy was burning up and covered in sweat. He felt useless every time this happened. He never knew what to do. At least the worst of it was over. Or so it seemed. *The pain has passed,* he thought. *Now he'll just sit there in that vegetative trance. But for how long? A few seconds? A few minutes? An hour?* They'd had him checked out at the clinic several times, but even the doctors were stumped. They'd told them to try epilepsy meds, but those only made things worse, so they'd stopped using them.

He averted his eyes abruptly as his hearing amplifiers picked up an odd sound coming from the halls outside. The noise soon grew to a roar. It sounded like an earthquake was tearing its way through the lower floors of the building. The closer the source of the commotion got, the more it sounded like clanking—lots and lots of clanking—and an unpleasantly familiar electrical whir. It only took him a moment to realize what was going on. "Abelardus fucking Brine," he shouted, bolting up from his chair. "This is *not* the time. Liz, you need to get the boy out of here!" His sudden outburst earned him a gaping look of bewilderment from his wife. "Get him out of here *now!*" he reiterated, giving her a stern look. "Now, Liz. Now! Do it!"

"Harrold!" Elizabeth harrumphed, clearly shaken. "What's gotten into you? I've never seen you like this before. What's going on? You tell me right now."

"Don't question me, Elizabeth!" Harrold barked. "I don't have time to explain. Just take the boy and go down the fire escape. Right fucking now!"

Elizabeth shook her finger at him, trembling. "This isn't funny, Harr! Not one bit!" The stern look he gave her then made her swallow her next words with a gulp. Reluctantly, she plucked the unconscious boy from his seat, and rushed toward the living room, confused and afraid.

Wasting no time, Harrold reached beneath the kitchen table and drew his Electrode Disperser from the holster that was fastened there. The smooth-curved weapon looked like a tactical shotgun, with some major differences. Instead of a loading port, it had a circular, numbered dial, and three rods tipped with metallic spheres protruded from its muzzle. The weapon was generally nonlethal to humans, but its discharge had a devastating effect on anything electronic. He turned the dial once around and the Electrode Disperser hummed to life. Wasting no time, he pivoted and dove to the side—split seconds before a hulking Mech Unit came crashing through the front door.

The heavily-armored machine ripped through a good part of the door's frame in the process, showering the room with wooden splinters and plaster debris. In its continued motion forward, it crushed the chair that Harrold had been sitting in only moments earlier. In a clumsy effort to lunge at him, it somehow managed to trip on its own feet. Thrown off-balance, the Mech Unit had nowhere else to go but down, and it completely pulverized the kitchen table when it fell on it.

Harrold was lying so close to it that he could easily make out the inscriptions on its dull blue chest plate. The white lettering read LEA MUUI A2-I6, or "Law Enforcement Agency Mech Unit Urban Infiltrator Alpha 2-16", for those that were well versed in police issue arms and combat machinery. Just below that was another inscription in a much smaller print.

If found inactive, please contact the LEA immediately or return this unit to Precinct 14. Thank you for your collaboration, citizen, and have a nice day.

Though far smaller, and less heavily-armored than the Street Sentinels that patrolled the city's dark underbelly, the Infiltrator remained a force to be reckoned with. While its movements were sometimes awkward in extremely tight spaces, its mobility by far exceeded that of its counterparts.

The Infiltrator's visual sensors blinked red, drawing him back to the urgency of the situation. "Run!" he yelled, rolling over onto his stomach. He rose to one knee as quickly as he could, aimed his gun at the fallen Infiltrator, and pulled the trigger.

To the naked eye, there was no immediate effect. In reality, thousands of microscopic conductors shot down the Electrode Disperser's barrel, and were channeled into a concentrated stream by the condenser rods. When the electrodes reached their target a fraction of a second later, the gun's muzzle sparked with a brilliant flash. A powerful current arced through the stream and short-circuited the LEA robot on contact. All that was left of it was a smoking heap of scrap metal that trembled as it tried to rise and failed miserably.

The same fate befell the next Infiltrator that entered the room. It fell back through the damaged doorway, wriggling and throwing off sparks on its way down. It hit the floor with a loud crash that kicked up dust and plaster.

Off to the side, he could see Elizabeth struggling desperately with the old, jammed window that gave onto the fire escape. She was trying to pry it open with her bare hands, but couldn't manage. She grunted in despair as she tugged and pushed at it, fighting back her tears and failing miserably. They trickled down her cheeks in rivulets, and a violent sob escaped her despite a visible effort to hold it in.

A wild scream ripped through her body the second the Mech Units in the hallway opened fire. Her high-pitched shriek was drowned out completely by the deafening roar of their fully automatic weapons. They spewed out salvo after salvo of hot lead that shattered glass and punched holes right through the outer walls of the apartment building.

Harrold dove and rolled to the corner of the kitchen least visible from the doorway. Crouching to avoid the hailstorm of bullets zipping by overhead, he glanced over at Elizabeth in the living room and cursed under his breath. "Move out of the way, Liz!" he yelled out. He tossed down his Electrode Disperser and drew two plasma pistols from the holsters strapped to his ankles. Quickly taking aim, he fired at the window with both guns. The glass pane shattered instantly and fell to pieces all over the floor. "Go!" he yelled, returning his attention to the gaping doorway.

It wasn't much of a doorway anymore, he noted. With the chunks of wall that had been torn out by the charging Infiltrators, and a nearly constant stream of gunfire, it looked more like the hole a wrecking ball might leave behind. He could see two more of those Infiltrators standing behind that hole, or *thought* that he could see two of them. There were probably more. The muzzle flashes from all their firing were almost perpetual, and made it hard to see, but it gave him a good idea about just how many there were. *It's a wonder we're still alive*, he thought, grimacing sourly as he discharged both of his pistols at the doorway. He fired both guns as quickly as he could, over and over again. No time was wasted with precision.

Some of the muzzle flashing died out as another Infiltrator crumpled to the floor. By Harrold's reckoning, it had taken four or five bursts to bring the thing to its knees. His plasma pistols were far less effective than the Electrode Disperser had been. Instead of disabling the robots at once, the searing heat they discharged punched deep gouges into their thick exterior casings. The intensity of the pistol's beam was just high enough to melt through some parts of their metal hulls and start electrical fires. He glanced over his shoulder at the electrode disperser, and was dismayed to find that it was broken. It had been hit by stray bullets.

The downed Infiltrator's right hand was engulfed in flames, the better part of its legs blown clear away or melting. Small fires broke out as it tried to use the wall to struggle to its inexistent feet. It was already wobbling when another Infiltrator shoved past it, knocking it to the floor. "Just... go... down!" Harrold bellowed, still firing away. His pistols were overheating and starting to burn at the palms of his hands. The pain was enough to make him grit his teeth, but he kept on, never relenting.

He took one last look at Elizabeth and his son. *My hearts,* he thought. Elizabeth was busy pulling away some of the larger shards of glass from the window frame, with Daniel cradled firmly to her bosom. *Please... please let them get away*. Then, when it felt like his fingers were starting to fuse to the pistols, he let out a vociferous roar and rose, guns blazing.

Tears welled in his eyes as he started a slow walk toward the gaping hole in the wall. As much as he hated it, he knew how this would end. He didn't know how they'd found him here—how they'd found his home, where he was most vulnerable—but it didn't matter. The only thing that mattered now was making sure that his family got away. He had to buy them some more time.

Another Infiltrator went down with a clank and a groan, but another took its place almost immediately. Smoky fumes were starting to rise from the palms of his hands. He let out another blaring war cry as he fired back at the muzzle flashes. One bullet ripped through his shin and stopped him dead in his tracks, and then another grazed his shoulder, but he refused to go down. He took another painful step forward, his battle cry turning to a scream of agony. "Elizabeth, run!" he howled, and then his consciousness ceased as his life escaped him.

Daniel came to with a gasp and his body started to convulse again almost immediately. His shaking was so violent that his mother nearly dropped him, but she caught him and pulled him close before he could fall. His memory of the past few minutes was fuzzy at best, and concentrating was nigh on impossible. He had no control over his body, and his ears were ringing from the constant din of machine gun fire. An intense pain gouged at his skull again and he cried out in anguish. When his mind left his body, he saw that everything in the apartment was broken or on fire. And then he was both his mother and himself. He was sharing her head, but retained his own. It was confusing, but at least the pain had subsided.

Gathering every last ounce of willpower that she had left, Elizabeth hoisted him up through the broken window and onto the fire escape. Without hesitating, she pulled herself up and started to squeeze through after him, ignoring the tiny shards of glass cutting into the palms of her hands and bared knees. "Go on, Danny!" she urged him, straining to be heard over the sound of gunfire. "Hurry up and go!"

Daniel stood before her and gave her a defiant look—as defiant a look as he could muster in his terrified state. His legs trembled as he clenched his fists, rivulets of tears streaming down his face. "No!" he screamed. "Not without daddy!" He was so choked up by the situation that the few words he did manage to say were nearly incomprehensible. "Not without poppa!"

When Elizabeth glanced over her shoulder into their half-destroyed home, she felt a cold, hard lump rise in her throat. The Infiltrators were still giving their apartment a solid thrashing, but no one was returning fire. Not a dozen feet from where she sat hunched over the window sill, Harrold lie broken, sprawled out on the floor in a pool of his own blood. His plasma pistols were smoking, but still clenched firmly in his hands. *He's gone,* she thought, stricken with disbelief. There was no denying it, though. He was barely recognizable. The occasional bullet made his body jerk around as the Infiltrators continued firing at him.

Her husband, her lover, the man she'd spent the past fourteen years of her life with was dead. Her life partner was gone. The father of her son was gone. *Father of my sons,* she reminded herself. Their oldest had been buried what seemed a very long time ago, but she would not lose another. She would not let them take him, too. Suppressing a sudden urge to retch, she stumbled out onto the fire escape, nearly collapsing in the process. She gathered herself, then took Daniel by the arm, and tugged him along with her, guiding him as they ran down the rickety, wrought iron stairs.

A flight and a half down, she looked up and over her shoulder, toward their apartment. Just looking back made her feel like she was tempting fate. The second she was about to look away, a balding man with shades popped his head out through the window. In the blink of an eye, he'd crawled halfway out and was aiming a pistol down at them.

As they wound their way down the steps, the man quickly zeroed in on them, and started firing off round after thunder-clapping round. The rain of .50 caliber bullets punched holes through the stairs around them in ringing twangs. It fueled their fear and hastened their descent.

Before long, the resounding cracks of gunfire gave way to a succession of clicking noises. The man had emptied his magazine. Cursing, he retracted inside the building and could be heard issuing brief orders barely audible from the street. The only clear and discernible thing that she could make out was an enraged, "Go! Go! Go!"

She pulled Daniel up into her arms the second they reached the bottom. Holding him tightly, she swiveled around and looked down both ends of the alley, trying to decide which way to go. To their right, the street was only a stone's throw away. It was close enough that she could read the burned-out neon sign above Tattaglia's Rib Shack, across the way.

To her left, the alley stretched out about three hundred feet into almost complete darkness. She knew what was back there, just beyond their line of sight. That way they'd find nothing but abandoned parking lots, derelict buildings and all-around shady business. *Our best option is to run into one of the buildings across the street, and hopefully lose them in a crowd somewhere*, she thought. The sound of fast-approaching sirens, and the red and blue flashes reflecting off of Tattaglia's storefront window made her change her mind rather quickly.

"Hold on tight, love," she whispered into Daniel's ear. She turned toward the far end of the alley and took off at a quick jog. Before long, the lighting got so bad that she could hardly see three steps in front of herself. Occasionally, she had to slow down to skirt around large piles of long-forgotten junk, or clamber over old concrete blocks that had fallen sometime over the years.

They'd gotten about halfway to the back of the building when the alley lit up like the sun itself. Still running, she glanced over her shoulder and saw exactly what she feared she might. Through the near-blinding glare, she managed to make out the shapes of two men standing behind a large spotlight that was pointed in their direction. Beside them was the silhouette of a hulking Street Sentinel that stood poised and ready to fire. It was about eight or nine feet tall, by her reckoning, and the turrets mounted on its shoulders were the size of garbage cans.

With adrenaline pumping through her veins like nitrous oxide, Elizabeth sprinted forward. She'd never run so quickly in her entire life. She could hear a faint thrum of machinery starting up somewhere behind them, and moments later, it was joined by a cacophony of whirring and drilling noises.

Small chunks of brick exploded from the walls. Windows shattered and sent down showers of broken glass. Sparks flew up and off the concrete all around them. Whistling noises seemed to come at them from everywhere, and were accompanied by bolder zips and whishes. That was the sound of unequivocal destructive power, of two miniguns being fired in tandem at five thousand rounds per minute.

Realizing how slim their chances of surviving would be if she just kept running in a straight line, Elizabeth veered hard to the left and crouched behind a large steel dumpster. Panting, she took a moment to catch her breath. Her heart was racing. She could feel it pulsing in her wrists and forearms.

Suddenly, her thoughts turned to Daniel. "Danny!" she shouted. She had to yell at the top of her lungs just to hear herself over the din of the turrets. The Street Sentinel was still hard at work pounding the alley. "Danny!" she yelled again, louder, but he remained unresponsive.

Fear gripping her by the throat, she held him out in front of herself to look him over. Aside from a couple nicks and scratches, he looked like he was fine. There were no bullet holes. There was no profusion of blood. Tears glistened on his cheeks and his eyes were bloodshot, like he'd been crying for a while, but he wasn't uttering a peep. It was like he was somewhere else, like he wasn't even there at all.

She shook him lightly and he blinked. Their eyes met and they held each other's gaze for a moment, and she knew for certain that he was back.

"When's the noise going to stop, momma?" he pleaded, fresh tears starting to form in his eyes.

She hugged him close and spoke directly into his ear. "I don't know, honey. Soon, I hope."

The second she said that, a large section of brick slid off of the wall on the other side of the alley, and toppled down to the pavement with a crash. It smashed into a mess of broken brick and old, crumbled mortar. A large chunk of it flew wild and narrowly missed her head.

Cringing, she turned her back to shield Daniel from any other fragments of masonry that might come their way. The sudden move made her realize just how much her arms hurt. Her muscles throbbed, and a lancing pain was shooting back and forth between her armpits and her elbows.

Am I hit? she wondered. A burning sensation started to flare up in both of her arms. No, she hadn't been hit, she knew, but the surge of adrenaline had worn off. Her muscles were so tense that the veins jutting out of her forearms looked like they were about to pop. Daniel wasn't exactly huge for his age, but he was still a big and heavy boy. Carrying him around for more than a minute or two at a time was an arduous task under normal, everyday circumstances. This was nearly torture. She had no idea how long she'd been carrying him for, but she couldn't do it any longer. Not if she wanted them to get away. Not if she wanted them to remain alive and unscathed. And she did, more than anything.

She set him down on his feet and cupped his face with both of her hands. She didn't like the idea at all, but she knew that they'd make better time if they both ran. "Can you run really, really fast, Daniel?" she yelled, straining to be heard. "Momma needs you to run as fast as you possibly can."

More sections of brick were sliding off of the walls on both sides of the alley, and a loud clatter inside the dumpster told her that they'd just had a very close call. After what seemed like an eternity, Daniel finally nodded.

"Good," Elizabeth shouted. "You're going to have to run down to the other end of the alley. Over there." She pointed in that direction and made sure he'd understood before continuing. All of the fallen bricks had kicked up a dense cloud of dust and crushed mortar, and it was hard to see. "Stay close to the wall. Keep low, like momma, and watch where you put your feet."

Daniel nodded again. "Okay, momma. I will."

He hadn't yelled, but Elizabeth had heard his tiny voice almost perfectly. Her ears were ringing from the constant chaos of the miniguns, but she could actually hear him now. The drilling had stopped. There was still a faint hum in the air, but the loud drilling had stopped. *They stopped firing*, she thought. Two loud clicking noises echoed down the alleyway and the drilling started up again with a vengeance. "Guess not," she groaned. There was a succession of clunks and clanks as bullets punched through the dumpster, leaving large holes where the spotlight shone through in beams. She'd felt almost safe hiding behind the dumpster's thick plating, but that false sense of security was gone now.

"It's now or maybe never," Elizabeth told herself. "Go, Danny! Go now!" She had to yell again just to be heard. "Momma's right behind you! Run!"

Daniel darted off like a gutter rodent flaring danger. Scurrying between some obstacles and hopping over others, he made it all look rather easy.

Elizabeth was hard-pressed just to keep up with him. Bullets whizzed by all around them. Shattered glass and chunks of brick rained down on the pavement, which was already heavily littered with debris. Sparks danced and kicked up all around them like so many sparklers at a Founder's Day parade.

Short of breath, low on hope, it took everything Elizabeth had to keep putting one foot in front of the other. When Daniel rounded the corner up ahead and disappeared from sight, it gave her the courage that she needed to make one final sprint. *I have to make it*, she thought. *Just a little bit farther. I have to make it, for Danny. I can't leave him all on his own, all alone to fend for himself. Not now, not like this. He's too young, too innocent, too unprepared for the harsh realities of this cruel world. We've always been there for him. He'd never make it on his own.*

Those thoughts kept her going while she dashed toward the finish line. At the end of her wind, she finally closed the gap and rounded the corner of the building. She'd made it, but there would be no moment of relief for her, no time to rejoice. She was so tired and had gained so much momentum that she wasn't even able to stop herself when she bumped into Daniel, who was standing frozen right in front of her.

He didn't even flinch when she plowed into him from behind. In a perfect marriage of awkward movement and motherly instinct, she picked him up on the fly and set him down a few feet farther, then finally managed to stumble to a halt.

Clinging to him still, as much to steady her own feet as to keep from dragging him to the ground, she looked up and froze as she saw it—the reason Daniel had stopped dead in his tracks. A towering metal beast two times taller than any man she'd ever met was standing less than a stone's throw ahead of them. She knew that it had to be some kind of Mech Unit, but she'd never seen one like it before. The oversized rifle in its oversized hands was aimed directly at her stomach, at Daniel.

Without thinking twice, she shoved her son to the pavement, sparing him from the molten beam of energy that burst from the Mech Unit's rifle and sliced through her midsection like a hot knife through butter. Exhaling, she looked at her son one last time—with love, with desperation, with fear—and then her eyes rolled skyward, and she fell lifelessly to the ground.

As her life fled from her body, that part of Daniel that had shared her mind returned to him. For the first time in a while, he had all of his wits about him. But now he was all alone.

A tension had been building up inside of him. As they ran for their lives, that tension had soured and burned like acid in the pit of his stomach. It was like a giant abscess swelling with fear and anger. He'd repressed it as best he could, but when she went down, that abscess burst. His restraint gave way like a rickety old sluice battered open by an angry storm.

With tears streaming down his face, furious and terrified, Daniel pushed himself to his feet and leapt at the Mech Unit, screaming, "Momma!" at the top of his lungs. The situation was reminiscent of a movie he'd once seen a very long time ago, when he was only four years old. In the final scene, he recalled, two armies had stampeded toward each other across a dry and barren landscape. With their swords held high and waving wildly above their heads, the members of the much smaller force bellowed out defiantly as they closed in and clashed with the army of evil. In the end, the good guys had overcome nearly impossible odds, and won the day.

Images of triumph flashed in his mind as he made a valiant charge of his own, but that didn't help him, and no amount of courage would. All it resulted in was him slamming into a thick wall of steel. He stumbled back as soon as he crashed into the Mech Unit's legs. The colossal hunk of metal was unfazed, but a throbbing pain now pulsed through his arm and shoulder. It took him a couple seconds to steady himself, and he came dangerously close to keeling over like a drunken hobo in the process.

Raising his balled fists, he cried out again and stepped up for another go, flailing his arms around wildly as he advanced. In his mind, trumpets blared as the cavalry charged. This time, he stopped short of the giant and raised his hands to hit it, instead. With sweat and tears burning at his eyes, he could hardly see where he was aiming, but that didn't stop his relentless flurry of ineffective punches. He was standing so close to it that he could hardly miss it if he tried. Every punch produced a tinny, clunking noise, and left the nonresponsive machine unscathed. There wasn't so much as a scratch or a dent in it, but red smudges started to appear wherever he'd hit it. It never occurred to him that the red smudges were his own blood. His fists hurt, but that only made him flail harder.

"Stupid meanie!" he yelled, pounding away at it. When the pain in his bruised and split knuckles was too much to endure, when his arms were so tired that they seized up and refused to move altogether, he dropped to his knees and started bawling uncontrollably, sputtering out the occasional, "Momma."

Until then, the Mech Unit had remained silent, but it finally turned toward him, and spoke in a raspy, modulated voice that sounded to him like a message one might receive on a two-way radio. "Secondary target eliminated," it said, as though reporting back to someone that wasn't there. Its voice sounded strangely human beneath the static, broadcast-like crackle. "Apprehending tertiary target now. Over."

Daniel hobbled over to his mother's side and slumped down in the crook of her arm. He used the back of his sleeve to wipe at the tears and sweat still stinging his eyes. Loud clanking noises made him look up, just in time to see the Mech Unit's massive hand swooping down on him.

Frank William Fasaro thrashed around in that hazy place somewhere between sleeping and awake. He tried to open his eyes, but they wouldn't budge. He struggled to get up, but his limbs wouldn't move. And then he was dreaming again, and no longer himself. Now he was Daniel MacBride, a terrified boy of five, and he'd just watched helplessly as a towering hunk of scrap metal had killed his mother.

He'd never seen a Mech Unit that huge before, or anything even half as frightening, but now everything was dark, and he couldn't see at all. When his mother had crumpled to the ground before him, he'd taken a run at the thing, kicking and screaming with tears streaming down his face, but then something had hit him. Something had hit him hard, and everything had gone black as night. He was still kicking and screaming and the salt of his tears was still burning his eyes, but everything was dark, so dark. He could hear the voice of a woman calling out through that darkness. It was distant, at first, but it grew closer. "Frank," the voice called out, and suddenly he found it familiar. He couldn't put a name to it, but he knew that he'd heard it before.

It didn't matter anyway. His mother was dead. *That stupid robot killed her!* A violent sob racked his chest and he wanted to scream, but couldn't. Something was pressing hard against his lungs. He was just a little boy, he knew, but he *would* kill it. He'd kill it 'til it was good and dead. If only he could *see* it, he would. It had killed his mother, and those other dumbots had killed his father, too. He felt a spasm of emotion wash over him again, and this time he howled out a tortured, "No!"

"Wake up," Vanessa pleaded, shaking his shoulder. "Franky. Wake up!" She shook his shoulder again, harder.

Frank gasped sharply and sat up as he came to. His ears were ringing and everything was a blur. Panting, he glanced around the room, his eyes darting left and right. When he was satisfied there was no imminent danger, he sighed once, released his death grip on the bedsheet and sagged back onto his pillow.

The olive-toned woman lying next to him leaned over him watchfully then and laid her fingers down carefully on the side of his face. Her touch was cool, soothing. "Shhh..." she whispered, stroking gently along his temple and the line of his hair. "You were dreaming again. It's over now."

It is over, he allowed. Relief started to wash away all of the fear and anger that he'd felt gripping him only moments earlier. He was relieved to see Vanessa, relieved that all of it had been nothing more than a bad, albeit realistic dream. He'd been having the same one almost every night now for the past few months.

No matter how many times he told himself it wasn't real, it never stopped *feeling* real. It was crazy and he knew it, but that didn't change a thing. *I'm Frank William Fasaro*, he thought. *Not this "Danny" kid.* For some reason, he reminded himself of that every time he woke from the dream. He'd grown up in a good, relatively safe neighborhood. Not the slums, like in the dream. His parents wouldn't have had it any other way.

Vanessa continued caressing the side of his face with the back of her hand. She really did have a gentle touch. If she kept it up, she might just put him back to sleep. "The agency is working you too hard, honey," she said softly, her voice tinged with concern. "They're wearing you out. If you're not coming home all bruised and beat up, then we can at least count on you being exhausted. And then you can't even get a good night's rest, with all these weird dreams you've been having."

Frank didn't know how to respond to that, so he didn't. He was tired, and groggy, and didn't like what he was hearing. It sounded an awful lot like a conversation they'd had before, and it wasn't one that he felt like having again, at least not in his current condition. Instead, he remained silent, and listened.

"Maybe it's time for a little vacation," Vanessa more than just suggested. She looked away then, the city's lights filtering in through the blinds momentarily bathing her figure in a dim glow. "And if that doesn't help," she added, turning her gaze on him once more, "then it might not hurt to see a psychologist."

Despite the darkness of the room, he could tell that she'd seen him roll his eyes just then by the way that she exhaled markedly. Or maybe she hadn't seen a thing, and just knew him too well.

"Now hear me out, okay?" Vanessa pleaded. "I'm not saying that you're crazy or anything like that, but these dreams of yours are *not* normal. To be honest, they're kind of starting to freak me out. You shouldn't be thrashing around in your sleep the way that you do, or waking up in a cold sweat all the time. A psychologist might be able to help you understand why you keep having these dreams, maybe even help put a stop to them."

"Sure," Frank sighed sarcastically. The conversation wasn't going to just go away, and it put him in a sour mood. "And maybe if I'm *super* lucky," he added, feigning enthusiasm, "they'll diagnose me with whatever the latest make-believe disorder is." He couldn't stand shrinks. Half of everything they said was baloney. "You think they'll put me in the loony bin if they find something? Maybe stuff me full of pills? Needles? Or hey, why not just skip all that and go straight to electroshocks?"

Vanessa groaned loudly, and her reaction didn't surprise him. She did sometimes say that he liked to avoid the issues, and make light of them instead of facing them head on. She was probably right about that, but he didn't much care. He didn't want to talk about it. He just wished she'd drop the subject altogether.

"Psychologist, not psychiatrist," she breathed, forestalling his next quip. "I know that you don't trust either, and I'm not going to pester you about it. Just promise me that you'll think about taking some time off, okay? You've hardly missed a day's work in over a year. You've got over a month's worth of vacation time piled up. You do realize that they're going to give you a cash-out if you just sit on it, right?"

Frank let out a long sigh before answering. "Yes, Vanessa. I know. I *did* read the fine print before signing up, *thank you.*" Realizing that he might have sounded a bit harsher than he'd intended to, he sat up then and took her hands in his own. "Sorry," he said. "I'm a grumpy asshole. You don't deserve that."

Vanessa nodded. "You are grumpy, but it's okay. I've gotten used to your post-hibernation antics, Franky-bear. You *are* going to think about taking a vacation, though. You *really* need one."

Frank scrunched his face up and wrinkled his brow, mildly annoyed. "Maybe, okay? It's just not a good time right now."

"Why not, Frank?" Vanessa asked. "It never seems to be a good time with you."

Frank rubbed at the sides of his head. He felt a headache coming on. "There's just too much work right now."

Vanessa rolled her eyes again and threw up her hands, clearly irritated. "What work, Frank? Please tell me. Are you even on a case right now?"

"No," Frank breathed, "but that doesn't mean that I'm sitting around doing nothing all day."

Vanessa patted his back reassuringly. "I'm not saying it does, honey, but I'm sure they can find someone else to pick up the slack while you're away."

Frank leaned back against the tufted headboard and exhaled emphatically. How could he explain this to Vanessa in a way that she'd understand? He let his face sag into his propped-up hands and started rubbing at the sides of his nose, a telltale sign that the migraine he'd felt earlier really was on its way, and that its arrival was imminent. "I'm not sure if you've heard this, Vanessa, but crime is on the rise in all but a few of the city's sectors."

Vanessa furrowed her brow and planted her fists on her hips. "Ohhh no," she grumbled. "You are *not* going to sit there and tell me that that's *your* problem, Franky. You are not." She crossed her arms then, and by some trick of feminine magic, she managed to look even more disapproving than she already had.

"But it *is* my problem," he replied forcefully. "I'm an officer of the law, Vanessa, and things like this really do matter to me. I didn't join the agency just to sit on the sidelines, especially not at a time like this."

Vanessa turned toward him and threw her leg over his lap, straddling him. "Listen," she said, choosing her next words with care, "I understand that you're devoted to your job. Really, I do. It's kinda cute... in a messed up kind of way. But weren't you the one going on about how big the agency was, not so long ago? You're not the only officer in your precinct. What difference would it make if you took a couple weeks off?"

He'd never thought of the implications of that in great detail, but he wasn't in the right frame of mind to start now. With her mounted over his groin the way that she was, he could hardly think straight. He was no longer tired and he'd forgotten all about his headache. "Maybe none," he finally conceded, straining to concentrate, "but I have to make myself available right now. We're understaffed as it is, and I haven't exactly been employee of the month. I've been around... but it's complicated. I need to prove my worth to the agency, and maybe a little to myself."

Vanessa took a long, drawn out breath. From the look of it, she was on the verge of unleashing a longwinded rebuttal. She opened her mouth to say something, but then decided against it at the last second, opting to fall over onto her pillow, instead. "Oh, applesauce," she muttered in a pouty way.

Frank suppressed a sudden urge to grin. There was no point arguing with him when he'd made up his mind about something. He knew that much about himself, and he knew that she knew it, too. He also knew that she found his tenacity appealing, when their arguing didn't go on for so long that it pissed her off. Even then, good arguing sometimes led to good make up sex.

"You know," Vanessa said, sounding defeated, "you sure are hardheaded when you want to be."

Reaching over, Frank cupped her chin with his hand and gently turned her face toward him. He was hardheaded in more ways than she knew. His other head was only getting harder. "I know," he admitted, "but I promise that I'll think about it."

"You will?" Vanessa asked, smiling.

"I will," he answered. "I'll *think* about it. Tomorrow. After I've gotten some rest. In any case, I know what I need right now, and it's not a vacation." With that, he placed his hand on her hip and let it rest there.

"Is that so?" Vanessa asked, quirking her brow.

Frank nodded over at her, grinning slyly. "It is. I just need to think about something else for a while." He slid his hand over her backside then and gave it a good squeeze. It was so perfectly round and firm that just grabbing it drove him near mad with desire. It didn't help that he'd just woken up, or that she was as beautiful as she was naked: completely.

Vanessa looked unsure. "That may be easier said than done."

"You have a point," he admitted, "but that's exactly what I need to do, and I know I can do it." He gave her bottom another squeeze then, and pulled her in toward him.

Vanessa propped herself up on one elbow, facing him. "And how exactly do you plan on pulling that one off, if you don't mind my asking. All you ever think about is work."

"With help," he answered matter-of-factly, then added, "and that isn't the *only* thing I think about," as an afterthought. As far as he was concerned, he'd just made as obvious an advance as he could, but she just wasn't getting the message. *She must be tired,* he concluded. *My stirring did wake her after all.*

A look of confusion crept onto Vanessa's face. "With help? I thought you didn't want to see a psychologist."

"A psychologist?" Frank asked with a laugh. "I don't want to see a shrink. I want you to help me take my mind off things." He tugged at her again, a little more forcefully, and pulled her in close, 'til her pelvis butted right up against him. The heat of her thighs against his groin made him want to take her right then and there. If she couldn't feel his manhood grinding up against her and figure out what that meant, he almost had a mind to pull her right down on top of it.

"You perv," Vanessa laughed, pulling back suddenly.

She was more than pleased to oblige, however, and Frank did forget about his work the second she draped herself over him and started to kiss his neck. When she inched her way downward and disappeared beneath the covers, he even managed to forget about the dreams, at least for a while.

CHAPTER
2

Icon

Leonard cracked his knuckles against the side of his face as he stood by his office window, casually observing the streets below. As usual, the Plaza district was abustle with all kinds of activity. Giving his balding head a good scratch, he let the blinds down and waddled over to the side of his desk. "Can I get some coffee in here?" he barked, a little gruffer than intended.

The captain was a stocky man of forty-six. His shoulders were wide and his bones were big. Despite an abundant gut that strained his belt, the man was built strong. His intense, brown eyes held a power all their own. They gave him the look of a person that meant business, but were sunken and creased from stress and a lack of sleep. His bushy mustache was trimmed at the corners of his mouth, and what was left of his brown hair formed a U-ring around the back of his head. They somehow managed to soften his image.

Maria's response came in over the intercom almost at once. "Yes, Captain Boston. Right away, sir." And then she whispered, "But Leonard? You don't need to yell. I can hear you just fine." A few seconds later, the door to his office opened up and Maria walked through it holding a steaming pot of coffee. "Even when you forget to use the intercom," she added with a smirk.

He felt like a bit of a schmuck. Maria's desk sat just outside of his office, and he'd left his door cracked open, to boot. There *wasn't* a need to yell. He could have just used the intercom, but it was one of those things that he never really thought to do, in part because he didn't *want* to. The switch sat right next to the panic button. Despite them being so clearly labeled that even the basest simpleton could figure them out, the possibility of accidentally hitting that big, red button unsettled him.

Leonard's fingers were big and thick, and even though he wouldn't admit to it outright, more often than not, they were also clumsy. The switch and the button were just too damned close to each other for practical use. The last time he'd tried to use the intercom, the SWAT team had burst into his office unexpectedly, and he'd spilled hot coffee on his junk.

That was just the tip of the iceberg, though. There were a lot of things about his office that annoyed him. It was cramped and it was dingy, and that was something he could deal with, but it also had microphones and cameras. It had little ones, hidden ones, sneaky friggin' bastard ones. They were all linked directly to the surveillance room. The precaution had served its purpose in the past. If someone he brought in started to get funny with him, he could have a couple armed units in his office almost as quickly as he could give the unfortunate bastard the finger and say, "Fuck you." Having his office bugged up the wazoo was a nice little security feature, but it was also a pain in the ass. Just passing gas became a potentially embarrassing undertaking.

"Sorry Maria," he mumbled, smiling nervously as he rubbed at his neck. "Morning's got me a little backward, is all. Still kinda groggy, you know?"

She smiled back at him understandingly as she set his freshly filled cup of coffee down on the corner of his desk. "Leonard, it's okay. I know the feeling all too well." She leaned across him to grab the documents from his junk box, then gave him another reassuring smile and turned to walk back to her desk.

He couldn't help but watch her plump bottom sway as she left the room and closed the door behind her. "Damn..." he whispered, allowing himself an indecent thought or two. Oh, what he wouldn't do for just a few minutes in the supply room with that ample-bosomed vixen. He sucked in his belly then and adjusted his pants, trying to cut his straining belt some slack. Damn thing kept digging into him.

He looked at the engraved plaque on his desk then with some regret. *Captain Leonard Boston*. Twenty-seven years busting his hump for the agency had earned him this closed office and that hot, blonde dish that sat outside it. A desk job had its advantages, granted, but his prodigious gut seemed to be one of the more direct consequences of his promotion. He walked around to the other side of his desk and sank into his chair. Yeah, he'd choose a laser pistol and a hostage situation over this mundane paperwork any day of the week.

He leafed through the mess of papers on his desk and pulled out a page at random. "Same old crazy bullshit as always," he muttered as he gave it a quick once-over, "just a lot more of it than there used to be." He scratched at his chin then and gave the media report a closer review. "Marketplace massacre kills six. Terrorist group claims responsibility for subway catastrophe..." He trailed off with a groan, crumpling the paper up before tossing it back on the pile, disgusted. The agency just wasn't what it used to be. The punks they recruited nowadays were useless young gun wannabes and show-offs. If it weren't for the Mech Units, the city would be in total freakin' chaos.

"Sir?" Maria's sweet voice on the intercom wrenched him back from his current train of thought.

He looked at the intercom switch on his desk for a moment, indecisive and weighing the odds. Clearing his throat, he undid the top button of his dress shirt and cracked his knuckles, preparing to tackle the switch head on. Leaning in close, moving slowly, meticulously, and with the care of a model car assembler, he finally flicked the switch, and let out a sigh of relief.

"Are you alright, sir?" Maria asked, probably concerned by the sound of heavy breathing that was no doubt coming through on her end.

"I'm fine, thanks," Leonard responded. "What is it?"

There was a brief pause before Maria answered. "I forgot to tell you something earlier..."

Leonard drummed his fingers rhythmically on his desk as he waited for her to go on. "Yeeees?"

A few more seconds went by before Maria answered him. "The commissioner's people called about fifteen minutes ago. He wants to see you in his office at eleven. I asked why, but his assistant wouldn't say."

Leonard's tension rose and his face turned beet red. "What?" he yelled. "That two-bit freakin' clown wants to see me in *his* office? At eleven? This morning?" His sudden outburst and the sound of his fists smashing down on his desk rang out over the intercom with a static crackle. "His office is all the way across town!" If he was a bit grumpy earlier, he was well on his way to being full-blown pissed off, now.

"S-sir?" Maria asked, her voice trembling nervously.

Leonard couldn't hear her. He was too caught up in his own fit of rage to hear anything. *Commissioner Caldwell*, he thought, grimacing sourly. *That old, hairy, overgrown nut sack! He probably wants to bust my balls over the latest rash of killing sprees, but does he realize even for a second that our precinct's got the lowest crime rate in the entire freaking city? No. Of course he doesn't! The smug bastard's too busy reading the headlines while drinking champagne and eating caviar with the president! I want to see HIM in MY office so I can tell HIM what a lousy friggin' douche bag HE is, and to get me a bigger friggin' budget if he wants us to be more cost-effective!*

"Sir?" Maria's voice came in over the intercom again, louder.

This time, he heard her. "Yes, Maria. What is it?" He was trying hard to contain himself, but was still obviously miffed.

There were a few seconds of lingering static, and then she spoke. "Detective Fasaro is here to see you."

He rolled his head back suddenly and groaned. He had to admit that Frank was an okay kid. The guy had potential, at least. He got things done, and when he wanted to, he showed a lot of heart. There was no denying that. Somehow, though, despite all that, despite having been around for a few years, he still managed to act like nothing more than a run-of-the-mill *rookie*, like most of the other assholes the academy sent his way.

At least he wasn't cocky, like most of those other jack-offs were. Still, he didn't have the balls *or* the brains that it took to be as good as the guys that *he* used to work with, back in the day. Okay, maybe he had *most* of the balls and *some* of the brains, but he still fell short, as far as he was concerned. Those used to be prerequisites to joining the Law Enforcement Agency, but they sure as shit weren't anymore. Not by a long shot. To top it off, the kid was always late—chronically late.

All in all, his feelings toward the guy were pretty love-hate. Sometimes they leaned a little more toward love, but not today. Today he was in a hateful kind of mood, but his hate for Frank was really more of a hard love. It was turning out to be a really shitty morning, and this was the last thing that he had time for. If anyone else had come to see him, he might have kicked them in the ass and said, "Thanks for comin' out." But he'd see Frank, even if it was for some trivial bullshit. And it most likely was. He grumbled and let out a loud, defeated sigh before muttering out a begrudging, "Send him in."

There were three rapid knocks at his door and Frank stepped inside. "You wanted to see me, sir?" he asked, then closed the door behind him.

Leonard swiveled his chair around toward the window as Frank stood there. He glanced at him over his shoulder then and arched his brow. "Not really, no," he replied snidely, "but here you are." He took a sip of his coffee and turned around to set the cup down on his desk. "So what do you want this time, Fasaro? You here to rat yourself out again?"

Frank cleared his throat. "Well sir, I—"

"So you're late. Again," Leonard announced dramatically, cutting him off. "Whoopty-friggin'-doo. I should be used to that by now, don't you think?"

Frank tried to get a word in, but he spoke over him. "Being late every day isn't going to net you any promotions, kid, but you aren't in this for promotions, are you? So who friggin' cares? I'm not your mom."

Frank cleared his throat again. "Sir, I just wanted to—"

Leonard cut him off again. "This better not be about the drug bust you pulled off at the old train yard last week. You want a vacation, is that it? Listen, kid, don't go thinking I'll be lenient with you, or give you any extra R&R just because you got lucky and did a good job back there."

Jumping on the occasion, Frank butted in. "I don't want a vacation, sir. That isn't what this is about."

Leonard furrowed his brow. "Then what the fuck do you want?" he barked. "I don't have all day!" If you wanted to survive in *his* precinct, you got used to his tirades and outbursts. Most of his men got it, and Frank was no exception. The kid learned early on not to let it get to him.

"I really am sorry I'm late," Frank calmly stated, joining his hands behind his back, "but that's not why I'm here, either."

Leonard cursed under his breath and gave him the evil eye. It was a look that said to cut the crap and get straight to the point.

Frank must have gotten the message, as he blurted out a plain and simple, "I want to be transferred to Special Assignments."

Leonard froze in place, both fists planted firmly on his desk. The irritation in his eyes faded and gave way to amusement. Even he was surprised by the burst of laughter that escaped him then.

He pounded his desk with the palm of his hand, laughing 'til he was beet red in the face and nearly gagging.

After a few seemingly interminable seconds, he finally caught his breath and managed to settle down somewhat. "You gotta be kidding me, kid," he snickered. Try as he might, it was hard to remain calm, and he still sounded like he was on the verge of breaking into another fit of hysterical laughter. "If things were like they used to be, you'd have been fired a long time ago. But things aren't like they used to be... so instead, here you are in my office... asking me for a transfer to Special Assignments."

Frank frowned despite himself, obviously caught off guard. "I just want to help," he said in a subdued tone.

"If you *just* want to help," Leonard barked, "then you'll do whatever I damn well tell you to. Is that clear?"

Frank inhaled deeply and balled his fists at his sides.

Glimpsing the first spots of crimson blooming in Frank's cheeks, Leonard realized that he'd struck a nerve. If he kept it up, things were going to get ugly fast. Guys like Frank, guys that seemed so damned calm all the time—maybe *were* calm *all* the time—they still had buttons they didn't like getting pushed, and when those buttons *did* get pushed, it wasn't pretty.

The last thing he needed this morning was a yelling contest in his office. The kid had heart and he was patient. He had to give him that. Being overly hard on him and laughing in his face probably wasn't the best way to discourage him from jumping ship to SAU. If he wasn't careful, he might push him even farther down that path. The kid might decide to go above and beyond him for permission to transfer, just to prove that he could. And it would be a relatively easy thing to do, what with the way things were. But he could *not* let Frank join Special Assignments. He'd have to be more careful about what he said from here on in, and how he said it. He had to find a better approach.

Drawing a blank, he decided to put his money on the method he knew best: honesty. In an effort to stamp out the fuse that he'd just lit, Leonard mustered up all of the calm and politeness that he could stomach without puking. "Don't take it personal, Franky. I got the commissioner breathing down my neck on a daily basis 'cause this city's going apeshit bananas. We've got shootings, hostage situations, shit getting blown up. People are dying. Too many of them. But despite what you probably think, heroics aren't really what this city needs right now." *What it needs is a bigger police budget and better training for new recruits,* he added for himself as an afterthought. *And some equipment that isn't as old as the commissioner himself wouldn't hurt, either.*

"What does it need then, Captain?" Frank asked, having regained most if not all of his composure.

Leonard walked over to the window and motioned for Frank to follow. "Come take a look at this and tell me what you see."

Frank got there just as the captain had finished raising the blinds. He looked out the window, scanning left and right. "What am I looking for exactly?" he asked.

"The big picture," Leonard replied, leaning against the wall with his shoulder, legs crossed at the shins.

Frank scrubbed his fingers through his hair. "Okay. The big picture." He shook his head like he was unsure what he was looking for, or if there was even really a point to the exercise. It was obvious from the way he surveyed the scene below that he was concentrating hard. "It's a beautiful day," he finally said, more to himself than for the captain's benefit. "The sun must be shining *somewhere* behind all that smog, 'cause everything's lit up with a dull, grayish hue. There's almost no point having the streetlights on. *Almost.*"

He paused for a moment as he took more of it in. "The streets here are pretty clean," he added. "There are all kinds of shops and restaurants lining them in every direction. This part of the Plaza is bustling. People are milling around like ants. They're all heading somewhere or doing something... getting things done, despite all the shit going down in the rest of the city, what with the terrorist activity and the crime sprees and all. I can even see some kids down there playing in a fountain across the street." The answer to what he was looking for must have dawned on him then, because his eyes lit up like light bulbs. "This sector is teeming with people, with activity, but everyone is calm. It's a good, safe area."

Leonard nodded. "It is." He strolled past Frank to the other corner of the window and asked, "Do you know how many men I need to keep on patrol here every day to keep it that way?"

Frank looked up briefly as he scoured his memory for an answer. "In a commercial sector," he stated matter-of-factly, "the manual recommends keeping twenty-four officers on patrol. And that's a bare minimum. I know you're pretty orthodox, but the Plaza's kind of big as far commercial sectors go, and it's perfectly under control, so... thirty-six?"

Leonard shook his head slowly. "Not even close."

"Okay, how many then?" Frank asked, arching his brow.

"None," Leonard replied, smiling with a certain degree of smug satisfaction. "None whatsoever."

Frank looked like he had a hard time believing it. "How can we keep the peace if no one's on duty?" he asked, skeptical.

"Surprising, isn't it?" Leonard asked. "Even though there aren't any officers on patrol here," he added, walking back to his chair and sinking in, "most criminals wouldn't think twice about pulling something. And that's because of our icon."

Frank scratched at the back of his head, obviously stumped. "Well, I thought I was onto something for a second, but now I'm just confused," he admitted. "Our *icon*?"

Leonard sighed as he swung around in his chair. "Yes, our icon," he said. "The image that we project. Or the image that represents us—the law." He peeked at his watch then before continuing. "Precinct headquarters itself, visible for all to see for about a mile around, is a real big chunk of that icon, but it's not the only heat we're packing. No, there are so many officers moving through here on a daily basis that it gives the impression we have a really strong police presence. It doesn't really matter that they're only passing through."

Frank smirked despite himself. "It's a wonder we need police at all. Just put some signs up all over town. *Be nice, or else. We're watching you. LEA.*"

Leonard furrowed his brow. "I know you're only kidding, but cut it with the crappy jokes, and just listen to me for a second, okay wise guy? I know this is getting kind of long, but there *is* a point, and I'm getting to it."

"Sorry, Captain," Frank breathed, walking back to the front of the desk to take a seat in the visitor's chair, opposite Leonard. "You have my full attention."

Leonard waited for Frank to settle in then kicked his feet up onto his desk. "Image might be getting us by for now," he admitted, "but we can't depend on it forever. It'll probably save us ninety-nine times out of a hundred, but there'll always be a few nutjobs out there that just don't care if we're around or not. If some psycho decides to walk into a hotel with a bundle of TNT strapped to his back, then we might just be in trouble. And I say *might*, because we still have a lot of officers moving through here daily, so even if nobody reported the incident, one of our guys would probably pick up on it anyways. Our response time would be affected, sure, but we'd pick up on it... eventually... hopefully before the bomb went off."

Frank's brow creased with worry. "So why not assign a few guys to the plaza then?" he asked. "Are we *that* understaffed? Is it really that bad?"

Leonard rubbed at the stubble on his face and patted what little hair he had against his sweaty scalp. "Yes, Frank, it really *is* that bad. It's never *been* this bad before. The city's a clusterfuck right now. We've got the lowest crime rate in Innerstadt, but it's still awful. I've got the commissioner being a real monkey on my back, and even though it's through no fault of my own, it is for a reason. It's a war out there, Franky."

He pulled his feet off his desk, rose, and walked back to the window. He was getting too riled up to stay seated. "It's a war from the inside, where civilians make up most of the casualties. And don't be fooled, I'm not just talking about the terrorists, here. Most of this is their fault, obviously, but the agency's been spending so much manpower trying to find and eradicate them that it doesn't have a whole lot left for anything else. I've lost so many guys to *Special Assignments* right now that I can't even cover the entirety of our own sector. Needless to say, *real* crime is on the rise. And by that I mean crime that doesn't involve explosives or nerve gas or whatever-the-frig else those terrorist crap bags have up their sleeves.

"Maybe the shit we deal with on the daily isn't as shocking as a terrorist attack, but it's just as dangerous… just as tragic. I guarantee it. Believe you me, there's an entire army's worth of pissant lowlifes out there just raring to do their neighbors in, just so they can get their mitts on all their shit. In the long run, they'll rack up even more casualties than the Awoken, and it pisses me right the fuck off. In a lot of places, it isn't even safe to walk down the street in the daytime. And this shit's going down in sectors that used to be considered good, safe neighborhoods. Or safe commercial districts, just like this one."

The longer he went on, the more Frank's brow creased, the further down his shoulders slumped. Kid obviously had no idea that the situation was this bad, that their problems were this broad and all-encompassing.

Leonard opened the window to let in some new air and continued talking, uninterrupted. "You know, counter-terrorism is risky business all across the board. It's expensive and it's dangerous. Almost every day, a Special Assignments officer bites the dust. And if it's not in our precinct, it's in another. Every time one of our guys gets whacked, I need to pull someone else from their regular duties to take their place. Don't forget that we have the *lowest* crime rate in the entire friggin' city. That means that no matter how bad we have it here, there are other precincts out there that have *much* higher casualty rates than we do. I can't even remember how many guys I had to transfer out last month alone. I lost count, but I guarantee you it was a lot. It was way too many. No, what we really need is better trained recruits and a much bigger budget, but we aren't getting either."

"Isn't that an even better reason to transfer me to Special Assignments, sir?" Frank asked. "It seems like the only real way out of this mess is to tackle the terrorists head on. Pour all of our resources into it if we have to—go after them hard. We can't just ignore them and keep going on with our everyday business. If you want to kill the snake, forget about the tail and cut off its head. Sure, crime would be bad for a while, but won't it be worse if we don't take care of these slimy bastards once and for all? Pretty sure we wouldn't have these problems if we wiped them all out. Seems pretty straightforward to me."

Leonard rolled his eyes and grunted in disbelief. "I hear the commissioner has a job opening for a spokesperson, if you're interested. You pretty much just recited his current call to arms; hit most of the buzzwords and everything. I won't hold it against you *too much* 'cause you're young and ignorant, but it's just plain stupid. Commissioner Chucklefuck should know better, even if he is just an overpaid bureaucrat. He doesn't see the big picture. All he sees are numbers and taler signs. I'm sure he could get us the funds we need if he wanted to, but he *doesn't* want to. He's too busy blaming all this on everyone else's incompetence to really see what's going on. He has no idea how far beyond us this is, even though we've told him at least a hundred freakin' times already. He's got a point about the incompetence, to a certain extent, but things would never have gotten this bad to begin with if he hadn't whittled away our budget over the years."

Leonard slid a cigarette out from the pack that he kept on the windowsill. They were Schreiber Lights. The doctor had ordered him to quit five years ago, but as far as he was concerned, the good doctor could go fuck himself. He walked back to his desk, took a seat and opened up his top-right drawer. Lying amidst a mess of stationery odds and ends were his antique 9mm pistol, a half-empty, rectangular 40-ounce bottle of Wüstewasser whiskey, two plain shot glasses and a heavy silver ashtray. He took out the ashtray and both shot glasses and set them down on his desk. "If I have to go see the commissioner," he complained, unscrewing the cap on the whiskey bottle, "I'm going to need a little of this." He filled both glasses to the brim then pushed one across the table toward Frank. Grimacing, he struck a match on the underside of his desk then lit up and leaned back in his chair. The first drag was rough on his throat, but he liked the feel of it all the same.

"Diverting everything into counter-terrorism sounds like a good short-term solution," he said, thin streaks of smoke escaping through the corners of his mouth, "but it's not. If it was done *right*, it could work, but what he has us doing now is suicide. There's no point in building up huge concentrations of men. It just gives the bad guys bigger, easier targets to blow up. Counter-terrorist units have always been small for a reason. They've always been made up of only the best, smartest officers for a reason. Cut off the snake's head, you say? We'll never even *see* the snake's head the way things are going now. They don't exactly advertise, you know, or hold up signs that read, 'Here we fuckin' are!' The Awoken are sneaky friggin' bastards. They hide from us in plain sight. They watch us. They strike at us from the shadows. *They* come after *us* is the point I'm trying to make. And all Chucklehead over there has done is offer them bigger, juicier targets to shoot at."

Leonard took another long, drawn out drag on his cigarette and flicked the loose ash onto the floor. "The only way to make counter-terrorism work is to spend more on advanced training and better tools for our intel boys. It might take some time to train the units effectively, but it'd be a heck of a lot less expensive in money and in lives in the long run. If we did it that way, we'd have a chance. It wouldn't be a quick fix like the commissioner wants, but we'd have an actual *fighting* chance. What he's doing now is gambling. He's gambling the city, and that's a big friggin' gamble. What happens when we get so low on manpower that we can't even ensure basic safety levels? We've already sunk that low in a lot of places, but what happens when it's like that all over the place? Really *all over* the city?

"Chaos, Franky. Total freaking chaos. And that's *exactly* what the terrorists want. They won't have to work so hard at killing people no more, 'cause people will be killing each other all on their lonesome. Oh, the commissioner will be just *thrilled* then, won't he, when the Awoken's numbers have swollen so out of control that we're left with next to nothing. Eventually, they won't even have to kill anyone, at least not the way that they have been, because by then they'll have exactly what they've been after this entire time."

Frank was leaning forward in his chair, with his elbows on his knees and his chin propped up on both of his fists, listening intently. "And what is it exactly that they're after?" he asked, genuinely concerned.

"Power, kid... it's all about power. It's *always* about power. They want to overthrow the government and set up their own. They want to make their own rules, be the ones to call the shots." Leonard crushed out the rest of his cigarette and sighed, then looked off into space for a moment, lost in thought. "Now don't take this the wrong way," he said, breaking the silence, "but if we keep going the way that we're going, we'd probably be better off if they just got what they wanted now. I'm not saying I want it to happen, just that something has to change, and change fast, 'cause the way I see it, we're losing this war, and at the rate we're going right now, we'll be lucky if we last another six months. And that's if things don't get worse."

His closing words struck the kid like a punch in the gut and it showed. "Six months," Frank muttered, mostly to himself. "Why doesn't everyone know about this right now? What are we going to do about it?"

"The answer is simple, kid," the captain stated matter-of-factly, spinning once around in his chair. "National security. The government isn't saying shit because it wants to avoid mayhem. The last thing we need is a general state of panic. They're keeping this hush-hush to avoid chaos. At least they're doing *that* right. Even if we knew for a fact that people would take it well, what would we tell them? 'Please avoid leaving your homes?' We can't do that, Franky. We can't *afford* to do that. This city's the only place we've got on this piece of shit planet we call home. Who's gonna come help us get through a situation like this? No one is. If production stops, we're all pretty much screwed. People *have* to keep going on with their lives, understand?"

Frank nodded. "It's so simple, I'm not even sure why I asked. I guess we're just so used to being well-off that it's easy to forget how fragile our situation really is. We've got a well-designed system here, but nothing's perfect. There isn't a contingency plan that could get us through that kind of crisis for any extended period of time. If people decided to barricade themselves in their homes, everything we've worked so hard for—everything the founders worked so hard for—would crumble away within weeks. The food stores would dry up, and with nowhere else to get provisions, we'd pretty much be fucked. How many innocent people would have to die before the situation stabilized again, *if* it even stabilized again? A thousand? Tens of thousands? I don't know. Might even be higher than that."

"Sometimes I don't think you're an absolute idiot," Leonard commented woodenly. That was a compliment, coming from him. "As for what we're going to do... well we'll do everything that we *can* do, the *only* thing we can do. I'm gonna do my best to pressure that asshole Caldwell into dishing out more funds, and you're going to do your best to project our icon wherever this city needs you to."

Frank ruffled the hair at the back of his head. "Okay," he answered uneasily. "How do you want me to do that, again?"

"Haven't you been listening at all, kid?" Leonard huffed. "I need you to get out there and do your job. It's as simple as that. I'm not even asking you to be the best, Frank, just to do your best. Go out there and flash your badge around. Flash our *colors* around. Go out there and remind the people of Innerstadt that we're still here, that we're still looking out for them. Go out there and let all the lowlifes and crazies and would-be criminals know that as long as we got breath in us, we won't be putting up with any of their shit."

He got up from his chair and walked over to where Frank was sitting. "If you still want to play hero, and run off to go fight the terrorists head on," he stated blandly, "then don't worry, your time will come. It's inevitable. Let me warn you now, though. When that day comes, you'll wish that it hadn't. It'll be clear to you then that you're just another martyr."

He turned to face Frank then leaned in and put his hands on his shoulders, looking him square in the eyes. "If you want to be a *real* hero," he said, his voice unusually emotive, "then forget all about this *SAU* bullshit for as long as you can. Do your job. Help give this city what it really needs: hope. And try not to die while you're at it. We can't afford any more losses right now."

He'd never admit it, but that wasn't really what he wanted to say. That wasn't why he wanted Frank to be careful. The way things were nowadays, he couldn't turn down requests for transfer to Special Assignments. Not legally. He could get fired for it if he did. Regardless, he'd been protecting Frank ever since the new SAU recruitment policy had come into effect. That piece of crap policy had increased the number of recruits precincts were required to transfer over to SAU by astro-fucking-nomical proportions. It had left him and other captains with less than the bare-bones essentials to work with. At this rate, he wouldn't be surprised if they asked him to hand over all the unborn babies in his left nut.

They'd even inquired about Frank specifically, at one point. He'd made up a bogus excuse then to avoid handing him over, and he'd keep on making excuses for as long as he could. Frank might get on his nerves from time to time, but he was one of the few people he could actually stand, one of the few guys he could actually depend on. He would *not* send him to the slaughter. Not if he had a say in it. Not without a fight.

"Just point the way, Captain," Frank said. He sounded like his confidence had been renewed. "I won't let you down, I swear. I won't let the people of this city down. Where does Innerstadt need me most?"

"Atta boy, Franky," Leonard exclaimed, patting him on the shoulders profusely. "It's good to see that we're on the same boat, even if it is sinking." He looked at his watch then and cursed. "Have to get to that meeting with Commissioner Chucklehead." He walked to the back of his office and grabbed his gray trench coat from the coatrack. Then, after slipping it on, he paced back to his desk, and started rummaging through the clutter of junk there. "Where'd I put those fucking reports," he muttered. "I can never find anything when I need it."

He looked up at Frank then, if only for a moment. "A few sectors have only partial coverage right now," he jabbered out in a rush. "Could be some that don't have any at all. We're working with a few of our neighboring precincts right now. Lending a hand where we can, because we can. We're in better shape than some of those guys are, for now. Check with dispatch. They'll know where to send you."

Frank saluted him briskly as he rose. "Go get 'em, sir," he said as he headed for the door. He had his hand on the doorknob and was about to turn it when Leonard told him to wait.

"I'm just curious," Leonard said. "If you're so into heroics and all that, then why didn't you join the SWAT team when you had the chance to? I know you did all the tests and trials. I saw your file. You completed all of them successfully."

Frank hesitated a moment before answering. "I wouldn't say that I'm into heroics or whatever. I just want to help out however I can." He paused again briefly before continuing. "When I really started looking into SWAT, everyone and their brother wanted in. There was obviously no shortage of manpower there. Grunt police work, on the other hand... nobody wanted to do that. So I changed my mind, backed out. Figured I'd be more useful just doing what we do. As for the whole SAU thing, I wasn't even sure what it was all about, to be honest. I'd seen the posters, heard some rumors. Seemed like it was pretty important, but nobody wanted to sign up. It was too dangerous, people said. So I thought maybe I'd be more useful to the city if I joined SAU. Cause no one else wanted to. That make any sense to you?"

Leonard forgot about the reports he was looking for. He'd stopped rifling through the pages on his desk and had a blank expression in his eyes. Maybe he'd been wrong about the kid. Maybe he was a better cop than he gave him credit for. Maybe even as good as the lawmen he used to run with. "Yeah, Franky," he said, snapping out of it. "It makes perfect sense." He hesitated a moment before adding, "You be careful out there, you hear?"

CHAPTER
3

Bertha on the Beat

When Frank walked out of the captain's office, the first thing that he noticed was how quiet it was. There was none of the usual hustle and bustle that the place was known for. The entire floor was as close to dead silence as he'd ever heard it. There was no talking over the phone, no typing, nothing. A quick glance down the hall revealed why. All along it, people's heads were poked out of their offices and cubicles, and seemed to be fixed in place, all eyes gazing blankly in his direction. *Well, this isn't strange at all,* he thought. He felt like he was in one of those dreams that he'd had as a kid where he was naked in front of a packed auditorium.

Hesitantly, he started down the hall at a stroll, toward the elevators. He noted some familiar faces along the way. There was Marty Grewell from accounting, with his too-big forehead and thick mustache. Ella Gustavson, usually bubbly and a vision of beauty, wasn't quite as attractive with that look of worry creasing her face. James Horwick, Sven Dresden, Jaimie Witt. They were all looking in his direction, but he couldn't say why.

As he moved farther down the hall, he soon realized that they weren't looking at him at all. Their eyes were riveted on the door to the captain's office. It was still extremely weird, but at least he didn't feel like the guy who'd forgotten to put his pants on before coming in to work anymore. A faint scuffle of boots tickled his ears as he reached the elevators, but he took no heed of it. He pressed the button to call the elevator up, waited for the doors to open, and stepped inside.

"Hey!" a familiar voice called out. "Hey, Icon! Wait up!" A second later, Andrew Gilroy rushed inside the elevator, just as the doors began to close.

Andrew was an imposing man. He stood well over six feet tall, had a slim but powerful build, and mocha-colored skin. He kept his head well shaven, and the tip of a sinuous tattoo could be seen climbing the back of his neck.

Frank knew what the rest of the tattoo looked like because they had the exact same one. It was a concentric spiral made up of a thick blue line that started at its center and wrapped itself around that point six times, spacing itself out a little more with each loop. After the sixth loop, the line broke off from its circular trajectory and arced upward, dithering off at the base of the neck. Covering the vast majority of the spiral's center was what looked like the head of a growling wolf, proud and menacing. It was inked in blood red in a style that seemed simple at first glance. Closer examination would reveal a more intricate design that favored subtle lines and elegant, symmetrical curves.

Frank had designed the tattoo from fragments of memories that he couldn't quite place. They were primarily symbols that he'd seen somewhere, at some point in his life, and hadn't entirely forgotten. He and Andrew had decided to have the drawing inked on their backs when they graduated from the academy. To them, the symbols represented strength, loyalty and brotherhood. They were emblematic of a pact that they'd vowed to never break; an engagement not only to the agency, but also to each other.

"Hey, Andy," Frank said, leaning forward to hit the "Garage One" button. "Wait, what did you just call me?"

Andrew exhaled dramatically and sank back against the elevator wall with a hollow thud. "Right," he answered, his voice dripping with disbelief. "Just pretend like you didn't hear me." He shook his head from side to side, then threw up his hands and breathed out an annoyed, "Shit, son. Sometimes you're as big of an idiot as the captain says you are."

A stranger might not have realized it, but Andrew was laying it on thick. The subtle tug at the corner of his mouth soon turned to a twitch, then cracked into a full-blown smile as he spat out, "Can't figure why he chose to project your icon all over this fine city's face. Everybody knows that mine is way more magnificent than yours is. There's a whole lot more of it to go around."

Despite the dark afterthoughts lingering on in the back of his mind, Frank couldn't help but chuckle at least halfheartedly at the blatant but confusing use of sexual innuendo. Sighing, he leaned against the back of the elevator and looked up. He was mildly embarrassed by the situation he'd just been in, for the most part because he hadn't even known what was going on until someone had pointed it out to him. Crossing his arms, he straightened himself and turned to Andrew. "Was the intercom on the *entire* time I was in there?"

"Sure was," Andrew confirmed with a nod and a pat on his shoulder. He was still smiling, but that smile was fading. The two watched silently as the illuminated floor numbers scrolled down on the panel above the door.

"It was kind of funny, at first," Andrew said, breaking the silence, his jet black eyes growing more and more serious as he spoke, "but when the captain got on about how shitty everything is right now..." The elevator door slid open and they got off at the Garage One level. "When he got on about how messed up this city *really* is..." He raised his hands palms up and shook his head, at a loss for words.

Frank gave Andrew a pat on the back as they stepped aside to clear the way. "It's a tough pill for me to swallow too, Andy, but we have a real chance to make a difference here. I know things don't look too good right now, but nothing's over yet."

"See, and that's exactly why not!" Andrew exclaimed, his eyes lighting up like he'd just remembered something important that he'd forgotten to say. "That was some seriously messed up shit back there," he confided, "but if it wasn't for the way that you and Snarky McGruff took it all in stride, *I'd* have taken it a lot worse than I did—a *lot* worse."

Frank didn't know what to respond to that, so he waited and listened, and hoped that the conversation wouldn't turn to praise. Too many compliments made him feel uncomfortable, even when they came from good friends and were completely sincere.

Andrew crossed his arms and shook his head adamantly. "After what the captain said, I was about ready to put my foot so far up the commissioner's ass, he'd have gotten my boot in his goddamn teeth. My *word*, Frank, I still am! I really hope Boston can talk some sense into that stingy butt nugget. Probably won't, but I can hope, right? You know, I never really cared much about what top brass had to say, but you can bet your bottom taler that from now on, I'm gonna be watching this closer than Ultimate Death Match on Sunday night pay-per-view."

The irritation in Andrew's eyes subsided as he continued speaking. "I'm really rooting for the captain right now. I really, really am. Coming from me, I think that says a lot. And *you*! Lordy Lord, Frank... *you*! You know, you might not always have a whole lot to say, but when you finally go and open up, I don't just *hear* what you're saying, I *feel* it in my bones. It's not even *what* you say, either; it's the *way* you say it. It's the reason *why* you say it. You might come off as kind of 'boy scout' sometimes, but I assure you that there was anything but. Shit, son. We got ourselves our very own Undercity Ranger, right over here! Makes me want to be a better—"

"Dude. Shut up," Frank said, waving him off with the back of his hand. "Seriously. That's enough. Please." He didn't like being put on a pedestal. Not in the least. He'd gotten through most of his life by keeping quiet and avoiding attention whenever possible. It was just the way that he was, and Andrew knew it full well. He started to walk down the garage's main catwalk, his friend following close in tow.

The first-level garage was cool, damp, and little more than a spacious concrete warehouse. But at least it was well lit, Frank thought. Bright fluorescent lights were fixed to the walls and hung from the ceiling at regular intervals. They must have made life far easier for the dozen or so mechanics that he could hear drilling and clanging away, somewhere in the distance.

As the pair continued traveling toward the other end of the garage, they spied the first signs of the mechanics hard at work. In the distance, a jet of sparks sprayed out onto the catwalk from one of the bays on the right. Someone was busy welding *something* together again. With the city's current difficulties, the mechanics corps would be working long into the night down here. Many of the docking bays they passed were empty, many more than usual.

As recently as two months ago, the sunken areas on either side of the catwalk had been filled near to capacity with all kinds of vehicles. Now, it looked like half of the docks were empty. When the new SAU recruitment policy had come into effect, Special Assignments had started commandeering all of the better rigs. The majority of those vehicles wound up destroyed or were never seen again. Some of them *were* returned, but in very bad condition. With the latest rash of roadside bombings, and all of the heavy firefights breaking out, the grease monkeys would have their work cut out for them.

Frank arched his brow and glanced over at Andrew suddenly. "Hey, weren't you supposed to be tied up in your office today?" he asked. "I thought you had a huge backlog of paperwork that you had to get through. Reports to file and whatever."

Andrew glared at him with wide eyes and evident mock resentment. "Oh, you did *not* just ask me about my paperwork," he said, wagging his finger from side to side. "Oh nuh-uh. Nah. No way." He crossed his arms then and flicked his head to the side dramatically, away from Frank. "Bitch tells me to shut up, then wants to talk about my reports and shit? Girlfriend, you need to learn you some manners."

"Okay," Frank sighed exaggeratedly. "I'm sorry I cut you off. What were you going to say?"

Andrew smirked and shook his head from side to side. "I was just saying that the way you reacted to the captain's news back there made me want to be a better cop. Take that however you want to, Frank, or don't take it at all. That's your call. But the point I was trying to make is that if it wasn't for that, I'd be in my office right now, trying real hard not to think about running home to board up my damn windows."

They walked on in silence for a while before Andrew added, "How could I sit in my office and file reports all day when I know how much this city needs us right now? Captain said some sectors had no coverage at all. You know what that means, right? It means that if shit goes down, no one's taking care of it. *No one*, Frank. The other precincts are even worse off than we are. *They* ain't doing shit about it. File reports *my ass!*"

Frank slapped him on the back and grinned. "Well, it'll be good to know that you're out there with me, Andy, even if we end up working opposite ends of the track. We're gonna take this city back—block by block if we have to. Show everybody we're still here." As an afterthought he added, "I know that we're going to have to get out there and grunt it out as often as we can, now, but we'll still need to be organized. In other words: you'll *still* have to get to those reports, eventually."

"Oh like hell I will," Andrew objected energetically. "I threw *both* damn boxes out the window before coming down here, man. They're gone. Just spread their wings and took flight."

"Wait, you did what?" Frank sputtered in disbelief. "You're shitting me, right? You can't be serious."

"Hell *yes*, I'm serious," Andrew replied in a huff. "Probably looked pretty cool from the street, too—like paper rain. I'm never filing another damn report again. What's the boss gonna do about it, anyway? Fire me? Shit, son, he'll be pinning a medal on my lapel before this is over and done with. Trust me."

Frank laughed despite himself. "No, *you* trust *me*. Chances are he's gonna kick your ass 'til it's more blue than it is black."

"You're probably right," Andrew conceded, shaking his head. "It's a scary thought, but what's done is done. There's no going back on that now." He hesitated briefly before adding, "Franky, you know more than anyone how much I like to clown around. Shit, you're almost as bad as I am. We're like two jokers gone missing from that old deck of cards, off fucking around someplace, up to no good. Sometimes, I joke around so much that people wonder if I'm ever serious. Now I know that you're not one of those people, but I'm still gonna warn you. What I'm about to say isn't just serious, it's *dead* serious, and if you laugh, I'm'a knock all those pretty little teeth right out of your mouth."

"No promises," Frank replied, "but my dental plan is shit, so I'll try my best."

"You know, we've been through a lot together," Andrew said, and they had. They'd met in the first grade, and had quickly become fast friends. "We've known each other what, twenty years now? Maybe more? That's a damn long time, man, and all that time, we spent most of it together. If we weren't just hanging out in your backyard, we were out getting into some kind of trouble." They might be representatives of law and order now, but they'd gotten into their fair share of hijinks in their earlier years.

"Hell, the only reason I signed up for the academy in the first place was because you were going," he confided. "Through all of that, through good times and bad, you've always been there for me. And I like to think that I've been there for you, too, or at least tried to be. I wanted to thank you for being there for me again today. If it wasn't for your example, I think I might have messed up something awful. So... thank you. You've always been like a brother to me, and I appreciate that." A look of relief washed over him then. "That wasn't half as hard as I thought it would be."

Frank smiled and reached out toward Andrew, who held out his arm in anticipation. They grasped each other just above the elbow, then pulled in close for a one-armed hug and a few pats on the back. "There's no need to thank me," Frank said with a grin as they broke away from each other. "Little brother from another mother. You've been there for me just as much as I've been there for you, okay? You've helped me out of a tight spot or given me an example to follow more times than I can remember. We're just doing what we do. Right?"

As much as he tried to ignore it, he couldn't help but find his colleagues' collective reaction to this whole situation concerning. He couldn't really blame people for being scared. Admittedly, it was some pretty scary shit. But the kind of paralysis he'd witnessed outside the captain's office troubled him, as did the subtle but unusual displays of emotion from his peers. Was this how people were supposed to react when their way of life came under threat? He imagined it was. Perhaps what really bothered him was his own calm. He knew full well that the situation was dire, but it was like his emotions were stuck in neutral.

He'd heard that hardship could bring out facets of people's personalities that they might not even be aware of. Before today, he'd never seen the captain as anything but gruff, determined, and disagreeable—an aged and somewhat rank amalgamation of piss and vinegar. But for the briefest of moments, he'd lowered his guard and opened up just enough to let out a gleam of... what had that been, exactly? *Warmth?* He had a hard time even imagining it. Warmth and the captain went together like ice cream and mayonnaise. But he'd seen it. He'd *felt* it.

And Andrew, who was usually so carefree that everyone envied him for it, was as close to a nervous wreck as he'd ever seen him. He might try to hide his anxiety behind a facade of lighthearted banter and juvenile humor, but beneath all that was a man struggling to control his fear. He'd already come close to panicking once today. He was coping now, but would it take very much to set him off again? In his current state, he wasn't so sure.

"Hey, isn't that your bike?" Andrew asked, pointing just ahead and to the right, to the bay they'd seen the welding sparks shooting out from earlier. "Dock twenty-eight, right?"

Frank stopped walking as he felt a lump rise in his throat. That was his dock, alright. New jets of sparks sprayed out from the bay. *They could be working on someone else's bike,* he tried to convince himself. *I'm not the only guy with a rig in dock twenty-eight.* Just then, he remembered that he was, as of last week, when Tom Borland and Jack Fehr had gotten shipped over to the Barrios precinct. The captain had let their vehicles follow them because the Barrios didn't have anything to spare.

Suddenly filled with dread, he gave in to an overwhelming urge to run. Pushing off the guardrail, he sprung forward and made a mad dash toward dock twenty-eight. When he reached the short staircase leading down, he grabbed onto the railing, swung to the right, and hopped the entire flight. The soles of his boots clapped loudly against the concrete floor as he landed.

The scene before him made him stop dead in his tracks. There, splayed out across the top of a reinforced workbench, were the remains of his beloved hoverbike. Looming over the dissected carcass, crackling and sparkling welder in hand, the mechanic—a man of considerable girth—was busy chopping his bike into tiny bits and pieces. Or at least that's what it looked like to him.

Andrew came down the stairs at a jog behind him, and the two of them stared on blankly through the flashes and sparks. A few seconds later, the mechanic looked up and saw them standing there. Hesitantly, the man turned off his welder and raised his helmet, revealing the dirty, sweaty face of Salomon Grundy, one of the senior mechanics. At present, that face was wrought with uncertainty and apprehension.

"What happened to my bike, Sal?" Frank asked curtly, finally working up the will to speak. He was still in a bizarre state of shock. He wasn't exactly in *love* with his vehicle, but it had gotten him from point A to point B ever since he'd graduated from the academy. It was a good bike. It was *his* bike. Seeing it strewn out there in pieces was disheartening.

Salomon cleared his throat and pulled his helmet all the way off. "Oh, uh... hey," he sputtered nervously. "Listen, I didn't really have a choice here, Frank." He looked around quickly before setting his gaze on the two of them again. "I wanted to try to fix it," he pleaded, "I really did, but the boss said it was only good for spare parts. It was messed up pretty bad."

"Sal," Frank said, raising his hands in a calming motion, "I know that it's not your fault, okay? I just want to know what happened to my bike." He was already starting to get over the loss. Once the initial shock had passed, it wasn't such a big deal.

Salomon wiped the sweat from his brow with an old grease-stained rag. "Sorry, Frank," he sighed, "I haven't been getting much sleep lately. None of us have, down here... and those SAU guys..." He rubbed at the back of his neck as he leaned heavily against the workbench. "Those SAU guys are making our lives absolutely miserable. For real."

"It's okay, Sal," Frank assured him. "These are hard times for all of us. You don't have to apologize." He walked over to the table, across from Salomon, and set his hands down on the cool metal surface. *So many tiny pieces.* He couldn't help but wince at the sight of them. "So," he breathed, "I'm still curious to know what happened here."

Salomon grunted deeply in response. "Special Assignments happened." He scrunched his face up with disgust and added, "They did like they always do. They borrowed it and they broke it... and they were major pricks about it too, as usual."

Frank sighed. Had he really asked the captain to transfer him to SAU this morning? He was glad that the boss had talked some sense into him. "Okay," he said, ruffling the hair at the back of his head. "Thanks. I'm gonna need something to replace it, though. What can you hook me up with?"

Salomon got up and motioned for Frank to follow. "I'm glad you asked, my boy," he said, leading Frank and Andrew around the corner, into the dock itself. "I have exactly what you need." He walked to the middle of the room then stopped, took a deep breath, and flamboyantly proclaimed, "Voilà!"

Frank and Andrew looked around the room, then at each other, their confusion apparent. "I don't see any bikes around here, *Salmon*," Andrew chided. "You been huffing butane again?"

Salomon rolled his eyes and shook his head. "Look harder, Mister Smarty Pants. *Right* over there." He motioned toward an old motorcycle that was propped up against the wall not twenty feet in front of them. Grinning, he crossed his arms and added, "Boys, say hello to Bertha."

Frank's eyes followed Salomon's guiding hand and settled on the primitive-looking motorcycle. "What? That pile of junk?" he stammered, incredulous. "You've gotta be kidding me, Sal." He could hear the nasal sound of Andrew's stifled laughter building to an imminent eruption behind him.

"Hey, watch what you say about Bertha," Salomon warned. "You'll hurt her feelings. She may be a little old, but she's still a mighty fine broad... uh, bike. I restored her *myself*," he added with a point of pride. Judging by the sound of Andrew's wheezing, his efforts to contain himself were failing. Right on cue, he gave up trying, and burst into full, unabridged laughter.

"Sal," Frank pleaded, then trailed off. The bike did look like it was in fairly good condition for what it was: an antiquated piece of crap. It was nothing at all like his hoverbike. Instead of an enclosed cockpit, it had a long, open-aired leather seat, which looked relatively comfortable, but spelled out D-A-N-G-E-R in more ways than he could count. On a hoverbike, the pilot had no choice but to lie down facing forward. There was almost no room for superfluous maneuvering. The whole concept of *sitting* on a bike was completely foreign to him. He couldn't even imagine riding the thing without it resulting in complete and utter disaster. He could already picture himself smeared across the street like a dollop of red goop.

There was no smooth, armored plating, either. Except for an encased area under the seat, and another, smaller one near the front, beneath what looked like handlebars, everything looked open. Everything looked *exposed*. He couldn't get over the fact that it had wheels, of all things. He moved in closer and squatted beside it for a more thorough inspection. Exposed was a vast understatement. There were parts here that he couldn't even name, and seeing them made him anxious. He was afraid something might break off if he decided to touch it.

Yellow and orange flames, running from front to back, were painted over both of the glossy, black casings. They seemed to dance and lick at the air as though blown to the rear by strong winds. It was an odd but strangely attractive paint job. He'd never seen anything like it before. On the back casing were the words "Blitz Racing" in a bold, silver lettering.

He got up and rubbed at his temples. "Sal," he pleaded again. "Do you really expect me to ride this thing? No one in their right mind would ride this thing." If anyone in his own lifetime had, he didn't know about it. It wasn't even street legal. He'd piloted one in a VR simulator at the academy, years ago, but that had been nothing more than a glorified video game, and wasn't even in the curriculum. It had been part of an optional program he'd taken, a specialization course on adaptivity in emergency situations. "It has a combustion engine," he exclaimed, like that should explain everything and get him off the hook. "Shouldn't this thing be in a museum? I mean... do we even have *fuel* for it?"

Salomon walked up to him and patted him on the back. "It has a full tank of gas and we have enough stockpiled here to keep it running for a very long time. I know it's far from standard issue, but the captain wanted this to be *your* replacement vehicle. Ask Little Joe if you don't believe me."

Frank sighed and shook his head. Joe Littell alias Little Joe headed up the mechanics corps, and despite his nickname, there was nothing little about him. The chief made Sal look like a lightweight. "That won't be necessary, Sal." He'd never doubted his words before, and he wasn't about to start now.

"Look," Salomon said, crossing his arms, "I know it sucks, really it does, but these are hard times for everyone, like you said. We're running real low on roadworthy vehicles as it is. We've had to uh... get a little crafty. We don't got a whole lot of choice in the matter, understand?"

Andrew had quieted down somewhat, and was currently busy wiping tears from his eyes. "Well, Frank, speaking of Joe... I have to go find him before I head out." With that he waved briskly, hooted out a, "Good luck with Bertha," and walked off, a huge grin splitting his face in two.

"I'm glad you find this amusing," Frank called after him dryly. "Give my regards to Little Joe. I hope you find a nice little tricycle waiting for you in your dock, with bells, a horn, training wheels... the whole works. They had to get a little crafty, hadn't you heard?" He heard Andrew burst into another fit of laughter the second he walked out of sight.

He turned his attention back to Salomon then. "Okay, Sal. So how are we going to manage this? I don't even know how to pilot one of these things. Not really."

Salomon looked up pensively before replying. "Well, as far as piloting goes, shouldn't be all that different from your hoverbike. Granted, it's not the same as far as the body or the mechanics are concerned... but you should find the controls pretty similar to the ones you're used to. Just try it out. You'll get used to the traction pretty quick. Trust me."

"You mean to tell me that you've ridden one of these things before?" Frank asked, arching his brow.

"Are you fucking crazy," Salomon answered plainly. "I'm paid to fix these things, not ride 'em. Fuck, I don't even *know* someone that has. It's a bit of a collector's item, if you know what I mean. Heck, this model was first built in 2035. But how hard could it be? It's got brakes, handlebars... et cetera, et smettera. Haven't all the vehicles you've piloted before had those exact same things? Or, you know... their equivalents? Besides, people used to ride 'em all the time. If our caveman ancestors could do it, I'm pretty sure you can figure it out, too. Just trust me."

Frank felt like asking him how he'd managed to restore the motorcycle to working condition without even testing it first. He felt like it, but refrained from doing so. Arguing now would be a waste of time. It was going to be this or nothing. "You got the keys to it?" he asked, resigned to his fate.

"They're in the ignition," Salomon replied tiredly. "Have fun with her. Me, I'm gonna go take a nap." He started to walk off, but stopped suddenly. "Hey, Frank!" he said, raising his tone to be heard over the sound of the engine. Frank had already hopped on the bike and was revving it thoroughly. "Be careful in the bends! Never forget: Traction!"

Frank couldn't make out everything he'd said, but he'd gotten the gist of it, and that would be enough. "Traction!" he called out, giving him the thumbs up, then, "Later, Sal! Thanks!"

Salomon waved once and hit a big white button inside a recess in the wall. The gigantic bay door rumbled and groaned as it started its slow rise.

Frank guided his bike under it at a turtle's pace as soon as he had enough clearance for his head. He had to steady himself on either side with the plants of his feet as he did. Slowly but surely, he climbed the slight incline through the tunnel that led to the surface. Before passing the final threshold to the streets above, he stopped for a second to gauge the feel of the bike between his legs.

He could already tell there was going to be a huge difference in handling. He constantly had to shift his weight or put his feet down to keep the bike from tipping over. He imagined it wouldn't be nearly as difficult to keep it well-balanced once he actually got it on the road and running at a steady pace. He *hoped* that would be the case, at least. It was nearly impossible to tip a hoverbike over, even on purpose. This thing seemed to want nothing more than to fall over and take him with it. It was going to require some getting used to, and a whole lot of focus.

When he wheeled the bike outside, the sky was dark, and the entire city was bathed in orange light and shadows, but it was still a beautiful day by any standard. He could clearly see a faint aura radiating from the nearby street lamp, and the glowing headlights of vehicles as they came around the corner of Wilderweg and Hauptstrasse. Pensive, he looked up, remembering the dream and Daniel's thoughts on the subject.

Sometimes, it really *was* hard to differentiate between night and day, but this day was a bit of an exception. The sky was barred by thick clouds of smog, as always, but it was much brighter out than he was used to for this time of morning. It was so bright, in fact, that he found it almost bizarre. On an average day, early evening could be a shade off from late morning, or it could look exactly the same. This looked more like late afternoon on a clear day. He'd be completely disoriented if he didn't have constant access to the time.

He pushed back the sleeve of his jacket then and glanced at his Communications Band. It was just past a quarter after nine. Depressing the small, green button on the top-right side of its face, he raised it to within a few inches of his mouth and said, "Officer forty-two dash zero sixty-seven, reporting for duty." There was a faint buzzing from the tiny speaker grafted to the inside of his left ear, followed by a barely audible beep that signaled the receipt of an incoming transmission.

There was a low, static sound over the line, and it gave way to a clear and amiable female voice. "Morning, Frank," the voice said. "You late again, honey?"

Frank grinned as he revved his engine into the open line. He was starting to appreciate the loud noises that the bike made. He let the sound of the engine die down a bit and answered, "Yes, Chloe. I'm late. Again."

"Holy shit!" Chloe squealed. "What was that?" She went silent for a moment, then voiced an understanding, "Ah... so that's what Bertha sounds like."

He revved the engine again and it growled furiously. *Did everyone know about this in advance,* he wondered, *or does Andrew just have a really big mouth?* "Yes," he said, mildly embarrassed as he noticed all the attention he was drawing from pedestrians and drivers alike. A large group of people waiting to cross the street at the closest intersection were all staring at him, and some vehicles were actually slowing to a crawl as they passed him by.

"I see you've got quite the gathering of attentive fans down there," Chloe teased. "Didn't think you were that popular, now did you, honey?"

Frank looked up and over his shoulder, to the seventh floor. There she was; third window from the left. He couldn't exactly tell what color eyeliner she was wearing, but he saw her well enough that he was sure it was her up there, spying down at him. He waved his hands over his head, and when he was sure that he had her attention, he gave her both fingers, high and proud.

"Hey," she moaned, "that's not nice. Your public is watching you, Frank. Think about the children."

From her silhouette, he could tell that she had her thumbs in her ears. If he knew her at all—and he liked to think that he did—she was probably sticking her tongue out at him, too. "Yeah, okay. The children. Well, tell your mom that I'm sorry, kid. I should try to be a better influence on you. Anyway... the captain said that you'd know where to send me this morning."

"Oh, did he now?" she asked. "Well in that case, why don't you head over to Xeno's to fetch me a decent cup of coffee. This oily black stuff from the cafeteria is *nasty*."

Frank let out a loud sigh directly into his Communications Band. With any luck, it would come out as loud and annoying static on the other end. "As much as I'd love to be your personal errand boy," he said, eyeing the growing crowd of onlookers warily, "there's a mob of zombies down here, and I'd like to move out before someone tries to eat my brain. In other words, are you actually going to dispatch me somewhere, dispatcher?"

The sound of Chloe's pronounced exhaling crackled fiercely in his earpiece and made him wince. "Okay, fine," she groaned. "Have it your way, party pooper. You've got a choice: Langdon district or Sherwood Park. Neither of them have any coverage right now. Was the same for Dartmuth Station up until about two minutes ago, but Andy beat you to it."

Dartmuth Station was a pretty rough district. Most cops steered clear of it, when they could. It was the kind of place you were assigned to when you drew the short straw. Frank was at least glad to see that he'd had as much influence on Andrew as he'd said he had. "If you hadn't stalled for him so much, he wouldn't have beaten me to anything," he said with a semblance of mock accusation.

The sound of Chloe's laughter made the speaker in his ear screech loudly. "Sure. Whatever you say, Frank," she replied dismissively. "Don't be paranoid. He was already on his way to Dartmuth Station when you called up. You're just super slow. Now are you going to make your choice or what, Mister *I'm-too-busy-to-talk-to-you-right-now?*"

It was an easy decision to make. Compared to Langdon district, Sherwood Park was a piece of cake. "Simply the best," was the slogan they spewed out all over the media to attract big spenders. It was by and large the wealthiest residential sector in the city, and one of the *only* districts where you could still find housing that didn't come in the twenty-some-story plus format. Mansions aside, it was all designer-quality commerce and fine dining, affordable almost exclusively to the city's elite, fancy-pants population. He wouldn't even buy a cup of coffee there. Not on his salary. Not with their steep prices. He'd sooner invest in a new pair of pants in another district.

Langdon district was another story entirely. It wasn't exactly a cesspool, but it had its fair share of problems all the same. Hard drugs, illegal prostitution rings, racketeering, corruption, violence; it had a little bit of everything. It wasn't the worst district in the city, not even by a long shot, but organized crime had crept in over the years and established itself enough to cause some serious issues. A few up-and-coming street gangs were running the show, for the most part. They were sharing the reins rather peacefully, for the time being, but these things had a way of degenerating. An eventual turf war was not unlikely. Either way, he'd have his work cut out for him there. As an added bonus, it bordered on Dartmuth Station, so he and Andrew might be able to relay each other if there was an emergency.

"Just put me down for Langdon," he answered, still eyeing the swelling crowd nervously. He was starting to feel like an ambulant museum or some kind of freak show on wheels. It was time to leave the crowd behind and get to work. He revved the engine again. The sound of it was really starting to get addictive. "Oh, and Chloe," he added after some hesitation, "have you noticed how damned bright it is outside? I haven't seen this much light in the sky since... I'm not sure that I ever have. It just feels kind of weird to me. Nice, but weird."

"Uh... Frank?" Chloe asked, sounding awkward. "Are you okay? Like... have you been getting enough sleep lately? It's been pitch-black out there for at least the past ten to fifteen minutes, and honestly, it wasn't a whole lot better before that. I'm not even kidding. Looks like a thick cloud cover rolled in over the smog."

Frank furrowed his brow. With the dreams waking him all the time, maybe he *wasn't* getting enough sleep lately, but that wouldn't enhance his vision. She was probably just messing with him. "I've been getting plenty of sleep," he lied. "Thank you."

"Then maybe you should get your eyes checked," she said, "because it's dark as ever outside. I swear." There was a moment of uncomfortable silence before she asked, "Hey... are you and Vanessa coming to see that movie tonight? You know the one with the tough cop and the stupid cop? Andy said he was coming for sure." It was an obvious attempt to lighten the atmosphere by changing the subject.

"No," he answered gruffly. With that, he revved his engine exaggeratedly one more time and took off. His tires screeched loudly as he merged onto Wilderweg in the northbound lane. He really hadn't expected the bike to be so jerky on takeoff, but he compensated by shifting his weight and recuperated with relative ease. *Traction*, he reminded himself. *Never forget: Traction!*

Until then, he'd despised the attention the bike had drawn, but when he saw how people reacted every time it ripped out a new and exciting noise they'd never heard before, he felt like laughing. Their facial expressions ranged from bedazzled ooh-ahs to outright terror.

"I'll see you at eight o'clock then, showoff," Chloe said. It reminded him to switch off his CB. A little uneasy on his bike, he decided he'd take it slow at first, riding well below the speed limit until he felt more confident with his new set of wheels. He was as good as an expert when it came to hoverbikes, but this was a whole other ballgame. His reduced speed might be an annoyance for any drivers caught behind him, but it might also give him a chance to enjoy the scenery for once.

The buildings in the Plaza were relatively low compared to those in its neighboring districts. Looking up from ground level, the wall of gradually steeper skyscrapers made him feel like he was at the bottom of a vast gorge, and Wilderweg, stretching farther north than the eye could see, was like a canyon bed, its smooth flow of sparse traffic the trickle of a dying stream.

The way north led to progressively older parts of the city. Much of the Wilderweg stretch, the outlying boroughs and the northeasternmost reaches had remained intact over the centuries. The districts there were durable and easy to maintain, just like the founders had intended them to be when they'd first built them, in a time long before official records were kept. The buildings there were considered eyesores by modern standards, but investors still found a use for them in industry, small business and low-income housing. The poor had to live and work somewhere, after all.

Frank looked at the cracked pavement zipping by beneath him. He'd have to be extra careful. The roads in the older parts of the city were oftentimes neglected and riddled with potholes. He tried to avoid picturing what a motorcycle crash would look like, but found that it was easier said than done. He felt completely exposed on the back of this crude, metal beast. One wrong move or a simple lapse in attention could send him flying off the bike at a breakneck speed.

There was a large, green sign hanging from the overpass up ahead. "Now entering Compton," it read in tall, white letters. He squinted as he rode into the darkness beneath the overpass. When he emerged on the other side, the aesthetic differences were visible immediately. Compared to the Plaza district, everything here looked a little duller, and like it was in need of a good wash. Low two and three-story businesses lined the sector's main artery. Behind them loomed drab-looking apartment buildings that rose high into the urban canopy. A labyrinth of covered skywalks connected the buildings and made it hard to see the sky from the street.

All those skywalks made him feel caged in, repressed. From below, he thought they looked like a giant sewer grate. In such a confined space, the neon signs in the windows of practically every business seemed to meld together into one multicolored, glowing mess of light. The ambiance they created was not unlike that of a nightclub or a seedy casino. Some people found the lighting here "dazzling", but Frank saw it as seizure-inducing, at best. Either way, almost everyone seemed to agree that it was inadequate, as far as practicality and safety went.

He could easily envision some poor soul getting mugged somewhere in all of these shadows. A little injection into the local budget to provide them with more streetlights would do no harm. It would do a world of good, actually, but it wasn't likely to happen. The president, like virtually every other president before him, clearly preferred to invest in the nicer parts of town. The old districts were all too often overlooked. Regardless, Compton wasn't that bad of a district. Things would only grow worse as he continued down this road.

Three red lights and eight blocks later, the skywalks gradually started to give way to the sky again. Small business became more and more scarce and large warehouses and factories became more prevalent. Mulholland was one of the city's largest industrial parks. There were only two others larger than it, but none were even half as dirty. Everything here seemed to be covered in a thin layer of soot. Every other building had a large smokestack, or a set of large smokestacks that belched out a putrid, yellowish filth that shifted as it rose high into the sky. Instead of dissipating with the wind, the toxic blend merged with the smoke spewed out by the other factories. Together, they formed one great cloud of airborne pollution that no doubt contributed heavily to the city's perpetual blanket of smog.

As the citizens of Innerstadt knew all too well, horrible odors were a fact of life. *The Stink*, as people called it, reared its ugly head on a daily basis, but it was almost always unexpected. It didn't matter which part of the city you were in, either. There was no escaping it. The wind carried *the stink* to the farthest reaches of the city. Over the course of the day, it would travel everywhere at least once. It was the kind of odor that made people wrinkle their noses and give each other accusatory looks when they first smelled it. It was a stench like something borne by the bowels of some dead or dying beast then left to rot in a hot place for days. It made people curse and cover their noses with kerchiefs, or wave their hands in front of their faces with a look of disgust. It stung nostrils and clung to fabrics, and drove some of the wealthier citizens to burn their clothes. That odor stemmed from this place, and seemed to permeate the area in permanence.

It was like the whole sector had been drenched in rot and left to soak in it. It was disturbing to think that nearly one third of the city's food was manufactured here, and even more disturbing to think that the horrible smell came from the production process itself. Synthetic cheese, synthetic meat products, laboratory-grown fruits and vegetables; most of them were made or grown right here, and few were those who knew the secret of what exactly went into them. Fewer still were those who really cared, so long as dinner was on the table when they got home from work. There were also breeders here, raising animals for human consumption, but they were few and far between. Only the richest could afford authentic chicken, pork, or beef, or as they were more commonly referred to, the *real deal*.

Seafood was more affordable and readily available to the general public. If he continued down this road past Langdon district, he'd eventually reach Portsmuth, the city's sole source of fish and shellfish. The port, as many called it, bordered on nearly three quarters of the city's artificial lake. Three quarters of its *attainable* shore, at least. The rest of the lake was hedged in by the city's virtually impenetrable ramparts. Consequently, over half of its perimeter remained inaccessible. Approaching to within five-hundred feet of the rampart was a severely punishable offense, so exploitation along the wall was absolutely out of the question. Punitive patrols were frequent and unforgiving, so stakeholders in fishing enterprises didn't dare venture that far out from shore. Those that did were promptly sent to the bottom.

If he looked east, he could just barely make out the high ramparts. For the briefest of moments, he wondered what lie beyond them. His curiosity was as spontaneous as it was fleeting. If the government claimed that a slow and painful death awaited anyone that dared to venture outside of the city's protective walls, it was probably for a reason. Radiation levels were extremely high out there, and that was all he needed to know.

Langdon's taller buildings soon appeared on the horizon. As he neared the sector's limits, traffic condensed and slowed to a near halt. Rolling along at a snail's pace with the growing and impatient mob, it took nearly fifteen minutes for him to reach the first residential towers on Langdon's outskirts. Blaring sirens drew his attention and he half-stood from his bike to survey the area. He could clearly see that there'd been some kind of traffic accident up ahead.

An ambulance was parked in the middle of the street a few hundred feet up the road, and another was on its way from the opposite direction. In the midst of all that was an overturned transport. It looked like there'd been some kind of spill, but he couldn't tell what it was; not until the smell of it came downwind and gave it away. "Holy mackerel," he breathed. The breadth of the street was covered in a thick layer of trout. Upon closer inspection, it looked like the entire silvery mass was wriggling. The transport was most likely on its way from Portsmuth to some marketplace when it lost control and tipped over, spilling its jittery cargo everywhere.

Traffic had come to an utter and complete stop. Up ahead, no one was getting through, and there were no side streets to use as alternate routes. To make matters worse, it could take a while for the cleanup crews to arrive and clear the fish and the overturned vehicle from the road.

There was a subtle buzzing in his ear, followed by a barely audible beep. "Report in," a vaguely familiar baritone ordered over the comm-link. His smooth, practiced tone carried well over the static interference.

Frank pushed his sleeve up and activated his communications band, then raised it to within a few inches of his mouth, and responded in a crisp tone. "Officer forty-two dash zero sixty-seven, reporting in."

"Detective Fasaro," the voice said more than asked. "What's your current situation?"

"I've just entered Langdon district via Mulholland Park, but there's severe bottlenecking around the outskirts. There's been an accident up the way, on Wilderweg at the height of Munnstrasse. Looks like a fish truck got flipped over on its side. The streets are badly congested from Wabashallee to Munnstrasse. I guess you could say I'm *dead in the water*."

There was a brief moment of silence before the dispatch officer responded. "We've received an anonymous call from your sector. Reported assault in progress over at Griswold Thurman High School, at the corner of Pine Crest and Park Hill." There was another moment of awkward silence before he asked, "Are you able to disengage from the traffic? If not, I'll call in some help from Dartmuth Station, instead."

"Don't bother doing that unless you absolutely have to. I'll find a way out of this mess." Griswold Thurman High was practically around the corner. There was no way he was going to let them pull Andrew off his rounds for this. Not over something as trivial as a traffic jam, he wasn't. He was fairly certain that his friend had bigger fish to fry, and it would probably take him longer to get there, anyway. "What do we know?" he asked him as he dismounted from his bike.

"Not much," dispatch responded. "We've got two victims: a male and a female. According to the caller, they're being assaulted in the big park behind the school. Expect as many as four armed assailants, possibly more. That's all we've got."

"Okay. I'm on it," Frank said. He started to guide his motorcycle through two lanes of bumper-to-bumper vehicles. "I'm heading over there right now."

He turned his communications band off and signaled to the driver of a red compact hovercar that was blocking his path. "Move back," he shouted. The driver, a nervous-looking man in his thirties, went into reverse immediately. He backed up all of two inches before hitting the car behind his. The impact was light, but stopped him cold.

Frank grimaced and pushed his bike between the compact hovercar and the bigger luxury craft in front of it. It looked like there was just enough room to squeeze the bike all the way through. Exhaling, he climbed onto the red car's hood, crouched down and tugged his bike through the tight space. Once he got to the other end, he hopped down and had to yank hard to dislodge his bike. His efforts left a few scratches on both vehicles.

The luxury craft's driver was a hairy, potbellied man with blonde hair that was twirled at the front. He was wearing a dark gray suit with sleeves that were drawn halfway up his forearms. He stuck the top half of his body out the window, glaring at Frank while shaking his fist and yelling, "You're gonna pay for that, you little punk! Do you have any idea whose car you just vandalized? Do you have *any* idea who *I* am? *Do* you? *Huh?*" The man had gone beet red in the face and was trembling with rage.

Frank sighed as he pushed his bike up onto the sidewalk, then got on and started it. "Take it up with the city," he said. "They'll reimburse you for the repairs. Now, if that's everything, I have an emergency situation to deal with." He gave his bike some throttle then and started advancing slowly down the sidewalk.

"Take it up with the city?" the man barked, incredulous. He tried to grab Frank by the arm as he passed by on his motorcycle, but couldn't reach him, and decided to smash his fists down against the outside of his door instead. "The only emergency you have is right here, pal!" the man roared, bashing his fists down again. "Now get back here and pay for my damages *right now,* or I'm gonna snap your neck like a twig!"

Frank furrowed his brow, but ignored him and continued on his way. He didn't know who the man was, and he didn't care to know, either. He could have fined him for threatening an officer of the law, or even arrested him for attempted assault, but he didn't have time for anything but the task at hand.

He coasted along at a reasonable pace for a short while, but soon slowed to a crawl as he approached the crowd of onlookers that had gathered near the crash site. He had to signal wildly, and shout for them to get out of the way so he could wade through them safely. They parted before him without hesitation as soon as they heard the rumble of his engine.

He was making good progress when the sound of a slamming car door somewhere behind him got his attention. He looked back to see where the noise had come from. "Crap," he muttered, shaking his head in disbelief. "I do *not* have time for this."

The fat man in the little suit had gotten out of his vehicle and was heading straight toward him with great, shoulder-bobbing strides. The fire in his eyes looked like it could burn a hole through a brick wall. "*Nobody* walks away from me like that when I'm talking to them!" the man bellowed, pointing Frank out as he marched in his direction. "Nobody!"

Frank returned his attention to the path ahead. He was almost the entire way to the scene of the accident. The only thing standing between him and his next objective was a milling crowd of gawkers. *That and a shin-deep pile of trout*, he thought, grimacing. It spread out from the building ahead to the overturned transport. There wasn't the slightest gap in between. He had no choice but to go through it.

"Police, coming through!" he shouted. "Clear the way!" Those standing immediately in front of him parted ways almost instantly, stepping into the street or backing up against the wall to let him pass, but people weren't reacting quite as quickly or moving nearly as fluidly a little farther ahead. Moving slowly, he closed the gap to the next buildup and realized where the problem was stemming from.

From that point on, the crowd thickened. A little farther ahead, it was even spilling over into the street. That was probably where the spectators had first started gathering after the accident had occurred. Near its center, the crowd had grown so dense that people had very little room to move. To Frank, they looked like so many huddled sheep, unable to make a decision or even move on their own. Consequently, they were immobilized in the mire. Each one seemed overwhelmed by the other's inability to make a decision. They lacked an authority figure to tell them what to do.

They were like people caught in a burning office building that could smell the fire and see the smoke, but failed to acknowledge the situation because no one else was doing so. It had happened before. He'd seen it with his own eyes. It was normal, expected human behavior. Maybe they'd seen someone die, or thought that someone had died in the accident. That kind of thing could sap a person's decisional capabilities. From the look of things, with the extent of the damage and the number of vehicles piled up behind the transport, it was a likely scenario.

Frank wasn't completely indifferent to their plight, but he had a job to do. The paramedics would soon have everything under control here anyway, and all he could really do was tell everyone to disperse and carry on. At that precise moment, somewhere not that far away, people that he *could* help were being assaulted. If he could just get past this somehow, if he could just get there in time, then maybe, just maybe he could help those people. Maybe it was already too late, maybe it was already over, but he couldn't just assume that. He had to do everything that he could to get there as quickly as possible.

He cleared his throat, and repeated his earlier warning in a raised voice. "Police, coming through! Clear the way!" He didn't get the reaction that he was hoping for. People were too absorbed by what was going on. Albeit slightly delayed, almost as though they were being woken from a trance, the closest layer of the crowd did eventually look toward him before stumbling out of the way. He repeated himself again, louder, and it produced much the same result. Rinsing and repeating the process over and over again, he slogged through the crowd, slowly but surely. Those that had moved out of the way for him squeezed in against each other the second he passed them by, resealing the gap that was left in his wake.

When the final layer of the crowd parted, clearing the way to the relatively open sidewalk, he heard the infuriated voice of the portly man cry out again from somewhere behind him. "Where do you think you're going, punk?" he demanded. "You can't run from me! You *are* going to pay for this!" He started cursing then, loudly and repeatedly. "Hey! Get out of my way, you fucking idiots! Do you know who I am? Do any of you fucking fuckwits *know* who the fuck I am?"

The furrow in Frank's brow deepened and he grimaced sourly. If he wasn't in such a hurry, he'd cuff the guy and make him sweat for a while. He could understand a certain level of frustration on his part, but chasing down an officer of the law over something as trivial as a few scratches on a hovercraft bordered on madness. With a bit of luck, the crowd would keep the angry man at bay at least long enough that he could continue on his way.

Wasting as little time as possible, he accelerated generously and closed the distance between himself and the spill. He slowed on his approach, and waited until his front tire squished into the first fish on the edge of the pile before sticking his feet out to the sides. As he'd expected, riding through the truckload of trout was no easy task. One second he'd had good traction, and the next it was like his tires were spinning in butter. Using his feet as guides, he brought the bike almost the entire fifteen or so feet across at a glide. As he neared the other extremity of the spill, the bike's rear end started to fishtail out of control, but he managed to straighten it out just as his front tire gripped the rough asphalt on the other side, and he kicked up a brief spray of fish gunk as he sped up.

Things started to look up as he approached the next side street. At first glance, no one seemed to be waiting to get onto Wilderweg at the intersection there. As he slowed to round the corner onto Munnstrasse, a quick scan of the area confirmed that his observation had been right. The only traffic on Munnstrasse consisted of vehicles turning right from the opposite direction of Wilderweg in an attempt to bypass the traffic jam.

Dropping down from the sidewalk to the pavement, Frank sped westward on Munnstrasse's clear, eastbound lane. He veered off into the right-hand side as soon as he'd put enough distance between himself and the vehicles trying to get out of the traffic. Riding more freely now, Frank realized with some relief that his earlier prediction had been right on: the bike was much easier to handle at faster speeds. And surprisingly, he was comfortable with it. Considering the urgency of the situation, he figured it was as good a time as any to see how fast Bertha could go. Increasing the throttle generously but gradually, he watched the indicator on his speedometer climb. Forty, forty-five, fifty miles per hour and rising after only a few seconds, and he wasn't even trying. Since no one had thought to install a siren on this rig, he'd have to be a lot more careful about his speed around intersections.

The shoddy, often derelict-looking buildings lining the street seemed to whiz by at an incredible speed. The Old Worlders had known what they were doing when they'd designed this bike. Its acceleration put any hoverbike's to shame. If the roads were this clear all the way to the high school, he'd be there in no time at all.

Remaining as alert to his surroundings as he possibly could, he checked off street names as he passed them by. Bennettweg, Archerstrasse, Schultzweg, and finally, Pine Crest Allee appeared just ahead. He slowed to thirty miles per hour as he made his approach. When he'd gotten to within a stone's throw of it, he grimaced as the lights changed from green to orange. In a second or two, the light would turn red. Unlike his brief trip down Munnstrasse, there seemed to be at least moderate circulation here, with vehicles lining up at the intersection.

It was a do or die situation. He could either slam the brakes and come to a screeching halt, or speed up in an attempt to get through the lights before they changed, hopefully without getting run over by a dump truck. Taking a deep breath, he glided into the left lane to give himself a wider berth. Then, when he engaged the intersection, he leaned hard to the right. The rear end of the bike started to slide out, and he skidded through the intersection, barely avoiding incoming traffic as he rounded the corner onto Pine Crest Allee. He came out of the turn like a bat out of hell and had to counter-steer to straighten his rig. He breathed out a sigh of relief, but didn't slow down. *Can't stop yet*, he told himself. He repeated it over and over like some sort of mantra. The clock was ticking. He *had* to get there before it was too late.

Seconds later, he was closing in fast on Park Hill Weg. He could see Griswold Thurman high school up on the left side of the road, just past the Park Hill intersection. If his memory served, that was where the front entrance was, and that would be his insertion point. With all the noise it churned out, Bertha—the Blitz—was quite the attention getter. If he rode straight to the back of the school, he'd draw everyone's attention straight away, and he couldn't have that. If he was going to succeed here, he was going to have to exploit every advantage that he possibly could. Even a modicum of surprise could go a long way.

After zipping through the intersection, he eased up on the throttle and coasted along the street on nothing but the bike's forward momentum. When he came parallel to the school's front doors, he squeezed the brakes smoothly and came to a stop, then waited for two incoming vehicles to pass him by in the other lane. After they had, he turned left and rode up to the sidewalk in front of the school. Once immobilized, he cut the engine then hopped off the bike and set it down on its side. If Bertha had a kickstand, he didn't know about it. No kickstand. No siren. He couldn't help but wonder what other surprises she might have in store for him.

He looked up the stairs leading to the front doors and started climbing them at a jog. It was no wonder they'd christened the street Park Hill. The stairs ran about seventy feet up a relatively sharp incline. The ancient stone building on high looked out of place and out of time. It was reminiscent of something from an age long past. From a time before the old world ceased to exist at the drop of a bomb—at the drop of a series of nuclear bombs.

Gaining the top of the stairs, he reached inside his jacket and drew a pistol from the shoulder holster concealed there. While his semiautomatic Barringer Mark II wasn't as fancy as the standard issue laser pistols most officers carried, its .44 caliber rounds packed quite the punch. Though considered outdated by most, Frank liked the extra weight of the heavier gun in the palm of his hand. Despite any of its technological drawbacks, he found that it had a decent range, and maintained a good rate of fire without sacrificing precision. The matte black pistol wasn't much to look at, but it was a family heirloom of sorts.

It had once belonged to his grandfather, William Bernhardt Fasaro, and despite its advanced age, it had been extraordinarily well maintained. He'd practiced firing it long before he'd ever considered joining the academy. He'd grown so used to it that he had a hard time imagining using anything else. If given the option, he wouldn't. It had taken quite a lot of negotiating to convince the captain to let him keep his sidearm. There were comparable weapons available in the armory, but this was the one that he wanted to use. When the weapons lab gave the OK, the captain couldn't really say no.

Moving furtively, Frank rushed to the school's facade. As he reached it, he swiveled around and pressed his back to the cold, hard stones. He sidled the wall to the northeast corner of the building, then stopped and peeked around it hesitantly. There was nothing out of the ordinary on the school's north face, but after concentrating for a second, his ears tuned in to what sounded like a distant scream. It seemed to be coming from the school's west end, from the park itself.

Holding his pistol at the ready, he rounded the corner and ran westward. He sprinted nearly the entire distance, but slowed to a light jog as he neared the northwest end of the building. Backing against the wall again, he inched his way toward the corner, and once he'd reached it, he repeated his previous maneuver, peeking around it for a better view.

He spotted one of the suspects about ninety to a hundred feet ahead and to the left. The man was standing with his back to him behind a tall, stone obelisk. Frank's view was partially obstructed by the monument, but he was able to pick out a few details. The suspect was wearing black synthetic leather with gray stripes from the tips of his toes to the nape of his neck. His long, brown hair looked greasy and was tied high at the back of his head in a crude ponytail. It looked like he was holding something in his right hand, but he kept fidgeting around nervously and it was hard to tell what it was.

"This is how you repay me?" a shrill voice cried out in anger. Despite the limited visibility, Frank could tell that the man with the ponytail wasn't the one doing the yelling. His body language alone made it very unlikely. He heard the sound of a woman whimpering then, but it was drowned out as the voice continued. "I feed you. I clothe you. I even find you your fix when you need it... and *this* is how you repay me!"

There was obviously more going on here than Frank could see. He had to get a better view. Running into things headlong wasn't always a good idea, and he wouldn't do so unless he had absolutely no other choice. About twenty-five feet directly in front of him, a low hedgerow ran a straight line westward, into the distance. It was relatively thick at the base, and though he wasn't entirely sure, it appeared to cut off somewhere past the obelisk. If he was cautious, he might be able to use it to sneak in closer and get a better look. It was risky, and would leave him exposed for a few seconds, but it was the only option he saw.

He watched the man in the synthetic leather, waiting for the best time to act. When he was as satisfied as he would be that the guy wasn't looking his way, he crouched down and dashed across the lawn, then ducked behind the hedgerow with a barely audible thud and a light ruffling of leaves.

As he inched his way forward, he peeked through gaps in the hedgerow, keeping tabs on the one and only suspect that he could actually see. From the look of it, he was probably just the hired muscle, standing around trying to look tough while remaining completely silent. A loud smacking sound resounded then, and it was accompanied by a woman's violent sob.

"I warned you, Kristal," the man's voice grated angrily. "I fucking *warned* you. But did you listen?" Kristal's only response was another of her agonized sobs. "No," the voice answered for her. "You had to go and do the one thing I told you *not* to. You stupid whore! You sleep with whoever the fuck I tell you to and no one else. Paying customers *only*. Is that so hard to understand, you dumb bitch? You're fucking useless to me in *love.*" He wriggled around that last word like it left a bad taste in his mouth.

A pimp and his bodyguard, Frank thought. Through sheer inadvertence, he crushed a dry branch under his foot then and it snapped loudly. Suddenly, the thug with the ponytail swiveled in his direction. He had a look of suspicion about him. Frank froze and his heart started to beat a little faster. Waiting motionless, he held his breath for what seemed like a very long time. When the seedy figure shrugged and turned back to his business, he let out a quiet sigh of relief.

Paying closer attention to his footing, he continued on his way, carefully sneaking toward the other end of the hedgerow. As he neared its edge, he got down on his stomach at the base of the bushes, then inched his way forward until he could peek past it, toward the monument. The view was far better from this vantage point. From there, he could see the entire picture, and the entire picture was less than promising.

The crying woman sat huddled in a ball near the foot of the monument. Five dangerous-looking men loomed over her in a haphazard circle. Apart from their common taste in leatherette jackets, they seemed like a perfectly mismatched band of misfits. At least at first glance, they did. Upon closer examination, he noticed that they all had a thin strip of dark purple cloth tied around their right bicep. It was most likely a sign of allegiance to whatever gang they belonged to. Their overly obvious leader, the shortest of them all and the one doing all the talking, wore a silly-looking melon hat with a fuzzy, neon green feather sticking out at the back. A little off to the side, a naked man, bruised and battered, lay writhing in a pool of his own blood. He could almost swear he could hear him moaning.

The urgency of the situation had just escalated to a whole other level. At first, Frank thought he might be dealing with a case of flesh peddler's restitution. Occasionally, when a working girl wanted to leave her old ways behind, start over again, her pimp would offer her an opportunity to buy back her freedom. The girl was given a ridiculously short timeframe to gather an exorbitantly high buyback fee, purportedly to compensate for some of the pimp's lost prospective revenues. Most that tried couldn't hope to respect the deadline given, but even if they did somehow manage to, they usually turned up dead a short while later.

It wasn't exactly a common occurrence, but it happened a lot more often than it should. The only reason prostitution rings were able to survive in their city was secrecy. An unhappy working girl was a liability, even more so if she had intimate knowledge of key players and the ins and outs of the operation. The same could be said for anyone that had managed to get away from it all. No smart pimp would take that risk. For most of the women in these rings, there was no way out. The flesh peddler's restitution scheme was an effective way of recouping some of the losses on a girl before shutting her up forever.

If this had been a buyback, he'd have had a lot more time to analyze the situation. If it had been a buyback, the best course of action might have been to lay low and do nothing at all, at least for a while. If it had been a buyback, the pimp might have jostled her around a bit and issued an ultimatum, and in a case like that, it could have been reckless to intervene before the girl was left on her own. It could have aggravated the situation and resulted in a lot of unnecessary bloodshed and collateral damage.

But he'd witnessed buybacks before, and this was looking less and less like a classic case of one. From the look of it, bloodshed was going to be inevitable. There wasn't much he could do for the victims but strike fast and strike hard. He didn't like it, but all the right alarms were sounding off in his head. For all the venom the pimp was spitting out, he'd never once mentioned money, and he didn't seem like the kind of person that doled out second chances out of the goodness of his heart. Furthermore, he'd brought four of his men with him and had left the girl's boyfriend in what looked like critical condition. It was a bit much for an ultimatum. It looked like they were simply going to rub the both of them out.

He had to engage them immediately and without warning. There was no other choice. It was textbook procedure. When a citizen was in danger, he became judge, jury and executioner, and it was his responsibility to remove them from harm's way by whatever means necessary. If he had to get a little blood on his hands in order to do that, it was his prerogative.

Rising to one knee, he held his pistol out at eye level and clicked the safety off. Just then, the leader of the pack reached behind his back and drew a pistol that had been tucked away under his belt. Frank took a deep breath, lined up his sights, and just as the man brought his gun around on the girl, he squeezed the trigger. A loud clap thundered out as the .44 round punched through the back of the pimp's melon hat and exited through his forehead with a brief but violent spray of blood. His body jerked once as he dropped to his knees, then fell forward and landed face down beside Kristal. The woman had gone completely hysterical as soon as the shot had gone off. From the look of her, she was certain that her end had come.

Before any of them could react, a second, third and fourth shot cracked through the air. The man standing farthest from Frank clutched at his chest and watched with horrified disbelief as a spurt of blood gushed through his fingers. His eyes rolled back into his head then and he slumped forward lifelessly. Nearly simultaneously, the man standing next to him lurched back as a bullet ripped through his left arm, just below the shoulder.

Frank pivoted and ducked behind the hedges just as the two other henchmen spun around and started firing in his direction. Bullets whizzed past overhead and shred through the foliage all around him. As he'd anticipated, with their leader gone, the other misfits would concentrate on him before turning their attention to their hapless victims. He'd just bought them a little more time. Unfortunately, the shrubs he was hiding behind offered little in the way of hard cover, and he'd be of no use to anyone dead. He peeked around the edge of the bushes and spotted a short, brick wall running north to south. It was close enough that he could get to it in seconds if he ran for it.

Throwing caution to the wind, he spun around and sprinted for the wall, firing *almost* blindly over his shoulder all the while. He put just enough precision into his shots that he was sure they would go too high to actually hit anything. The purpose of his firing wasn't to hit a target, but to suppress his enemies long enough that he could get to cover. He couldn't risk hitting either of the victims in the process. Shooting on the go was challenging at best, and he'd be damned if he accidentally killed one of the people he was trying to save because he'd tried to get in a lucky shot. The covering fire served its purpose, and fazed his enemies just enough that their shooting was as horrible as his own was. He fired the last round in his magazine just as he reached the wall's welcoming hard cover.

He scrambled forward frantically then stopped and sagged against the wall with a thud. In a matter of seconds, he ejected the empty magazine into his open palm, pocketed it and slapped a new one into place. He always carried around at least two spare mags of ammunition when he was on duty. Situations like this one were the reason why.

Turning, he held his gun up with both hands and rose swiftly. He had to drop back to his knees almost immediately as a new volley was fired his way. Both uninjured thugs had taken up positions behind the monument and were using it for cover. The third gunman—the one he'd tagged in the arm—had pretty much stayed put and was firing from a prone position.

Bullets whizzed by overhead and thunked into the other side of the brick wall. One shot hit high near its top and showered him with a cloud of grit. He wiped the dust from his eyes and, moving quickly, scurried half a dozen feet farther along the wall. Taking a deep breath, he rose again and aimed at the prone target. He squeezed the trigger three times in rapid succession. The first shot bounced off the concrete and into the great unknown, but the second and third bullets ricocheted into the man's collarbone and throat. The man's eyes went blank as they rolled in their sockets and his head sagged limply to the ground.

"Great! Just great!" one of the remaining two yelled out. "Let's get the fuck out of here *now*!"

Frank waited, poised to shoot, but couldn't get a bead on them. He could hear them running off, but they were obviously making painstaking efforts to stay out of his line of sight.

After hopping the wall, he cleared the distance to the two victims and knelt by the unconscious man, then took his wrist and checked his pulse. It was slow but regular, like the rise and fall of his chest. His glassy eyes stared blankly ahead. He turned toward Kristal then and he gave her a quick once over. She was spattered with blood, but he knew that it wasn't hers. She looked shaken, but otherwise fine. "Don't you worry," he said in a soothing tone. "You're safe now." She didn't respond, but he'd expected as much. She was somewhere else right now. Her fear had thrown her into a mild state of shock.

He opened the connection on his communications band and spoke into it. "This is officer forty-two dash zero sixty-seven calling dispatch. Dispatch, do you copy? Over."

"Roger, Sixty-seven," the same familiar baritone from earlier answered him. "I'm listening."

"Shots exchanged at Griswold Thurman High," Frank said. "Remaining suspects have fled the scene. Will pursue, but require immediate medivac for two victims at my location. Male victim is unconscious with multiple lacerations to the ribs. Some blood loss has been sustained, but seems to be under control, for now. Will require shock treatment. Female victim is pretty shaken up, but otherwise physically intact."

"I see your location," the dispatch officer responded. "Stand by." Less than ten seconds later, he added, "Medivac is on the way. Estimated time of arrival is five minutes."

Frank holstered his pistol, then laid his hands on Kristal's shoulders and looked her square in the eyes. Or tried to, at least. He wasn't even sure if she knew that he was there. "Kristal," he uttered softly, but that garnered no response. "*Kristal*," he said again—a little louder—shaking her shoulders lightly. "Can you hear me, miss?"

Slowly shaking off her torpor, Kristal finally looked up and met his gaze. She nodded weakly and let her head sag.

"Good," Frank said. "You had me worried for a second." She didn't look like she was going to answer him, but that was okay. He knew that she was listening. "You're going to be okay now, Kristal. You're *both* going to be okay... but you need medical attention." He paused for a second to ensure that she was still following him. "A medivac team is on the way. I need you to stay right here until the ambulance arrives. Do you understand what I'm saying? You need to stay *right* here, Kristal. Help is on its way right now."

Kristal sat quietly for a moment and finally nodded.

"Alright," Frank said. He knelt by the man in the feathered hat then and rifled through his pant pockets until he heard the familiar jingle of keys that he was hoping to. Straight-faced, he grabbed the pimp's keys and got up. The other men had run off and disappeared around the school's south-facing wall. Following them that way might not lead him past his bike, but he couldn't risk delaying himself further than he already had with a detour. He might need a vehicle to continue the chase, and there was a pretty good chance that they'd lead him to one.

Wasting no time, he started after them at a sprint. They might have a considerable lead on him, but his training and conditioning were a point in his favor. Innerstadt's police force might have its funding issues, but its officers were extraordinarily fit, and he was no exception. Years of hard work and dedication had honed his athletic abilities, and molded him into a runner that few could truly hope to compete with.

He rounded the corner of the school and spotted his quarry straight away. Both men were about halfway down the wall, by a handful of loosely parked hoverbikes, and were busy getting onto their rigs at a scramble. He hoped that they'd all parked together, because he wasn't going to be able to catch up to them before they took off. Since their victims were out of harm's way, he wasn't about to shoot them down in cold blood. Even if he tried to, he couldn't guarantee his accuracy from this far out.

Fueled by a profound disgust for what they and other crooks just like them had done, and by the thought of what they'd keep doing if he let them get away, Frank charged down the sidewalk like a stampeding bull. The sight of them taking off pushed him even harder. He could feel the beat of his heart drumming in his ears, but he ran faster, letting out a labored grunt as he reached his limit and tried to surpass it.

He watched as the two of them sped eastward down Park Hill Weg and turned left onto Pine Crest Allee. That was where he'd parked Bertha. If he'd known they'd go that way, he might have been able to cut them off, or at least buy himself a little more time. But he hadn't known, and he hadn't taken the shorter path, and regardless of that choice, he'd have to work with what he had and somehow catch up to them.

As he neared the remaining vehicles, he looked around for the fanciest-looking one and saw it almost immediately. It wasn't hard to spot. All the hoverbikes were open-topped Sports models, with low visor shields and a higher-than-usual elevation on their inclined seats, but the one with the eyesore of a custom paint job was a Strahl Kraft, he was sure. He could spot one from a mile away. The brand was quite popular with the street racing crowd. Consequently, they were a lot more expensive than other bikes of comparable quality were.

With its bright purple and yellow paint job, silver crown and scepter decals, and decorative lighting, there was no doubt in his mind that this one had belonged to the pimp. Guys like him were always flashier than the help. They wouldn't have it any other way. There had to be a very clear distinction between them and their entourage of common thugs. It helped reinforce the illusion of superiority. In his experience, the accessories that they used to fabricate such distinctions were oftentimes gaudy. They were meant to impress, and make it painstakingly clear exactly who the boss was. In a pimp's world, image was half of everything.

He hopped onto the Strahl Kraft as soon as he reached it. There was a low whir as he turned the key in the ignition, confirming that he'd chosen the right vehicle. The whir intensified and the hovercraft rose suddenly, then stopped once it had lifted a few inches off the ground.

Ever mindful of the urgency of the situation, he pulled out into the street, increased his forward thrust and headed for the intersection. He slowed a little as he reached it, but ignored the red light and veered hard-left. He floored it as he sped through the crossroads, and narrowly avoided a parked hovercraft that was merging onto the street.

Ahead, traffic was dense but fluid. He saw no sign of the fleeing criminals until he topped the next rise. There, from the pinnacle of Pine Crest Allee, he could see all the way down the slope that led to the harbor in Portsmuth. His quarry was turning right onto Grantstrasse, about a quarter of a mile up the road. "Stupid assholes," Frank muttered under his breath. They probably thought they'd gotten away scot-free. With the recent job opening left in their pal's wake, they were probably already thinking about climbing the rungs of the criminal ladder.

If he could help it, they'd have something else coming to them—a lonely jail cell, or a six-foot-deep hole in the ground. Despite his elevated kill ratio, he was not a butcher. He didn't go out of his way to ensure that he killed the bad guys every single time. To the contrary, he sought peaceful resolution. Sometimes, he thought it was just bad luck that had him constantly pitted against the ones that never gave up.

Any truth to that was yet to be determined, but there was one thing he was sure of: everyone was responsible for their actions— *everyone*—and those that died got what they had coming to them. As for these clowns, the choice was theirs. It always had been. Regardless of anything they might do in the following moments, their days of living in the lap of ill-gotten luxury would soon be over. At least they would be if he could help it.

Frank was closing in on the slower-moving traffic at an alarming rate. The tail end of the truck in front of him was getting closer and closer, but all he could think of was the smug look of satisfaction on the criminals' faces, thinking they'd managed to slip away. At the speed he was going, pockets of wind shook the bike whenever a vehicle whooshed past on his left, and he was hard-pressed to maintain his bearings every single time.

Just as he was about to rear-end the truck, he nudged his bike left onto the center line. It was a dangerously tight squeeze. With vehicles zipping past on his left and others filing by him on the right, there was no elbow room to speak of. He had to tilt his bike to the right, and then back to the left again just as quickly to compensate for a driver that was hogging a little too much of the road. A collision of any kind and on either side could have been the end of him. When he managed to straighten his rig, he had to duck low to avoid having his head taken off by a city bus' low-hanging rearview mirror.

A last vehicle whooshed by on the left and that lane was clear again. The taxi on his right slowed to a halt and he glided into the left lane to speed up. At the lights, he cut the thrust and turned his handlebars all the way to the right. His rig continued straight across the intersection as its rear end slid out, realigning it with Grantstrasse. His powerglide through the crossroads brought him face to face with an ice cream truck. He floored it again and managed to clear the way just in the nick of time. They'd come so close to a head-on collision that Frank could see the expression of sheer horror register on the truck driver's face as he slid past him, and the cup of coffee that slipped from his grasp as he braced himself against the steering wheel.

As soon as he cleared the truck, he veered into Grantstrasse's eastbound lane. To his surprise, he spotted the men he was looking for just a couple blocks ahead of him. They were cruising along at a Sunday driver's pace with the rest of the late-morning traffic. They didn't look like they were in much of a hurry. In fact, they almost seemed aloof, like nothing at all had happened. They even waited patiently at the stop sign farther up the road and took off in sequence. From the look of it, they thought that they'd shaken pursuit, and were trying to blend in with the crowd to avoid drawing further attention. Their lack of urgency was a painful reminder of the difficult times the city was going through. If the same situation had played out several years ago, multiple units would have been dispatched to the area within minutes to neutralize the threat. If they'd failed to get the situation under control quickly enough, an all-points bulletin would have ensued.

They no longer had the resources that they needed for that kind of response. There just weren't enough officers to cope with even half of the city's basic needs. He couldn't afford to call in backup units, and even if he did, it could take them forever to disengage from whatever else they might be busy with and actually get to the scene. Sadly, these guys seemed to know it. Every low-life criminal in the city seemed to know it. When he'd woken up that morning, however, he hadn't. Or he'd refused to see what was taking place right under his nose.

He still couldn't believe that he'd walked around with the wool pulled over his eyes for so long, that he'd failed to see the gravity of the situation, that it had taken the captain spelling it out for him to understand. He felt ashamed—ashamed and angry. He was angry at the nonchalance of criminals like these ones, at people who took the law lightly, who preyed on the weak to enrich themselves. He was also angry at leatherette jackets, for being the ugly, synthetic monstrosities that they were.

Putting these guys behinds bars would be a first step toward redeeming himself. It wasn't like he hadn't been doing *anything*, but he'd have done a lot more if only he'd known how bad things had gotten. It wasn't like top brass or the media were being open about it, but if he'd looked harder—just a *little bit* harder—he'd have figured it out all on his own. The criminal world had.

He cut his speed and was especially careful not to draw their attention on his approach. He wanted to gain as much ground as he possibly could before making his presence known. To some, he knew, it would seem like a stupid move. But it wasn't. He wasn't out to gun them down. Not yet. Not without giving them the chance to surrender, first. He didn't want to get too close, either. *That* would be a stupid move. Sneaking up on an armed criminal and yelling, *"Freeze, punk!"* might be good for the movies, but in the real world, it was a risk he didn't want to take. Startling them now would be dangerous at best. No, he didn't feel like dying just because he'd spooked Mr. Jumpy McFiggins. What he *wanted* to do was get just close enough that if they did decide to hightail it out of there—an outcome which was very likely in his opinion— then at least they wouldn't have very much of a head start.

He'd come back across Schultzweg and Archerstrasse, and was pulling up to where the two were stopped at the Bennetweg intersection when the larger one looked back over his shoulder. "Police! Put your hands in the air!" Frank yelled as he raised his pistol, confident that the jig was up. The thug's mouth dropped open the second he spotted him. His slack-jawed expression reminded him of something he'd seen in a horrible cartoon, and might have been funny in a different context.

"Oh, crap," the man said, loudly, but in a slow, drawn-out voice that was tinged with an equally amusing blend of terror and sheer disbelief. "He's back, Will. Will! He's back!"

"Well way to go, you fucking moron," Will spat. "Giving my name to the cops and everything. Has anyone ever told you how retarded you are?" He paused then to show that he was expecting an answer. "Well, Jimbo? Have they?" He didn't even look over his shoulder to see who was there. Apparently, he wasn't at all fazed by the cop that was parked behind him, or by the possibility that a gun was aimed at the back of his head. For all he knew, his brains were about to be splattered across the pavement in front of him, but he didn't seem to care.

Frank *was* aiming at the back of Will's head. He wasn't too worried about "Jimbo", but a man with his back to him could be up to anything, and his indifferent attitude irked him. "I said put your hands above your heads, where I can see them!" he ordered brusquely, gripping his pistol like he meant to use it. "Don't try anything funny with me."

Jimbo's hands went up immediately, Will's did not, and that was about as much of a reaction as he was going to get out of them. For all intent and purposes, it was like he was hardly even there at all.

"It's not like he knows that Will's short for Wilhelm," Jimbo slurred defensively, "or that your last name's Braun." The guy looked like he was genuinely oblivious to his slipup.

For a second, Frank wondered if anyone could really be that stupid, or if it was all just intentional. Maybe Jimbo had always had it in for Wilhelm, and now that they were both screwed anyway, he'd do everything in his power to ensure that he didn't walk away from this unscathed. He dismissed the theory as comprehension dawned on Jimbo's face.

Wilhelm's shoulders crisped visibly, and he squeezed his handlebars so hard his knuckles turned white.

"I said hands above your heads," Frank barked loudly. Jimbo fidgeted nervously and reached up even higher than he already had been, but Wilhelm remained motionless, pretending like he hadn't heard a single word.

"You hopeless fricken retard!" Wilhelm shouted. "Why the shit did you have to go and say that, huh?" He shook his head violently, steaming. "I don't know how you managed to stay alive as long as you have. It boggles my fricken mind. Really, it does." Jimbo started to apologize, but he cut him off before he could get a word out. "I don't want to hear it, Jim. Really, I don't. 'Sorry' don't change a thing. 'Sorry' don't make up for half the dumb shit you've said and done in the time I've known you. Not by a long shot. No sir, not even close."

Frank could hardly believe his eyes. In his experience, one of two things happened when criminals were confronted by the law. The more common of the two was surrender. Though there were many ways of surrendering, the reactions of most of the criminals he'd stopped before had ranged from resigned cooperation to bitter protest, and in most cases, everything had ended with arrests being made. The other thing that happened was resisting arrest. It was less common, but not at all infrequent. There were as many ways of resisting arrest as there were of accepting defeat, and the law's response was physical subjugation, though sometimes a firefight was inevitable. Again, in most cases, it ended with an arrest being made—or with people being carried away in body bags.

He wasn't sure what this was, so for the time being, he set it aside in its very own category labeled "What The Fuck". These clowns were like a living, breathing version of Eden and Oswald Brookes, lead characters in a documentary series called "In Our

Family". Copies of it were available for lease from the history section of the library Vanessa worked at. It was also one of her favorites, though he couldn't understand why. According to most scholars, the series offered new insights into the everyday lives of ancient Americans. By all accounts, it painted an accurate portrait of their culture and society in what many simply referred to as "the old days". How they could know that for certain was beyond him. He left that kind of thing to the experts. Fortunately for historians—and for Vanessa—the series had already been dubbed over from American to something that wasn't complete and utter gibberish when it had first been discovered.

"This is your *last* chance," Frank warned them in a firm tone. "Put your hands above your heads, where I can see them." With his pistol still trained at the back of Wilhelm's head, he cocked its hammer and added, "Now!" Their little display had gone on for too long already. He had to take control of the situation.

"Why don't *you* shut your fucking piehole?" Wilhelm grated defiantly, his voice dripping with disdain. He paused for emphasis then and added an exaggeratedly sarcastic, "Now," before flipping his head around to look Frank in the eye for the first time. His intense glare oozed loathing and condescendence. It was a little unsettling, but no big surprise. "In case you haven't noticed, I'm trying to have a conversation here, bullswine."

A subtle movement in Jimbo's eyes grabbed his attention then and he followed his gaze. Two more hoverbikes were speeding north up Bennetweg. They were heading straight toward them, and closing fast. Their riders wore the same purple armbands as the pimp and his crew. All of their stalling had been a setup, an ambush, and he'd played right into their hands.

They must have called in backup shortly after running from the park, and if they had geolocators, their buddies could easily have pinpointed their location, even on the move. Whatever their arrangements had been, they'd arrived quickly, and taken him completely by surprise. He didn't have to see their guns to know that they were carrying. It was a given. He had to act fast or he wouldn't stand a chance against them. As they made their approach, he stiffened his arms and pulled himself off the left side of his bike, crouching against it for cover.

Capitalizing on the situation, Wilhelm throttled up and got ready to take off. Just before he did, he whipped out a grimy-looking .357 and cracked out three shots before Frank could so much as react.

To Frank's surprise, Jimbo was the one that lurched back from the impact. First his left shoulder swung back, then his right, and finally, the third shot caught him straight in the midsection. The unexpected volley made him rock backward in his seat, then spring forward again in an awkward sprawl across his handlebars. *So much for Jimbo*, he thought with a certain degree of regret. The poor guy might actually have benefited from an extended stay in prison. He might actually have changed. Few criminals ever did, but he just might have. He could tell after just one brief exchange. It wasn't his fault he was stupid, or uneducated, or both.

The twisted look of delight plastered across Wilhelm's face as he turned to speed away made him sick to his stomach. The loud, "Oops!" and the hooting fit of laughter that followed were even worse. Grimacing, he raised his pistol and aimed it at Wilhelm's back, but the riders closing in on him opened up with their submachine guns, forcing him behind cover. Dozens of bullets chinked off his bike and danced off the pavement all around him. As they bore down on his position, the one in the lead swerved off and turned down Grantstrasse after Wilhelm, firing back at Frank the entire time. His blind spraying lacked any kind of precision, but created an effective crossfire.

He was pinned down on two sides. He was open to stray shots on his left, and if he tried to move, it would be even worse. After weighing the odds, he decided to risk it all. With the other rider closing in fast, there was a good chance that just sitting there would get him killed anyway. He had to act quickly.

Ignoring the projectiles zipping by him from both directions, he turned aslant and rose, firing off a hail of well-aimed shots that sent the closing rider reeling off the back of his hoverbike. The unmanned rig bore down on him and he braced for the inevitable impact, tightly gripping the side of his bike. The careening bike slammed into the front end of his well-grounded rig and its nose lifted into the air. It corkscrewed over his head and came down behind him with a smash, then scraped almost all the way across the intersection before grinding to a halt. He'd weathered the collision without flinching, but the jolt that he'd received had sent shockwaves throughout his arms. When they passed, his arms stung like a thousand angry bees.

He ground his teeth and winced as he got back on the hoverbike. It looked like it had seen better days, but the other bike had clearly taken the brunt of the collision. The damage to the Strahl Kraft seemed to be purely aesthetic. He did a quick check for the sake of security, and everything seemed to be in working condition, except for the smashed headlight. Ignoring the lancing throbs in his arms, he started after the fleeing men.

When he got to the Wilderweg intersection, he decided to turn left onto it. He very much doubted that they'd run south, into areas with increasingly elevated police presence. Chances were they were heading north, toward the docks. The harbor sector of Portsmuth was a veritable cesspool of unsavory activity, and the safest haven in the city for a pair of filthy little good-for-nothings like them. He realized that he'd chosen the right path when he discovered a trail of empty shells leading around the corner, where the other Johnny-come-lately had let off a spray of blind fire in his direction.

Traffic on Wilderweg had cleared up considerably and was fairly navigable. It didn't take long to hit cruising speed in these conditions, and maneuvering around what few obstacles there were was a piece of cake. He spotted them weaving in and out of sparse traffic a bit farther up the road. They sped past the on-ramp to the Uplands Autobahn and he was almost on them by the time they crossed the T-intersection at Vederweg.

The "Mad Backward Shooter" started firing at him over his shoulder the second he spotted him, spraying bullets all across the street in a blind arc. His firing was vastly ineffective and posed only a minimal threat, but Frank was still glad for the protective barrier that the bike's windshield provided. One lone bullet—one in dozens that were flying all over the place—somehow managed to hit it, but ricocheted off of it with an audible *chink*, leaving him unscathed. If not for the heavy-duty windshield, the bullet would have knocked him clear off the bike, and he was more than a little relieved that it hadn't, after the fact. At the speed he was going, if the shot itself hadn't killed him, the fall certainly would have.

He'd already been gaining on them steadily, but the pressure was on now more than ever to apprehend them promptly. He had to put an end to this before there were civilian casualties. He gave it—or *tried* to give it—and accelerated a little, but not nearly as much as he'd hoped to. He was already ripping down the road at full thrust, and hardly noticed an increment in speed, if there even really was one. Despite the oblique cityscape zipping past in a blur, he felt sluggish. If they weren't already pushing their rigs to the limit, he could be in trouble.

Almost as though he was thinking the same thing, the one that had been firing at him glanced over his shoulder then and gave him the finger. The wicked grin he was sporting nearly split his face in two. He turned his head around again just as he was about to enter the Ulfstrasse intersection.

Frank's brow creased as the man leaned forward and drew his limbs in tight to his body. From the look of it, he was about to floor it, or *thought* that he was about to floor it. The aerodynamic stance he'd adopted couldn't really mean anything else.

It all happened so fast. Just as Frank was about to engage the intersection, a large cube van came hurtling down Ulfstrasse from the left. It plowed into the biker in front of him like a freight train, sideswiping him right off the road. One second he was there, and the next he wasn't. The van's driver obviously hadn't seen him, as he'd made no effort to brake or even avoid him. Instead, he rammed into him headlong, carrying him and his bike at least as far as the other end of the intersection. Just how far, Frank would never know, as the gruesome scene was over and behind him in the blink of an eye.

He grimaced as he wiped some spattered blood from his brow. Even if the guy was still in one piece, there was no way in hell he was going to just get up and walk away from that. The shower of falling blood he'd sped through just after the van had crossed the intersection was evidence enough of that. For a split second, it had been like riding through a heavy mist and a light rain all at once. He pondered on the brute force required to do that kind of damage to a human body—to just pop it like a heated can of soda—and decided not to linger on it for too long. If he'd been going just a *little* bit faster, he would have been the one splattered all over the pavement like a dollop of red goop. The cleanup crew would have had to collect him in buckets.

But he couldn't let that distract him from the task at hand. Wilhelm had to be stopped, and fast. The hulking man had a lead on him, but Frank was still gaining ground steadily. Only a half-block's worth of street separated them. Congestion had started to build up again as soon as he'd passed Ulfstrasse. Pressed for time and determined to gain any advantage that he could, he weaved in and out of the traffic, deftly avoiding incoming vehicles and unanticipated, inanimate obstacles. He was forced off of the road more than once in his quest for the upper hand, but he skillfully steered clear of danger every time.

Wilhelm was so close that he could almost taste his fear. His body language suggested that seeing his associates fail miserably one after the other had gotten to him. He could see no trace of his previously arrogant demeanor. All he could see was the panicky intensity of someone that was doing everything in their power to escape and survive. If he reached out then, he could grab onto him and yank him right off of his bike. He could, and he knew that he probably should—he'd obviously given the man every chance to surrender—but he wouldn't, even though deep down, part of him really wanted to.

That part of him wanted to lie, and say that Wilhelm would get over the accident with a few years of physical rehabilitation, but he knew better than that. Every bone in his body would be broken, and that would probably be the brighter side of things. Sometimes he wondered why he even cared at all. The guy had just killed one of his own in cold blood, and for reasons he could only attribute to stupidity or something else he couldn't fathom.

He thought on it and drew nothing, but it didn't matter; he still cared. Sometimes he acted brashly, violently, but he never enjoyed killing. Not at all. It was a last resort for him, at least by agency standards. He was sure there were past scenarios he could have handled differently, using more peaceful methods. But he was also certain that those alternative approaches would have increased the likelihood of civilian casualties, not to mention the added risks to himself. His job was dangerous enough on its own without pushing his luck. The agency's methods weren't pleasant, but they were sound. They were tried and tested, and didn't leave much room for mistakes. That usually worked out for the best.

The brutal, unwavering ways of the law had saved his life on more than one occasion. Despite that, part of him wanted to go against the grain, just as he was doing now. Some might say that it made him a bad cop, and the captain would most certainly agree. The agency subscribed to the old Bad Apple theory. A rotten apple would spoil the bunch, as they said. The solution was to dispose of the bad apples as soon as they were identified. It almost made sense, at times, which rendered his occasional bouts of internal strife even more incomprehensible. Maybe he just had a hard time likening people to rotten fruit that needed to be thrown away like worthless trash.

With mounting frustration urging him to do what any other cop would, pitched against a sudden moral dilemma, his insides were in turmoil. He supposed his leniency might have something to do with wanting people—even the lowest forms of scum—to have as much of a chance at redemption as he could afford to give them. Beyond that, he couldn't say. Regardless, he had to find a way to stop Wilhelm, preferably one that didn't involve a nasty, spine-shattering spill.

The bike in front of him reversed thrust and slowed down then, just enough that he had to swerve left to avoid running into it. Just as he was about to overtake it, Wilhelm kicked the front end of his rig, redirecting it into oncoming traffic. He had no more than a split second to react.

Pulling even farther left, he gunned it and shot across the street, narrowly avoiding getting squashed like a bug on the grille of an incoming city bus. He'd cut his thrust and yanked his handlebars to the right when he was halfway out in front of the bus. By the time he reached the sidewalk, he'd managed to bring the bike around in the right direction and floored it. His rig kept sliding toward the left as he moved on, and it glanced off of the brick wall with a loud scrape. It ricocheted to the right after that and kept going.

He'd scraped his knee against the wall during the impact, and somehow managed to open a long gash along his elbow in the process. The burn in the affected joints was horrible, but he knew that they weren't serious injuries. The pain would eventually fade away, just like the jolt to his arms had. The stinging there felt more like a hundred angry bees now, rather than a thousand. For the time being, pain was the least of his worries.

He'd deflected from his anticipated trajectory and was moving fast. The bump had redirected him toward the street, and more immediately toward a lamppost—a large and very solid-looking lamppost of the cast iron variety. He pulled left, but knew that he wouldn't be able to avoid it completely. He wouldn't have enough time to turn. Just as he was about to straighten up, the tail end of his bike caught the post and his front end swung back toward the street.

He might have made things easier for himself if he'd tried coming to a complete stop, but he couldn't risk losing Wilhelm. Not now, not on his life. He yanked his handlebars left to avoid spinning out into the street, and started a wild fishtail straight down the sidewalk instead. His tail end swung out from one side to the other as he tried to compensate as best he could. The swerving gradually declined as he battled to keep from crashing, and he was finally able to get the vehicle under control again. Overturned garbage cans and debris were left scattered in his wake over the past half of a city block.

He looked ahead and to the right, but couldn't see Wilhelm anywhere. The guy had probably gained a considerable lead on him while he'd been busy trying to not get himself killed. Fighting off a rising sense of panic, he muttered a curse under his breath, and continued on his way. Agitated, he glanced down a side street on his left as he passed it, but saw nothing out of the ordinary there, and decided to keep going straight. He'd only had a visual on it for a fraction of a second, and couldn't help but wonder if he'd missed something. He could only hope that he hadn't.

Less than a minute later, he was relieved to have stayed his course when he spotted his quarry riding over the sidewalk and into an alley near the end of the block. Wilhelm hadn't seen him. Of that he was sure. He probably thought that he was dead, or out of commission somewhere back up the road.

Set on making an arrest before the opportunity vanished into thin air, ignoring the pain in his limbs, he pressed on. He threw caution to the wind on his approach, dipping far into the street to give himself a wide enough berth to turn down the alley without having to slow down.

The alley was as grimy and littered as any other. Barred service doors and rusty garbage bins lined the old brick structures on both sides. Brightly-colored graffiti adorned the walls in some places, contrasting oddly with their decrepit condition. The walls themselves seemed to be cracking under the stress of time, and the foundations had started to crumble in some areas. A tall fence cut the alley in two, and he could see Archerstrasse in the distance behind it. Wilhelm was up near the fence, and was busy pushing his hoverbike behind an open dumpster. It was obvious that he was trying to hide it.

Frank was nearly on top of him before Wilhelm realized what was going on. The look of panic in the crook's eyes was well worth the crushed knee *and* the gash on his elbow. "It's over, Wilhelm," he said, coming to a full stop. "Just give up now and let me take you in peacefully."

Until then, Wilhelm had been frozen still like a rabbit caught in the bright glare of an incoming truck's headlight, but he came to with a start then, and turned on his heels before sprinting toward the fence. "Of course," Frank muttered under his breath as he hopped down from his borrowed bike and darted after him. By the time he reached the base of the fence, Wilhelm had already scrambled halfway up it. "Just give up," he called out, irritation edging its way into his voice. "You're only making this worse for yourself." He didn't have to wait to know that the man wasn't going to heed his words. Pushing his sleeves up, he took a step backward and got ready to jump.

Without further delay, he ran a few steps forward and leapt into the air. He gripped onto the fence with his hands as he made contact with it, but didn't waste time seeking foothold. Instead, he pushed down and in with his feet in tandem, and propelled himself upward to find new grip. His ascension would be fast just as long as he managed to maintain sufficient momentum, but he was already starting to lose it. He'd caught up to Wilhelm about three quarters of the way up the fence. Feeling that his feet were about to slip, he released his hold on the fence and latched onto the man's leg at the knee.

"Hey!" Wilhelm barked, sagging heavily under the added weight. "Hands to yourself, bullswine!" He kicked his leg around in an attempt to shake him off. Frank's legs were dangling freely beneath him, but he managed to stay firmly latched on.

Wilhelm flailed his leg around some more and Frank nearly lost his grip, but he held on and the kicking soon slowed to a halt. The beast of a man grunted as he lifted him and his leg into the air in an attempt to return his foot to its hole in the fence. The maneuver was successful, but slow and laborious. Wilhelm's leg was getting tired.

"Let go!" he shouted, glaring down at him angrily. He freed up one of his hands and started taking wild swings at him. Once, twice, three times, and he connected with nothing. The fourth jab actually landed, but it ended up being little more than a poke on Frank's wrist. Wilhelm didn't have enough reach at that angle to do any real damage.

"You let go!" Frank yelled back at him. "It's over. I'm taking you in." He didn't know how he was going to back that up from his precarious position, but that was beside the point. All he could do at present was hold on, and watch as Wilhelm lowered his hands on the chain link fence to lessen the gap between fist and face. As he'd expected, the punches started raining down again. The new angle did make a bit of a difference. Some of Wilhelm's thrusts were getting through, but they were mostly ineffective due to their awkward positioning. It looked like a lot of clumsy arm flapping as far as he was concerned. He was partially shielded by Wilhelm's own leg, and the guy was hitting himself as much as he was hitting him.

Wilhelm growled as he twisted around to find an even better angle. Failing to find one, he reached up and started climbing again, slowly but surely. "You heavy piece of shit," he snapped.

Frank winced from the strain of holding onto Wilhelm's leg. If he didn't do something soon, he felt like he was going to lose his grip on the thug's slippery leatherette pants. Tightening what grip he *did* have with his right hand, he reached up with his left and grabbed hold of Wilhelm's belt, which prompted a series of guttural protests. Wasting no time, he let go of Wilhelm's knee, hoisted himself up and clutched a fistful of his jacket. He did *not* want to give the guy another chance to shake him off. One swift maneuver later, and he was straddling the giant's back in an awkward-looking piggyback ride.

As he wrapped his arms around the man's neck, he squeezed hard, forcing his chin up. He didn't really mean to choke him, but the effects were pretty much the same. If Wilhelm had tried to throw him off a second earlier, while he was busy scaling Mount Muscle Mass, he was fairly confident that he'd have let go and fallen to the ground like a sack of potatoes. Fortunately for him, he hadn't. He'd caught him mid-climb. Gigantor had been too busy seeking foothold to react. In any case, it was too late now. He was stuck on Wilhelm like a barnacle on a rusty bow. It would take nothing short of a crowbar to pry him loose. Infuriated, Wilhelm started to thrash around like an angry bull. The man was even stronger than he looked. "This... is what happens... when you don't cooperate," Frank grunted.

This only agitated the man further, and his wild flailing intensified, but remained largely ineffective. "Get off me now," Wilhelm gurgled through clenched teeth, making great efforts to climb the last bit of fence before reaching the horizontal support bar at the top. "Get off me now, or I swear... you're *not* gonna live to regret this, you little fuck!" Gripping the bar firmly with his left hand, he reached over his shoulder with the other and grabbed Frank by the hair.

Frank grimaced as he felt his roots start to pull up. He'd had enough. Using Wilhelm's stance against him, he freed up his legs and swung them around to the side, thrusting the plants of his feet into the fence. Then, tightening his grip on the man's neck as best he could, he contracted his legs and pushed against the fence with all his might. Wilhelm arced back violently as the top half of his body followed Frank. He stopped his backward plunge briefly as his left arm extended to its fullest. For a moment, it seemed like he might be able to hold onto the support bar, but his tired hand wasn't strong enough to carry their combined weight. His fingers slipped and both men plummeted in an eight-foot freefall to the hard ground below.

Frank let go the second he felt the resistance holding them up give way. Following the Break Fall principles he'd learned during his martial arts training, he brought his arms and legs in close to his body, squeezing his chin down to his chest. He was careful not to over contract his muscles. Instead, he tried to keep them as relaxed as he possibly could, and braced himself mentally for the impending crash.

When he did come down, he contracted his muscles almost immediately and rolled to the side, then swung his arm out and smacked at the ground with the palm of his hand. Wilhelm smashed down with a loud thunk in the exact same spot he'd been in only a fraction of a second earlier.

Rolls and tumbling were meant to reduce the damage caused by a fall through better distribution of impact throughout the body. While this was most certainly a tried-and-true technique, his usage of it had until then been limited to ground-level combat, as it should have been. Falling from that height had done more than just knocked the wind out of him.

Gasping for air but finding none, he pushed himself to his knees with some difficulty. A violent fit of heaving coughs racked his chest. When his dry retching subsided, he was finally able to draw a breath, but it was cut short by a piercing pain lancing through his side like a hot knife. Grinding his teeth, he grasped at his ribs and grunted at the contact. Softening his touch, he laid his hand on them again. It was still a painful procedure, but one that was slightly more tolerable. He wasn't entirely sure, but he thought he might have a broken rib or two. He'd have to control his breathing if he wanted to avoid feeling a stabbing pain with every breath. He'd take short breaths only, if he could help it. Slowly rising to his feet, he stifled another series of painful coughs and settled his gaze on Wilhelm.

The brute was alive and breathing, writhing in what seemed like a pain on par with his own. He was in bad shape, that much was clear, but the source of his torment was obviously of a different nature. He was groping at his lower back as he struggled to his feet. There was a faint popping sound as he straightened himself and he screamed out in agony.

"You filthy piece of shit!" Wilhelm bellowed. "You're gonna pay for this!" And then he took a step toward him, but stopped almost immediately, and howled out another of his tormented vociferations. He clutched at his lower back and screamed as though crazed. When the pang passed, he looked up at Frank, an intense hatred burning in his eyes. Gnashing his teeth, he used his forearm to wipe at the sweat that was dripping down his face, then pointed an accusatory finger in his direction. "Boy, I'm gonna teach you a lesson you won't soon forget."

Frank assumed a defensive stance as the other man hobbled toward him. He stood at an angle, knees bent and feet well parted. Though he connected a lot harder with his right hand, he led with it now, his right foot placed slightly ahead of his left. He kept his right arm extended in front of himself at shoulder height. His left arm was drawn back close to his chest, his balled fist poised at level with his neck. This was the Starke Note fighting style they taught at the academy, or a variation of it that he'd just cooked up to compensate for his injuries. His hope was that his modifications to the traditional stance would reduce the level of movement required of his right arm and upper body, and offer better protection for his injured ribs.

Though he wasn't yet a master of Starke Note, Frank had passed his trials with flying colors. At present, he was a Macht twelve of a total of eighteen. This accomplishment was denoted by a tattoo on his right shoulder. The emblem had two sinuous, parallel slashes with five crosshatches each. If he earned another slash, he'd be competent enough to start training other officers. Most of them never made it past Macht ten. Since Hiro Janssen, the agency's former Starke Note Meister, and the only Macht eighteen in the city, had been banned from practice for refusing to come out of retirement at the employer's request, the next highest in line was a Macht fifteen. All in all, Frank considered himself a relatively skilled fighter.

Wilhelm was slow getting to him. At the height they'd fallen from, and with the way Wilhelm had landed, it didn't surprise him at all. If anything *did* surprise him, it was that he'd gotten up in the first place. For all the guy knew, he might have thrown out his back, but he was still trudging along toward him with the obvious intention of beating the ever-living snot out of him. That on its own was a remarkable feat. He couldn't underestimate this opponent, not even for a second.

He maintained his stance until Wilhelm was within arm's reach. When he was in close enough, the thug's first reflex was to take a swat at his outstretched hand. Nimbly drawing it to the side, Frank avoided the lunge with ease. Then, in the same fluid motion, he followed up with a powerful, openhanded strike to the side of the man's face.

Caught completely off guard as he was falling through on his botched swing, Wilhelm reeled back a step and brought his hand up to his reddened cheek. A wild look of anger flashed across his face. Squaring his shoulders with a grunt, he raised his arms and assumed a haphazard posture he'd probably seen in a bad action movie. "So that's how you wanna play, huh?" he uttered with a growl, his words dripping with acid. "Like a puss? Well your little girl slaps can't hurt me, Nancy!"

Cracking his knuckles, he started to sidestep slowly, left to right and right to left, with a little hop to his step. Grinning mischievously, he threw a few jabs at thin air and followed up with a shadowboxed uppercut for good measure. "You wanna play, but I'm too fast for you and your little girly moves," he boasted. Stopping suddenly, he puffed up his chest and tapped it twice with his clenched fist. "I'm gonna show you how a *real* man fights, bullswine. I'm gonna show you how a man fights when he's born of the streets."

Frank waited patiently, completely indifferent to the bigger man's taunting display. To anyone with a modicum of combat training, what was meant to impress or intimidate would come across as little more than ridiculous. At a glance, all Wilhelm had going for him was his size and sturdiness, and even then, it wasn't all that impressive. He'd felled much larger foes before.

He tried not to focus on the overly apparent. Wilhelm was slow. His movements were clumsy. In most cases, this would mean nothing more to him than another advantage. But looks could be deceiving, and he couldn't allow himself to be so sure. A few seconds ago, the guy had been writhing in agony. Now, he was dancing around like their eight-foot fall was nothing more than a distant memory. It was possible Wilhelm had been faking it, and by the same token, it was possible he was playing down his abilities to lure him into a false sense of security. It was possible, but not very likely. The truth of it seemed to be that Wilhelm, with his bulging muscles and much-bigger-than-average build, was a rare breed of rubber bone.

Only an infinitesimal percentage of people had this particular trait. Frank did not. His cousin Carlos, on the other hand, had, and he'd also been the one to give him his first, painful lessons in the advantage it conferred in a fight. In the rough-and-tumble era of their teenaged years, they'd often sparred in backyards with Andrew and other childhood friends. Though Carlos had next to nothing in the way of coordination, and rarely hit anything with his wild, sweeping hooks, the guy had more chin than all of them combined. They could pummel away at him all they wanted, as hard and as fast as they could, but Carlos would *not* go down. When he did, it was only because he'd lost his balance, and he'd hop right back up again. The bouts usually lasted so long that he got tired and gave up. When he got into the hard drugs, first he became unstoppable, and then he started to wither away.

With some hard work and a lot of training, he could have been an excellent prizefighter. He could have been, if he hadn't died of an overdose at the ripe old age of seventeen. It was only one piece in a complicated puzzle, but his cousin's premature death had been the main catalyst that drove him to join the force. Putting the manufacturers and distributors of dangerous narcotics out of business remained his foremost long-term objective.

Even though there were no visible symptoms, Frank couldn't help but wonder if Wilhelm was hopped-up on something. Most serious criminals didn't use drugs. Not the kind that affected their judgment, at least, and certainly not when they were on the job. But he wasn't exactly sure how serious of a criminal Wilhelm was. At any rate, he hoped that he was as slow as he looked, because drugs or no drugs, subduing him wasn't going to be easy.

Wilhelm broke the mounting tension by pouncing forward and yelling out an emphatic, "Kablam!" as he threw a quick left hook. Frank leaned back and managed to avoid the blow, but just barely. He hadn't expected it, despite the verbal telegraph. The guy wasn't nearly as slow as he looked. Springing back at him immediately, Frank threw a left hook of his own, then followed up with an openhanded strike with his right, and finished off with a strong, two-handed shove to his solar plexus.

Wilhelm's head jerked to the right and then to the left as Frank's fist and palm connected with the sides of his face in rapid succession, and then he stumbled back from the powerful shove to his midsection, nearly toppling over in the process. Unscathed, he shook it off and rushed back in.

Reading Wilhelm's hotheaded charge with ease, Frank raised his knee as high as he could and kicked forward. The sole of his combat boot shot into the man's gut with force and precision, folding him in two and wrenching the air from his lungs. Denying him any chance to recuperate, he followed up by grabbing onto his jacket by the shoulders and pulling him forward as he thrust his knee upward. It smashed into Wilhelm's nose with crushing force, and spattered the bottom half of the man's face with blood as his septum broke.

Fending off the urge to hit him again, Frank backed away and watched as the thug sank to his knees, his head sagging limply between his shoulders. "Are you ready to be taken in yet?" he asked him calmly, though he was fairly certain he knew what his answer was going to be.

Wilhelm remained motionless for a few seconds, his eyes riveted on the small pool of blood that was forming at his knees. Finally, rising slowly, he wiped at the blood on his face with the sleeve of his jacket, spit out a mouthful of blood, and hissed, "It's gonna take a lot more than that to stop *me*, Nancy." Sneering, he unzipped his jacket, slid it off his arms and let it fall to the ground, exposing the chiseled muscles beneath.

Though he was well built—obviously, the man spent hours a day in a gym to maintain his physique—his chest and abdomen were covered by what appeared to be self-inflicted scars. The look was most definitely home manufactured, and the purpose of it was to make him look tough and scare off rival gang members. But Frank was neither impressed nor intimidated. He knew how to differentiate between a genuine knife wound and the work of a scalpel. The incisions had no doubt been made with great care, under the fluorescent lights of some third-rate public washroom. Even if the scars had been real, it wouldn't have mattered; he wasn't easily frightened.

After assuming his preferred action movie posture once more, Wilhelm stepped forward and came in swinging. What he lacked for in efficiency, he more than made up with relentless variation. Breathless, he shuffled his feet around, and occasionally switched up his lead hand as he unleashed a virtual deluge of erratic, seemingly random combinations.

Frank was hard-pressed to evade all of them. Anticipating his opponent's moves had always been the cornerstone of his fighting style, but that wasn't helping him here. The chaotic mess of jabs, hooks, and uppercuts made it tricky to predict what Wilhelm's next move would be. As hard as it was to believe, the thug's lack of any formal training was working to his advantage, and Frank found himself pushed into a solely defensive stance, unable to pierce through the barrage and strike back.

His superior reflexes compensated for his lack of foresight. He was able to avoid the majority of Wilhelm's blows with a simple sidestep, or a lean in the right direction, but the hits were coming in faster and harder, and there was no sign of them letting up. It wasn't long before he'd given up on moving out of the way, and resorted to blocking instead, an endeavor which quickly veered toward the painfully awkward.

Pain rifled through his entire body every time his arms took the impact of Wilhelm's sweeping hooks. When this was all over, he might just consider taking a break from the beat for a few days. He'd never been much of a desk jockey, but there was a certain, sudden appeal to pushing paper. The thought was cut short as one of Wilhelm's haymakers slipped through his guard, precursor to his jumbo-sized fist pounding heavily against his ribs. The agony was immediate and overwhelming. He fought to stay on his feet, but failed miserably. The sensation that his kidney had just burst like a swollen balloon and his sudden lack of breath forced him to his knees like the unseen hand of some invisible giant. He wanted to stay up—he made every possible effort to stay up—but his legs gave way and he collapsed like a house of cards.

"Booyashaka!" Wilhelm hollered, hopping back a step for emphasis. "Told you I was too fast for you, you dirty, bullswine bastard!" He followed up by throwing another series of showy punches at nothing in particular.

Frank's eyes were a blur and every gasp for air drew little more than a sharp pain. His ears were buzzing and Wilhelm's voice grew warped and distant. He couldn't make out what he was saying, but he was in too much pain to care. He watched helplessly as Wilhelm hopped back and forth and from side to side, jabbing into the air like he was locked in battle with some imaginary foe. His fleeting senses wavered in and out, almost as though his body was undecided on whether to hang on and weather the storm, or to simply shut down. Finally, bits and pieces of Wilhelm's delirious monologue filtered through, momentarily wrenching him back from his torpor.

"Born of the streets!" the thug shouted, tapping his chest with his fist. "Who's the big shot now, coppertop? Huh? Who's the big fuckin' shot? Am I under arrest, Mr. Officer, sir?"

Frank's eyelids flickered in a brief fit of spasms and he nearly retched. He managed to suppress another urge to heave, but he knew that it wasn't over. He paused, breathless, hoping nothing more than for it to pass. A violent jerk shook his body suddenly as he coughed, and brought up a sizeable giblet of mucus and blood. It forced itself up through his windpipe with a gurgling choke, freeing up his airway, then ran down his chin as he sagged forward, propelled by the force of his expectoration.

The right side of his chest cavity felt like it was on fire—a liquid fire that he felt he was drowning in. Despite the gravity of his injuries, he still had one good, fully functional lung left, and he realized that if he was careful and didn't overdo it, he could still breathe, if painfully.

Dipping into his last reserve of willpower, he focused all of his efforts on regaining control of his wavering senses, and finally got a grip of himself. Retaining the same vulnerable position, he remained motionless, his face unchanged. Wilhelm could have killed him a while ago if he hadn't been so busy gloating and showing off. He could have, but he hadn't, and Frank planned on making that his biggest mistake.

He just had to wait for an opening—just one—and then he could strike back. Hopefully, his attack would be decisive. In his current state, the effort would be taxing, and it wasn't likely he'd get a second chance. It would hurt a *lot,* but he was as good as dead if he didn't try.

He sat back on his heels, his head sagging forward limply as though he lacked the strength to raise it, and played out the "dead and done for" role as best he could. It was a relatively easy task, in his condition. He let his head sway slowly from side to side like a droopy noodle, and even let a long filament of saliva drool its way down to the ground. All the while, he kept a watchful eye on Wilhelm and his over-the-top display.

Wilhelm—who by all appearances was buying into his deception fully—was still dancing around throwing wild punches, but now he'd also started some ridiculous chant about being "The Man". Following every single one of the stupid things Wilhelm did or said was a little beyond his current capabilities, but he was still able to make out some of his rambling.

"My whole damn life, the man's gone and kept me down," Wilhelm proclaimed theatrically. "Now finally, I get my chance to stick it to him. It brings a tear to my eye. Truly, it does." He trailed off at that and sniffled, wiping an imaginary tear from his cheek with all the pomp of an elementary school drama. His following pause was marked and contemplative.

Frank sat poised and ready for action, attentive to Wilhelm's every move, the tone of his voice, his body language. *Ladies and gentlemen,* he thought morbidly, *Wilhelm Braun is about to leave the building.* Everything seemed to indicate that for better or worse, the show would soon be over. If he was going to find his opening, it would have to be soon.

There was a strong possibility that only one of them would come out of this alive. He wasn't exactly afraid of death, but he wasn't a big fan of dying, either. This wasn't how he wanted to go. Not at the hands of a guy like Wilhelm. And he didn't want to leave Vanessa behind, either, or his parents. Not in this mess, the closest thing to a civil war the city had ever seen.

Wilhelm finally broke his silence, and launched right into the second part of his poorly-performed, one-man play. "It brings me both great joy and great sorrow to have to dispose of you, my friend, because even a filthy bullswine like you must have a family." Hands clenched loosely behind his back in the classic gentleman's pose, he casually strode toward Frank, his nose raised snobbishly high. "I can't guarantee anything for your kids, if you have any," he cautioned, "but I do promise to take *good* care of your girlfriend at least once a week when you're gone. Maybe even twice, if I'm feeling frisky."

He stood directly over him, his fists poised casually on his hips. This was the moment Frank had been waiting for. The guy was so nonchalant about everything it was obvious he didn't see him as a serious threat anymore.

Wilhelm dropped the act suddenly, reverting to his usual, venomous self. "And wouldn't that be oh so *civilized* of me?" he asked with disgust, nearly spitting the last few words out. "Isn't that how you *civilized* folk talk, Mr. Fancy-pants policeman, sir?" He cracked his knuckles threateningly and wiggled his fingers before adding, "You cops are all the same. You think you're *so* much better than everyone else, walking around like you've got nightsticks shoved up your asses, talking all civilized-like, trying to stop guys like me from making an honest living."

Frank watched from the corner of his eye as Wilhelm turned a deeper shade of red. It would be any second now. He could feel it. He'd lash out and either live or die. All in all, the course of action was a little better than the alternative, which consisted of doing nothing and dying like a wretch.

"What gives you the right to make up the rules?" Wilhelm demanded through grit teeth. "What gives you the right to decide who lives and who dies? Can you answer that one for me, Mister Officer Sir?" His anger flared visibly as he went on. "What gives you the right to come here and interfere with my honest business, you weaselly little sh—" the rest came out a shriek of agony.

Frank's fist connecting with his family jewels stole his words and twisted them into something strident and unintelligible.

As Frank had anticipated, a jolt of pain lanced through his side as he lashed out. The tender muscles along his ribcage felt like they were going to rupture. That certainly wasn't going to feel very good in the morning. Grinding his teeth, he pushed himself to his feet with some difficulty as Wilhelm dropped to his knees before him. The pain hadn't registered fully for either of them when he wound up and swept his left hand across the man's face in a powerful openhanded smack.

In his bewildered state, Wilhelm went down like a rag doll. He squirmed around on the ground for a while, writhing in pain, then flipped over onto his stomach and stopped cold. It looked like the pain had been too much for his body to handle, and he'd just passed out.

Frank reached around the back of his belt and freed a set of restraints from one of the many clips that were affixed there. He removed its blocker—a gadget that spared him the trouble of having to unlock the cuffs in the middle of an arrest—and pulled them all the way open. *Just one more thing*, he thought, stepping toward Wilhelm's motionless husk, *and this will all be over*.

He wasn't exactly proud of the way that he'd taken the giant down, but he was alive—they were both alive—and that was what mattered most. He knew what the pain that he'd inflicted on the other man felt like all too well, and he wouldn't wish it on anyone. It was a searing, all-consuming agony that made your vision flash white and your body cramp up in shock. It made breathing difficult and could lead to a blackout. It wasn't exactly the kind of thing that one could take graciously. Though unlikely, he knew that a blow like that could even kill a man.

Regardless, he deemed that the situation warranted it. He could have just shot the guy in cold blood, gunned him down where he stood without a second thought. But he hadn't. The thought had crossed his mind, but he'd chosen not to go for the kill. Eliminating the threat would be the surest way to resolve the situation, but taking him into custody would give them the opportunity to question him, maybe glean new information on the city's prostitution networks. That was reason enough to keep him alive, as far as he was concerned.

He kneeled by Wilhelm, grabbed his wrist, and snapped the first loop of the restraints around it. The guy's arm was limp and lifeless, which made his task a little easier, but it still felt like it weighed a ton. To make matters worse, he was lying on top of his other arm. Furrowing his brow, he reached out, leaned over him, and took him by the shoulder, then braced to flip him over onto his side. With one hand on the cuffs and the other on Wilhelm's shoulder, he pulled, but budging the giant of a man turned out to be harder than he'd hoped it would be. Not only was he built like a fridge, but he was also covered in blood, sweat and some other gunk that he'd picked up while rolling around on the ground. His fingers couldn't get a proper hold. They kept slipping every time he managed to lift him up an inch.

He had to stop for a moment as his head began to spin. The injuries he'd sustained so far were starting to take a toll on him, and he felt more than a little woozy. For a second, he could have sworn that he'd felt Wilhelm's muscles tense under his hands, but his senses were getting so helter-skelter that it was impossible to tell if they really had.

Taking a deep breath, he let go of the restraints and gripped Wilhelm's shoulder with both hands, ready for one last and hopefully *successful* effort. When he *did* tug at the man, this time he flipped over a lot easier and a lot quicker than he'd expected him to. To his surprise, Wilhelm had come to. Or maybe he'd never been unconscious to begin with.

He spotted the short knife in the giant's free hand almost immediately, but it was already too late. Wilhelm slashed at his face as he rolled over, and cut a deep gash from the bottom of his left ear to the corner of his mouth. He screamed and stumbled back onto his ass as Wilhelm continued his rolling motion and pushed himself to his feet.

Frank followed suit and got up. He raised his hands defensively, but Wilhelm was already on top of him. He brushed a first stab at his midsection aside, but got clocked in the face by a violent right hook less than a second later. The blow resonated inside his skull like a firecracker going off, and droplets of blood sprayed from the freshly-cleaved wound on his face. He was still standing, but the ringing in his head was overpowering, and he couldn't react.

Before he knew it, Wilhelm had grabbed him by the back of his collar, and plunged his blade into his banged up ribs a first, second, and third time. Something inside of him let go then, and for the first time he found himself thinking, *so this is it.* Feeling wobbly, he dropped to his knees, clutching at his side, physically drained and robbed of all hope.

Grinning wickedly, Wilhelm pushed him in the chest with the tips of his fingers, and laughed a disturbingly gleeful laugh as he fell backward like a sack of potatoes. In his ears, Wilhelm's voice sounded twice as deep as before and echoed in a fading loop. He felt like he was floating to the ground beneath him, like the whole world had slowed to a near halt. He'd never wondered what dying would feel like—at least, he'd never dwelled on it before—but he was pretty sure this was it. He wondered why he'd never wondered about it before. He also wondered if it mattered, now that it was happening, and why he had so much time to wonder about it in the first place. His head drooped lazily to one side, which offered him a slightly better view of his assailant and his surroundings, and prompted another question. When had he even hit the ground? He hadn't felt anything on impact.

His questions would have to remain unanswered. He'd all but forgotten about them by the time Wilhelm dropped to his knees and started inching his way toward him, bloodied knife in hand. He tried to bring his fists up, but couldn't. His arms wouldn't even move. He just didn't have the strength to raise them.

Wilhelm pressed the tip of his knife to Frank's throat and grinned sardonically. "Always wanted to stick me some swine," he sneered. "Would be a crying shame to let you bleed to death before I got the chance to do it again."

Frank felt absolutely helpless, like he was caught in a dream in which he was trying to wade through waist-deep water, and getting nowhere fast. But this was a lot worse, because he could hardly muster enough energy to twitch, let alone move sluggishly. He felt like he should be panicking, but he wasn't. He was overly reflective, like his mind was compensating for the loss of his other senses. All he could do was watch and wait for the end to come.

The sound of boots slapping and scraping against concrete drew his attention. He wanted to turn his head to see where it was coming from, but couldn't. He was confident that the last thing he'd see before dying was Wilhelm's stubbly face, contorted with sickeningly twisted amusement.

He waited for the blade of the knife to strike across and slit his throat. He waited, but it didn't happen. Suddenly, Wilhelm looked up, the demented expression on his face giving way to alarm. The white-hot anger crept back into his face, and he muttered something that was almost assuredly profanity. He couldn't tell for sure, because his hearing had just let out altogether, and he was relying on what he saw.

Finally, the moment he had been anticipating came. He took a deep breath—probably his last, as far as he knew—and watched as Wilhelm drew his arm up over his head, poised to strike. Just as he started to thrust the knife down at him, a faint cracking noise broke the silence, and Frank was surprised to find that at least some of his hearing had returned. The noise amplified until it sounded like an explosion going off underwater, and that was followed by either an echo, or a series of muffled explosions. He wasn't sure if he was hearing them or feeling their vibrations.

Wilhelm's shoulder rocked back unexpectedly, and it sent his knife flying out of view. Suddenly, Frank understood what was happening. He understood, but it didn't matter. His body was failing him. He was sure that he was a goner now, no matter what happened next. Wilhelm's other shoulder lurched back, and he contracted violently as a bullet caught him in the chest. He jerked back over and over again as a salvo of rapid fire riddled his body with hot lead. The gunshots sent him reeling almost out of view—almost, until a shot to his forehead stopped him cold. He convulsed as he fell forward, sparks flying up off the pavement behind him. The only thing that had kept him up had been the force of the rounds punching through him.

"Cease fire!" he heard someone bellow out from a distance, though surprisingly clearly. "Cease your fire immediately! We have a man down over there!"

He didn't know how they'd managed to find him, but backup had arrived. "Get the medivac over here *now!*" that voice said. It sounded familiar, though he couldn't put a name to it. It didn't matter anyway. He was completely drained, and wanted nothing more than to close his eyes and go to sleep. "Don't worry about me," he wanted to say, though the words never left his mouth. "I'll be okay right after this nap."

His head lolled back then, and he stared blankly at the sliver of dull gray light that was shining through between the rooftops of the buildings that flanked him.

Apparently, his vision was failing him too, now, because what he saw up there made no sense at all. He didn't know what it was, but it was... something. That something—or *some things*—was difficult to identify, but whatever it was, it was quite obviously *there*, up in the sky and on the buildings. It was made up of odd shapes that didn't really fit into their surroundings or even with each other. They stood out like some kind of bizarre optical illusion. The longer he stared, the more certain he was that they all fit into some bigger picture that he couldn't quite make out. It reminded him of gazing into one of those abstract prints that didn't look like much of anything until he'd stared at it for so long that his eyes started to feel numb and lost focus. Any second now, three-dimensional shapes would start to emerge.

The illusion grew bigger and closer as he stared on. He couldn't help but wonder what it was. New parts of the puzzle came into place as the others drew nearer. They merged with the other shapes, finally forming a rough outline, but of what, he couldn't say. A man? Yes, he thought that might be it, though it made even less sense to him now that he saw the whole picture. It looked like a man with his arms folded, hunching over him with concern. He couldn't make out any of the details of the man's face, but he was sure that he was looking at him, watching over him. He wanted to keep looking, but his eyelids were growing too heavy. *Everything* felt heavy. Shrugging off that final urge to stay awake, he closed his eyes and went to sleep.

CHAPTER
4

Anomalies

"Interesting," Edward Munro mumbled as he shifted in his seat, leaning in for a closer inspection of the data set lying on his desk. "Yes, interesting indeed," he murmured a moment later, then trailed off as he combed his fingers through the thick mess of light gray locks that he called hair. He squinted as he adjusted his spectacles. "One might even say intriguing."

Leaning back, he slowly spun around in his chair then rose. He gave himself a quick once-over, then furrowed his brow and smoothed out his wrinkled lab coat. The drab old thing had a dreadful habit of bunching up on him, and if he wasn't careful, he'd wind up looking like Jack's mangy mutt. The unidentified stains and the layer of chalk on his sleeves, on the other hand, didn't bother him in the least. They were vestigial reminders of his numerous and oftentimes fruitful experiments, and he wore them like a badge of honor.

Clasping his hands behind his back, he strode past the oaken desk to stare at a large chart that was pinned to the main study wall. He removed his glasses, wiped their lenses on his sleeve, and squinted obtusely as he scrutinized over the algorithms that were scrawled upon it. "A most puzzling dilemma," he murmured as he slipped his glasses back into place.

"Indeed, Munro," said a nasal voice from somewhere behind him, which gave him a start. A tall, bald man in his mid-to-late fifties stepped through the gaping doorway then, and waited for the electronically-operated door to slide shut behind him before continuing. He had square shoulders on a thin frame, and looked relatively athletic for a man his age. "It is a dilemma that we have been unable to resolve *completely* for over twenty years."

Gritting his teeth, Edward swung around then, and spat out a bitter, "Yes. Over twenty years, and you still haven't learned to knock before entering."

The slightly younger scientist looked up and exhaled, loudly and exaggeratedly. "Don't get your testes in a knot," he sighed. "There *is* a reason for this little visit of mine." He strolled over to Edward's desk then, and spared the clutter of documents amassed upon it a disinterested glance.

"I couldn't care less about your reasons, Doctor Weissinger," Edward harrumphed, returning his attention to the chart.

Weissinger smirked mischievously and dropped down into Edward's chair. "I didn't think that you would," he chided, "but it's beside the point, yes? You weren't at the committee meeting this afternoon, Doctor Munro. Come to think of it, you weren't at last week's meeting, either."

Edward traced a finger across several equations scribbled on the chart and mumbled silently, performing quick calculations in his head. "Well, I've been busy," he responded distantly. He was far too absorbed in his own endeavor to show any real interest. "I have a lot of work to do."

Weissinger leaned back and kicked his feet up onto the desk. "We all do, Edward. The committee begins to wonder why you seclude yourself." He stretched his arms out them and placed his hands behind his head. "They begin to suspect that you've been withholding information from them. From us."

His accusatory tone irritated Edward to no end. Frowning deeply, he tore his eyes from the chart and turned to face him. "And what do *you* suspect, Weissinger?" he demanded sourly.

Weissinger stood abruptly, towering over him, and scowled down at him with contempt. "Suspect?" he barked, indignant. "Unlike the *other* members of the committee, I *know* that you've been withholding information from us, because I had the good sense to monitor your research."

Edward tensed suddenly, and an unexpected pang of anxiety set his stomach roiling. How could Weissinger possibly know? He'd barely even noticed the subtleties himself, at first, and he'd conducted his research in the greatest secrecy. Try as he might, he couldn't hide the emotional distress that he felt washing over him. Feeling defeated, he took a deep breath, then sighed dejectedly and let his shoulders sag.

"That's right," Weissinger continued sternly. "I know all about your little secret, Edward. Why you tried to hide it from us in the first place is well beyond my ability to comprehend. This matter concerns all of the Commission."

Edward winced and braced himself for the diatribe he knew was sure to follow.

"I don't know how many misfired synapses it took," Weissinger complained, "but you should *not* be holding out on us. Do you understand me? I don't care how many years of your life you've spent working on this. Your carelessness is endangering the entire program. Well?" he added after a moment of silence, planting his fists on his hips. "What have you got to say for yourself? You know this isn't going to go over well with the committee."

"Then you haven't told them yet?" Edward asked him in a tentative manner, feeling cautiously optimistic.

"No," Weissinger sighed. "Not yet. I wanted to hear your side of the story first. Why wasn't the committee informed about Sixty-Seven's condition? And please don't tell me it's because you're attached to your work. That's never a good excuse."

Edward hesitated briefly, gathering himself, and tried his best to sound convincing. "Well, you see," he muttered awkwardly before regaining at least some of his composure, "it is my belief that any negative action taken at this point in time would be premature and a hindrance to the program." He *had* to convince Weissinger to keep quiet about this. He was *not* about to lose all his years of hard work to those madmen.

"Premature?" Weissinger scoffed, furious. "*Premature?* He's been displaying *obvious* symptoms for over two months now. Your own records show it clearly!" Edward tried desperately to get a word in, but Weissinger spoke over him. "You know what kind of havoc a contaminated component can wreak upon its environment, Doctor, and of the rippling effect it has on others. It's why infections are terminated when symptoms *first* manifest themselves and *not* two months later. We're lucky the entire panel hasn't been spoiled. Now," he stated dismissively, clearing his throat, "what led you to believe that Sixty-Seven's termination would hinder the program?"

The scarlet had receded from his cheeks, confirming that his curiosity was winning over on his anger. The observation relieved Edward somewhat, for all that was worth. The cellular anomaly was under *his* microscope now. This might be his only chance to change the other man's mind, to keep him from going to the committee, or even worse, the council. "The symptoms were barely noticeable, at first. I very nearly overlooked them myself," he humbly admitted. "It required a great deal of patience and a little bit of luck to locate them. What astonishes me... what kept me from sharing this with the committee, was the discovery that they'd already been present for years, completely undetected despite our state-of-the-art equipment *and* routine psionic sweeps. I'll prove it, if you don't believe me. I'm sure you'll agree then that the records hold no antecedent."

Weissinger barely managed a nod, the stupor creeping into his eyes a sure sign of his sudden bewilderment.

"Ah," Edward said, allowing himself a slight grin as he realized just how taken aback Weissinger was. "You hadn't caught onto *that* with your monitoring, had you? You understand my motivation, now? We *cannot* let them pull the plug on Sixty-Seven, Jerg. Not now! This research cannot be sacrificed to the council and their flawed policies."

All things considered, Edward was pleased with himself. He was more and more convinced that the tides were turning in his favor. "These anomalies, this situation... they're an opportunity, Jerg. This could be our chance to resolve the issues that have been holding us back for so long."

Jerg shook his head slowly, coming to. "It could also be our downfall, Doctor," he cautioned. "Let us not forget the twenty-two subjects that we lost three years past as the result of similar efforts. It was duly qualified as negligent then, and it would be no different now, with this."

Edward stared at Jerg for what seemed a very long time, then took a deep breath and opened up the proverbial floodgate. "Yes. Yes, Jerg, yes. We did lose twenty-two subjects. *Once again* we are reminded of the *unfortunate* effects of the council's policies and their ironfisted rule over our program's committee. They sacrifice time, they sacrifice resources and they sacrifice *progress...* and for what? To save what work we've already accomplished? I think not. It may well be their intention, but their barbaric policies have adverse effects. They stall development in a serious way."

Edward paced around the room as he delivered his lively discourse, gesturing vividly and never breaking eye contact with Jerg. As soon as it looked like the other doctor was about to say something, he stifled him with a raised palm and talked over him. "The council's fear of change and the committee's fear of the council stall progress in a serious way, but I digress. Although outwardly a catastrophe, we gleaned a significant amount of data from that unfortunate situation three years ago, and the project throve afterward because of it. We learned because of it. We *grew* because of it. Besides... if the other subjects have remained intact, unaffected for so many years, why would they risk contamination now? The symptoms have been present and stable for years, so why, Doctor Weissinger, *why* in the ever-loving name of Science would we pull the plug *now*, after all this time?" Each word he spoke seemed to convince the younger scientist a little more.

"I begin to see your point, Edward," Jerg conceded, diffident. He wasn't used to being challenged, or surprised, or defeated, but the effects wouldn't last. It wasn't long before he'd regained his composure and added, "In a worst-case scenario, there is such a thing as acceptable risk. I don't see why your studies should be interrupted. So long as homeostasis is preserved in the testing platform, I'm not sure why *anyone* would object to them."

Edward suppressed a sudden urge to grin. Instead, he bowed his head briefly and drew his hands together over his chest before saying, "Thank you, friend. Thank you. You do understand it's imperative that we keep this affair secret, Jerg. We *must* remain silent about it, at least for now."

Jerg shook his head decisively. "I can't do that, Edward. It's strictly prohibited to hide such information from the committee. And I'm the chief of security. This *has* to go to the committee, if not to the council. There's no getting around it. What I can do, however, is speak before them on your behalf. I'll present your findings in a favorable light, of course, and try to ensure that they support your little... experiment."

Edward nodded briefly, certain of nothing but left with no other choice. "If you must, then so be it."

Jerg nodded back at him. "I'd better get to it, then. If they discover this on their own, before I can intervene, you'll most likely suffer severe penalties. And then our plan will die in the egg, before it even has a chance to hatch." He turned away from him then and stalked off toward the door.

Albeit brashly self-confident and temperamental, despite the contempt that some of their colleagues had for him, Weissinger was influential in his own way, Edward knew. The man had at least some sway with the committee, and that was something that could work well to his advantage.

"I'm warning you, though," Jerg called back to him from the doorway, "if anything should go wrong here, you'll be the one to blame. Not I!" With that, he casually disappeared behind the sliding door. He was also prudent. He was always prudent.

CHAPTER
5

The Long Way Back

Frank twisted and turned twixt the muslin sheets of his sweat dampened hospital bed, struggling futilely for a hold on reality. In his mind, Daniel sat cross-legged on the cold, dusty planks of his bedroom floor, bouncing a small rubber ball off of the floor and onto the wall and catching it again when it came back at him. He'd been doing the same thing over and over again for what felt like an hour now. It was supposed to be fun, but barely managed to keep him occupied.

He usually enjoyed this simple, if pointless game. It kept his hands busy and sharpened his reflexes. Playing little games like this one or reading some of the few books that his family owned took up most of his free time, and had spared him from complete and utter boredom on more than one occasion.

But not this time. He let his shoulders slump and watched the ball bounce past him on the next return. His depressing little bedroom was part of the problem. It was little more than a box furnished with a small, hard mattress in one corner and a rotting wooden dresser in the other. The few slivers of light filtering in through the boarded window cast a dull glow on the room.

Though he ignored the reasons why, times had been hard for his family these past couple years. They didn't enjoy many of the luxuries that they once had. Still, his father always ensured that there was enough food on the table, and he was grateful for that. But what he really needed was a friend, someone to play with, to spend time with. That was another problem he'd found himself faced with ever since Hopper had disappeared. Maybe that was when things had really started to go downhill for them.

He sighed deeply and looked down at the cracks in the floor. Passing the time would be so much easier if he was allowed to go outside, but his father expressly forbade him from venturing beyond the front door without supervision, specifically of the parental variety. With his father's long absences and his mother's busy schedule, he was almost always stuck inside.

He heard something in the doorway then and looked up. His mother was standing there, looking down at him with sad eyes. "Momma, why can't I go outside and play with the other kids?" he asked her. "Are you afraid that I might run away? Cause you know I'd never do that, right?"

Elizabeth cast her eyes down shamefully. "No. That's not it, Daniel. Please believe me," she entreated. "I want you to be able to play with other children. Really, I do, but..." She trailed off for a moment then sighed deeply before continuing. "Your father and I are concerned for your safety, is all. The world out there just isn't a place for children, Danny. It isn't safe."

Daniel's spirits lifted visibly. "But Poppa's gonna make it safe again, ain't he!" His innocent eyes sparkled brightly with a blaze of youthful pride.

"You know, Danny, you remind me of him when you do that," she said, smiling faintly. "Yes, he'll make it safe again, one day." She gave him a look that was meant to be reassuring, but still betrayed a certain quiet unease.

Daniel bobbed his head approvingly. "I hope so, too. Maybe Hopper will come back when it's safe. I really miss him."

Elizabeth shifted uncomfortably then and turned her face away from him. She could try to hide it, but he could still see the tears forming in her eyes.

"You miss him too, don't you?" Daniel asked, frowning as he pushed himself to his feet. "Don't worry. He'll come back some day, Momma." He walked over to the doorway then and hugged her tightly, closing his eyes as he did. "I know he will!" His well-intended gesture only wrenched more tears from her.

When he opened his eyes again, he was somewhere else. In the blink of an eye, he'd been transported to an entirely different location. He'd somehow found himself back in the comfort of his old bedroom in their Plaza condo, where they used to live. He didn't know how it had happened, but there he was, lying snugly under the warm covers in his cozy, queen-sized bed.

Had it all been a dream? Was he still dreaming now? He couldn't quite tell. Both realities were convincing, but this one seemed particularly vivid.

The shaggy scatter rugs on the floor and colorful portraits adorning the walls contrasted sharply with the sparse and dirt-poor furnishings of the decrepit room he'd been in only seconds earlier. His mother sat hunched over on the edge of his bed, sobbing uncontrollably. That hadn't changed.

But she looked younger now, somehow. Her long, auburn hair was untouched by the gray strands that had streaked through it only moments earlier. Her face, smooth and unwrinkled, was free of the lines that creased it previously. His father was sitting beside her, hugging her fiercely. There was something different about him, as well. He was garbed in one of those fancy business suits that he hadn't seen him wear in years, and though he was there with them in at least a physical sense, his eyes stared straight past them, into the void. They burned with an intense, unadulterated hatred, his lip curled back into a nasty-looking snarl.

Daniel had no idea what was going on. It reminded him of something, tickled his memory, but for the most part, it just scared him. He rolled over to turn away from the disturbing scene, and caught his breath as his eyes locked with those of an eerie old lady that was sitting directly beside his bed.

"Wake up, Daniel," the bug-eyed woman croaked.

He shuddered violently and burrowed deeper into his blankets, his escape reflex kicking in strong. Try as he might, he couldn't stop thinking about the spittle oozing through the gaps between the lady's lumpy, rouge-caked lips. The image was too freshly imprinted to simply suppress it. It felt like it would be engraved in his memory till the end of time.

"Wake up, child. Wake up," she uttered throatily, over and over again, like some kind of spine-tingling, demonic alarm clock.

Suddenly, his surroundings vanished entirely and everything went black, leaving him alone and in the dark. His parents, his room, even the bed that he was lying on just disappeared completely, but the old woman's repetitive croaking seemed to echo on inside his head. It was his only companion in this seemingly endless stretch of nothing. Eventually, the voice billowed out and faded altogether, leaving him truly and completely alone.

Frightened, he waited there in silence for what seemed like a very long time, staring blindly into the pitch-black void engulfing him. All he could hear was the sound of his own breathing. He was frozen in time, incapacitated by fear. In a way, the absence of sound was almost as bad as the old woman's unearthly mantra. When he'd finally gotten her out of his mind, her voice whispered into existence again.

"Wake up," she breathed, her words barely audible, but loud enough to make him question whether he'd really heard them or just imagined it. Again, the invasive silence fell. "Wake up!" the voice boomed out suddenly, removing all doubt and startling him from his dream.

Frank's eyes flickered open and he winced in agony as the bright light flooded in, burning his sensitive retina like the water of an over-chlorinated pool. He held one hand over his eyes and tried to focus on it, but everything was a blur. He moved his hand away, and gasped sharply as his vision returned and the chunky woman looming over him took shape.

"Wake up, sleepy head," the portly nurse sang out loudly. "It's time to change your sheets." Her shrill voice complimented her toothy smile perfectly. "And you have visitors... *and* you're being released today, too. Wowie zowie!"

Though weakened and lying stiff in a hospital bed he couldn't remember being helped into, strangely, all he could do was think about the dream. It had been so vivid, so real, like something that might actually have happened. *Nonsense*, he thought, dismissing the idea almost as quickly as it had popped into his head. He'd rather lie to himself and pretend like he'd never thought of it seriously before. A dream was just a dream, he reminded himself. There was no excuse for *crazy thoughts*. Still, he couldn't help but wonder who Hopper was.

The nurse stopped what she was doing all of a sudden and gave him a funny look. Had he said something out loud without realizing it? He'd have to be more careful. If he started taking these nocturnal visions too seriously, he could get himself into trouble. The last thing he or Vanessa needed was for him to get dragged off to the loony bin for med cocktails with his new pals Griswold Thurman, Napoleon Bonaparte, and Abelardus Brine.

Vanessa. He didn't need to see her to know that the warm hand that was now resting on the side of his face was hers. He strained his neck to look up at her, but she gently pushed his head back down onto his pillow.

"Don't get up too quickly," she whispered, her soft voice tickling his insides. "You'll hurt yourself." He had the distinct feeling that she'd stick by his side no matter what ill befell him.

Vanessa waved the nurse away and walked around the bed so Frank could see her more easily. Though he felt like an empty shell of the man that he used to be, he couldn't help but smile at how fondly she watched over him.

"Someone's here to see you, honey," she added, then helped him into a sitting position and put an extra pillow behind his back. His visitors were a welcome sight. Tom and Andrew had come to see him from the precinct. They were both in uniform.

"Hey, man," Andrew said, falling in beside Vanessa. Tom got up from his chair and followed suit. "How you doing?" he asked, careful not to speak too loudly. "And more importantly, what's it like to be famous?"

Frank offered him a puzzled glance. The last thing he could remember was getting into a fight with Gigantor the Magnificent, Shadowboxer Extraordinaire. He also recalled something about a rookie mistake he'd made in letting his guard down, but he'd already been in a bad way by that point, and could hardly fault himself for it. He had no idea how long he'd been out for. He had no way of knowing. It could have been a few days or even a few weeks, and it would have been all the same to him.

"Oh, come on, now," Andrew mock chided him. "There's no point in playing stupid with *us*, Mister Popular. Like you didn't know." He went and grabbed a chair from the corner of the room, put it down beside the bed, and sat down. "Your fans are gonna think you're avoiding them, Sunshine," he jested, "what with you being cooped up in here for the past month or so. Everyone's been talking about you these days. The trail of creeps you left behind before you wound up here got you some serious media coverage. They haven't run out of new material yet, but you've already become one of those annoying loops that they run over and over again on every single channel."

Frank smiled weakly but didn't have the energy to speak. He appreciated Andrew's attempt at humor, even if it did seem blatantly ridiculous to him.

"Yeah, you probably think he's joking," Tom said in a gruff, slightly less practiced tone, "but he's completely serious." The stocky, broad-shouldered man took a seat opposite Andrew on the other side of the bed and hunched forward before adding,

"One of those guys you ran up against the other day survived the massacre. Big, goofy guy... seemed kinda retarded. We brought him in for questioning, and got a heck of a lot more out of him than any of us expected to."

He paused briefly for emphasis and went on. "It led to some pretty major arrests, Franky. Media's been making you out to be some kind of law enforcement hero or something, since you started the ball rolling on this and everything. Heck, agency's been playing right along with it—go figure—and even the commissioner sang your praises during one of his media briefings. That's a heck of a lot more credit than he's ever given a badge before.

"Of course, Chucklefuck would do anything for a shot in the limelight, and he's probably gonna ride this hard for as long as he can. Kind of straying from the point here, though; point being that I can't blame you for trying, Franky, but you know you'll never dethrone old Tommy Gun here. I'm still number one in the ass kickin' department. You're not even close second." He grinned widely at that. "Anyway, we were in the area and thought we'd drop by to see how you were doing. We were worried about you. Doc says you're gonna be alright though, pal. You just need to take it easy for a few days. Get you some R & R."

A scraggly old man in white scrubs entered the room then. From the look of it, he was completely absorbed by the notes on the clipboard he was holding only a few inches from his face. "That's right, Mister Gostobalis," he said, wiping his forehead with the back of his gloved hand before waddling over to the side of the bed. "I'm your doctor, Francis Sloope." He nodded and half-bowed as he introduced himself. "It's good to see you up and at it, Mister Fasaro, in a manner of speaking. I have to say, this is the most responsive I've seen you since you first got here."

Frank found himself distracted momentarily by the doctor's big, bulbous nose, which jutted out from his face like a bizarre, superfluous appendage. He couldn't recall ever seeing one quite so big before. It was almost cartoonish in its proportions.

"Now, let's see," the doctor continued, eyeing his clipboard closely. "When you first arrived here, you had severe lacerations and more minor contusions than I cared to count. You fractured your arm in two places and suffered multiple stab wounds—*deep ones*. To top it off, you had a collapsed lung and more broken ribs than you could shake a finger at. Oh, and you went into a coma, though admittedly a short-lived one. Quite an impressive list, if dying young is your thing."

He eyed Frank disapprovingly then and carried on with his elaborate reproof. "No, you weren't much to look at when they brought you in, but aside from your punctured lung—which we had to drain constantly, mind you—most of your wounds were superficial. We had to keep you under after the more immediate danger had passed... to facilitate your recovery."

Vanessa started to say something then, but Doctor Sloope cut her off, and continued speaking over her. "He'll have been a lot better off for it," he said. "Trust me. Though not life-threatening, your partner's wounds were extensive. It would've taken him a lot longer to recover, and every waking moment would have been a lesson in agony."

"Instead," he added, looking down at Frank, "all you'll have to deal with now are passenger pains, but I'll write you up a prescription for those. While I'd firmly encourage you to explore new career options—preferably ones that don't involve guns or knives—you should be ready to go back to work in a few days. To a desk job, that is. If you rest well and avoid overexertion. I don't want you lifting anything heavy or moving around too quickly, but you probably won't feel like doing either of those anyway."

Frank managed a labored nod. It was all coming back to him now. He'd taken quite a severe beating back in that alleyway. He knew that the boss was going to chew him out for not requesting backup, but the perpetrators might have gotten away if he'd waited for help. And he'd gotten his man in the end, after all. Well, he'd almost gotten his man. He vaguely recalled someone rushing to his rescue. Someone else had gotten his man. Or had they? Suddenly, he wasn't so sure. Had all of it been real, or merely part of one of the countless dreams he'd been having over the past few weeks. He'd have to get his hands on the official report to know for sure. Still, his recollection of the man he was fighting getting shot to shreds was pretty convincing.

Doctor Sloope cleared his throat in an effort to get Frank's attention. "No difficult activities at all. Period." He eyed Vanessa suggestively then until he was satisfied that she'd understood the message. "You can pick up your prescription from the pharmacy on your way out. They're powerful painkillers, so be careful. In strong enough doses, they could knock out a pack of alley wolves and put them to sleep forever. Now, if there are no questions, I have other patients to attend to. I wish you a quick recovery, Mister Fasaro, and urge you one last time to get another job. Goodbye." The small man turned around promptly and left, disappearing from the room as unceremoniously as he'd entered it.

At Vanessa's request, Tom and Andrew helped Frank into a wheelchair. After a quick stop at the ground-level pharmacy, they escorted him to her hovercar in the basement parking lot, helped him into it and said their goodbyes. Before long, they were home.

The next couple days seemed to meld together into one endless, mind-numbing fog. Frank spent a great deal of that time lying in bed, trying to decipher the meaning of his recurring dreams. His painkiller-induced stupor made his efforts even more futile than they already were.

On the third day, he was finally able to start walking around on his own again. Late that morning, he listened as Vanessa took calls from both of their parents. They inquired about his recovery and her take on the situation. Before long, she'd "invited" them all to dinner. She didn't have much of a choice in the matter. They'd all made it perfectly clear that they'd have to check up on him personally, except for his mother, who was down with a case of the dripsy and would have to stay home. Frank was a little bit disappointed by the news, but understood that she just didn't want to give him her virus in his weakened condition.

The evening started out tame enough, but became increasingly embarrassing when Vanessa's parents broke out the old childhood photos. They had plenty of bizarre and awkward anecdotes to go along with them. Armand and Reina Durante were a regally-attired but truly down-to-earth pair. Flaunting humiliating pictures of their "baby girl" as they liked to call her, seemed to give them great joy. "You'll understand one day, when you have children of your own," they'd occasionally offer up in a suggesting manner. Their prized jewel was a picture of her in the bathtub at four years old, with a crazy look on her face, and with hair spiked up like the quills on a hedgehog's back.

While Frank did find that particular photo amusing, it gave him pause for thought. Most parents had pictures of their children smothered in spaghetti sauce or chocolate icing. With all of the pictures gathering dust on the walls in his parents' home, or lying hidden away somewhere in old photo albums, he couldn't recall ever seeing one of himself at that age. It was probably nothing, he knew, but his curiosity was piqued.

Vanessa's parents grew tipsier as the night wore on, and after a while, it became apparent that it was time to wrap things up. The two of them shared an acute penchant for fortified wine; if there was any around, it was a given that they'd need a ride home at the end of the night, assuming they even made it that far.

When Vanessa left to drive them home, Frank decided to ask his father about the curious lack of photos. On legs that were far more wobbly than he'd like them to be, he followed the sounds of clinking dishes to the kitchen, where he found his father washing them. "Come on, dad," he said as he hobbled over to join him. "You didn't have to do that. I thought you were just gone to the washroom or something. I was going to do them later."

"Oh, you were going to do them later," Gordon said in a mock chiding tone, then smiled wryly as he glanced over at him.

"That brings back memories." His smile widened then and he shook his head lightly, ostensibly reminiscing over one of them. "It's fine," he quickly added. "Really. It was a nice meal, and I just wanted to say thank you. Least I could do."

"If you insist," Frank replied with a shrug, "but hand over one of those dish towels, would you? Dinner wasn't good because of me. Vanessa's been doing pretty much everything the past few days." The two of them stood there working quietly for a minute when Frank finally decided to ask him the question flat out. "So why aren't there any pictures of me when I was little?"

Gordon was so surprised by the question that he dropped the glass he was busy cleaning. He managed to wedge it between the counter and the top of his foot just as it was about to hit the floor. "Why aren't there any pictures of you when you were little?" he repeated, slowly, like the words were complicated and he wanted to be sure he'd understood them correctly.

"Um, yeah," Frank answered tentatively. He'd felt foolish for asking the question in the first place, but hearing it played back to him made it even worse.

Gordon picked the glass up carefully and put it back in the sink, then dried his hands off on his shirt and rubbed at his chin pensively. "Well," he said, then trailed off. "That's a bit of an odd question, isn't it? Why do you ask?"

Frank thought about it briefly and shrugged. He knew that it was a strange question, but he wanted an answer to it anyway. "Just curious, I guess."

Gordon nodded then and looked around, almost as though he might find the answer to the question hiding somewhere in the kitchen. For anyone who knew him well, this was a sure sign that he was nervous and trying to avoid something. "Hem," he mumbled, his anxiety becoming more and more apparent.

Frank didn't understand what the delay was all about. It was a relatively simple question that should have garnered an equally straightforward answer.

"Oh, geez," Gordon finally sighed. His shoulders slumped forward heavily and he looked down at his feet. "Your mother is going to kill me. Founders be fucked, she is."

Frank's curiosity quickly turned to concern. "What is it?" he urged him. "What?"

Gordon took another deep breath before continuing. "I'm not sure how to tell you this, son," he managed to say, struggling with every word. He was far from expressive, especially when it came to matters of the heart.

"Magda's going to kill me, for sure," he whispered to himself, staring at the floor. He kept silent for a few seconds before finally adding, "You were adopted, Frank. I'm sorry. I'm sorry if this is coming out the wrong way. I thought for a second that it might be easier if I just came out with it, like ripping a bandage off, but this isn't the same thing at all, is it?"

"Adopted?" Frank said more than asked, practically stunned. He grabbed a nearby chair and let himself sink into it heavily. "But I... you... I mean..." he mumbled incoherently. An awkward moment passed and he looked up at his father, his face twisted with pain. "Why didn't you tell me this sooner?" he asked him with a voice that was shaky and wrenched with emotion. "Why didn't I know about this already?"

Gordon shook his head, at a loss for words. "Please, Franky, I'm sorry," he pleaded. "Your mother didn't want you to know." The guilty expression on his face betrayed his own feelings of responsibility. "She didn't think it was necessary. *In fact*, she thought it would only cause problems, because you *are* our real son, even *if* we don't share the same DNA. We didn't want to make an issue out of your being adopted."

Frank rubbed at his throbbing temples gently. He had so many questions on his mind, but his thoughts were bouncing back and forth so much that he couldn't think of one in particular to ask him. His head was all a jumble. The only thing he managed to come up with was, "Why?"

"Well," Gordon sighed, "your mother and I weren't able to have children of our own. She was barren and I've always shot blanks. Not a very good combination, those two. Even if we'd been able to conceive, the cost of a childbearing permit back then was insane. We might have been able to find the money *somehow*, but it would have broken us financially. And that wouldn't even have guaranteed us a child anyway.

"Even if we'd managed to raise the money, there was a good chance the request would have been denied. They didn't sell those permits to anyone that walked in off the street, you know. I was a policeman, Frank, just like my daddy before me. Not a lawmaker or a judge—no sir. The profession didn't have the clout that it does today. Not even close. Nowadays it's a different story, but back then, they didn't exactly encourage us to be fruitful and multiply. No, adoption really was our only choice."

Frank grimaced bitterly at his father's words. *Only choice.* That was just another way of saying "last resort", wasn't it? He opened his mouth to say something, but felt like he'd lost his tongue, and forgot what he was going to say in the first place. He closed his eyes then and took a deep breath in an effort to regain at least a modicum of composure. "Who are my real parents?" he asked. "My biological parents," he quickly added, realizing how hurtful his question might be. He suspected that he already knew the answer to that, but he had to ask anyway.

Gordon shook his head again for what seemed like the fiftieth time. "I'm not sure, Frank," he breathed. "The only thing the folks at the orphanage told us was that some homeless winos had dropped you off there one night and then never came back. They probably couldn't afford to—"

"Get out," Frank ordered, cutting him off abruptly. His mood had fouled instantly, and he found it nearly impossible to remain calm or think rationally. He just wanted to be left alone.

"Frank," his father pleaded. "Franky, I'm sorry. Really, I am. If I could go back and—"

Frank's icy glare silenced him more than any words could. "I said get out," he repeated, seething. He knew that he wasn't being fair, but he couldn't help it. His father had just announced that they weren't even related. They weren't of the same blood. And chances were he was an illegal baby, delivered without a permit, born without papers. That on its own could stifle his and Vanessa's own plans of filling out an application.

Having a child wasn't anything concrete yet, but they'd talked about it plenty, and they were really getting used to the idea of it. Now their chances could be seriously hampered. What pissed him off the most was that his father's delivery was made with the casual calm of a, "Hey, nice weather we've got going right now, wouldn't you say?" At least, that's what it felt like to him. "Like ripping a bandage off," he grumbled. "Right."

Gordon sighed deeply and offered him one final, apologetic glance before withdrawing from the room.

Frank felt like there was a massive tumor gestating inside his skull. He waited until he heard the front door close, then rose and pushed through the door to his bedroom. He strode to the side of his bed, grabbed the small prescription bottle from the nightstand and spilled its contents into the palm of his hand. There were only two painkillers left, but that was all he needed. He just wanted the pain to stop. He just wanted to go to sleep. Taking one extra pill couldn't really hurt, could it? He popped the pills into his mouth, turned the bitter things over with his tongue, and swallowed them down whole. They went down rough, but he managed.

The effects were nearly instantaneous. The pain was gone, but he felt woozy and had a hard time staying on his feet. It took him every last bit of coordination just to fall on the bed, and not the floor. He struggled onto his back and managed to push one shoe off with his foot, but was already snoring heavily before he could remove the second.

"Ooh," Daniel cooed, wide-eyed with amazement. He ogled the mesh of banged-up tin cans and thick copper wiring held out before him. Most people would think it wasn't much to look at, he realized, but to him it was a thing of beauty, in its own way. "What is it?" he asked, clearly impressed.

The boy holding the odd contraption pulled it away from him and cradled it in his arms possessively. "It's mine is what it is," he boasted in a snotty, better-than-thou tone. "It's a ray gun, and you're not allowed to touch it!"

Daniel was so focused on the crude toy gun that he didn't even see the other boy, but he could tell by the tone of his voice that he was about ten years old. "Where did you get it?" he asked him, hoping to find one for himself.

"Duh," the other boy groaned loudly, obviously annoyed. He whirled his finger around his ear and added, "I made it, retard! Don't you know *anything*?"

Daniel's face reddened as the heat rose in his face. "You're gonna get in trouble if momma sees that, Hopper," he warned him, gritting his teeth. "And don't call me a retard!"

Hopper sighed exasperatedly. "Fine, I won't call you retard, moron, but mom ain't going to find out about this, now is she? Not unless someone wants to enjoy the smell of their own poopy pants up close and personal."

Daniel shut his eyes tightly and put his hands over his nose. "No! No! No! No! No!" he stammered. "Not the poopy pants! I won't tell! I promise I won't tell!"

"Good," Hopper stated curtly. "Now I'm gonna go play, and you're gonna stay here and keep being an idiot, unless you have something better to do. Doubt it."

Daniel opened his eyes and started hopping up and down. "Can I come too? Can I? Can I? Can I? Can I?"

Hopper stomped his foot down and shook his head to the side. "No," he answered him in a firm tone. "You're just a dumb little kid. Dumb little kids don't play with guns, and I don't play with dumb little kids. Now leave me *alone*. I'm gonna go scare some girls with Tom. You better not follow us."

Daniel wriggled his nose and crossed his arms stubbornly. "Tom Tamlin is a big booger head!" he exclaimed defiantly. "He's always saying naughty words. Momma says he's a bad *influmence*, too," he added matter-of-factly. "He says so many bad words that one day his mouth is going to rot and fall right off his face. *Right. Off. His face.* Just you watch."

Hopper rolled his eyes in response and fell to his knees dramatically. "Oh my goodness, what shall we ever do?" he cried out exaggeratedly. "He says so many *naught words.* The next time he opens his filthy mouth, blood's probably gonna gush out of my ears." He let himself drop to the ground, agonizing all the way down, then played dead for a few seconds.

Daniel furrowed his brow in response, not at all pleased with Hopper's mock portrayal of him.

Satisfied with the results of his dramatization, Hopper got to his feet and dusted off his pants. "You should know better than to go crying to mom over everything, Danny. She has better things to do than listen to you whine, you big baby."

Daniel's anger flashed white hot, and he started to tremble like the world's smallest volcano, ready to erupt at any second. "I'm gonna tell on you anyway, Franky MacBride!" he shouted, shaking his balled fist at him. "Momma's gonna spank your bum so hard it'll turn blue and explode!"

Hopper—or "Franky"—snorted, gave him the finger, and hollered out a routine, "Later, retard!" before running off.

The split second before he'd turned and bolted away, Daniel managed to get a good glimpse of his face.

Frank woke in a cold sweat. The room was spinning slowly all around him, and the image of that little boy's face was still fresh in his mind. His throat was dry and it felt like he had something stuck in it. *That little boy*, he thought. *What was his name? Hopper? Franky MacBride? He looked so familiar. Bad-mouthed Franky MacBride looked like...* He looked kind of like he did when he was younger. More than just sort of. All that talk about photos and flipping through albums the night before had jogged his memory somewhat. He recalled seeing pictures of himself when he was around that age. The eyes were the wrong color, and his face looked a bit longer, but otherwise, the resemblance was just too uncanny to ignore.

He suppressed a sudden urge to throw up. The painkillers took over before he could get that far, and he fell asleep again despite the spinning. The rest of his night's sleep was devoid of dreams and was over in an instant.

He refused to think about any of it when he woke up the next morning. Careful not to wake Vanessa, he crawled out of bed and headed for the shower. The hot water pounded *some* sense into him, but his legs felt limp and his arms were like full sacks of potatoes. Even his high-energy breakfast and two cups of coffee failed to get him started. He wouldn't be taking two painkillers at once again anytime soon. Of that he was certain. He didn't like the idea of taking any in the first place.

He had every intention of going to work, but his arms were useless, and driving there on his own was a horribly bad idea. He wanted to get in early to beat the rush hour traffic, but that would require waking Vanessa to ask her for a ride, and he couldn't bring himself to rouse her from her sleep. Her parents lived halfway across town, and she'd most likely gotten home late.

After thinking the situation through, he decided to wait until she got up on her own, instead. It wasn't like he *had* to be there early, or even at all, really. As far as he knew, he had free rein on his return to work, at least for the time being. He found that a bit odd, considering the department was understaffed and spiraling deeper and deeper into chaos, but who was he to complain? He'd have thought that they'd push for an expedited return, but clearly someone important had a different take on things.

The only thing urging him back was his own boredom. He couldn't stand sitting around doing nothing, and he was starting to go stir-crazy. Satisfied with his decision, he put on a fresh pot of coffee, then tried to massage some life back into his arms as he waited for the black gold to brew. With a bit of luck, his arms would feel better before Vanessa even woke up.

Some wishful thinking and two hours later, Vanessa leaned over from the driver's side of her hovercar and kissed him on the cheek. "Are you sure you're alright, Franky?" she asked, eyeing him carefully. "You know, the captain said to take your time coming back. It's not like that paperwork of yours won't be there waiting for you if you decide to stay home for another week or two. Are you sure this is what you want?"

Frank smiled reassuringly, kissed her in turn and answered, "One hundred percent." He pulled the release on the underside of the dashboard and the passenger-side door started to slide upward. He leaned over to give her one last kiss before pulling himself away from the comfort of his seat.

"Catch you later, Van," he said, then watched the door slide shut all on its own. He waved as she drove off, then turned around and looked up at the imposing LEA building. Suddenly reluctant, he helped himself along the rail leading up the front steps with some difficulty. After a telling sigh, he straightened his uniform then pushed through the heavyset front doors.

The captain was standing at the other end of the hall when he walked in, and was busy reprimanding some rookie officer he'd never seen before. He had a feeling it was going to be a very long day. Out in the streets, he was spared from displays like this one, for the most part, but seeing as he was tied to the office, he probably wouldn't have much of a choice in the matter.

"And what's with this report?" Leonard snapped. "It looks like you wiped your ass with it, Jablonski. I hope I'm not touching shit right now." The cringing recruit's forehead was dripping with sweat and he looked like his knees were about to buckle. The look on the captain's face said it all. He wanted to smack some sense into the incompetent little simp. Frank was pretty sure he'd heard the captain say the same thing to him before, almost verbatim.

"You good-for-nothing simp," Leonard barked. "You just stood there like a turd on the side of the bowl and did nothing while those thugs roughed up and robbed a little old lady. And you failed to get *any* kind of statement from the witnesses. Un-be-freakin'-lievable. At least you called in the Medivac. At *least*. And it's a good thing, cause I'd'a beaten the snot out of you if you hadn't.

"Listen, kid. You haven't been with us all that long, and old Captain Leonard here ain't so sure you got what it takes to make it in the agency. Shit like this is *not* going to fly. Understand? I might be able to shape you into something useful yet—maybe—but it's lookin' like I've got my fuckin' work cut out for me, and I don't like that. You hear me? I want you to *show* me that you've got what it takes, kid. Show me that you've got some fuckin' balls. You think you can do that?"

The captain trailed off when he saw Frank walking down the hall toward him. "Hey, Fasaro," he called out. "There's my guy!" His friendly enthusiasm was unpracticed and awkward. "I wasn't expecting to see you up and on your feet so quick, but here you are. I gotta say, kid, you got yourself some cojones. Wasn't sure you did, but you do. Anyway... How you doin', Franky?"

"Uh," Frank mumbled, momentarily speechless. It sounded like the captain was trying to go easy on him, maybe even be nice. He wasn't used to that. "I'm... I'm okay, sir," he practically *asked*. He couldn't help it, but he was almost sure that the look on his face reflected his thoughts perfectly. *What the hell has the boss been smoking?* he wondered. It wasn't at all like the captain to give a shit, or even to ask as a formality.

Leonard gave him the once-over, clearly doubtful. "Bah," he grumped. "You can can it with the bullshit. You don't have to act all tough, kid. You look like a house of cards right now. Yeah, okay, you're standing there sure as shit stinks, but you look like you might fall over any second now."

Frank nodded reflexively and offered up a monotonous, "Yes, sir." This was the captain he was used to.

Leonard cleared his throat and scratched at the back of his ring of hair with a few brisk, brushing motions. Noticing the recruit still standing there watching him, he belted out a, "What the heck are you looking at, chucklehead?" It sent Jablonski into a startled, backward stumble. "What are you, deaf?" he barked, even louder. "Seriously. Why are you still standing there?" The new recruit turned tail then and ran.

Frank couldn't help but laugh. It took him a moment to realize that the boss was laughing too.

Leonard chortled, snorted and finally forced himself to stop in order to catch his breath. He coughed noisily into his balled fist then wiped the tears from his eyes. "I've got a job for you on the home front today," he wheezed. "I'm not sending you out like that; no siree, Bob. I want you to head up to Records Management and start processing some of the backlogged documents in the archives there. It's a boring job, I know, but someone has to do it, and it might as well be you."

Frank nodded, saluted casually and headed straight for the elevators. With any luck, the captain's good spirits would last until he was at least three floors away. It was odd enough seeing him in a good mood, he knew it couldn't last. He didn't want to be around for the next outburst.

A short while later, the elevator door slid open and Frank stepped out into the biggest mess of paperwork he'd ever seen. The fourth floor was well known for its clutter, but he hadn't imagined it would be this bad. Why the agency refused to hire civvies to put some order into this mess was beyond him. From the look of it, they were a few years behind with the processing.

He did a little exploratory roaming and was dumbstruck at what he found. There was shelving as far as the eye could see, or as far as the mess would let him, at least. Row upon row upon row of bookshelves stacked to the ceiling spanned most of the floor. Here and there, enormous piles of loose paperwork and unfiled documents littered the alleys, sometimes blocking them off altogether. In some places, haphazard piles had fallen over and lay in heaps, along with books that had fallen off of shelves that had been filled past capacity. He'd never seen so much clutter in the same place. It made it all seem very labyrinthian. At least the bristly, slate blue carpet was clean. It was a nice change to the dirty-looking tiles he was accustomed to.

After a few minutes of random wandering, he stumbled on what he took for an archivist's workstation, somewhere near the outer wall. Whoever had occupied the cubicle had left it in a state of disorder that was on par with everything else in the place. As mucked up as it was, he doubted he'd find anything better, and decided to stake his claim on it. He shrugged off his leather jacket and slung it over his shoulder, then grabbed a pile of reports from a nearby cabinet marked "MIA".

He threw his jacket over the back of his new chair, pushed a heap of records off his desk and onto the floor, then dropped his own files onto the cleared surface and took a seat before the black and green screen of his antediluvian terminal. Normally, he'd have stifled the exaggeratedly long yawn that racked his body, but there was no one else around to hear him anyway. He'd only just gotten there, but he was already dying for another coffee. An extra bold anything would do just fine.

The files he was currently thumbing through were about officers that had gone missing in the line of duty. Most of the reports had been written subsequent to their disappearances, but there were a lot of other documents that had been started by the officers themselves and just never completed.

The thought of it all made him shiver. The number of files in the "MIA" cabinet was staggering. Even though there wasn't any evidence to back it up, he knew that most of those officers were dead. It wasn't like they'd been whisked away to some faraway location. They couldn't have just run away. There was nowhere else to run to even if they'd wanted to. Leaving the confines of Innerstadt's walls meant certain death.

Two mind-numbing hours and six files later, he had a newfound respect for anyone that had the perseverance to endure an office job as tedious as this one. First, he had to group everything into case files, which was a real pain in the ass if the case files weren't already indicated somewhere obvious, or even created yet. Then, he had to fill out a metadata sheet for each document individually. Finally, he had to scan each document. One by one. And enter all the metadata into their records management system. And smack his head when he realized that he'd forgotten to do something, and have to go looking for it again, and start over. This wasn't what he'd joined the agency for. No way, no how. He wished he could be out there in the streets, doing something important—not that this wasn't important, but it was boring as fuck. In any case, he was nowhere near recovered, and he knew it.

His thoughts wandered to the dream he'd had the night before. Shortly after waking from it, he'd shrugged its content off as a figment of his imagination, but after further consideration, he wasn't so sure. There were too many coincidences to just write them off. Finding out that he'd been adopted certainly changed things. It opened up a whole slew of possibilities he'd never even considered before. Maybe he'd been a snot-nosed, ten-year-old brat that gave his little brother the finger a lot, cursed profusely, and hung out with some kid by the name of Tom Tamlin.

He considered it briefly, but it didn't really fit. His childhood memories of Andrew and of his parents—his *adoptive parents*, he somberly reminded himself—went farther back than that. He just couldn't accept the idea that he'd lived two lives simultaneously while only remembering one of them. That period of his life was pretty much accounted for.

It didn't make sense, but very little of any of this did. His father—*Gordon*—had told him that his biological parents were homeless, and that they'd one day decided to drop him off at the orphanage, probably so they could afford to buy their next bottle. That competed directly with the idea that the dreams were visions from his past. If his drunken hobo parents were real, then his dreams definitely weren't.

He couldn't help but entertain the possibility that his father had lied to him about the entire thing. And why wouldn't he? Gordon had lied to him for years—for his entire life. But what would he gain in doing so? What did he stand to lose? He was a full-grown man now, not a child, so it wasn't like Gordon had to worry about losing him to his biological parents.

Maybe he'd just been afraid that he'd lose his shit over it. If his dreams really *were* memories, wouldn't that mean that his real family was dead, that they'd been brutally murdered? That might warrant a ridiculous cover-up. Maybe. He realized that he'd probably never find out, and it probably didn't matter anyway. Still, he couldn't help but think about it.

In one of his previous dreams, Daniel had said something about "Hopper" disappearing. Maybe his father had told him the truth, or at least part of the truth. Maybe he'd run away as a kid and gotten nabbed by a couple of vagrants who'd sold him to a shady orphanage for some cheap hooch.

The fact that he could account for most of his earlier life was still problematic to this theory, but there was no ignoring the persistence of his dreams. He had to be having them for a reason. They couldn't just be random. But try as he might, he couldn't link them to anything he remembered experiencing. He couldn't pinpoint any one thing that would have influenced him to such a degree that he'd dream about it constantly, and with such eerily repetitive consistency every single time.

He thought about it for a while and decided to give in to his curiosity. Cautiously, he leaned back far enough that he could see into the passage, took a peek to ensure that no one was around, and then ducked back inside his cubicle.

Even though there was nothing wrong with what he was doing—at least not technically, he didn't think—he was a little paranoid about getting caught in the act. He felt silly for it, but it couldn't really be helped, even if he knew that he'd been a lot less nervous over much, much worse.

Shrugging it off, he took a deep breath, tapped away at the keyboard, and brought up the LEA archives application. Wasting no time, he started scouring through old reports from the past fifteen to twenty-five years. He was looking for anything even remotely similar to a raid on a family residence that had resulted in civilian casualties.

Several hundred results were returned almost immediately, but they weren't what he was looking for at all. Most of these unfortunate incidents had been logged as counter-terrorism ops. That seemed like it had to be some kind of mistake to him, like something that wouldn't happen all that often, but it wasn't the time or the place to stray from the task at hand. If the captain caught him screwing around on the clock, he might have to stay late to make up for it, and he'd promised Vanessa that he'd come straight home after work.

He sighed and pressed the escape key twice, which returned him to the main prompt. Undeterred, he clacked at the keyboard again and waited as the Citizens Registry loaded up.

This other database contained bits and pieces of personal information on almost everyone in the city. It had dates of birth, places of residence, family relations, criminal antecedents, and far, far more. The agency might be falling behind with its archiving, but that certainly wasn't the case in its "invasion of privacy" department. It employed a virtual army of civilian staff, headed up by a crack team of expert investigators, to ensure that the information it contained was valid and up to date.

If someone had shady relatives or questionable business ties and the right flags were raised, criminal analysts were consulted to review their file and assess their threat level. The agency used this information to decide who to keep tabs on. That wasn't its only use, but it was one of its primary functions. Most people accepted the fact that the agency kept these tabs. Some did not.

Reticence toward this data collection was understandable and to be expected, at least to a certain degree, but certain unsavory individuals took their opposition to the extreme. Some malcontents liked to claim that the government was a gentleman's club for the privileged elite, a legitimized front for tyranny. According to this sorry lot of good-for-nothing rabble-rousers, the powers that be did nothing but spout lies in a bid to placate the troubled masses, effectively pulling the wool over their eyes and misappropriating just enough of their freedom that it went unnoticed.

These were the people behind the recent spike in crime. They were armed, they were dangerous and they called themselves *The Awoken*. These self-proclaimed *freedom fighters* said that they were the voice of the people, but Frank saw them as nothing more than a plague on society. They hindered progress and threatened the very survival of the human race. He knew quite well that some of the city's methods were invasive, that some of them infringed on personal liberties, but he saw these so-called injustices as minor and a necessary evil.

In a perfect world, things might be different, but they didn't live in a perfect world. The world they lived in was as far from perfect as it possibly could be. Innerstadt was the last pocket of human civilization in an otherwise hostile environment. Though it wasn't always perceptible, their survival hung in a precarious balance. Their history could be traced back with relative accuracy several hundred years, and the past couple centuries or so had been relatively fair, but Innerstadt had gone through hard times in the past. It had teetered on the brink of annihilation on more than one occasion, and these sordid events lived on in history books and collective memory alike as vivid reminders of the fragility of not only their way of life, but also the human race.

These hardships, this history of struggle had made the city what it was. It was a last bastion of hope for humankind. If its government had to rule with an iron fist to keep it that way, then so be it. He had no objections.

Unsure where his thoughts were taking him, he reminded himself that he wasn't looking for terrorists. If he could, he'd find and deal with the lot of them, right down to the very last, but he was looking for something else right now. That *something* might seem trivial in comparison, but it didn't feel that way. What he was looking for was his past, his history, his identity. What he was looking for was himself.

He examined the Citizens Registry menu and frowned. The system looked familiar, but it had been a while since he'd worked with it. He navigated to the query panel and muttered as he was forced to run through a series of standard, bullshit disclaimers. "The information you are about to access is confidential and *blah blah blah,*" he murmured. "Do you agree to comply with *blah blah blah?* Yes." The software had obviously been updated sometime in the past few years, but the layout had remained relatively similar, and he was able to launch right into his investigation with very little readaptation.

"Frank MacBride" yielded no results. He had as much luck with "Daniel MacBride", "Harrold MacBride", and "Elizabeth MacBride". After inputting just about every variation of those names that he could think of, including searches by surname only, he sighed exasperatedly and double-tapped the escape key, which returned him to the program's main menu once more. He stared at the screen for a while, trying to think, but drew a blank.

He heard the scuffle of feet in the distance then and decided to close the program in a hurry. There was no way he could explain what he was looking for without either lying or coming across as completely insane. Because he was the worst liar ever, and because he'd rather avoid being ridiculed by his colleagues, he chose to keep his preoccupations to himself. As far as he was concerned, he might as well dismiss what had just happened as a momentary lapse in reason.

There was no Elizabeth MacBride. There was no Harrold or Danny. The only near-matches he'd found were a Derek MacBruis and a Maudeline McBraida, and neither of those were very close at all, as far as he was concerned. After stretching his arms again, he jumped right back into his work. He had a few more hours of filing to do before he could go home.

CHAPTER
6

The Committee

Jerg took a seat amidst his fellow scientists and waited for the austere-looking woman at the head of the long, granite table to get the meeting underway. Even though some of his peers were making it frightfully obvious that they were less than pleased to be called away from their work so suddenly, the commissioner didn't seem the least bit worried by it. She looked calm, stolid even.

Jerg knew full well that many of his colleagues disliked the commissioner. Some of them said that she was a temperamental know-it-all. Some others went so far as to call her a bureaucrat or an empty suit—behind her back, to be sure—but that meant little to him coming from a group of whiny complainers that didn't know how to behave in front of the Committee. Most of them were lucky to have even made it through the selection process. As far as he was concerned, they were lucky to have even been considered in the first place, the ungrateful pantywaists.

The rabble of haggard, dried-up geriatrics hardly looked like researchers in a first-class, top secret organization. While some chattered over algorithms to diversified psionic equations, others partook in heated debate, or bickered angrily over being dragged away from their laboratories to be in attendance. The heavily-armed sentinels standing guard by the entrance, with their straight-backed demeanors, and their radiant white uniforms, were a much-needed reminder that this was a government-funded operation, and not the lounge of a luxuriously-furnished psychiatric ward. Though, now that he thought of it, they could easily pass for orderlies.

The commissioner, Stephanie Richardson, was a very serious, very intelligent woman. Though few of Jerg's colleagues recognized it, he certainly did. Many of them questioned her rigid, results-oriented governance and unforgiving work ethic, and while it was a fair criticism, at times—at least in part—Jerg saw in her other qualities that were befitting a leader of such men. Though she did have to step on a few toes every now and then to maintain order, she was extremely lenient with regards to the poor attitudes and eccentric behaviors of her staff.

Most of their problematic and downright unpleasant habits were side effects of severe alienation. For the most part, their lives were restricted to the confines of their laboratories, their living quarters, and a very restrained, predetermined set of high-security testing areas. Their access to the outside world was limited at best. Since receiving any visitors inside of the facility was out of the question, they were occasionally granted leave to go topside, but these topside passes were issued sparsely.

In light of that, she thought it only fair that they should be afforded a certain degree of tolerance. Everything considered, the Commission's mandate and the superior intelligence required to carry it out was all the incentive she needed to keep her people happy, or at least try to. They were, more often than not, a very difficult bunch to please.

Her employees were almost preternaturally gifted in their very specific concentrations. In the realm of science and technology, they were the absolute best, the cream of the crop, and that was exactly what the Commission of Higher Sciences needed. They were all brilliant in their own way, and in others they were no smarter than she was, and that was also what the Commission needed. More so than its employees realized.

Despite their soaring IQs, most of them were so highly focused in their specializations that they lagged behind in most everything else. They were as good as handicapped in the outside world. This double-edged blade kept them from asking too many questions and prevented them from seeing the bigger picture. Jerg saw all of this very clearly. He understood the organization more than anyone else, perhaps even the commissioner herself.

"Order!" Richardson barked, her sharp command silencing the squabbling scientists almost immediately. When the crowd had quieted completely, she tacked on a, "Thank you," in a tone of voice that was almost just as brusque. "I do realize that you have very important things to do, but I'm certain that our chief of security had a very good reason for requesting this meeting. Isn't that so, Doctor Weissinger?"

"Indeed, madam," Jerg responded, taking his cue. He rose then to address the assembled committee members. "An extremely good reason, I assure you." He nodded curtly then and drew his lips back in a feeble attempt at a smile before proceeding. "I come here today bearing news of a potentially game-changing discovery— a discovery that *had* to be brought before this forum. I thought it absolutely crucial that I share it with everyone here gathered, as it may affect all of them."

"This should be interesting," Richardson said. "Please, go on."

"As I was saying," Jerg began, drawing his words out slowly and with great care, "I, along with Doctor Munro—who could not be here today, unfortunately—have made a groundbreaking discovery." He'd no doubt deny it later, but he was relishing his moment at the center of it all. With his arms folded neatly behind his back, he paced around the table as he addressed his audience. "One which seems to pose a threat, at first glance, but that—in reality—presents us with opportunities to enrich our knowledge base and further our studies."

"Oh, cut the fluff and get on with it already," an exasperated complaint rang out sharply from the far end of the table.

"Gentlemen," Richardson interjected promptly, "your work will still be there waiting for you when you return to your labs. It won't just get up and walk away. Not unless there's a glitch in the containment system, in which case I'll have to have a little chat with our good Doctor Weissinger here after the meeting." The ensuing wave of laughter lightened the atmosphere around the table somewhat, though at least one attendee retained his scowl.

Jerg waited for the noise to subside and bowed his head in appreciation before picking up where he'd left off. "I'll get straight to the point, then. Doctor Munro and I have discovered that a certain test subject was nearing the critical stages of awakening. As you all know, these 'tainted' elements have always had a negative impact on their environment, their nasty effects rippling out and drawing others into similar states of rejection. This time, however, would be very different, as we would most certainly see no such effects. Having said that, I think it imperative that we delay the termination of said subject until further research can be conducted on the matter."

"And how in the blazes can you be so sure?" a short, red-haired man of considerable girth spat out bitterly. "You have *no* way of proving that!" He pushed up from his chair at once and glanced around the room to his colleagues, saving a stern look of contempt for Jerg. "If you ask me, gentlemen, *Mister* Weissinger here is just blowing out a lot of hot air!" He gestured mechanically with chopping arm motions as he added, "A whole. Big. Lot of it," speaking slowly and with deliberate pauses, as though he felt it added weight to his argument. Several others nodded, hooted or even slapped their hands on the table repeatedly in demonstration of their agreement. It was a typical display of skepticism for this lot, and nothing out of the ordinary.

Jerg smirked maliciously, suppressing a sudden urge to clamber over the table and smack the pompous buffoon right across the face. *Jenkins, you portly sloth*, he thought, seething. *You're a blind fool. You're all blind fools.* Not so very long ago, he'd been just as blind and ignorant as they were now, but he was still going to relish putting them in their place.

He was all too aware of the fact that they'd never really liked him. Oh, they were cooperative enough when it came to sharing information. He'd developed quite the network of contacts inside the Commission. But they thought they were better than he was. Evidently so. Though he *was* a scientist in at least the technical sense, he wasn't as well-versed as they were in their areas of real science. He had the cognitive abilities, but lacked their erudition, and they looked down on him for it. During the greater part of his life, he'd been recognized first and foremost for his work in law enforcement, not physics. That reputation had stuck. To them, he would always be the bumbling policeman, good for twirling a nightstick, eating kale doughnuts, and little else.

"Perhaps," Jerg riposted with relative calm, "you should have a glance at the readings that I brought with me before spouting off at the mouth with your blind accusations." He straightened himself then and placed his hands on the high back of a vacant seat before adding, "Seriously, Jenkins. Go right ahead. I'll wait. And while we're at it, the rest of you should see this, too. I insist. It's all over there, by my seat."

Jenkins eyed him suspiciously for a moment, then motioned for someone to hand over the documents. The lanky woman sitting in the seat next to Jerg's—Doctor Meridiani—scooped the bound stack of papers up and slid them across the table to him.

Jerg watched with great anticipation as Jenkins removed the elastic band that was holding it all together, then leafed through each page one by one.

After a minute and a half of awkward silence, Doctor Jenkins looked up at him, a perplexed expression etched upon his face. "These are cerebral activity reports for subject Zero Sixty-Seven," he said, his voice tinged with uncertainty.

"Well bravo, *Mister* Jenkins," Jerg offered up sarcastically. "Truly, what a remarkable feat. Congratulations are in order, I think. You've managed to decipher the carefully encrypted... oh, that's just the title. The one that's clearly written across the front page. Never mind." Despite efforts to the contrary, he couldn't help but grin as he watched Jenkins slink a few inches lower in his seat.

Jenkins was without the shadow of a doubt the only other scientist in the compound with a temperament that rivaled his own. His fuse was even shorter than his was, however, and it was Jerg's principal advantage in their frequent quarrels. Watching him cower in confusion like a beaten dog was extremely satisfying.

"If you study them very carefully," he added with a certain degree of pomp, "you'll notice that some of the so-called *normal* signatures repeat on a daily basis. The pattern they form is unlike that of most infections, true, but if you follow them back far enough, you'll find that they behave in very much the same way. The development of these patterns—or their emergence, if you will— was just much, much slower. These same sequences were present, if sparsely, as many as seven years ago, maybe more. Over time, they slowly increased in frequency. I'm sure you'll agree that these are similar to the symptoms that the system looks for routinely, but for some reason—possibly because of their slower overall progression—the system seems to have overlooked them here."

Jenkins studied the pages once again, then looked up and nodded despite himself. "It's true," he murmured, resentfully, "but I still don't see why any of this is important to us, aside from the fact that the subject will have to be purged from the program."

"Let me see that," Jenkins' neighbor demanded, snatching the report away before he could so much as protest. Soon, half a dozen curious scientists were huddled around it, surprise dawning on their faces as the data sunk in.

"Oh!" one of them exclaimed suddenly. The man was David Kight, the lead for the psionics division. "Oh, yes. I see it, now. Good find, Doctor Weissinger. *Excellent* find."

Jerg concealed a satisfied smile. He wondered if Doctor Kight had come to the same conclusion as he and Doctor Munro had.

"Perhaps," the enthusiastic man continued, "and I don't want to overstep my bounds here, or make any wild assumptions, but perhaps we've finally achieved what we've been working towards for so many years. After all this time, gentlemen, ladies, can you imagine? Perhaps we've finally found a test subject that has fully adapted to our psionic tampering. One that resists, maybe even ignores its own defense mechanisms."

He rose then and fanned his hands slowly as he spoke, almost as though to stifle some foreseen objections. "Granted, there are a lot of good subjects that haven't *spoiled*," he conceded, accompanying that last word with quotation mark gestures. "I'm not saying otherwise, but if you take a look at all of the rejected specimens to date, you'll notice a very strong trend there."

He grabbed at his chin then and paused for a moment. His eyes went from intense to distant and then back to intense again in the space of a few seconds. "To date, the appearance of even one symptom has almost always spelled out imminent *corruption* for its host," he added, offering them his patented finger quotes once more. "Even if the breakdown *isn't* immediate, it always ends up catching up with them sooner or later. It's always a precursor."

His eyes went through that transformation of theirs that let everyone around him know that he was drifting again, most likely looking for the best way to put his thoughts into words. Though usually sharp, they now looked glassy, like he was daydreaming. "In theory," he advanced, starting at a slow mumble and quickly working his way back to cruising speed, "since we don't know what triggers the symptoms, or sets off the defense mechanism, any of our so-called 'stable' subjects could 'become infected', or 'go bad' in the blink of an eye. If this, one of our oldest subjects, has had the symptoms for years now, and hasn't been picked up by the system as a contaminant, it could mean very good things for our research moving forward."

"Where the cerebrum is concerned," another man added idly. Half a second later, he tacked on an embarrassed, "Of course, what else would you mean? I understand what you're getting at perfectly, Doctor Kight, and I couldn't agree more." The much older scientist stopped then and mumbled something incoherent.

Jerg recognized him as Ludovic Plattz, an eighty-something-year-old with a skeletal build and scarce white hair. The man had a keen eye for details, but was notorious for drifting off into space in the middle of a conversation... and sometimes staying there. He also had a habit of going off on wild tangents that seemed completely disconnected from his original train of thought.

Rumor had it that his peculiar quirks served him well as the lead for cellular engineering research. Doctor Plattz had gone into reflexive inertia and Jerg was about to speak up when the man came back from his trance, beating him to the punch.

"If we could find out why this subject endured where others failed," Plattz picked up, "we could better select future candidates for the rehabilitation program. Better yet, we might find a way to modify our current subjects in such a way that the defense mechanism becomes a nonissue. If we could achieve that, ladies and gentlemen, we'd have much better end results."

"Spot on," Jerg said, beaming. "I'm glad that you understand the magnitude of this discovery." Not all of them were as slow as Doctor Jenkins after all. In all fairness, some of them were quite sensible, but needed hard evidence to convince them of anything. He was almost certain they'd be amenable to his way of thinking. All he needed now was the commissioner's approval. "Would you like to see for yourself, Commissioner?" he asked, hopeful.

"No," Richardson replied, sighing deeply. "I'm afraid that won't be necessary." She sounded extremely disappointed.

Jerg blinked twice in surprise. Why was the commissioner not impressed? Everyone else was, and with good reason. He'd even managed to impress himself. This unprecedented event was remarkable, to say the least.

"I'm sorry, Doctor Weissinger," Richardson said, *almost* apologetically. "While it is an impressive discovery—and one worthy of commendation—it isn't exactly *yours*. Yours *or* Doctor Munro's, for that matter. Getting straight to the point, it's already been brought to my attention."

"It has?" Jerg asked. Feeling a little flustered, he cleared his throat and added, "By whom, madam, if I may?"

"You may," Richardson answered plainly. "The situation was brought to my attention yesterday by Emril Langsarks, our newly-appointed emissary from the Ministry of Inner Workings. Mister Langsarks will be working very closely with us over the next few weeks. As per his recommendations, *and* pursuant to council regulations, the subject is to be terminated as soon as our schedule permits. In fact, plans to dispose of this potential source of infection have already been made, and will be set in motion soon. As per usual, protocol will be followed to avoid disrupting the platform's homeostasis."

None of the other scientists raised their voices to protest. Not even one. Their recent surge of enthusiasm turned just as quickly to embarrassment, and those that were still standing wasted little time regaining their seats. Seething, Jerg clenched his fists and shook in a visible effort to keep his anger under control. *Useless, spineless fools,* he thought. *They're nothing but mindless sheep, blindly following their shepherd without so much as questioning her judgment or challenging her decisions. Fools and cowards.*

It racked his brain why a MIW agent was poking his nose around in their business, too. The intrusion infuriated him to no end. He couldn't *stand* interlopers. Unwarranted interference in his work was right next to murder on his list of unpardonable offenses. For anyone with a masochistic bent, it was a surefire way to make top tier on his shit list.

Having worked for the police for the greater part of his career—endeavor which saw him make his way through the ranks from Investigator to Head of Tactical Operations, and culminating as Head of Criminal Psychology—he understood that most of his colleagues saw him as an outsider, which was exactly what he considered Langsarks to be. The main difference between the two of them was that *he* actually belonged there. Despite his lack of higher credentials, *he* was a man of science. Langsarks, on the other hand, was not. Langsarks was nothing more than a money man. All MIW agents were. All MIW agents *had* to be in order to fulfill their ministry's mandate. They were money men and silver-tongued vipers, right down to the very last.

The Ministry of Inner Workings was a central agency. It functioned as a liaison between the other government agencies and departments. Whether anyone liked to admit it or not, they held the reins of power. In short, they provided the departments with direction in order to optimize their efficiency.

They also held the purse strings. They gave funds and they took funds away, seemingly at their leisure. Ultimately, they had the power to realign departmental priorities. Since they reported directly to Innerstadt's president, Mister Sigur Van der Veen, no one could deny their authority. An order from MIW was like an order from the president himself.

While most agreed that a central arbitrator would discourage the departments from vying for resources, and that standardized policies would keep them from setting off in their own directions, very few people enjoyed having their work tampered with on such a personal level. Fewer still were those brave enough to voice their disapproval when such incidents occurred. Jerg was one of those rare skeptics that believed that the ministry was superfluous and a drain on public funds. If the president wanted things to be done a certain way, he firmly believed that it was his responsibility to communicate directly with the departmental heads themselves, instead of employing an entire agency of accountants and shifty sweet-talkers to do the work for him.

Yes, it would involve President Van der Veen getting his pretty little hands dirty, but what other, more important things did he have to do besides run government? Play golf with leaders of industry? Shake hands with celebrities and smile for the cameras? Due to their complete lack of expertise, the Ministry's objectives were often ludicrous in their scope and nearly impossible to achieve. The president would better understand this if he dealt directly with the experts themselves, instead of relying on the opinions of profit-driven suits. What a MIW *penny-pincher* could bring to the Commission of Higher Sciences was well beyond him.

"But madam," he pleaded. "Think of the possibilities!"

"*But* nothing, Weissinger!" Richardson barked, cutting him off abruptly. "My decision has already been made." She sighed softly then and straightened her tie, visibly attempting to calm herself. "I understand that you're disappointed with this turn of events, Doctor, but really we have no other alternative. Yesterday morning, I might have been as excited about this as you are now, probably even more so. But events that you aren't aware of have put everything in an entirely new perspective for me."

All eyes turned to the main doors as the guards stepped aside to admit a tall man in a jet-black suit. The sleek briefcase that was cradled under his right arm matched his black-within-black eyes perfectly. The lithe but imposing man strode to the nearest vacant seat, set his briefcase down on the table and sat.

"Please forgive me for my lack of punctuality," he entreated in a clear but reverberant voice. "Some complications arose in the testing platform and they required my immediate attention." The barely visible wires just below the skin on both sides of his head suggested heavily of cybernetic augmentation.

"There's no need to apologize, Mister Langsarks," Richardson replied. "You haven't missed anything important. Welcome. We were just talking about you, actually."

Jerg scowled. Why would Richardson allow that *thing* direct access to the testing platform? Even he had to jump through hoops just to get in there, and he was chief of bloody security. Admitting untrained personnel to the platform was plain stupid.

The risk of it being disturbed by a foreign presence was far too great. And they were worried about homeostasis? *Pshaw.* Their success hinged on maintaining a certain illusion of stability, and they were already hard-pressed to keep a reasonable balance.

"Is that so?" Langsarks stated more than asked, the tone of his electronically-modified voice inanimate and uninspired. "Only good things, I hope."

"Why yes, of course!" Richardson exclaimed. "I was just telling the staff about your most recent discovery." Her oily smile nearly split her face in two. "Doctors Weissinger and Munro have come to similar conclusions to your own, though they obviously lack some of the details that you were able to uncover. Would you be so kind as to explain the situation to Doctor Weissinger and the others? I think it primordial that they understand exactly why we *must* eliminate subject Sixty-Seven at all costs."

Jerg was fuming. *That fool,* he thought. *Insinuating that that "Machine Man" was smarter than he was? What gall!* He felt the heat rise in his face so abruptly that he could easily imagine tendrils of smoke seeping out through his ears. This "half man" had better have a very good explanation for him.

Langsarks stared at Richardson for a long moment before voicing a bland, "Of course." He held the commissioner's gaze a moment longer before turning his head away to address Jerg directly, effectively singling him out. "While I was accessing the platform's security grid—"

"How *dare* you do such a thing?" Jerg snapped, jumping from his chair to point an accusatory finger in his direction. "Your incompetence is going to endanger the entire program!"

"Order!" Richardson barked. "That kind of outburst will not be tolerated, Doctor Weissinger! I will not warn you again!"

Jerg sighed in exasperation and sunk into his chair, trying desperately to pinpoint exactly where everything had gone wrong. He was usually able to pull the other scientists' strings like they were puppets, and the commissioner had more often than not been a complete pushover. What had gone wrong was that *thing* sitting across the table from him... that *intruder!*

"Mister Weissinger," Langsarks put forth firmly, "it's by my good grace and my good grace alone that you're even afforded an explanation at all. My reasons for entering the platform are a question of national security, and since your clearance is insufficient, it's really no concern of yours. If you insist on questioning my motives, I'll have no choice but to report this to the proper authorities as a serious breach of conduct *and* security. Understood?"

Visibly satisfied that Jerg's protests were over and done with, at least for the time being, he went on. "Good. While accessing the platform directly could present certain risks, ones I'm confident you're all aware of, it enables one with the proper training to accumulate data in a much clearer form. The end-user reports that the system generates for you are obscure, at best. Though this lack of precision in the reporting system is understandable, when we take into consideration all of the heavy encoding involved, it also cripples your ability to detect certain infectious elements in a timely and efficient manner."

He paused then, and with the complete lack of emotion on his face, one could only wonder if it was meant to dramatize what he was about to say. "Infectious elements such as the one that I took note of during my last sweep of the platform. The subject in question has been making unwarranted and inappropriate use of the program's integrated databases. In the last week alone, incursions have multiplied considerably, escalating from one isolated incident to a series of frequent, almost routine checks. One of the databases in particular was accessed six times yesterday alone, but never for more than ten minutes at a time. Does this sound even remotely like normal behavior to you, gentlemen? Does this sound like a risk that can be ignored? The answer is *no,* and if we don't do something about it now, this sort of thing will continue to happen and it *will* spiral out of control. If that doesn't sound like a threat to you, then I don't know what would."

He paused momentarily to examine the faces of those gathered around the table, then added, "I have considered all of this very carefully, and measures have been taken to rectify the situation. Subject Sixty-Seven has been scheduled for termination, along with several others from the newer cohorts. These subjects have been identified as unfit for long-term rehabilitation. You may not like it, you may not agree with it, but my decision is final, and it's already too late. The wheels are already in motion."

He paused again to gaze at his auditors. There was something very much like condescendence in his look. "Ladies, gentlemen," he finally added, then turned to address the commissioner directly. "We should consider ourselves extremely lucky that more damage wasn't done." He glanced down at his phone then and frowned deeply. "If I may, Commissioner Richardson, my attention is required elsewhere immediately."

The commissioner nodded emphatically in response. "Yes, of course," she said. "Thank you, Mister Langsarks." She watched as Langsarks rose from his seat and strode briskly from the room. "Meeting adjourned," she called out once the door had closed behind him, then added, "I'd like to speak with you in private, Doctor Weissinger. Right now." She rose swiftly and walked over to the door to her office, then glanced at the dissipating crowd a moment longer before pushing through.

A few of the retiring scientists gave Jerg odd looks before they disappeared behind the sliding doors that led back to the main complex. Sighing reflexively, he knocked on the table with the knuckles of both hands in tandem, slowly and repeatedly.

Was he going to receive a sermon over his little outburst, he wondered. He had every reason to be angry. He had every *right* to be angry. That bucket of MIW bolts had no *real* proof that subject Sixty-Seven was a danger to the rehabilitation program. It was a possibility, true, but still. Who did he take himself for, threatening him like that? This was too big of an opportunity for him to just throw it away the way that he had. A little resistance should have been expected, even encouraged. With that in mind, he gave the back of his bald head a good rub, pulled away from the table, and followed after Richardson.

After entering the office, he closed the door behind him and took a quick look around. It wasn't nearly as imposing as some of the other executive suites he'd had the displeasure of visiting over the years. Many of the executive cadre had the unbecoming habit of flaunting their wealth and status.

Many years ago, back when he was an officer of the law, he'd get sick to his stomach every time he had to report to the director of ATSOF's office. The place had been so gaudy it had looked more like a throne room than it had a functional working area.

To the average Joe, the commissioner's office would probably seem like a downsized palace, but for anyone who knew the ropes around government, or had spent any amount of time working in it, it didn't take long to dispel the illusion. The commissioner did not share the upper echelon's taste for wanton luxury and frivolous overspending. That much was clear.

The dimly-lit room was actually rather small, though it would have been quite comfortable if not for the tight squeeze around the woman's desk. It made the area behind it look like some sort of back store, where no one but the she was meant to go. Whether this effect had been intentional on her part or not remained a mystery, but he happened to agree that being back there was no one's business but her own.

Imitation mahogany bookcases lined every single wall. They were stacked to the ceiling with dusty tomes, and topped with ancient-looking medical and scientific paraphernalia, trinkets of civilizations long expired. Richardson's apparent infatuation with the old and antiquated never ceased to amaze him. How could a woman of her standing bother herself with relics of the past when there was the present and the future to worry about? Didn't they have enough problems to deal with already without wasting time longing for bygone days?

The desk that Richardson was sitting behind as she puffed on her sickeningly sweet-smelling clove cigarette looked like it might have been carved from real wood. It *looked* authentic enough, but it was most likely a synthetic reproduction. Even if there were any real wood supplies left—anywhere besides the presidential park, that was—taking a blade to the stuff was illegal, and carried a very hefty fine. Considering the severity of the penalty involved, not many would give themselves the trouble of actually making it into something. Just selling it would be a painstaking endeavor. *Could be an antique*, he mused. That would be less complicated.

"Have a seat, Jerg," Richardson more than just suggested, vaguely motioning to one of the tall chairs opposite her.

After a curt nod, Jerg pulled the chair back and sat. He wasn't as furious as he'd been a moment earlier, but he certainly wasn't pleased, either, and he didn't have all day to just sit there waiting. Apologizing now might save him some time. He had to get back to work. He had to let Doctor Munro know that his efforts had failed. Edward would *not* be pleased, but there wasn't really much he could do about that. Success just wasn't a possible outcome. "I am so deeply sorry for my outburst," he said, feigning remorse. "I will try my very best not to let it happen—"

"It's already forgotten, Jerg," Richardson stated, cutting him off abruptly. "That's not why I called you in here."

Jerg blinked. Well at least he wasn't going to be scolded for his behavior. "What is it th—"

"Would you let me *speak* without interrupting me just this once?" Richardson snapped, causing Jerg's eyes to go even wider with surprise. *Someone* was feeling edgy today. Scarlet tinged the commissioner's cheeks and forehead and her lip was pulled back into an austere-looking frown.

"Now," Richardson added, "I'm going to pick up where I left off, and you aren't going to say a damned thing until I'm finished. Is that clear?" She waited for Jerg's reluctant nod before continuing. "Good. I'm in no mood to argue."

She straightened her tie and took a deep breath. "When you first arrived here all those years ago, I saw in you a competent, young man with a good mind and the will to push it as far as he needed to in order to get the job done. Though you didn't have a naturally scientific bent like most of the others here, your brand of intelligence proved to be a great asset to the Commission. Over the years, it became apparent that your temperament impaired your ability to work well in a team environment, but still, your logic and understanding of the human mind allowed you to thrive, and you became more and more invaluable to us and our operations. In more recent years, your work on the containment modules proved to be most helpful. Your diligent work as chief of security has helped to ensure that they remain in good working condition, and that everyone here remains safe."

She brought her palm flat down on the table then and gave Jerg a long, hard look. "I'm not telling you this to flatter you, Jerg. I'm saying it because I want you to know that despite what you're about to hear, your work here has been appreciated." She swiveled halfway around in her chair then, ignoring the wild look of bewilderment in Jerg's eyes. "And while your work here *has* been appreciated, I'm appointing Emril Langsarks as the new acting chief of security, at least for the time being. You'll be joining Doctor Kight and his team, and assisting them with their very important work on psionics."

"But... but I... I..." Jerg sputtered, flabbergasted. Suddenly downtrodden, he gazed at the floor blankly and slowly shook his head from side to side. This couldn't really be happening to him, could it? He'd been chief of security for years—for many *long* years—and never once had so much as a minor incident escaped his attention. He'd been ever vigilant in his role.

Despite his pristine record and unwavering loyalty, now the commissioner was transferring him to the psionics division, and replacing him with that uppity misfit, Langsarks—an *aug*, of all unlikely things? Was this her way of rewarding him for all of his

efforts, for all of his years of dedication and hard work? Was it
really? It wasn't exactly a move down in the world, but he enjoyed
his job, and he did it well. He was so shocked by the prospect of it
that he couldn't even bring himself to anger. In his astonishment,
the only thing he could manage was silence.

"If none of this sounds fair to you, that's because it's not,"
Richardson droned out remotely. "If there was another way to do
this, I would, but my hands are tied. Believe me. You have until
tomorrow morning to clear out your office. Dismissed." She lit
another cigarette then and took a long, drawn out drag on it before
sinking back into her chair, as though oblivious to Jerg's presence.

Jerg glowered as something dark and spiteful triggered inside
of him. The commissioner's indifference to his plight struck a nerve,
and filled his mind with very twisted, very unprofessional thoughts.
The nonchalance with which she'd just brushed him aside was
something that he would never forget.

Even if the order to have him transferred had come from
above—which is what he imagined the commissioner had meant
when she'd said that her hands were tied—she should have provided
him with earlier warning. She *should* have spoken up for him, and
gotten the point across that he was essential to the Commission's
security operations.

It enraged him, but there was no point in arguing about it.
Instead, he rose swiftly and straightened his lab coat. Sparing the
commissioner one final, defiant look, he smiled coldly, then turned
on his heels and strode from the office. He marched straight
through the conference room and past the guards at the entrance.
The sound of his shoes clapping on the cold, concrete floor soon
echoed through the halls as he stalked down them, weaving through
the brightly-lit maze of subterranean corridors. He ignored the
curious glances from his meandering colleagues and walked past
them without even acknowledging them. *Nosy rats*, he thought.
He didn't bother responding to the white-clad sentinels that saluted
him crisply as he strode past them, either.

Jerg respected the uniformed men under his command, but he was in no mood for decorum. *Blast it*! Soon, they wouldn't even *be* under his command. The thought that they'd be following Langsarks' orders was unsettling, at best. It made him feel queasy. He doubted that any of them knew it yet, or that they'd take it very well when they found out. Most of them had developed a very profound sense of devotion toward him over the years, and many of the younger recruits idolized him for his past exploits.

Sometimes he wondered why he'd even left the force. He'd been one of the top dogs in his day, and many of the tactics taught at the academy today were of his very own device. It wasn't like there was room for advancement in the Commission, either, and he wielded a lot less authority than he had in the past. Yes, he remembered his less subservient days in the Anti-Terrorism Special Operations Force fondly. But even back then, alas, he'd served the Commission in one capacity or the other.

The respect that his subordinates had for him was what little consolation kept him going through those mentally taxing years. They remembered. Oh, yes. They remembered well. It more than pleased him to hear younger men speaking of his achievements over lunch in the cafeteria. At times, they went on and on as though the work of his earlier days was the stuff of legends.

"Hah!" Jerg laughed dryly at the thought. It made him feel so ancient. With any luck, the men would give Langsarks a hard time just to spite him. It was one thing to be given a title or rank, but quite another to command the respect that a leader needed to make a unit run like a well-oiled machine. *Just look at me,* he thought sourly. *My entire life has been about following rules and regulations, about respecting established hierarchy, but here I am hoping that his men will disobey his direct orders.*

This wasn't like him at all, but he considered the change in programming justifiable. There was something terribly wrong with Emril Langsarks. The man was an interloper, to be sure, but that wasn't all. He plain and simply didn't belong. For that matter, there was something awfully wrong with Commissioner Richardson as well. Her recent behavior was deplorable. He took a deep breath then and found himself much calmer. *Good*, he thought. Edward's office was just around the corner, and he had no reason to take his frustrations out on him.

CHAPTER
7

Misfired Synapses

Edward fidgeted with the dials on the side of his microscope, trying to adjust the instrument's focus, but with little success. "It's no use," he sighed, straightening himself. He moaned dejectedly as he stretched the aching muscles in his back. His spine was excruciatingly stiff. He'd been looming over the examination table all day, analyzing tissue samples, and hadn't had the good sense to sit down and relax for even five minutes.

After the day he'd just had, he was more than happy to drop into his chair to review the pile of reports lying on his desk. The results from the tests he'd conducted earlier in the day had come back negative of abnormalities, further supporting his theory concerning subject Sixty-Seven. The tissue samples were normal in every way. There wasn't a doubt about it.

Though his theory remained inconclusive, he wasn't frustrated by his lack of substantiating evidence. What pieces of the puzzle he *had* assembled provided a better picture for those who couldn't understand the purpose of his endeavor, and still supported that his theory was correct. He would find the answers to *all* of his questions, in time.

Research such as this required a lot of time and effort. He was always ready to put as much effort into his projects as needed, but time was one resource that he did not have in endless supply. He was getting older, and it was becoming more and more apparent with every passing day.

There were still a few good years left in him—at least he thought there were—but he wasn't entirely sure that they'd be enough. He'd worked for the Commission almost his entire adult life, and though they'd made significant progress in the field, they were far from perfecting the art of cerebro-engineering.

Truth be told, he wasn't as worried about perfecting it so much as he was about protecting his own work and bringing it to fruition. Unlike many of his peers, who were in this for personal gain and recognition, he'd grown quite fond of every aspect of his work. Not only of the job itself, but of the test subjects that made all of it possible.

While the Commission treated them like nothing more than disposable guinea pigs, Edward knew those that he worked with, and cared for all of them. He saw them for what they truly were: human beings. And they *were* human. There was no denying that, no matter how inert they might be. True, they were easily spoiled, rendered useless to the program, and whenever that happened, they posed a serious risk to its overall progression, but there was no good reason they couldn't be transported to other testing areas once they'd reached the critical stages of contamination. It didn't need to be the end of the line for them. He could easily think of dozens of other applications for them.

There was absolutely no need for the Commission to have them butchered once they deemed them useless. He sincerely hoped that Jerg's meeting with the commissioner had gone well. He needed more time. He needed *much* more time. He simply couldn't afford to lose Sixty-Seven. He was his very first test subject, and without question, the principal beneficiary of the majority of his time and effort. Without exaggeration, he'd nearly created him from scratch. In an odd way, he felt like Sixty-Seven was his child, his baby, and if he wasn't careful about it—which was usually the case—that was plain for anyone to see. It was no mystery why he got so touchy when it came to his work. He'd been gibed about it on more than one occasion.

Three loud knocks at his already-open door followed by a brief silence heralded Jerg's arrival. The man stepped onto the threshold and cleared his throat extensively before entering his quarters. From the sour expression on his face, Edward gathered that he came bearing ill tidings. There was a somber resignation in the way that Jerg held himself, and that made his heart sink a little. He'd try not to jump to any conclusions, but it was hard not to be melodramatic at a time like this. So much was at stake.

"Hello, Edward," Jerg mumbled weakly, his voice faltering. "Are you busy right now?"

"No, I'm not busy," Edward sighed. "Come in and have a seat." Jerg stepped forward and sat in the chair opposite him. Maybe his news wasn't going to be as bad as he thought it was. All he could do was hope.

"Been hard at work, I see," Jerg muttered pointedly, nodding at the pile of reports sitting on Edward's desk. "Trying to find anatomical differences between your specimen and the rest?" He scratched his head and looked at his feet for a second, clearly unsure of what to say next. "So," he added, "have you had any luck with that?"

"No," Edward replied, shaking his head slowly. "No luck at all. They're anatomically different, yes, but only as much as they should be. It will take much deeper studies to get to the bottom of this. I've only just begun to scratch at the surface here." It didn't seem like Jerg was picking up on his subtle cues. *Well*, he wondered, *will I or will I not be allowed to continue with my research?* He was starting to get annoyed. "Jerg," he sighed loudly. "Do you have *any* news for me? Concerning what we discussed the last time you were here. How did it go with the committee?"

"Oh, yes," Jerg blurted out. "My apologies, Doctor. I was just about to get to that." He drew a deep breath then and wiped some of the sweat from his glossy forehead before continuing. "I did my absolute best to defend your position, Edward. Really, I did. But unfortunately, it seems like they already knew about your discovery, and there's—"

"What?" Edward snapped, cutting him off abruptly. "How in Phlogiston's defunct theory could they have known? How could they have already known about it, Jerg?" He shook his head in disbelief then, and added, "I'm sorry. Please... please go on."

Jerg continued as though Edward had never interrupted him. He gave him a brief summary of the meeting as he remembered it, putting much of his focus on Langsarks and his responsibility in the affair. "And so you see," he concluded, seething, "he has convinced the commissioner that your work must be expunged. There's no changing his mind about it. I know. I tried."

Edward groaned miserably. The news couldn't have been more horrible. He felt like he was going to throw up. *I have to remain calm*, he reminded himself. *Panicking will get me nowhere. There has to be some way around this.* He was a very resourceful man. He wasn't going to give up, not even if the commissioner herself told him to.

"I'm sorry, Edward," Jerg mumbled. "I know how you must feel—really, I do—but we have no choice in this."

"No," Edward retorted firmly. "That's where you're wrong. I *do* have a choice. I'm not going to just sit here and continue on as if nothing at all has changed while those... those *monsters* butcher my work. They won't get away with this, Jerg. I won't let them get away with it. I won't."

"Don't do anything stupid, Edward," Jerg warned him. "I understand that you're upset, but being rash won't help. And you aren't the only one with problems." He sighed deeply before forcing out, "I'm no longer Chief of Security. I've been stripped of my rank and my post has been handed over to Langsarks."

Hearing about Jerg's predicament silenced Edward, if only for a moment. "I'm terribly sorry to hear that, friend," he said, so quietly that it was almost a whisper. He couldn't even begin to imagine how the other man felt. What he feared might happen to himself had already started happening to Jerg.

He had to act quickly, or it would be too late for him, too. The notion that popped into his head just then made him shiver. Thoughts like this one were dangerous even in their conception, but it might just work. It would be risky, to be sure, but he saw no other alternative. He was going to leave the Commission high and dry, and he was going to bring his work with him. It was crazy, he knew, and it was criminal, to boot. No one had ever managed to steal anything of significance from the Commission. Not since its inception, over a hundred years ago. Or so they said. But he'd manage it, somehow. He had to.

Jerg wouldn't be a problem, because he was going to come with him. If he had to brainwash him, or smash a bottle over his head and drag his unconscious husk all the way to the surface, he *would* come with him. Doctor Weissinger wouldn't agree with him from the get-go. He'd probably even be pretty categorical in his refusal, but he would manage to change his mind. He'd always been able to, though never for anything quite so important. But a little flattery went a long way with Jerg Weissinger, and the pickle he found himself in with the loss of his position made his eventual success even more likely.

CHAPTER
8

The Tip

The silver name plaque on his desk read "Captain Leonard Boston", but at present, Leonard looked nothing like an officer of the law. His collar was untied and his hair was disheveled. His lip was hooked back in a nasty-looking snarl, and a deep-seated hatred burned fiercely in his eyes.

He was sifting through some rather graphic photos that had been taken at a recent crime scene. The Awoken, that malevolent group of terrorists and self-proclaimed messiahs, had struck again. This time, they'd strolled into an inner-city mall in broad daylight, sealed the area off, and started preaching their usual bullshit about the world not being real. And after they'd finished delivering their delusional sermon, they'd started firing at anyone and everyone they could find on the premises.

Most of the rotten bastards had managed to get away before the police had shown up, and those that were left behind had taken their own lives to avoid getting captured, the piece-of-shit fucking cowards. Among the thirty-one confirmed dead were three-year-old Samantha Wilssen and her parents, Bobby and Veronica. Theirs was the photo that he was looking at now.

Even after everything he'd seen in his long career, sometimes it was hard to believe how gruesome a wound a conventional firearm could cause. Try as he might, he just couldn't understand how anyone could do something so horrible, and to a little girl, of all people. It was sickening.

If he wasn't seeing so red, he might feel depressed. Why did this crap have to be at the top of his stack today? Why? "Damn it!" he bellowed, banging his fist down hard on his desk. "If I ever come across one of those founder-fucked, psycho retards, I swear I'm gonna... I'm gonna..." he trailed off then, squeezing his fists in anger. He was madder than a wet hen, and he knew it.

He took a deep breath and closed his eyes in an effort to calm himself. His heart was pounding. The doctor had warned him about his high cholesterol and blood pressure. If he didn't cool it, he was going to blow a gasket one of these days. He exhaled, took another deep breath, and opened his eyes a few seconds later.

He was about to reach for the next photograph when his phone rang. He muttered angrily as he answered it. "Boston," he spat out dejectedly. "What is it?" Luckily, social skills weren't prerequisites in the Law Enforcement Agency, because they were far from being his forte. He listened to a few seconds of silence before speaking up, annoyed. "Listen, punk, I don't know who you are, but I don't have all day, and if—"

"Captain Boston," a static-garbled voice on the other end of the line said, cutting him off. The sound of it was so heavily modulated that it was difficult to understand what he was saying. Whoever it was, they were obviously using one of those electronic, voice-altering doodads.

"Who the fuck is this?" Leonard barked.

"It doesn't matter who I am, Captain," the caller replied calmly. "What does matter is the package waiting for you under all that clutter on your desk."

"What are you talking about?" Leonard spat, glancing at the window reflexively. He was all alone and the blinds were shut.

"What is this?" he demanded, pushing the mess of photos and documents around his desk. Before long, he found a thick, legal-sized, padded envelope that was wrapped in shipping paper. He picked the package up and turned it over in his hands. It was surprisingly heavy for something its size. "What is this?" he asked again, raising his voice in frustration. "Answer me."

"Proof, Boston," the electronically-modified voice replied. "Proof that your men aren't as loyal as you might think they are." With that, the anonymous caller hung up, leaving the captain no further explanation.

Leonard realized how stupid he must look, just sitting there, staring blankly, but he couldn't help it. He couldn't help but wonder who the wiseass had been. He hung the phone up with a sigh, set the package down on his desk, and stared at it for a few seconds. What he really wondered was how the guy had managed to get the package past security without anyone knowing about it.

Maybe it was someone on the inside. Who else would want to rat out a dirty cop besides a good cop or another dirty cop that had it in for him? He'd want to be anonymous too, if he were in that position. Sometimes, he wished he could be anonymous himself, and he didn't even have anyone to rat out. It wasn't always easy being the boss.

Wasting no more time, he ripped through the thin brown paper that the package was wrapped in and opened it. Inside, there were photos, legal documents, video disks, and more. Just from the sheer bulk of the material, it looked like it would take him hours to pore over everything. He grabbed a video surveillance disk from the top of the pile at random, and popped it into the viewer in the corner of his office.

The viewer's screen remained black for a few seconds until the picture finally came into focus. The high quality of the disk made it easy to tell that it had been taken from a security camera at Chez Joignon, a ritzy French restaurant just off the Red Light district. He wasn't really into any of that posh bullshit, but he'd had to go there a few times recently on business. He'd also been something of a regular despite himself, back in the day. It was the kind of place that Commissioner Chucklehead frequented regularly.

The camera was zoomed in on a cluster of four tables. Most of the patrons that night were just well-dressed nobodies, but he recognized the occupants of the fourth table immediately. The man on the left was John Grimm alias Havoc. Opposite him was Jimeno Giuterrez. They were more than just nefarious miscreants. They were two of the top leaders of the Awoken.

There was another person at their table, but he had his back to the camera. Leonard watched intently for nearly ten minutes, but the third person hadn't turned around even once in all that time. It was really starting to get on his last nerve. The penalty for aiding and abetting known terrorists was no laughing matter. Not unless you were a macabre motherfucker with a death wish. Whoever this guy was, he was in some serious trouble. Especially if he was a police officer. "Come on," he snapped, losing his patience. "Show your face, you greasy slimeball. Turn, already!"

Almost as if on cue, a clumsy waitress tripped on the rug as she entered the scene. The tray she was carrying tipped over, and some of the drinks on it fell over and spilled down the third man's back. After crisping his shoulders, the man got up, turned around, and raised his fist like he was going to punch her.

Leonard's jaw dropped. He couldn't believe his eyes. This had to be some kind of mistake. It had to be a joke. "Franky," he whispered in disbelief, his voice trembling. He pressed the pause button and zoomed in until the image was twice its original size. That was Frank's mug, alright, but he still couldn't believe it.

For some reason, Frank's absence had gotten him thinking about the nature of their love-hate relationship, and like it or not, he was pretty sure he'd pinned the tail on the proverbial donkey of the thing. Their heated discussions, his mixed feelings about the kid—he'd had a pivotal realization about all of that. And it was one that he would never share with anyone—*ever*—especially not with Frank. Especially not now. He'd never had children of his own. His wife had died too young for that. But if he had—if he'd had a son—he imagined he might have been a lot like Frank.

Somehow, buried somewhere deep beneath his crude, tough guy exterior, he had a soft spot for the kid. If he was honest with himself, he'd even go so far as to say that he thought of him as his own son, in a way, and that he acted accordingly. That was why he treated him the way that he did. That was why he'd turned down his request for transfer to Special Assignments. With almost everyone else, he was just another grumpy asshole, but he treated Frank like he would a delinquent teenager.

Frank Fasaro was a pretty decent cop and a genuinely good kid. Of *that* he was certain. This had to be some kind of setup. It had to be. The evidence must have been doctored. Someone could easily have edited him into the video. Why anyone would want to mess with Frank that way was beyond him, but he wasn't about to just accept or reject it without a serious investigation.

There was one easy way to find out if this disk was authentic. He'd have to track down eye witnesses. For starters, he'd find that ditsy waitress and run the surveillance disk by her. She'd have to remember a man that had nearly knocked her lights out. Of course, Frank was still frozen on-screen with his fist in the air, so he didn't know if he'd punched her or not.

He didn't really feel like finding out, but he'd resume playback anyway. He'd go looking for this broad after he'd finished looking at the rest of the evidence. For all he knew, the whole pile was fake, but he'd check it out if it took him all night. He didn't have much of a choice. It was his job.

CHAPTER
9

Sneaky Friggin' Bastards

Leonard would have gotten out of his run-down hovercar and hollered, if he thought it would help move traffic along any faster. He almost had a mind to anyway, just to vent his frustration, but it would require way more effort than he felt like putting into it. Instead, he decided to stick his head out the window and scream, "Honk! Honk!" at the top of his lungs. He retracted his head back inside the vehicle, furrowed his brow and decided to follow up with the real deal.

He started off by pummeling his horn over and over again in a rapid succession of brief, but biting toots, then concluded his *symphony of exasperation* with a long, drawn-out trumpet blare of a honk. Having vented at least a little of his pent-up anger, he tugged at his shirt collar and sank back into his seat.

He coughed raucously, cleared his throat and took a last drag on his raunchy cigar before flicking the smoking stub out the open window. Smoking usually relaxed him, but he'd run out of his usual Schreiber Lights an hour ago, and all he'd managed to find in his glove compartment was that old, piece-of-shit stogie that left a bad taste in his mouth. It did nothing for his patience, which was already starting to wear thin. The oily taste of resin clinging to the inside of his mouth made him feel noxious, and his throat burned so much that it felt like a hole was being bored through it with a hot poker. As if that wasn't already bad enough, the chill night air was making it hard to breathe.

He rolled his window up as a fit of hoarse, dry gagging racked his chest. His face was starting to turn red when he was finally saved by the liberating sensation of a phlegmy cough. He opened a crack in the window just wide enough to hock a loogie through it without splattering it all over the inside of his car, then sank back into his seat and sighed. If his job didn't kill him, cheap stogies would. He was more than aware that his health was going south, and fast, but he didn't really care. Everyone had to die of something, and he wasn't ready or willing to make any major concessions just for a *shot* at an extension to his miserable life. Admittedly, the wheezing was getting old, but the fact remained that he loved smoking more than he hated it.

He bashed the steering wheel with his fist and used it to brace himself against the violent heaving of his chest. Just to sprinkle a little salt on his open wound, he was feeling queasy, too, and the spicy khesh he'd had for supper had nothing to do with it. The evidence he'd finished examining a couple hours ago had left him feeling morose and sick to his stomach.

Though corruption in law enforcement was common enough to be considered an unfortunate fact of life, the agency had never been infiltrated by so many dirty agents at once. He wished he could pin the blame on poor administration, but the cold, hard truth was that anyone and their mother could be a criminal in disguise. There was no way to keep them all out. All they could do was get rid of the ones they knew about.

The photos and surveillance disks he'd received linked five other officers to the Awoken. For a number of reasons, it made perfectly good sense that most of them were recruits. As crappy as the situation was, it usually didn't take all that long to root out a bad cop. The greener they were, the quicker it was to get rid of them. The ones they *really* had to worry about were the sly old dogs that had managed to stay concealed for years through diligently applied prudence. Just the thought of it put him in a sour mood.

Part of him was resigned and believed that the accusations were probably true. That was the cool and calculating side of him that had developed over his long years of service as a captain. That facet of his mind accepted that Frank Fasaro and those new recruits were just cold-blooded terrorists, like the rest of the Awoken and their murderous brood. It was this harder aspect of his personality that had kept him going through thick and thin, and helped him endure the horrible reality of the nightmare they called life. That side had seen it all at least twice, and nothing really surprised it anymore.

There was another part of him, however—a smaller, *better* part of him—that didn't want to believe that the men under his command were capable of such atrocities. It was that lingering trace of trust and idealism, hidden somewhere beneath his rough exterior, that kept him from acting on anonymous accusations without first gathering sufficient evidence to make a rational decision. That and his unquestionable professionalism, of course.

None of the so-called proof he'd seen so far was enough to tip the scales. Maybe his cynical, realistic side would be wrong. Maybe this was all just the work of some vengeful scumbag that had a bone to pick with the LEA. Then again, maybe Frank W. Fasaro was nothing more than a two-faced rat, just waiting for the perfect opportunity to blow them all to smithereens. He didn't believe it for a second, but anything was possible.

Hopefully, this little trip to Chez Joignon would provide him with at least one piece of the puzzle. An eyewitness would be crucial in an investigation like this one. If he could find that waitress from the surveillance footage, he'd be able to confirm whether or not Frank was guilty. He really hoped that his better side was right.

He'd dispatched teams to investigate all of the suspects over an hour ago, but hadn't heard back from them yet. If the *evidence* he'd looked at earlier was authentic, then something would have to be done, and soon. The Awoken were a mob of bloodthirsty murderers and one of the most ruthless terrorist organizations the city had ever contended with. Even just a handful of these crazies could wreak absolute havoc, especially if they had access to state-of-the-art hardware and key outposts used by the city's one and only line of defense.

He sighed heavily and set his hands down on the steering wheel, gazing blankly out the window at the passersby. At this time of the evening, the streets were jam-packed with people. Hundreds and thousands of them went about their lives—their real lives: the ones that started after they got off work and hit the town. They milled through the streets like maggots on the bloated and rotting carcass of the city they called home.

They trudged along with the traffic and on the sidewalks on their way to shopping centers, theaters, restaurants and their homes, oblivious to any imminent danger they might be facing. If the dirty cop allegations were true and weren't dealt with quickly, then not only would the lives of his men be threatened, but so too would those of thousands of innocent others.

Disgust twisted his mouth into a nasty-looking snarl as he spotted a group of wild-haired teenagers loitering around outside of a tattoo parlor. As far as he was concerned, some of Innerstadt's citizens weren't worth saving, but it was still his job to protect them. Those misled, juvenile delinquents, with their spiked collars, flashy chains, and greasy, unkempt hair... what did they think they were accomplishing? It wasn't their "look" that bothered him so much as their arrogance and their flagrant disrespect for the law. That's what that whole rebel hoodlum getup of theirs was really about: utter and complete lawlessness. He couldn't help but wonder what the world would be like if ignorant little simptards like these ones really got what they wanted. No laws, no rules, just anarchy and chaos. If that was where the world was headed, he was pretty sure he didn't want to be a part of it anymore.

Maybe it was just his imagination, but he could have sworn that their numbers were swelling with every passing year. One day, they'd grow to be a majority. It was a frightening but realistic prospect. Imagining the changes that they'd make to the legislative system—if there was even one left by the time that came—made him all the more squeamish. For all any of them knew, the next generation would abolish the sets of laws that everyone had come to accept, if not always embrace. What could they bring to the table? Legalized drugs for all? *Hip* dress codes? Honest guys like him would probably be the first ones to lose their jobs. *Wouldn't be all that big of a deal, though*, he assured himself, smirking. He could always dye what was left of his hair blue and get a job at Sal's Scrote Piercing Emporium.

"Finally," he snorted as traffic started to move along again. A cacophony of tooting horns sounded as he tried and failed to start his hovercar's stalled engines. "Alright, alright!" he barked, flashing a middle finger at the angry drivers behind him. "Keep your pants on, assholes!" The engines wheezed, stuttered and finally started to rumble again on the fifth try. He had to get his mind back on the task at hand. The restaurant was only a few blocks away. He crept along with the heavy traffic for a few more minutes before finally pulling up to the place.

A slick-haired valet in a blue uniform with golden lining greeted him as he stepped out of his hovercar. "Keys?" the young man beckoned, offering his open palm.

"Sure thing," Leonard said, tossing him the keys. "Just make sure you don't scratch through the rust, you hear?" It took him a second to realize that the valet's open hand, which was still thrust out at him, meant he was expecting something more. He fished a few talers out of his pocket, dropped them into the kid's hand and watched him smile sourly. "What?" he asked him in an annoyed tone. "You want me to write you a blank fucking check?" He fought back the urge to verbalize his annoyance further. All the kid was doing was parking his piece-of-shit, rust-bucket of a car. Snotty little brats like him got on his last nerve fast and stayed there. He spared him a final, irritated look before turning around to glance up at the restaurant's brightly-lit sign, which read "Chez Joignon" in red neon letters. After an exasperated sigh, he stomped up the red carpet that led to the front doors.

The doorman welcomed him with a nod as he walked past him. Inside, everything was just as he remembered it. He wasn't exactly a fan of French cuisine or even of this restaurant in particular, but his late wife *had* been, and consequently, he'd been around before. Everything about the place was a little too chic for him, a little too sophisticated, but they'd had their fair share of precious moments here despite that. So many special occasions had been celebrated here, and more anniversaries than he cared to count. If he thought about it too much, he might get nostalgic.

The main dining area was a vast, open chamber with dark marble flooring and plush blue and red draperies that hung from every wall. Elaborate, eye-catching chandeliers illuminated the dozens of round, white tables below, where the city's crème de la crème sat reveling in lively conversation.

He recognized some of the flashier, louder patrons almost immediately. Members of the so-called elite always stood out like a sore thumb. They were rich, powerful and influential members of society like Thomas Reinhardt, CEO of Reinhardt Bovine and Dairy, or Innerstadt News Network's Jane Eckard, possibly the biggest pair of titties in the history of holovision. They sat flirting with each other rather shamelessly at a table near the far end of the dining hall.

His Excellency Sir Reinhardt was married, though not to Miss Eckard. Not very surprisingly, he didn't seem as interested in her winning personality as he was in her other *"assets"*. He knew that he shouldn't expect any better from piece-of-shit snobs and HV personalities—*arrogant fucking misfits that they were*—but was a little discretion really too much to ask for? Their adultery was blatant. Sometimes, the whole lot of them made him sick.

Another boy wearing the restaurant's blue and gold uniform approached him then, and asked if he could take his coat. This one looked like he was thirteen years old, at most. "I'm gonna hang onto this, kid," Leonard muttered absentmindedly, then wandered over to the reception area.

The headwaiter was a tall man with an almost skeletal build. He stood proudly behind the heavily-gilded podium, chest puffed up, giddily turning away an almost constant stream of would-be clients. He tilted his head and flashed Leonard an oily smile as he noticed him approaching. "Bonjour, monsieur," he said in a tone that was halfway between confused and condescending. "How can I be of assistance this evening?" At that, he eyed him warily for a moment, and added, "Do you need directions, perhaps? I hear there's a Burger Shack two blocks north of here, nestled cozily between the Satin Strips dance club and a poor peoples' refuge. If the burgers there are too rich for your budget—I mean *blood*—I hear that the refuge also serves soup. That might be a bit more within your range. Bye-bye now."

Leonard had remained silent throughout the entirety of the headwaiter's cavalcade of barely-veiled insults, but beneath his mask of calm reserve, he was seething. Normally, he'd have nipped the guy's snobbish arrogance in the bud and sent him crying to his mommy. Normally, he'd have grabbed him by the collar and yanked him down a peg or two. Just this once, he'd try to let it slide. He wasn't looking to cause a scene. Not yet.

And then he changed his mind. Pissing on Leonard Boston was never a good idea. Not unless you were looking to get a boot jammed up your ass. "You slimy prick," he spat. "I'm exactly where I need to be." He reached into his coat pocket then and fumbled around for his police badge. "And the question isn't whether or not I'm able to afford eating here, it's whether or not you can afford to have me shut this place down."

The headwaiter's face grew paler instantly. "Monsieur health inspector," he spluttered. "I am so sorry. I didn't mean to—"

"Can it, already," Leonard groaned, flashing his badge in the headwaiter's face. "I'm not a health inspector. I'm a cop."

The sickly look on the headwaiter's face dissipated almost instantly. "My apologies, sir," he said, bowing his head slightly. "You see, we're quite used to people eating here and then running away when they see the bill. It's incredible how fast they can run when they realize that they cannot pay. It really is alarming. But where are my manners? I am Jean-Pierre, the headwaiter here at Chez Joignon." He bowed again then, more deeply than the first time, and nodded in introduction. "How may I help you this fine evening, Mister..." he asked, trailing off.

"It's Boston," Leonard muttered pointedly. "*Captain* Boston. Don't you 'Mister' me. And I'm looking for one of your girls."

Jean-Pierre rubbed at his chin meticulously before asking, "What do you want with her? If you give me a name or tell me what she looks like, I might be able to help identify her, but I'd like to know what for, first."

Insignificant twit, Leonard thought to himself. *Who the fuck do you think you are?* If anything got on his nerves—and it was no secret that an awful lot of things did—there was nothing worse than a blatant lack of respect for authority. Jean-Pierre might not realize it, but he was *this close* to getting his arm twisted behind his back and kissing the floor.

"What I want with her is police business, *sir*," Leonard spat, his words sharp with contempt, "and though I could waste my breath describing her, I won't. There must be five other bimbos working here right now that fit her description to a T. I want you to round up your staff. *Now*."

"But sir," Jean-Pierre protested, going pale and panic-stricken once again, "that's impossible! I *cannot* tell the whole staff to stop working, not even for five minutes. This restaurant has a reputation to maintain. Chez Joignon is famous not only for its refined menu, exquisite wine list, and luxurious ambiance, but for its impeccable service, as well."

"So you saw that commercial too," Leonard grated, mildly satisfied that he was able to rattle the headwaiter so easily. "Fine. You can ID her for me, then. Is there someplace out of the way where we can look at this surveillance disk without being bothered? Sometime today, preferably."

"Yes, of course, Monsieur, Capitaine," Jean-Pierre said with a sigh, clearly relieved. "There's a playback unit in the security booth. I'll take you there now." He waved a nearby waiter over and instructed him to take his place, then motioned for Leonard to follow him, and led him across the teeming dining room floor.

Leonard kept a sharp eye out for the ditzy blonde waitress as they waded through the crowd, but he didn't see her anywhere. His immediate view was obstructed by clusters of uppity-class snobs and fancy-pantsed has-beens. He wasn't much for stereotypes unless they were his own. Then they were canon. He couldn't really help it; the "aristocracy" made him sick.

He didn't hold the rich, the famous or the powerful in very high esteem. He was willing to wager that none of those creeps worked even half as hard as he did. As far as he was concerned, it was just one of those certainties of life. As long as there were honest, hardworking folks out there, sweating and bleeding just to earn their bread, there'd be unscrupulous, lazy weasels with a knack for profiteering just waiting to purloin their earnings away.

It was the natural order of things; an order that he was tasked with preserving, even if it sometimes made him sick. He couldn't let his personal views get in the way of him doing his job, even if it disgusted him. He never had before, and he wasn't going to today. Hanging around with the *gentry* wasn't exactly his idea of good, wholesome fun, but he couldn't complain. Hadn't he been the one just itching to get away from his office and back into the field? He had been, he knew, and he'd have to deal with it and get on with the task at hand.

He followed closely as the headwaiter pushed through a set of heavy double doors at the back end of the dining room. On the other side, he led him a short distance through a concrete tunnel, then ducked into a small room on their right.

The sparsely decorated chamber was no more aesthetic than the bare hall outside was. All but one of its walls had been painted in spatters of lima bean green, and several rows of shelves littered with all kinds of worthless junk were lined up near the far end of the room. "Please, pay no mind to the poor appearance of this place, Capitaine," Jean-Pierre pleaded. "We are going to redecorate it very soon, though we have no set use for it, really. For now, we already have enough room in storage, and the place is too cold for a proper employee's lounge, so we just put a few miscellaneous items here for safekeeping. Here. Have a seat," he offered, pulling over a flimsy-looking wooden stool. "I will go get the playback unit. Just a moment, please!"

"I think I'll stand," Leonard murmured, pushing the stool away with his foot. "This thing looks like it's made of popsicle sticks or something. Rather not ruin my suit when it breaks."

Jean-Pierre chortled gleefully as he sashayed toward the other end of the room. "You are a very funny man, Capitaine Boston," he managed to say between roiling bouts of nasal laughter. "Perhaps you should consider another line of work, yes? Like a humorist, or... a comedian, as they say."

Leonard wasn't sure what the guy found so funny. His shift in attitude and his over-the-top fruitiness were creepy as fuck, as far as he was concerned. Grumbling under his breath, he wrinkled his brow and eyed Jean-Pierre as he disappeared between two shelving units, then emerged a few seconds later towing a large, black case with a grainy finish to it on the floor behind him.

Jean-Pierre set the case down a few feet in front of him, knelt to open it, then took a seat on the stool he'd pulled up earlier. "Alright then, Monsieur le Capitaine," he said, clasping his hands with a clap. "On with the film! Would you like some popcorn?"

"Haw, haw," Leonard uttered dryly, smirking. "You're just the funniest little man this side of Nuremberg, aren't you?" To his great disappointment, his sarcasm was lost on Jean-Pierre.

"Before we even look at this," he added with a sigh, "can you tell me where you were the night of the incident? Uh, last Tuesday. If you can, try to avoid any unrelated details like what kind of fruit salad you had for breakfast and what color crap it made. I don't want to hear about the haircut you considered getting, either, or how you cancelled your reservation with your stylist because you weren't ready to commit to a new look. Skip the bullshit and stick to the facts or you're going to piss me off."

Jean-Pierre rubbed at his chin, appearing lost in thought and anything but offended.

Leonard felt surprisingly let down. The guy got in a huff quicker than explosive diarrhea if there was a problem or even a *potential* problem with the restaurant, but he seemed like he was completely impervious to insult. He was fairly certain that he could badmouth this guy's momma all day long and it wouldn't even bother him in the least.

The seconds seemed to stretch on before Jean-Pierre finally looked up and shook his head. "I was working that day," he professed, "but I went home in the early afternoon. I'm sure of it. I wasn't feeling good. Not at all."

"Fair enough," Leonard grumped, turning his back on him. He scratched his head as he walked over to the open case. When he reached it, he slipped his stubby fingers inside his coat's inner pocket, fished the surveillance disk out, leaned forward with a grunt, and slid the disk into the playback unit's reading slot. "This footage was captured by your security cameras that night," he said. "All I need you to do is identify the waitress in the recording. That's it. Simple as that." A moment later, a holographic image appeared where once there was nothing.

Jean-Pierre nodded once then watched attentively as the surveillance disk started to play through the events of that night.

Nothing of note happened for the first few minutes, and his mind started to wander visibly, but he blinked out of his blurry-eyed daze as two women walked into the scene. "Ah, je vois, je vois," he said, quickly glancing up at Leonard. "The lady with the menu is Ginette, and the one pouring the wine is Elsa. It's one of them you're looking for, non?"

"Non," Leonard answered reflexively. "Uh... no. It's not. Give me a minute." He groaned loudly as he leaned forward again and grabbed the remote from its resting place beside the playback unit, then straightened his back with a pop, and started to fumble around with the controls. After a few seconds too many, he found the frame selection menu, and awkwardly worked his way through it. "There," he said. "That should do it. Frame twenty thousand." The bright projection changed to that of the clumsy blonde waitress stumbling into the scene. "That's her," he barked, pointing her out. "Who is she and where can I find her?"

"Oh!" Jean-Pierre exclaimed emphatically with a conspicuous smack to his forehead. "That, Monsieur le Capitaine, was our very own Anna Lucia Gordon, and a very lovely waitress she did make, even if she was a bit of a klutz. Unfortunately," he added, then trailed off momentarily before picking up in a far more serious tone, "she doesn't work here anymore. She hasn't worked here since the night of the incident."

"What?" Leonard barked. "Why not?"

"Well, you see, Monsieur le Capitaine," Jean-Pierre replied, sounding more than mildly embarrassed, "while what happened to mademoiselle Gordon is quite sad, really, and deserving of our sympathy, Chez Joignon *cannot* allow itself to employ waitresses that are... let us say, lacking a certain appeal. It's her face, you see. It... well, her bruises are simply too horrible for her to continue working here. I know it sounds cruel, yes, but the decision was not mine to make. To be quite blunt, it saves a lot of trouble with complaints from upset patrons. We offered her the possibility of returning to work here again. At a later time. If her face healed up properly and she no longer looked like an ugly duckling. It would only be fair, I suppose. It's like she's on leave—without pay or the promise of a guaranteed return to work."

Jean-Pierre looked down then and combed his fingers through his hair as he mulled something over in his head. "She isn't in any kind of trouble, is she?" he asked, his eyes filled with apprehension. "I sincerely hope that she isn't. You see, I've tried to contact her myself several times since then, but her phone seems to have been disconnected. I think she may have moved."

Leonard's eyes found Jean-Pierre's and they stared at each other for a second. He considered his next words carefully before responding. He felt his stomach roil again, and tried to reassure himself that despite his nagging feeling, there was nothing to worry about here... yet. So the chick really did get slugged in the face. So what? He'd already seen as much on the surveillance disk. It didn't prove that Frank had anything to do with it. Someone else could have punched her out. It could still just be a case of really good editing. It wasn't likely, but it was possible, especially if someone was trying to frame him.

He could think about it all he wanted, but he knew that he'd draw nothing more than a blank. He just couldn't figure out why the police hadn't been advised about all of this earlier, officially. The likelihood that he wouldn't get to interrogate Anna Lucia worried him, but he found some consolation in the fact that there *had* to be other witnesses to that night's events. Her assailant couldn't have chosen a more public arena to commit his crime in. All he had to do was figure out who was who on the surveillance disk and hunt them down for questioning.

"No," he finally sighed, having wrapped his head around Jean-Pierre's question. "She's not in any more trouble than she was the night of the incident. At least not with the LEA, she isn't. As far as I know, she got popped in the mouth for dropping a tray, and last time I checked, being butterfingered isn't illegal. Even if she'd dropped it on the president himself, there wouldn't be all that much we could do about it, so you can rest easy, if that's what's bothering you."

Jean-Pierre exhaled extensively, relieved. A weight seemed to have been lifted from his shoulders. "Yes, well I feel much better now," he breathed. "With the law, one can never be too sure."

Leonard dismissed that last comment of his as involuntary arrogance and ignored it. "Who else was around that night?" he asked. "Can you think of anyone else that should have been here? Anyone at all? You can start with those you identified on the surveillance disk, unless you can do better."

"Well," Jean-Pierre started to say, then hesitated a moment before adding, "There is this one girl... Antoinette. She's another of the regular waitresses here. She's usually on the same shifts as Anna Lucia, and works a section of tables near hers. Actually," he whispered, then trailed off momentarily before shaking his finger like he'd just had a realization, "she should be here tonight!" He gestured triumphantly then, his eyes shooting wide open. "I can go fetch her for you right now, monsieur, if you can wait a minute." He leapt from his stool then and stormed out of the room before Leonard could even voice his approval.

"Yes," Leonard murmured to himself. "Why of course. Take all ze minutes you need. Lé baguette, hon hon hon." With a bit of luck, one of his problems might soon be out of the way. He could only cross his fingers until Jean-Pierre returned, and return he did, only a minute later, as promised. He was smiling like the cat that ate the canary when he stepped through the gaping doorway.

Trailing close behind him was perhaps one of the most stunning redheads Leonard had ever seen. She had a full mane of flowing russet hair and a body that was built like an hourglass. Her low-cut uniform exposed just enough of her cleavage to make it easy to imagine what the rest of her ample, alabaster bosom looked like. Even more compelling were her shapely hips, which looked like they'd been conceived with childbearing in mind. If that wasn't enough to get his engine running—and boy oh boy was it ever—

her face wasn't too hard on the eyes, either. She had high, elegant cheekbones, a small, delicate nose, and voluptuous, pursed red lips that wanted nothing more than to leave their mark on his cheek. Or so he liked to think.

He wasn't even going to get started on her abnormally-bright, emerald green eyes. Considering the gravity of the situation, he felt doubly ashamed for ogling her like an old, creepy pervert. But he couldn't help it. She was a real looker—a perfect ten, and then some. He soon realized that his palms were sweaty, and that he'd been outright staring at Antoinette ever since she'd first entered the room. Back in the day, he could have faced off with a band of armed robbers and kept a straight face, but here he was building up a cold sweat over some broad. He felt like an imbecile.

"I uh... hello, miss," he bumbled quietly, trying vainly to conceal his obvious and sudden nervosity. He cleared his throat and ushered her along toward the stool. His cheeks were red with embarrassment. He couldn't even bring himself to look her in the eyes. "My apologies," he spluttered, failing in his second effort to get a grip of himself. "I'm Captain Leonard Boston, from the Law Enforcement Agency, and I have a couple questions to ask you. Please, take a seat."

Antoinette smiled a bit and blushed as she accepted his offer and sat. Maybe she'd read his mind—or his body language—and was flattered by the effect that she was having on him. Or more likely, as he saw it, she was completely weirded out and embarrassed by it. "Merci," she said, smoothing her skirt out before crossing her legs. Her voice, soft as velvet and sweet like honey, warmed Leonard's ears and made him smile against his will. "This is about Anna Lucia?" she asked, her voice tinged with concern.

"Yes," he confessed. "This is about Anna Lucia. Were you here the night that she was assaulted?"

"Oui, Monsieur le Capitaine," she whispered loudly, then glanced uneasily from him to Jean-Pierre and back again. "I was here... but I didn't see anything."

Leonard sighed dejectedly and rubbed at his face. "Are you absolutely sure?" he asked. "One hundred percent?"

Antoinette looked up at Jean-Pierre again, her lip aquiver, then nodded vigorously, a few tears shaking free in the process. "Yes," she said, wiping at her eyes. "I'm certain of it, Monsieur. I did not see anything."

As enthralled as he was by her, Leonard couldn't help but find her behavior suspicious. Something about it just wasn't right. She seemed disturbed, like she was holding something back, not telling the whole truth. She might just be upset over the aftermath of the whole ordeal, but he couldn't know for certain.

He was about to ask her why she hadn't seen anything—an event he considered unlikely, taking the proximity of the two girls' working areas into account—when a call came in on his cell phone. The vibrant ringing in his coat pocket nearly gave him a start. He took his phone out, exhaled loudly and stomped out of the room without excusing himself.

Some of the gizmos that the market churned out these days really got on his last nerve. The cell phone was one of them, even if it was nothing new. It was a technologically primitive survivor from the old days. Although one might be led to believe that the side effects of a globally-waged nuclear war would leave the world devastated, and in a sorry state of technological torpor, human beings were surprisingly resilient little fuckers, and resourceful, to boot.

The simple cell phone, along with a slew of other gadgets, had somehow managed to survive the cataclysm, and helped serve as a model in the reconstruction of a lost wealth of scientific knowledge. Though the city had come a long way in the past few hundred years, surprisingly little had changed in the area of telecommunications, and the cell phone was mainstay. Why they remained in the dark ages in that respect was completely beyond him, considering the fact that they'd surpassed their predecessors in almost every other way. Regardless, the cell was there to stay, and he was stuck with it.

For his sake, he hoped that some technological advancement would provide a less annoying means of communication in the near future. The government already had some pieces of the puzzle in place. The internal earphones the force was equipped with were proof of that, but the grafting of such devices in civilians was prohibited for political reasons including but not limited to the preservation of national security.

It wasn't like the government didn't have the resources it needed for a rollout of new communication tools, either. They'd become a nation of accomplished recyclers. While most of the world was uninhabitable, a lot of its natural resources were still out there, waiting to be plucked up by those willing to risk the seismic quakes and deadly radioactivity—those willing and authorized to do so by the powers that be, at least.

Foragers were handpicked by the government, and only the best and the fittest made the cut. It was dangerous work, but the rewards for particularly successful forays had the potential to make a person rich for the rest of their days—if they managed to make it back in one piece, that was. Hazmat suits helped with survival outside the city limits, and allowed government-backed corporations to set up excavation sites in the nearby mountains. But the suits themselves were only moderately dependable. They oftentimes broke down under heavier exposure to radioactive emissions, so venturing great distances into the wastelands was next to impossible, unless you wanted to suffer gene mutation or develop symptoms of the "slow death". The latter was a real treat if you happened to be a suicidal masochist.

According to the president—and every other president to have sat in the Bundespalast before him—Innerstadt was one of the few remaining cities to have survived the Great War. Efforts to establish long-distance communications with the rest of the world had proven futile, but continued nonetheless.

Details remained sketchy, but the government alleged with great certitude that these other peoples had been unable to cope with the radiation and had eventually died out, like everything else. The people of Innerstadt were the lucky few, the brave souls chosen by fate to carry man's torch through the night and into a brighter tomorrow. Or so went the government's pitch.

Before worldwide broadcast had died out completely, news had already spread that the earth's biggest population centers had been hit hard. In a dark, somewhat twisted way, he almost found it funny that all of it had started because of a fluke accident.

Near the pinnacle of the twenty-first century, the president of the United States and Northern Territories of America ordered a massive air strike on Tehran with the goal of delivering an important message to fundamentalists and terrorist organizations alike. In a gross miscalculation of proportions unequaled in history—according to the experts, at least—several unmapped nuclear warheads were detonated during what was supposed to be the bombing of small arms and chemical weapons caches.

The resulting blasts were of such incredible magnitude that the city was almost completely obliterated. In a heartbeat, the biggest population center in Iran was all but wiped from the map, and its immediate neighbors suffered heavily due to the resulting fallout. Some people nowadays claimed it was impossible, that they'd just nuked them straight out, but this was coming from the same tinfoil-hat crowd that blamed everything under the sun on moonbats and lizard people, so it was hard to take seriously.

Leonard couldn't say either way, if he was being honest, but he trusted the pros, and according to them, that horrible incident would send a wave of uncertainty rippling throughout the entire civilized world. It would *not* go unnoticed or unanswered for. The whole world was stewing with fear and anger, and grudges as old as time quickly bubbled to the surface.

From the onset of the tragedy, enraged American protestors gathered in the streets of their capital cities to call for the deposition of their president, Bors Hawthorne. Tensions mounted, and what began as isolated incidents soon escalated to a series of bloody confrontations between angry citizens and local law enforcement. It wasn't long before the armed forces were called in to stamp out what had by then been labeled an insurgency.

This only fanned the flames at home, and worsened relations with the international community. The president, ruling with an iron fist from his golden tower, came under even greater fire from those who still dared to speak up. Extremist factions opposing the current administration soon sprang into existence nationwide, while others yet—these little more than local pressure groups like so many others—suddenly became much more vocal. Other groups, some of them longstanding militias based in the Deep South and Midwest, were quick to declare their eternal and undying fealty to the ruling president and his dynasty. Their drives for recruitment increased, and thanks to an emergency relaxing of possession laws, they began to arm themselves more openly. Before long, they were sending out patrols to hunt down the "protesterous traitors".

The troubles spread further yet, and the entire nation, including the Canadian territories in the north, was thrown into an even greater state of unrest. The president was quick to label any new opposition an enemy of the state, and order their dismantlement. The institution of a *Shoot on Sight* directive for all police forces was meant to deter further rebellious attitudes. Near complete chaos broke out when the videotaped beheadings of traitors captured by the Holy Knights of Jesus militia found its way to the independent media. Otherwise peaceful people fled their homes and joined militant organizations for protection from the growing threat.

When the violence escalated to proportions resembling civil war, the UN "offered" to send in troops to help quell the rioting. President Hawthorne, as bold and self-confident as the country he represented, met their offer with a prompt refusal. His arrogance and blatant mismanagement in that time of unprecedented crisis soon earned his country a revocation from the UN.

The Eastern Alliance, comprised mainly of Russia, North Korea, Syria, and what remained of Iran, viewed the USNTA's instability as the perfect opportunity to exact revenge. They'd stacked up a myriad of grievances against them over the years, long before the millions of deaths caused by the strike on Tehran.

Without so much as a warning, nuclear missiles were launched at strategic locations throughout the United States and its northern territories. New York, Montreal, Ottawa and Washington were among the first to fall. Many other missiles were launched soon after in what could have been called a carpet bombing. Though the Americans were protected from missile attack by a space shield program that had been set up sometime around the turn of the twenty-first century, the salvo of nuclear warheads bearing down on them was so dense that not all of the bombs could be stopped.

It wasn't long before the rest of the world was sucked into the vortex of destruction. Willingly or not, every nation in the world was affected by the carnival of bloodletting that would bring the human race to the brink of extinction. The sky was seared and the seas went black, and the civilized world as everyone knew it ceased to exist.

No one knew exactly when these events had taken place. Most of their historical recollection was passed down by way of oral tradition, and what documentation they did have was of little use to them due to the loss of the ancient tongues and calendar. Some bits of footage had been salvaged and eventually translated, but the value of this partial data was questionable at best. Many historians agreed that the events had transpired, but none of them seemed to be able to agree on a reliable timeline.

Most of those that managed to survive the final waves of the war later died from exposure to radioactive fallout. The deadly particles continued to rain down and spread out over the entirety of the earth's surface. Innerstadt had remained virtually untouched, however, and continued to grow into what it was now: a filthy, rodent-infested metropolis that was constantly at odds with threats of overpopulation, hiking pollution levels and an all-consuming fear of the outside world. The water tasted bad, the food smelled funny, the healthcare system was a running joke, and they were perpetually teetering on the brink of one disaster or another, but it was home. And at least they were around to complain about it.

On the bright side of things, Leonard thought with a hint of sarcasm, they got to enjoy an abundance of high-tech gadgetry, such as the cell phone that was ringing in his hand for about the umpteenth time. He really had to quit it with the late-night Innerstadt History Network. Maybe if he watched some geeky tech channel instead, he could figure out how to answer his piece of shit phone in under two minutes. "Okay, already," he muttered, holding the ridiculously small phone to his ear. "Who is this?"

"It's me, Captain," Tom answered, his voice coming in loud and clear, if a little haggard.

"This had better be good, Gostobalis," Leonard said in a huff. He'd been expecting Tom to call sooner or later. "What do you want? You got something for me?"

"I'm afraid so, boss," Tom replied gruffly, "and you're not going to like it." He fell awkwardly silent for a moment before adding, "No, you're not going to like it at all. I can hardly believe any of this myself. What I got going on over here nearly made me lose my lunch. Still think I might."

"And?" Leonard barked, clearly impatient. "What is it? Just spit it out, already!"

"I'm at Frank's... Fasaro's. We found... what we found is... it's just horrible, boss. You should come over here and see this for yourself. I just don't—"

"Look," Leonard hissed, cutting him off, "I don't really have a whole lot of time for this right now. I'm in the middle of an investigation, got it? So just fucking say it. *Please.*"

"We found bodies, Sir," Tom breathed. "Four of them. Maybe more. It's kind of hard to tell right now." His voice was shaky and strained in a sickly blend of horror and disbelief.

Leonard picked up on it immediately, and wouldn't really hold it against him, even if it was hampering with his ability to communicate effectively. Gostobalis and Fasaro were friends. The thoughts going through the kid's head right now would be enough to shake his foundations pretty solid. Somebody had just messed around with his reality. He knew what that felt like all too well, and he was starting to feel it again already, but he couldn't afford to let it show.

It was the curse of his chosen path. His role was to lead by example and inspire confidence in his men. He wasn't supposed to get scared or upset. Panicking now would get them nowhere. It would only be detrimental to Gostobalis' ability to carry out his duties. "Go on, Tom," he said, his tone of voice much calmer than it had been the first time around. "Please." To an outsider, he'd still sound stern, but Tom should recognize this as empathy, or as close to it as he could expect from him.

Tom paused, took a deep breath and exhaled loudly before mumbling out the rest of his report. "They're mangled something awful, boss. We can barely tell heads from tails. There's a lot more than just that, though. There's much, much more. We also uncovered a substantial cache of weapons and illegal substances, and I don't just mean narcotics, but there are a lot of those, too. There's enough chems here to make a bomb that could take out four city blocks, easy. I wouldn't have believed any of it if I hadn't seen it with my own two eyes. Seriously, boss, I think you better come down here and take a look at this yourself. I know it seems obvious, but I'm not sure what to make of all of it. Or maybe I just don't want to believe it."

Leonard sighed heavily and closed his eyes. He rubbed at his brow to try to soothe his aching head, but it was to no avail. That feeling of nausea he'd felt earlier was back in full effect, and it had brought its friend Migraine to the party. Just when he thought it couldn't get any worse, it did. None of it made any sense, *least of all* this. But *why* not?

The witness he'd spoken to hadn't been able to identify Fasaro on the surveillance disk, but part of him had been hoping for that all along. He had to admit that he'd felt somewhat relieved when she'd failed to identify him. He just didn't want to believe that Frank was guilty. Sure, that girl *what's-her-name* with the huge rack had acted kind of strange about it, but that didn't mean jack shit, obviously.

Truth was, until he found solid evidence, he could still hope, just like he had until his damned phone had gone off. He would have kept digging, but it was pointless now. His priorities had changed. *Of all things,* he thought, grimacing bitterly. *Gruesome murder and possession of prohibited explosive substances.* There were mutilated corpses in his apartment, for fuck's sake. What more proof did he need?

Maybe he'd been a fool to think Fasaro was innocent. All Frank had going for him up until then was a lack of conclusive evidence, but the rest was enough to condemn him, he was sure. It was hard to think with the bizarre feeling gnawing away at the back of his mind. What was that, he wondered. Disappointment? Attachment? It didn't matter. None of it did. He had a job to do, and he couldn't let his emotions get in the way of it.

"Sir?" Tom asked in a careful tone. "What should I do?"

Leonard took another deep breath and clenched his free hand at his side before breathing his grim response. "No offense meant, Tom, but we both know what Fasaro is capable of. I don't want you running into him without a full squad to back you up. Go hunker down in the alley across the street, mind your own business and sit tight until I get there with backup."

"You got it, but backup's already on the way," Tom replied woodenly before hanging up.

Leonard stared at his cell phone for a second before folding it up and tucking it away in his coat pocket. He'd call in another backup unit just in case, and maybe something a little more heavy-handed, too. He might even put out an all-points bulletin from the CB in his car, just as soon as he hit the road. He couldn't take any chances with a guy like Fasaro.

He stared long and hard at the entrance to the back room. The headwaiter and the redhead waitress would still be waiting for him. Morose, he decided against announcing his departure. They were inconsequential and the clock was ticking. Besides, that Jean-Pierre guy gave him the heebie-jeebies, and he deserved nothing better for the disparaging comments he'd made earlier.

He might need to grill them further, eventually, but he'd deal with that when the time came. Until then, he had somewhere else to be. Frankly, he'd rather not be involved in any of this debacle. He could easily call the shots from afar on this one, or delegate the responsibility to a subordinate, but his conscience dictated otherwise, and left him with little choice. He felt responsible for what had happened, and obligated to intervene directly. Frank had been like his protégé, in a way. He grunted hoarsely then and pushed through the doors to the main dining room. He wouldn't waste another minute in this den of elitist snobs.

The exaggerated look of glee on Jean-Pierre's face melted away the second the captain left the room. All that was left in its place was a halfhearted smile and a remote look of nervous unease. He strained his ears to try to listen in on the captain's conversation, but couldn't make out much of anything, despite the strength of the man's voice. It sounded like he was muttering under his breath.

A short while later, the talking stopped, and he heard the sound of heavy footsteps leading away, back toward the dining room. Uneasy, he tiptoed to the entrance and poked his head into the hallway. His thin lips curled into a satisfied grin when he found the captain gone. He fingered his mustache thoughtfully and wandered back into the musty supply room. Antoinette sat waiting nervously, her eyes creased with concern. "Oh, don't you worry," he cooed. "There's nothing for you to worry about. You did exactly as you were told, and you did very well, might I add. Your cooperation won't be forgotten."

The pouty frown he offered her as a botched sign of empathy wasn't helping. From the look of it, she found it disturbing. For some reason, that amused him. "You can go back to work now, if you wish." Despite his wording, the tone of his voice made it clear that it wasn't really a suggestion.

Antoinette rose slowly from her stool and nodded, carefully avoiding his gaze as she did. "Yes, of course," she mumbled faintly. She started to walk off then, her head lowered subserviently.

He smiled again as he watched her leave the room. It was a cold and calculating smile. The girl was bothered, true—she was probably even terrified—but he didn't think she'd pose a threat. No, none whatsoever. She was too afraid to get in the way. She was too well controlled. Even if her conscience did get the better of her, there were ways of snuffing out such annoyances. He had practical experience in such matters.

He'd dealt with bothersome people before, and he wouldn't hesitate to do so again, if he was asked to. He *knew* that killing people was wrong, perhaps even horrible, but he didn't feel like a monster for any of it. What he did, he did out of necessity, out of a sense of self-preservation.

Better you than me. That was his motto. If he failed the Masters now—or maybe even just once, ever—it would be his neck on the chopping block. He'd probably end up wearing a pair of cement boots, along with all of the other wretches that didn't know how to keep their mouths shut, just like that stupid wench, Anna Lucia. It was her fault and hers alone if she was resting eternally at the bottom of the lake. Eternally, or until her corpse bloated and was eaten by fish. He shivered at the thought of it.

He could only hope that telling Antoinette to lie had been the right thing to do. Nothing scared him more than the thought of dying, but there was probably nothing to worry about. If he was lucky, he might even be rewarded. Still, he couldn't help but wonder what the Masters had in store for him.

There was only one way to find out for sure; he had to ask. It might seem like a ridiculous move to some, but they'd hear about what had happened here sooner or later. They always did, and if he'd made a mistake, it would be better for him if he told them about it himself. Nervous and hesitant, he walked to the other end of the room and paused deliberately. Decided, he grabbed the phone from the wall and laid it on his shoulder. He took a deep breath before punching in the number he'd been instructed to use for emergencies only, and with great discretion.

Closing his eyes, he took another deep breath, then held the receiver up to his ear. For a few seconds, he listened to the faint buzzing tone that the phone made when it was ringing at the other end of the line. He was about to hang up when he heard a low *click* followed by a brief silence.

"Hello," a deep voice grumbled suspiciously from the other end of the line. "What do you want?"

"Uh, yes... hello," Jean-Pierre mumbled incoherently. *Gather yourself, you fool,* he had to remind himself. He cleared his throat and tried his best to regain his composure. "It's John Paul Dubuc," he said, the tone of his voice surprisingly confident in his own ears. "D-y-b-u-k. I must speak to the Masters immediately. It is a matter of utmost importance." Despite his determined efforts to remain calm, he couldn't help but tremble just a little. Dealing with the Masters was always a terrifying experience.

"Silence!" the man at the other end of the line hissed loudly. "Do *not* forget yourself, whelp. You should know by now to show respect to your betters."

"My apologies," Jean-Pierre yipped, suddenly overcome with fear. It was more than obvious to him now that he was speaking with a Watcher. The Watchers scared him just as much as the Masters did, possibly more so. The invisible hand of their influence reached far, dipping into every nook and cranny in the city, and the cruelty of their disciplinary measures was without equal. The latest rumors circulating in the circle of aspirants said that they killed over very little, even on a whim, at times. While he rarely put much stock in hearsay, these were stories that he just couldn't afford to ignore.

Just one word from the man was all it would take to ruin his life completely. One word could burn the restaurant to the ground, or put an end to his life. The Watchers were nearly untouchable, and that further fueled his disquiet. Not even the Masters would dare raise a hand against them. It didn't matter if they were higher up in the organization's strange hierarchy; the Watchers were never to be harmed under any circumstances. They were the eyes and the ears of the Masters, and doubled as their bodyguards. Death soon found any who struck out at them. The Masters themselves were not exempted from this rule.

Only the Grand Anarch himself could take a Watcher's life without fear of reprisal, but he wasn't even sure that the man was anything more than a myth. He'd heard stories, and the Awoken swore by his existence, but few were those that claimed to have even caught a fortuitous glimpse of him.

In any case, it wasn't his place to question authority. He was nothing but an insignificant worm in all of this. Perhaps he'd be something more, someday, but for the time being, he'd consider himself lucky just to walk away from this conversation unmarked. He had to remain focused at all times. The wrong words or a simple slip of the tongue could sign his death warrant. "I am so truly sorry, sir. I meant no disrespect at all, I promise you. Please, I beg of you... may I speak with the Masters now? I swear on my life that it's urgent. I wouldn't be calling you otherwise. Please. You must understand that."

After a brief moment of hesitation, breathing heavily into the phone, the Watcher responded in a calm but condescending tone. "You're a worthless cur. Your beggary means less than nothing to me, just like your life. *You* must understand *that*. Regardless, you may share words with the great Masters, if such is their desire. Remain on the line until I return or until the Masters say otherwise, or you're a dead man. If I find out that this line has been tapped or tampered with in any way... you're a dead man. If this isn't as urgent as you say it is... you're a dead man. Do you understand?"

"Yes," Jean-Pierre yelped. "Completely." He was going to say something more, but realized that this was one of those golden opportunities to shut the fuck up, so he held his tongue, instead. Looking down, he realized that his legs were trembling and that he'd started to soil himself. He'd always known that he was a coward, but sometimes he managed to forget about it for a little while. This was *not* one of those times. The next few seconds of silence felt like an eternity to him.

"I understand that you have a matter of some importance to discuss with me." John Grimm's smooth and urbane voice almost startled another yelp from him, but a hand quickly raised to his mouth helped muffle the cry.

"Yes, Master Havoc," Jean-Pierre conceded, managing to sound completely calm despite himself. "I would not waste your time with trifles."

"Well, how very considerate of you, *Monsieur* Dubuc," John Grimm cooed, sounding genuinely grateful. "Please, go on."

Jean-Pierre held his hand over the phone's receiver and let out a sigh of relief. Everything was going to be okay after all. *This* Master seemed a little more understanding than the Watcher had been. The Masters were far more dangerous in the greater scheme of things, of that there was no doubt, but they were also more tolerant of the lower-ranking members and aspirants. Or so he'd heard. This too was a rumor he preferred to believe.

"There was a man from the Law Enforcement Agency here just recently," he continued, rubbing at his forehead, "a certain captain by the name of Boston. He was inquiring about the incident that took place here the other night, with you and Master Giuterrez, and the young blonde gentleman. He wanted to speak with a witness to the event. I couldn't say why for sure, because he never revealed his intentions, but that is what he wanted. I gave him a witness to speak to, but instructed her to lie and say that she didn't see anything. I'm not sure if the captain's curiosity was satisfied by our little masquerade, but he didn't press the matter. In any case, he's gone now: empty-handed. I just thought that you'd like to know this."

"Yes," Grimm replied smoothly, "I was expecting Boston would come snooping around sooner or later. And he's no longer there, you say? Pity. Any incriminating 'evidence' you could have fed him about the *young blonde man* as you call him would have been extremely helpful. But you had no way of knowing what to expect, so I won't hold it against you. By the will of the Grand Anarch, this man's right to live has been forfeit. In fact, his death has become *my* master's latest obsession."

He paused briefly then and exhaled dramatically. "It's a real shame," he sighed. "Just a few choice words could have sealed his fate. No matter. You have done well, *Monsieur* Dubuc. Well indeed, under the circumstances. I thank you for your caution. In his great wisdom, the Grand Anarch would be most pleased by your devotion to our privacy. You will find a handsome reward waiting for you on your return home, and I wouldn't be surprised if you became eligible for nomination into the brotherhood in the near future. Now if that's everything," he murmured, lowering the tone of his voice almost dismissively, "I have other pressing matters to attend to."

"Yes, yes of course, Master," Jean-Pierre blurted out in a hurry. "Thank you for your time." He sighed heavily as he heard the line hang up. "Dear me, what a headache," he groaned, rubbing at his eyes to try and ease away some of his anxiety. "Sometimes I wonder if these *bonuses* are really worth all of the trouble." He paused reflexively for a moment then laughed. "What am I saying? Of course they are."

CHAPTER
10

Mystery Meat

Frank grinned contently over a steaming plate of bacon fried rice, lòu-mihn noodles, General Mao chicken, and a mysterious mass of meat and pastry dubbed "the King Chu special". Vanessa had hardly even touched her plate yet, but he was already well into his second. Ever since he'd started walking freely again, he was constantly hungry.

He'd always had a healthy appetite, but it had never been this voracious before. It didn't matter how much or how frequently he ate, there always seemed to be room for more. His stomach was like a bottomless pit, and he was more than happy to try to fill it.

The doctors assured him that his wolfish hunger was quite normal, and a very good sign that a quick recovery was on the horizon. *Wolfish* truly was the best way to describe his insatiable need for sustenance. He shoveled down most of his noodles before Vanessa could stab a second mouthful of grilled vegetables with her fork. As mouthwatering as everything was, he ate with such ravenous enthusiasm that he could hardly even taste it. He chewed everything quickly before swallowing it down with a barely audible gulp.

They'd chosen to dine at a restaurant by the name of Uncle's to celebrate his return to work. It was a cozy little gem on the edge of the Portsmuth and Langdon sectors. The sloping street outside offered a fantastic view that stretched all the way to the lake. As far as anyone knew, Innerstadt was miles away from the nearest coast. Because of the city's near-complete isolation from the rest of the world, this should have made survival all the more challenging, but its founders, in their wisdom, had been blessed with the foresight to dig a vast artificial lake, and populate it with a great variety of freshwater fish and mollusks.

Other forms of aquatic life were genetically modified and introduced into the lake, and generations of intense mariculture had helped develop a sustainable freshwater ecosystem. Though a crucial resource, it wasn't an inexhaustible one. But even with tight preservation laws, the lake produced enough food to keep the restaurants and downtown markets well-stocked year-round. Pretty much everyone agreed that it was a boon to society, even though it sometimes seemed like more human bodies were fished out of it than trout. Unfortunately, it had become a notorious dumping location for organized crime syndicates.

Despite the advanced hour, the restaurant was nearly empty. Usually, the place would have been jam-packed with the late-night crowd, but for some reason, only a scattered handful of hungry customers sat eating at its small, round tables. The dim lights and the pleasant sound of conversation drifting from one table to the next imbued the place with a calming atmosphere. The tall windows flanking the front door on each side offered a spectacular view of Mercerstrasse, which was busy as ever with its shops and markets and peddlers, each one claiming to sell bigger or better trinkets at a lower price.

The currant-colored carpet on the restaurant's floor was bristly and plain in design, but the velvety-soft tapestry that ran all the way around the circular dining room drew the eyes of even the most disinterested of patrons. At least until the novelty of it wore off.

Traditional depictions of ancient China sewn into rich, colorful patterns made up the greater part of it. Where the sections of the tapestry started and ended, imposing red dragons sat poised atop thick brass pillars their lower bodies and tails were wrapped around.

The authentic silver, detailed earthenware and high-backed chairs brought the restaurant up a notch, and made it seem a little out of place among the decrepit but colorful shacks in its vicinity. The furniture, all lacquered in a warm shade of green, was of synthetic origin, but hard to distinguish from real, carved wood. It wasn't exactly Chez Joignon—not by a long shot—but it was quaint, with good food at reasonable prices. All in all, he much preferred restaurants like this one. If they'd chosen Chez Joignon, they'd have gone home broke or hungry, or possibly both.

Vanessa smiled timidly from across the table as she tapped at its smooth surface with the tips of her fingers. "What?" she asked him with a shy giggle. "Don't look at me like that, you troglodyte. I'm just not really hungry, that's all!"

"Are you sure?" Frank mumbled through a mouthful of rice, his words muffled so badly they were almost unintelligible. He swallowed carefully and blushed as he reworded his question. "What I mean to say is... is something bothering you? You look kind of worried."

"No," she sighed, shaking her head from side to side. "I'm fine, honestly. Thanks though." She gave him a warm, reassuring smile then, and stretched her arms behind her head. "Though, now that you mention it," she breathed, donning a sly air, "I am a little concerned about all that food you've been packing away. You're going to get really fat if they keep you cooped up in the office much longer."

She broke into a small fit of laughter, then dabbed the tears from her eyes with her shirtsleeve. "Really, though," she gasped, "everything is fine." She took a deep breath to calm herself before continuing. "I'm just happy you're okay. I don't know what I would have done if I'd lost you."

Frank smiled a bit and shoveled another heap of rice into his mouth. He never could tell exactly what Vanessa was thinking. Sometimes he was a little daft when it came to women, but he wasn't sure that explained it—not at all, really. Maybe he was just overly concerned with her well-being. Her presence alone was oftentimes enough to make him feel a little foolish, and that probably didn't help him out much, either. Sometimes, she just made it really hard to think straight.

He loved her more than he loved anything else, and that was more than just a token thought. He hoped that he wouldn't have to, but he'd die for her, if it came to that. She made him forget about the stress of his job. She made every aspect of his life a little more appealing. Even though he couldn't stop thinking about what his father had told him the other night—he was virtually plagued by the thought of it—to some extent, she managed to make even that easier.

His appetite dwindled and died out altogether at the thought of it. He set his utensils down and stared off into the busy street outside, overcome by an intense, broody contemplativeness. His persistent and now seemingly related dreams had never ceased. Every night, when he closed his eyes to sleep, he found himself trapped inside another person's body, another person's mind.

Daniel MacBride, his nocturnal host, was a curious youth whose very life seemed anchored in tragedy. The young boy was usually the focal point of the dreams, and the lingering thoughts he woke with were his, for the most part. At best, those thoughts were chaotic and confusing.

Curiously, he also perceived the thoughts of most of the other characters that cropped up in his dreams. Or at least snippets of them. Occasionally, he saw segments of the dreams through their eyes. When this happened, it felt like his conscience was split in two. A part of him left this Daniel character to latch onto the newcomer's mind, while the other part of him remained behind. These double perspectives were almost always precursory to a migraine, and even if he was just dreaming, the headaches felt real enough to him. That might explain why he didn't remember the split segments of dreams quite as well as he remembered everything else. Maybe.

He had a strong feeling that the cause of the dreams would forever elude him and remain a mystery. One thing he *was* certain of was that he'd never heard of anyone else experiencing anything even remotely like this. He'd heard of recurring dreams before, but dreams, even recurring, were *never* so linear. It wasn't natural... normal. There *had* to be a reason for all of it, an explanation, but what that was, he just couldn't say.

"Why do you suppose he waited until now to tell me the truth?" he asked her, glancing up slowly as though suddenly waking from a trance.

"I know this isn't easy for you," Vanessa said, smiling faintly, "but please don't stress yourself out over it. I'm not complaining—trust me, I'm not—but you've been bringing this up for days now, and you get so sad when you set your mind to it that it hurts just to see you this way. I want to see you *smile* tonight, Franky. I really do. We're supposed to be celebrating."

"I know," Frank sighed, shaking his head a little, "and I'm sorry—really, I am—but I can't help it. Why do you think he waited until now? He could have told me at any time, but he didn't, and not knowing why is eating me up inside. I can't help but wonder what else he and my mother have been hiding from me, what other terrible secrets they might have."

"I wish I knew what to tell you," Vanessa replied, frowning commiseratively. "Maybe *this* right here is why they didn't tell you in the first place." She placed her hands over his and leaned in closer to look him in the eyes. "Seriously," she sighed, "just look at how you're taking this. Do you think it would have been any easier if they'd told you when you were younger? Or would it have been *that* much harder to go through life knowing that you were adopted? Your parents *love* you, Franky. They wanted to protect you. They *still* want to protect you. If you ask me, that's all that really matters, isn't it?"

Despite the growing uncertainty gnawing away at him, Frank considered her words briefly and acquiesced. "You're probably right," he conceded, though he wasn't sure he believed it. "I'm probably just worrying over nothing." But was he *really*? Very little of what his father had told him had made any sense at all. It was a shock, to say the least, but he was sure that he'd feel better about it if he knew the whole truth in its integrality.

"Of course you are," Vanessa stated matter-of-factly. "Now cheer up." She sipped at her glass of white wine then and added, "Or I'm going to have to get you crazy drunk."

"I'm not sure I could stop you if you tried," Frank jested, trying his best to smile. His poor attempt was good enough for Vanessa. She'd already poured him a glass of wine and was in the process of refilling her own.

Maybe a few drinks *would* make him feel better, and help him forget about this adoption business for a while. Strangely enough, even though he'd been the one to bring it up in the first place, he didn't want to talk about it anymore. He could rack his brain till the sun stood still; it would get him absolutely nowhere. It was too frustrating, too *depressing*, and Vanessa was right, after all; this was supposed to be a celebration of sorts. Moping wouldn't help anything, even if he did feel like he was neglecting something important. He smiled weakly then and accepted the glass that Vanessa handed him, shrugging off his negative thoughts to offer her his full attention.

"To you," Vanessa proudly stated, holding her glass out.

"To us," Frank added, gingerly tapping his own glass against hers. He took a sip of his wine then, or tried to, at least. He was more of a gulper, but he did do his best to refrain. He was no sommelier, but he could recognize a Riesling when he tasted one. This one had a dry, somewhat sweet flavor to it, with an aroma not unlike that of lanolin. There were notes of peach, and lemon, and something he could only describe as gasoline. He turned the bottle around then to read the label. It was an Edelfäule on the Wall. He'd never heard of it before, but it went down well and it didn't taste half bad.

His premonition had been correct. A few drinks later, he was feeling a little tingly inside. He wasn't as *crazy drunk* as Vanessa might have hoped for, but he felt a little light-headed nonetheless. *If I drink just a little more,* he thought, grinning foolishly, *I'll be laughing off my rocker. Or crying like a moody little schoolgirl.* Getting drunk usually had one of two effects on him: ridiculously over-the-top and inexplicable happiness, or overwhelming sadness. It was often one extreme or the other with him, and he didn't feel like making a fool of himself, especially not tonight.

Frank William Fasaro knew how and when to say *no*. He didn't really like getting into an alcohol-induced stupor, anyway. He much rather preferred the mundane joys of reality perceived through sober eyes and with a keen mind. Getting completely smashed just didn't seem worthwhile to him.

He was fairly certain that the average Joe would disagree with him, but as far as he was concerned, being drunk was very much like being sick. It wasn't that he didn't enjoy laughing like an idiot every now and then, but just as with disease, he always valued *"normal"* that much more once the grueling nausea had worn off. Sometimes, people failed to realize just how good things were until they lost them. Prime examples of these, in his opinion, were a cool head and self-control.

"I couldn't eat another bite if I wanted to," Vanessa moaned, setting her fork down with a thump. "I feel like I'm going to pop." She flicked her hair over her shoulder then, leaned back in her chair, and exhaled noisily.

Frank grinned widely and shook his head a little, briskly stroking his chin through the rough, reddish five o'clock shadow that he'd once again "forgotten" to shave off. He didn't feel like he had time for that kind of thing lately, or more accurately, he just didn't *feel* like doing it. "Believe it or not," he teased, "I couldn't eat another bite either. Oh, I'm just as famished as I was the second we walked in here, but that stocky-looking guy near the door to the kitchen keeps giving me the evil eye. I think he might kick me out if I go back for more."

"And I wouldn't blame him," Vanessa laughed. "You eat like a pig. I don't know how you do it. If I even *thought* about eating half as much as you *usually* do, I'd look like a beluga, and have all kinds of loose blubber to spare."

"You?" Frank gasped in mock astonishment. "A beluga? Well, I would hardly say that, Vanessa, though I'm sure you'd make for a perfectly adorable one, if you were. Yeah, I could picture it. Beady little eyes. A short beak. Melon-shaped head. Turning all the man-whale heads your way. Luckily for me, I don't have to worry about getting crushed to death by any jealous man-whales, because my girlfriend's human. And the most beautiful, sexiest one in the city, at that."

"You're such a try-hard," Vanessa groaned emphatically, the annoyance in her tone lacking any real conviction. She always loved it when he complimented her, even when he did so in an excessively cheesy way. She could try to hide it all she wanted. It wouldn't work. No matter how much she appreciated his attention, he usually managed to embarrass her somehow, leaving her blushing and bashful. "It almost sounds like you're trying to flirt with me," she added in a playful, teasing way, shyly glancing at him through her lustrous mane of dark hair, which had unfurled down the sides of her face as she'd lowered her head. "Charming."

"I wasn't sure that's what I was doing," Frank said, beginning to blush a little himself, "but hey, if it works..." He grinned widely then and looked down. He felt oddly shy all of a sudden. His heart felt like it was overclocked. Beads of sweat were starting to form on his forehead. He exhaled slowly, mustered up all the courage he could find and looked up, the faint trace of mischief disappearing from his eyes, replaced by a look of utter seriousness. He hadn't exactly *planned* on doing this—not as a segue to belugas—but the moment felt about as right as any other.

"Vanessa, I'm really lucky to have you," he whispered loudly, "and I don't know if I could ever tell you that enough." For a moment, he was afraid he wouldn't find the words that he needed to go on, but as their eyes met, he found comfort in them, and the words started to flow more freely.

"I'm only being honest when I say that I'm more or less just the average Joe, but with you sitting across the table from me, I feel like a king among men. Every time I see you, I feel like I've won the monster of all jackpots, and I'm not just talking about the way you look. Don't get me wrong," he injected precipitously, "I really *like* the way that you look, but this is about so much more than just that. It's about love, Vanessa, and I am so grateful that I have yours. It's made me so happy. You've made me so happy. Life without you would be bland in the worst possible way. I'd get by, I suppose, but it would all seem pretty meaningless. Every day with you feels almost surreal."

He felt a sudden wave of nervous incoherence washing over him, but gathered himself in the depths of her eyes and pressed on. "No matter how hard life can get at times, you always know exactly what to say or what to do to pick me up and keep me going, and that's something that I can't imagine living without. Not anymore. Sometimes I feel like you know me better than I know myself. You're funny, smart, caring, beautiful, and I could go on like this for a while. You make me feel alive, Vanessa, really and truly alive. Without you I'd just be *living*, day by dreary day. It wouldn't matter what I did or what I accomplished: it would all be meaningless. You give it all a reason, Vanessa. You give *me* a reason—not just to live, but for everything I do."

The stunned look on Vanessa's face didn't exactly inspire confidence, but it was too late to back down now. "I really wish I knew how to tell you just how much I love you," he sighed, reaching across the table to take her hands in his own. "I wish I could just lay my heart out before you and make you understand how much you mean to me, but you know that I've never been good with words. Whenever I try to talk about my feelings, my thoughts get all jumbled up and everything comes out wrong."

Feeling helpless before her continued silence, he stared into her eyes for what seemed like a very long time before adding, "We've been living together for three years now... three *wonderful* years. I suppose I was a little bit wary about it, at first, a little unsure about the future, but those days of uncertainty are over."

Breaking from her apparent state of inertia, Vanessa brought her hands up and cupped them over her mouth. The delighted look in her eyes more than hinted at the strong emotions she felt washing over her. Though unvoiced, the questions she was asking herself might as well have been written in big, bold letters in a thought bubble floating above her head. Is he saying what I think he's saying? Is he really going to ask? Her thoughts were an open book for anyone nearby to read.

Emboldened by her reaction, Frank gained in assurance and continued on with more fervor. "You're my best friend, Vanessa. You're always there for me when I need you, no matter what. When I'm sick, you nurture me back to health. When I've had a really bad day, you're kind, and funny, and uplifting. When I've just had enough of everything, you're patient, and generous, and forgiving. You're all of these things and more, and I could never have asked for a better person to share my life with."

His emotions were astir at the sight of Vanessa's glistening eyes, and he was hard-pressed to hold back the tears he felt welling up in his own. Clearing his throat, he took a moment to regain his composure, then knelt beside her. "Vanessa," he said, looking up into her eyes, "will you be my wife?"

He reeled and nearly fell back as Vanessa leapt from her chair and grappled him in a fierce embrace. Though he'd hoped for a similar reaction, he hadn't exactly expected it, and it caught him completely off guard.

"Yes!" she cried out, squeezing him so hard that he could barely manage to breathe.

"Yes?" Frank asked, though he wasn't sure why. He'd clearly heard what she'd said. Maybe his nerves were to blame. Despite having lived together for years, the prospect of engagement had always been a sensitive issue for him, not because he was afraid of commitment, but because he wanted this moment to be perfect for Vanessa. Maybe it was because he was so happy he just couldn't believe it. It didn't really matter either way. He knew what her answer had been. Deep down, he'd always known what it would be, but that hadn't made it any easier.

"Yes!" Vanessa repeated, gushing. "Of course I'll marry you, you big lummox! Now shut up and kiss me!"

Frank was more than happy to oblige her. Wasting no time, propelled by an overwhelming sense of blissful delight, he took her head in his hands and kissed her then—a strong, passionate kiss—down on his knees in the middle of the restaurant floor.

When their lips finally parted, they looked at each for a few seconds before breaking into a collective fit of elated laughter. He realized that they were making quite the scene, even more so when a few of the other patrons started to clap, but he didn't care. He'd never been so happy before in his entire life.

CHAPTER
11

Probable Cause

Leonard glanced at his watch reflexively and muttered a few incoherent words under his breath. Sometimes when he was nervous or upset, some of the background chatter in his mind leaked out into the ether, and he was barely even aware it was happening, let alone conscious of what he was saying. He was just too caught up in his thoughts to focus on anything else. If he knew himself at all, with the torrential shitstorm currently splattering up the inside of his skull, he'd likely said something that most people would consider vulgar or wildly inappropriate. Or both.

He did a quick once-over of Frank's living room and glanced at the three officers that accompanied him before returning his gaze to the streets below, careful to remain concealed behind a narrow slit in the blinds as he did. It was a futile exercise, he knew, but it gave him something to do while they waited.

The guys beside him were on lease from Special Assignments, and their rapid deployment order had come from the commissioner himself, apparently. It was an unexpected but welcome gesture on his part, especially in light of the current shortage of manpower. Old Chucklehead had to get it right sometimes, he supposed. The borrowed guns were about as talkative as a rotting corpse, but he wasn't really in the mood for chitchat any-fucking-way.

As tough as his hide was, the current situation had torn his perception of things asunder, and he preferred to obsess over the task at hand. The operation he was running had been planned by the book. The extra men had given him the leeway to do that. He just hoped that it would be enough. Frank was a dangerous man—more so than he'd ever imagined.

The SAU officers were all decked out in blackened Kevlar body armor. They were experts in close quarters combat and tactical maneuvers. He had two spotters from his own precinct outside, ready to signal when Frank arrived. Two more men on the inside would help cut off his retreat in the unlikely event that the ambush failed and he tried to make an escape.

Everyone had assured him that it would be enough, that he was under no obligation to be there himself, but he insisted on participating anyway. He understood their point of view, but found it about as appealing as a steaming pile of turd. There were other, similar operations running simultaneously to their own. All of the officers that had been linked to the Awoken by that anonymous package he'd received were going to be taken into custody at the same time, or as close to it as possible. At least that was the plan. That way, they wouldn't be able to warn their leaders or each other once the shit hit the fan.

His role was supposed to be one of organization. He was the *captain*, for fuck's sake. He didn't *have* to get his hands dirty. He didn't *have* to, but he would. He felt responsible, somehow. He'd given Frank undue priority for years, thinking he was something he wasn't. After spending so much time around him, he'd almost come to think of the kid as his own. *Almost? Bullshit.* That was how flawless the dirty little rat's infiltration had been. At first, that had really gotten in the way of his judgment, but not anymore. *Now*, he was ready to face him and the rest of the Awoken, if it came to that, and he would not hesitate to use lethal force if he had to.

It broke his heart. Really, it did. Even with the cold hard truth shoved so far down his throat that it made it hard to breathe and upset his stomach, he just didn't want it to be true. It almost made him feel like puking, but he couldn't let that get in his way.

What would he look like to the rest of the agency if he didn't see this thing through? What would the men under his command think of him? What would the *city* do with the captain that had let a proven criminal slip away without consequence? And not just any criminal, but a traitor of the worst kind, one that had been in his service just a short while ago.

He had to make an example out of Frank and the others, had to make them pay for every one of their crimes against humanity, even if it kept him up at night. If it had been just his own ass on the line, things might have played out differently, but it wasn't his ass, and he had no other choice. He had to do what he had to do, or there would be hell to pay.

"Alpha One, reporting in," said the voice of Lieutenant Caldwell over the portable radio that was strapped to Leonard's shoulder. The lieutenant's words were clear and carried well despite the faint crackles and screeches of the radio. Leonard had been given the chance to have one of those communications doohickeys grafted to the inside of his ear canal a few years back, but he'd turned the offer down categorically. The technology was superior to anything else, apparently, but he was no technology dweeb, and he refused to be a guinea pig. "Looks like Fasaro's vehicle pulling around the corner," Caldwell continued. "Will advise."

Leonard's breath caught. The rest of the team stopped what they were doing—namely cleaning, dismantling and reassembling their gear—and turned their attention to the radio. Their eyes were riveted on it like it was a ticking time bomb, ready to go off at any second.

"Yeah," Caldwell breathed, breaking the silence, "that's him all right. Do you want us to engage now? We have a clear visual and positive identification."

Leonard pressed one of the buttons on the topside of the radio, and turned his head to speak into it. "Absolutely not," he answered in a huff, the urgency in his voice apparent. "Not unless you want to spend the next two weeks having my boot surgically removed from your ass, Alpha One. You stick to the plan, you little cock weasel, or so help me, I'll gladly give up a boot. Do I make myself perfectly fucking clear, Lieutenant Clusterfuck?"

"Crystal clear," Caldwell answered, unfazed by the captain's livid reaction. "Alpha One standing down."

When you reported to the likes of Captain Leonard Boston, you either grew a thick skin or got out fast. As far as Leonard was concerned, Caldwell was a good man, if a little too enthusiastic at times, and his skin had grown nice and hard. He could take it. He was impervious to the almost daily insults that he threw his way.

"The vehicle has come to a stop," Caldwell said. "Stand by."

Another lapse of tense radio silence ensued. The living room seemed like it was completely devoid of sound, except for that of the radio's faint, static crackling.

Finally, after what felt like an eternity to Leonard, Caldwell spoke again. "He's exiting the vehicle now," he said, trailing off. "There's someone with him, but I can't get a clear visual. Light build, possibly female." A few seconds later he warned, "Careful, Gamma Two. It looks like they're coming in the side door, right next to your position."

"Roger that, Alpha One," Sergeant Bedford replied, his voice cool, calm and serious. "Going ghost."

"Yeah, you better be," Leonard grumbled under his breath. His heart felt like it was lodged in his throat. The play-by-play color commentary wasn't helping his nerves one bit. More than anything, he was impatient for this fiasco to be done and over with. "Into position, Bravo team," he barked, waving the men off to their predetermined hidey-holes.

He took his own place around the corner from the condo's front entrance, just out of sight of the others, then fished a bottle of liquid antacid out of his inner coat pocket. "Fuck my life," he groaned angrily, then screwed the cap off and chugged down the last half of it.

"They're on their way up now, Captain," Bedford whispered loudly. "Gamma One and Alpha Team, close in and secure the ground-level perimeter."

"Be careful, Gamma Two," Leonard breathed into the radio. "I want radio silence from here on in." He screwed the cap back onto the empty medicine bottle, tossed it over his shoulder, and wiped the residue from his lips with the sleeve of his coat. "This is it, boys," he called out to the other men in the room with him. "If you don't fuck this up, you'll be up for commendations. If you do, you'll never live it down, if you're even alive to hear about it. So let's try not to fuck this up."

CHAPTER
12

Surprise Party

Frank's elbow bumped against the elevator's keypad for the third time in just as many minutes. They'd stopped on four floors and had accidentally queued up a few others, but they didn't care, even if they lived on the twenty-fourth. They were too enthralled by their amorous shuffle to even notice.

It was getting harder and harder to keep his balance under the constant assault of groping hugs and feverish kisses. It was a dance that he'd never had the chance to practice inside of a rickety old elevator, let alone master. The steps got all the more difficult to keep up with when the clothes started coming off. With his shirt unbuttoned and pulled back over his shoulders, his belt undone and trousers starting to slip loose, they jolted and plonked against the wall every time the elevator buckled unexpectedly.

Public displays of affection weren't exactly Frank's thing—at least not when they were considered indecent exposure or lewd conduct, they weren't—but he just couldn't resist Vanessa, and she was on him like white on rice. He didn't have the will *or* the desire to wait until they got back to the privacy of their own home, behind closed doors.

If Vanessa's flattering comments could be trusted, then his performance in the bedroom was nothing to smirk at, but he'd rarely felt this enamored or impassioned before. He felt driven by something stronger than himself, and he liked the effect that it was having on her. Controlling his urges seemed like a pointless and even counterproductive endeavor. His only current regret was that she was wearing a lot more layers than he was, and that was something that he planned on remedying in the near future.

When the elevator finally reached their floor, they were still having at each other like a pair of love-drunk teens at the after-prom. Neither of them noticed the prominent ding of the elevator bell. Consequently, the door slid open and they stumbled clumsily into the hall. Clutching at each other's clothes—the fact that they were still on was an anomaly all on its own—they paused, looked each other in the eyes and laughed blithely.

Ever the ambitious one, Vanessa took him by the hand and led him the rest of the short way to their condo. One of their neighbors—a frail, elderly woman with more wrinkles on her face than a crumpled ball of tinfoil—opened her door as they passed her by, and gasped loudly before slamming it shut again. This triggered another wave of laughter from the both of them. Mrs. Appleby would probably be waiting for him with a can of pepper spray the next time he offered to take out her trash.

After stopping in front of their door, Frank took Vanessa's free hand and spun her around, bringing her face to face with him. He let his hands fall to her hips and pulled her in close, then kissed her slowly one last time before producing a key from his pocket and sliding it into the lock. "I want you so much right now," he whispered, then pushed the door open and led her by the hand as he walked through. Despite his keen senses, for all of his training, nothing could have prepared him for what came next.

Vanessa was still closing the door behind them when Frank noticed a subtle movement from the corner of his eye. Before he could so much as turn around, a pair of gloved hands shot out from behind his head and wrapped around his nose and mouth, cutting his breath off almost completely.

Almost immediately afterward, a man in blackened body armor moved in and grabbed Vanessa by the arm. He pressed a stunner to her abdomen and discharged it, which sent her sprawling to the floor like a limp noodle.

A strong dose of adrenaline coursed through Frank's veins as he watched her go down. He tried to scream out in anger, only to find that his voice was muffled by the leather gloves that were smothering his face.

Struggling wildly, he wriggled his head around and managed to loosen the stranglehold just enough that it allowed him to close his mouth on one of his assailants' hands. He bit down as hard as he could, but his aggressor's only reaction was to retighten his grip. The glove's thin plates of armor coupled with the rigid hide that they were grafted to left the man's fingers unscathed, but his teeth were sore all the way through to his jaw.

With the second man lunging toward him stunner in hand, he waited for him to close, then kicked out in a last-ditch effort to avoid electrocution. His right foot shot out and struck the top of the man's hand, which sent the stunner skittering across the floor. Leaving him little time to recover, he grabbed onto his strangler's clenched forearms for leverage, and launched his feet straight into the other guy's abdomen. Caught off guard by the strength of the blow, the second man groaned loudly, and staggered through the front door before falling flat on his back.

Fueled by a near panic-leveled fear for Vanessa's well-being, he balled his fists and brought his elbows crashing down into his aggressor's ribs once, twice, a third time, but without result. Never relenting, he swung his elbows out again, and they finally found a gap in the man's plated vest.

A pained grunt heralded the loosening of the man's grip on Frank's head. The slipup was only momentary, but he'd felt the change, and it was all that he needed to turn the situation around.

He spun about and grabbed his assailant by the vest, still entangled in those powerful arms that wanted to hedge him in, but lacked the coordination to do so. First, he yanked at the man's heavy body armor, pulling him one way, then, while his feet were busy trying to keep up, he put the brakes on and shoved him hard in the other direction. The man lost his grip on him completely and went crashing into the open closet.

Frank turned and looked down at Vanessa, who was splayed out on the floor like an old rag doll. Her breathing sounded a little more labored, a little harsher than usual, but the rise and fall of her chest indicated that she was still all right. Chances were she was off in la-la land, he figured, dreaming hazy dreams of purple puppies and giant poppy flower seeds.

His eyes darted toward the sound of wheezing coming from the hall, past the front door. The man that had stunned Vanessa had pushed himself up on all fours, and was staring down at the floor beneath him.

In a moment of vengeful fury, Frank scanned the floor and quickly found the stunner he'd used on her. Grimacing, he picked it up, walked out the front door, and knelt by the struggling man. "You ever gotten a good jolt from one of these babies at maximum voltage?" he asked, seething. "It's kind of unfair for you that you have to use it on others when you haven't even had the chance to experience it yourself. Wouldn't you say?" He pressed the stunner to the man's jugular then and added, "How about I give you a taste of this thing right here, right now? Huh? Just a little one. What do you say, Sparky? You want a taste?"

He wasn't used to this much emotion bubbling over, and it almost got the better of him. He wanted to discharge the stunner into the guy's neck. He *really* wanted to. He wanted to make him suffer for what he'd done. He wanted to, but he knew that it could be fatal. Killing a criminal in the heat of action was one thing, but killing him when he was down—killing him in cold blood—that was something else entirely, and he was no murderer.

Following his better judgment—if a little begrudgingly—he slipped the stunner into his pants pocket and decided to kick the man in the gut, instead. The guy grunted hoarsely on impact and rolled into the fetal position.

"You stay down until the police get here," Frank hissed, "or you can be damn sure there'll be more where that came from." The man didn't answer, but he wasn't really expecting him to. It was probably for the best. He was seeing a volatile side of himself that he didn't like. When Vanessa was in danger, it appeared, it was difficult to remain in control. If the guy had given him sass, he'd have been hard-pressed not to kick him in the teeth. He might not have, but the thought had already crossed his mind.

He glanced down the hall to the left, following a faint noise that he'd heard coming from that direction. At least, he could have sworn that he'd heard something, but there was only silence now, except for the sound of his own breathing. He shot another look down toward the right end of the hall as he heard the noise again, more distinctly. It was the sound of footfall. Yes, it was the sound of feet stepping lightly in a stealthy and barely audible run. It was coming from both directions now, ever more clearly. Could it be the police, he wondered. No, he hadn't called anyone at the agency yet. The situation was eerily familiar, like something right out of his dreams.

When the sound of running reached the stairwells at both ends of the hall, he decided to duck inside of his condo to call for help. Vanessa was still lying there in the entrance, unconscious and breathing in a heavy rasp. The pair of legs protruding from the closet door suggested that the second assailant was still down for the count. Furrowing his brow, he pushed back the sleeve of his shirt, activated his communications band, and waited for the static sound that signaled connection, but there was nothing. He waited a full ten seconds, and still, nothing. In all his time in the agency, his comms equipment had never malfunctioned—not even once. He tried again, but got more of the same.

It was practically impossible and at the very least extremely untimely that his CB should fail him now. These simple devices were made to take a beating. They were designed to withstand much harsher punishment than they usually received, and saw very regular maintenance. It was almost like the signal was being blocked deliberately, but by who or why he couldn't say.

Something he saw then made his jaw drop, and the truth struck him suddenly like a ton of bricks. He crouched down by the sprawled-out husk of his dozing adversary and stared fixedly, his mouth hanging ajar as though the muscles in his face had gone completely numb.

The men's gear and their armored clothing looked more than just familiar. It had been aesthetically modified, to a certain extent, but he knew exactly where it had come from. Only one place manufactured equipment like that, and only one organization was authorized to use it: the LEA. These guys were most likely with Special Assignments. It would explain the modifications. It made no sense whatsoever, but it was the only explanation he could think of. It made him feel sick to his stomach. Why would the agency do this? He was a little lazy in the morning sometimes, but aside from that, he was a good cop, and he knew it.

It had to be some kind of mistake. He knew that he'd done nothing to warrant anything even remotely like this. Reluctant, he pushed himself to his feet with some difficulty. The reality of the situation had shaken him to his core. There had to be something that he could do. They had to listen to him if he tried to explain himself, didn't they?

The truth of it was that they didn't, and he knew it. The SAU was an executioner, not a negotiator. Its agents followed orders and they followed them well. So well that they hardly *ever* made mistakes. If someone had designated him as a target, he could forget about trying to explain anything to anyone. They wouldn't stop until he was dead or in custody, depending on the nature of their orders. Considering the brutality of their approach so far, his only chance at getting out of this—*their* only chance at getting out of this—was to run; to run fast and run far. Clarifications would have to wait until later.

To his greatest dismay, there were two problems with his two-point plan. First, he wouldn't be able to move very fast with Vanessa in her current condition. Second, even if he did manage to carry her out somehow, there just wasn't very far to run to.

He was so perplexed by their predicament that he hadn't even noticed the wailing sirens of the approaching backup units. He did, however, turn his head at the intermittent flashes of red and blue that lit up the living room like a Founder's Day light show.

So they have the building surrounded, he thought. *That was fast.* He took a moment to analyze the situation and digest what it meant for them. Obviously, escape was out of the question. There was no way that he could sneak past all of those police officers with Vanessa slung over his shoulder. He walked over to where she was lying and knelt beside her, a resigned air of defeat hanging over him like a shroud.

I could stay, he thought, brushing a lock of hair from her eyes, *and fight*. He'd already beaten two of them down and had hardly broken a sweat. Maybe they weren't as tough as everyone made them out to be. Maybe they were just *Joe Anybodies*—run of the mill cops like a lot of the guys that he'd worked with in the past— drafted into service that they were or weren't ready for, whether they liked the idea or not. Not everyone had been willing to volunteer like he had, he knew.

That was nonsense all across the board and he knew it. The men and women of the Special Assignments Units were the best the agency had to offer. Fighting them head-on in a *last-standish* faceoff was ridiculous and out of the question for more than just one reason. Just trying would be like something right out of a really bad action movie.

First and foremost, he was an officer of the law, whatever the agency thought of him right now. He'd spent most of his adult life serving and protecting the people of Innerstadt as best he could. Getting to where he was in his career had been a challenging and lengthy process requiring reams of hard work and determination.

If he fought back, he'd be giving them probable cause. He'd be tossing away everything that he'd worked so hard to achieve. His values, his work ethic, none of it would mean anything. He'd be no better than any of the criminals he'd helped put away.

He hadn't thought about it earlier, but the arrival of the other police units offered another possibility: surrender. For obvious reasons, he couldn't do that with SAU. He'd most likely end up dead if he tried. With a little luck—okay, with a *lot* of luck—he could turn himself in to the regular forces. At least that way he might avoid bloodshed. If he succeeded, his fate would be in the captain's hands, and there was no one he trusted more with his life than Captain Leonard Boston.

His greatest challenge would be getting outside. The agency would probably form a perimeter and sit tight, and he didn't want to risk an encounter with SAU while he sat around waiting for them to come in and get him. He was concerned about leaving Vanessa behind, but it would probably be best if he did.

The police couldn't possibly be after her. As far as he knew, she'd never done anything wrong in her life. They'd probably only neutralized her because she was with him. It wasn't like he could do much for her if he stayed, anyway. In fact, the closer he stayed to her, the more danger she'd be in. He was sure of it. It still pinched his heart and made him feel like a worthless sack of shit to just leave her there, but his mind was made up. If he pulled this off, everything would sort itself out. He had to believe that the captain would make sure of that.

Glancing toward the doorway, he quickly took stock of the situation and decided on the best course of action. The quickest way out wasn't necessarily the best. Going down the fire escape would get him to the ground in a couple minutes at most, but taking it would leave him open the entire time, and it would only get worse as he neared the street. They would probably have sharpshooters covering the windows by now, so it would be best to avoid open areas altogether.

There was another option. It seemed a little ridiculous, he knew, but it was still worth trying, even if he couldn't be sure it would work. In the past, he'd often noted—sometimes with disgust—that the walls in the bedroom were paper thin. One day, while he'd been rummaging through the junk in the back of their closet for some knickknack or another, his neighbors had started up with their weekly vociferations, and the sound of it was so clear that he could have sworn he was standing right next to them.

Moving some boxes around had lit the closet up with a faint glow as he'd uncovered a weaker part of the wall where the plaster was cracked and falling off in chunks. As he remembered it, he could have put his foot right through that wall with relative ease. He'd planned on having it repaired, but luckily for him, he'd never gotten around to doing it. He wasn't sure what the rest of his plan was yet, but busting through the wall into the next apartment over was as good of a place to start as any.

Wasting no more of what little time remained, he slammed the front door shut and slid the deadbolt into place, then knelt and carefully pulled Vanessa off to the side. Whatever happened, he didn't want her to get trampled when they blasted through the door and stormed into the condo.

The sound of footfall had drawn closer, and had grown from a stealthy jog to an all-out stampede. They must have realized that there was no point in sneaking around when he'd slammed the door. They knew that he was onto them now. He looked at Vanessa one last time—lovingly, longingly—then pulled his eyes away and headed for the bedroom at a sprint.

As he darted into the living room, he saw something swing toward him in his peripheral vision. He tried to avoid it, but it was already too late. A loud *thwack* resounded inside his skull, his vision flashed white, and an intense pain exploded in his head.

He felt his body go limp, and when his vision returned to normal a second later, he was lying on the floor. A burly SAU officer stood grinning down at him in his dark uniform. The man was holding an assault rifle by the cannon, and had it slung over his shoulder like a baseball bat.

Standing off to the side and somewhat behind him was the captain. He could hardly believe his eyes. He wasn't sure that he wanted to. Had he come to help him, he wondered, or had he come *for* him? His thoughts were too jumbled by the searing pain to tell. He reached out to him briefly, and then his hand fell to the floor as darkness engulfed him.

CHAPTER
13

Down in the Dumps

Jerg took a long, hard look at himself in the bathroom mirror. For the first time in years, he'd foregone shaving long enough to have a noticeable five-o'clock shadow. The dark circles under his eyes betrayed a moderate case of sleep deprivation. If he'd had any hair at all, he'd have left it unwashed and disheveled.

It had been two whole days since the commissioner had "transferred" him away from his position under duress, two long days during which he'd been at odds with his colleagues, with the organization, and even with himself.

Things might not have seemed quite as bad as they did if he hadn't been so tired all the time. During the day, it was a constant battle just to stay awake. At night, there was no finding sleep. His eyes were heavy, and at times they stung so much that he found them welling up with tears. Whether it was really the case or not, he felt like he was getting a little crazier with every passing hour.

He'd lost all interest in his performance the second the commissioner had tossed him aside like a piece of trash in favor of that walking cyber surgery ad, Langsarks. He'd always been assiduous in his work—*always*—but he was finding it nigh on impossible to motivate himself now. He'd even called in "unfit to work". He couldn't remember when the last time he'd done that was, possibly because it had never happened before.

For a while—sometime after Langsarks had stolen his job, the rotten weasel—he'd convinced himself that it would be in his best interest to remain loyal to the organization, to do whatever it was they needed of him. But the more he thought about it, the more he played everything over again in his mind, the angrier it made him.

He had absolutely no interest in participating in the applied sciences aspect of the Commission's operations, and he'd be surprised if he could find even one person that didn't already know it. *Psionics,* he thought, in a sour mood. *Pshaw! Reporting to someone young enough to be my child!* He *could* do it. He *would* have done it if there had been an actual *need* for it, and if the commissioner had shown even a minimum of appreciation for his past services. But he wouldn't do it now. Not for all the money in the city's coffers.

As far as he was concerned, he'd been grievously wronged. Why would he cooperate? He'd been spited, unfairly demoted. He was so insulted that he'd considered taking an early retirement. After sleepless hours of nocturnal deliberation, he'd decided that leaving would equate to giving up, and he was not a quitter. He would *not* give any of his "colleagues" the satisfaction of seeing him go that route. If anything, he'd stick around just to be a thorn in the sides of those that got on his nerves, and there were more than just a few of those. In fact, that included just about everyone, so he was going to have his work cut out for him.

His thoughts turned to Doctor Munro then. In some twisted way, he was glad that he wasn't the only one to suffer. Misery *did* love company, as they said. On the other hand, he was genuinely sympathetic to the doctor's plight.

Munro might not have lost his job, but he'd soon be losing a project that he'd been pouring his soul into for the greater part of two decades. It was his first major assignment at the Commission, and one of the first undertakings of its kind. It had been almost entirely his idea to begin with. In a way, losing it would most likely feel like he was losing his job.

If the same thing had happened to anyone else, he wouldn't have given a rat's behind, but this was different somehow. Doctor Munro happened to be a halfway decent person. Sure, he got into about as many quarrels with him as he did with anyone else, but Munro never questioned his intellectual capacity. While everyone else criticized him over his alleged incompetency, the only thing Munro ever reproached of him was his bad manners, and he could live with that, because it was a valid point. He *was* rude when he wanted to be. He *did* have bad manners. He knew it full well, and he didn't expect anyone to appreciate it.

If there was one person at the Commission that he could think of as an ally, one voice of reason in this mess of demented geniuses, it was Doctor Edward Munro. He'd never considered him a friend, per se, but he was the closest thing to one that he had.

Sure, most of the sentinels were loyal, some a little too devotedly for his taste, but it wasn't the same. The men under his command—the men under his *previous* command, he reminded himself—were all either aspiring or recycled lawmen. They were drawn to the weight that his name carried in law enforcement circles like flies were to a bloated corpse.

There wasn't a single one of them that didn't want to shake hands with the living legend that had influenced the Academy's curriculum in such a glorious way. He'd almost singlehandedly rewritten the agency's method of operation. Following fifty years of methodical stagnancy, his accomplishments were unparalleled. Absolutely everyone wanted to meet the author of such and such textbook on combat or illicit substances or suspect identification. They all wanted to gain his favor, and could he really blame them? As far as they knew, he had important ties and could help advance their careers. The people that held him in highest regard would do anything for him, but only because they wanted to use him. Such was the price of brilliance, he supposed.

Men like those made the very best lackeys. They were always happy to get the job done. If he wanted it, he could have an army of devout followers at his beck and call. His status had its fair share of advantages, but the sad reality of the situation was that he couldn't confide in any of his old subordinates. He couldn't speak to them as equals. They just wouldn't understand. They *couldn't* understand. But Munro did. He was his only outlet.

Rubbing the tired from his eyes for about the umpteenth time, he decided that it was time to quit moping around and go share his misery with another human being. It had never been in his nature to complain, but with everything else in his life spiraling out of control, he knew that venting his frustration would make him feel at least a little better.

With an inkling of regret, he eyed the stubble on his chin one last time before picking up his razor. He'd started to fancy the look. It made him feel like a bit of a rebel. As fitting as it was in his current state of mind, he'd be in good company, and knew that he should at least try to look presentable. He finished his late-morning grooming without dillydallying, threw on his long, white lab coat, and headed out the front door with renewed incentive.

CHAPTER
14

The Great Convolution

Edward rummaged through the clutter on his desk, muttering expletives mild enough to get him laughed at by a fourth grader. "Oh, hotdog," he grated, seething. "Where in the blue blazes did I put that fandangled thing?" He was starting to get particularly flustered when he finally found what he was looking for. "Ah!" he cried out triumphantly, both surprised and relieved. "Eureka!"

He held the folded document up and kissed it, then eyed it suggestively and added, "I'm *so* glad that I won't have to start *you* all over again," as though it could actually understand the words coming out of his mouth.

Never mind the fact that he could have gotten into serious trouble if the wrong person had stumbled on it and figured out what he was up to. He doubted it was incriminating enough to warrant sanctions all on its own, but if someone smart enough got hold of it, it could seriously hamper his plans. It could also link him to his crime after the fact, even if he *was* successful. He'd have to be far more careful in the future.

He laid his arm down on the edge of the table and swept it all the way across to the other side, spilling the mess of reports and loose spreadsheets onto the floor. Normally, he'd exercise a little more prudence with his work, but he didn't care about any of his other assignments anymore. They were all trivial next to the project that the Commission was trying to rip out from under him. Before long, they really wouldn't matter at all, regardless of the success or failure of his plan.

Stealing government property was a serious offense. Stealing *top secret* government property was far, far worse. Soon enough, he'd either be sitting behind bars in a squalid jail cell or gathering his own data—a whole new *wealth* of unexplored data—so he didn't much care what happened to the other junk he'd been producing for his superiors. Most of it was good for the garbage bin as far as he was concerned. He didn't have much use for rationalization and hogwash justifications.

He set the document down on his desk with care, unfolded it and smoothed out its deepest creases. At first glance, it looked like nothing more than a crude drawing some five-year-old would be extremely proud of. Art had never been his forte. Upon closer examination, one might have guessed that the crude drawing was a poorly penciled map of the Commission's facilities.

Drawn in thick grease pencil, wobbly lines depicted living quarters, corridors, boardrooms, and even the cafeteria. The big hamburger that he'd drawn in the middle of it had taken him nearly ten minutes to complete, and looked more like a bloated crab than it did anything else, now that he looked at it again. He'd used a variety of colored pens to delimit vents and ductwork that seemed to have been set without rhyme or reason.

The truth of the matter was that he hadn't had time to figure out where most of the ducts ran when he'd drawn the map the day before. In an effort to fill in the many gaps, he'd run a series of extrapolations and did some overly complicated math. After wasting a lot of time, it wasn't looking very good at all, so he just started guessing. Considering the importance of those ducts to the "escape" portion of his plan, things weren't boding well at all. As much as he'd like to go back and finish gathering accurate data, he was running out of time and was left with few options. He'd have to proceed on schedule, even if it meant going in half blind, which would hurt his chances of success to the Nth degree.

He realized that his plan was ridiculous at best, but it was the only one that he had, and he doubted he'd have time to come up with something better. He was a smart man, but this sneaking around business was well beyond him. This shortcoming would probably get him killed, but he couldn't turn back now. He wouldn't let the Commission get away with the destruction of his life's work. He *couldn't* let them. He was willing to die to prevent that, if need be, though he much preferred to stay alive, if possible.

He looked at the map for what seemed like a very long time, mulling over it carefully. His eyes eventually began to blur, but he continued staring blankly, almost as though in a trance. Maybe he'd missed something, he mused. Maybe there was something obvious here that he just wasn't seeing. Sometimes the best solutions were hiding in plain sight. "There has to be another way," he muttered, absentmindedly shaking his head from side to side. "There just has to be."

"There just has to be another way to what?" Jerg asked from directly over his shoulder, his head appearing suddenly in his peripheral vision as he leaned over him.

Edward nearly leapt from his chair, he was so startled, but he managed to snatch the map up and draw it in close to his chest, instead. He'd exercised all of the self-control that he had just to keep from yelping loudly. "You!" he snapped. "You're never going to learn, are you? For the love of Pete, Jerg! You scared the bejesus out of me."

Jerg laughed unexpectedly at that. It was a sudden, genuine feel-good laugh. "A little jumpy are we, Edward?" he asked, laughing once more for good measure.

Edward exhaled sharply, flustered. The surge of panic that had all but choked the breath from his lungs had flared up and died out like a flash fire. "Only when someone sneaks into my office and tries to give me a heart attack," he said, tipping his words with a little more acid than he'd intended to.

"Oh, come now," Jerg chuckled, patting him on the back. "You know that I'd never do that."

Edward gave him a long, hard look that oozed of blatant disbelief, but remained silent. He was far too busy trying to hide the map in the crook of his arm to give reply. He'd already thought about letting Jerg in on his little secret, but had since grown wary of the outcome of such a decision.

"I see that you're not convinced," Jerg remarked casually. "Regardless, you never answered my question."

"What question?" Edward asked, irritated.

Jerg sighed extensively before answering. "So you're deaf now too, old man. I said, 'There has to be another way to what?'"

It was Edward's turn to get an eyeballing this time, and the look that Jerg had in store for him spoke volumes. It wasn't cold or hard or even reproachful; it just said, "Are you daft?" He tried his best to think of something clever to say, but drew a complete blank. All that came was an awkward silence. He felt failure creeping up on him like a runny fart. If Jerg couldn't flare his unease, then the man didn't have half of the discernment that he thought he did.

Jerg rubbed at his barren scalp and laughed again. The sound of it was just as unexpected and alien to Edward as it had been the first time around. "Incredible!" Jerg exclaimed, shaking his head with disbelief. "Has anyone ever told you just how horrible you are at keeping secrets?"

A lump rose suddenly in Edward's throat. He was fairly certain that Jerg *was* onto him. He *could* just be messing with him or taking stabs at random. It wouldn't be unlike him. Either way, the situation was precarious, and all he could do was sit there and say nothing, frozen like a hare in the headlights, seconds before a dump truck splattered its entrails all over the road.

"You're not actually going to go through with it, are you?" Jerg asked him, sounding incredulous. "You'd be an idiot to try."

"Try what?" Edward managed to ask, his voice wavering.

"You know *exactly* what, Doctor Munro," Jerg responded firmly, though lacking any undertone of hostility. "I'm not stupid. I saw that little drawing of yours and understood what you were up to immediately. It's patently obvious, frankly."

Every muscle in Edward's body stiffened and locked up, and he started to sweat from places he never would have suspected. He imagined this was what rigor mortis might feel like if the mind went on after the body died.

"Oh, quit your fretting, Edward," Jerg pleaded, a rare look of concern touching his usually stolid features. "You look like you just saw a damned bloody ghost. It's not like I'm going to turn you in or something, is it?"

"It's... it's not?" Edward asked, blinking.

"No," Jerg calmly replied. "It's not."

Edward breathed a long, deep sigh of relief. He went over the situation briefly in his mind, then arched a bushy brow in Jerg's direction. "And why is it not?" he asked, very obviously confused. "Didn't you tell me *not* to try anything stupid the last time we spoke? This would probably qualify, I think."

Jerg cupped his chin between his thumb and his index finger and looked up contemplatively as he reflected back on it. "Why yes, yes I did," he answered. "But what I should have told you was to not try anything stupid *without* me. I've had a lot of time to think about what happened, and I don't see myself staying here and really *committing to* my work. Not after what they did to me. Not if I want to participate in the final stages of this research in any significant way. It's not like I owe the Commission anything anyway. In fact, I'd go so far as to say that they owe *us*. We practically did all of the groundwork that got this project started in the first place. But I digress. I want to participate in your work, Edward, and I won't take no for an answer."

Edward remained silent as he let what he'd just heard sink in. Though he'd originally intended on involving Jerg in his plans, his hopes of that actually coming to fruition had soured. At some point, he'd started having doubts about the doctor's reaction to his proposal. He'd all but dropped the idea, but now those doubts were turning out to be unfounded.

"Are you sure this is what you want to do?" he asked. "You understand all of the risks involved? We'll be outlaws no matter the outcome. If we succeed, the government will come looking for us, and if they find us, it won't be to offer us their congratulations. If we fail—if we're caught before we even get out of here—well... I think you see where I'm going with this. We won't even get a chance to further our research. I'm sure that the consequences of failure will be none the more clement."

"Yes," Jerg answered confidently, "I'm well aware of all that, but we're not going to get caught. No one knows the ins and outs of this facility better than I do. *No one!*"

"And what makes you so sure that's going to be enough?" Edward asked him. "Don't get me wrong... I have full confidence in your abilities, but I have a hard time believing that this would be easy for anyone."

"Well for starters, I practically put the current security system in place with my own two hands," Jerg answered matter-of-factly. "That and the fact that I command the loyalty of the sentinels should be all we need." He put his hands on Edward's shoulders then and looked him square in the eyes. "All I have to do is ensure that my most trusted men are posted to the sectors we'll be moving through. It's as simple as that. I'd have them cleared out altogether, but Langsarks might notice that and find it suspicious.

"He wouldn't, however, notice something as small and trivial as a change in rotations. If I've gauged him accurately, and I'm fairly confident that I have, I'd say that Langsarks is interested in the rehabilitation program's Interface more than anything else. He probably couldn't care less about physical security. The sentinels will not be a problem because they are discreet. They will not *see* anything and they will not *hear* anything unless I want them to. They'd carry our secret to the *grave* if I asked them to."

"Well, that's reassuring," Edward breathed, "but they won't have to. With two missing scientists, it shouldn't be long before the Commission pins the *theft* on us. It's inevitable." He set the makeshift map down on his desk then, and flattened it with the palms of his hands. "There's one thing in all this that still bothers me," he admitted, "and that's how the sentinels are going to explain what happened to Langsarks. Just what are they supposed to say? This could result in their termination... or worse. They could be linked to us in some way, made accessories to our crime. I don't want anyone else getting into trouble over this."

"First of all," Jerg responded, snatching the map up before crumpling it into a ball and sliding it into his coat pocket, "we'll want to get rid of this and anything like it if we want to avoid getting into more trouble than we've bargained for. Trust me, we won't need it. As for the guards, I want you to let me worry about them. What you need to do is concentrate on the task at hand and get ready to do this in the near future. Can you do that, Edward?"

"So soon," Edward said more than asked. "Yes, I suppose we'd need to act quickly, wouldn't we? Otherwise, we might be too late. Yes. Yes, I'll leave those other details to you."

Jerg gave him an encouraging clap on the back in response. "Perfect. Now let's go over what needs to be done."

CHAPTER
15

Franky in Chains

There was a steady thrum in Frank's ears when he came to. All he could see was a dull amber glow, and it took him a few seconds to realize that his eyes were closed. "Where am I?" he murmured, his voice hoarse and his mouth dry. He tried to wet his lips with his tongue, but it felt like it was made of sandpaper. "Need... water," he moaned quietly. He couldn't remember the last time he'd been so thirsty.

He forced his left eye open with some difficulty and a brilliant light flooded in through the open slit. His right eye didn't seem to want to follow suit. The white hot glow was blinding, and felt like it was boring a hole through the throbbing mass inside his skull. His eyes twitched suddenly and he brought his hand up to shield them, but it jerked to a rattling stop halfway there.

His arms were chained down, but to what, he couldn't tell. He could feel manacles digging into his wrists, and if it wasn't his imagination, it also felt like parts of his forearms were caked in layers of dried blood, most likely from cuts that kept reopening. The chains on his arms had about a foot's worth of slack, and that allowed them at least a certain degree of freedom, but his legs remained completely still despite his repeated attempts to move them. He thought that they might be clamped together with some kind of thick fetter, tightly bound in place by chains or straps or some other tough material.

"Where am I?" he murmured again, louder, more coherently than the first time around. He had no recollection of how he'd gotten into this mess. Only bits and pieces of fleeting memories remained of his clash with the Special Assignments Unit.

"Why, you're in your very worst nightmare, of course," a stranger answered in a voice that was dripping with contempt. "I *do* hope that you enjoy your stay with us, Mister Fasaro. Officer Jablonski certainly did, at least for a *while*. But he appears to have checked out early. A pity, truly."

Though spotty at first, Frank's vision slowly returned then as someone swiveled the floodlight away from his face, lighting up the area directly in front of him. The rest of the room was plunged into almost complete darkness, and it was difficult to make out anything but vague silhouettes there. The macabre scene before him, however, stood out starkly, and in far more detail than he would have liked it to.

Limp and discolored, strapped to a metal chair that was rigged in much the same way his was, sat the lifeless and bloated corpse of a man he'd known only as *the rookie*. Jablonski's glassy eyes were bulging, and his face was contorted from the horrors he'd experienced in his dying moments. He looked like he'd been severely roughed up before his body had capitulated. There was a black swelling under both of his eyes, his nose looked like it had been broken in at least two places, and there were trickles of dried blood under his eyes, nose, mouth, and ears.

"He really did seem like he was having a good time near the end," the voice explained with mock regret. "Until he overdosed on the *Fair Lady*, that is." He laughed dryly then before adding, "I suppose he wasn't as tolerant to the stuff as we'd hoped. You *precinct boys* are a little soft in the belly."

"You're going to pay for this, you monster," Frank snarled, then spit dryly into the darkness. "You mark my words."

"Oh, am I now?" the voice chortled derisively. "And what do you gentlemen think about that?" More laughter erupted from somewhere in the darkness. There were at least two other distinct voices in that sinister cacophony, but they were nondescript and did little to shed light on the identity of his abductors.

If what he remembered was accurate, he didn't really have to guess very hard at who they were. He was most likely in police custody. As far as he could tell, he might be in a LEA compound, but from what he'd seen and heard in the past minute and a half, he'd bet his bottom taler that his captors were with SAU. Those guys got serious hard-ons when it came to punishment, and were rumored to torture and even kill their prisoners. Whoever they were, they'd done a real good job on his eye. "What do you want with me?" he asked in a tone that was both defiant and resolute.

There was a moment of silence then, but it didn't last very long. Soon, the sound of booted feet clapping on concrete at a run heralded the apparition of a brawny figure before him. A man clothed in a black uniform charged out from the darkness behind Jablonski, and was on him in the blink of an eye. It all happened so quickly, he wasn't sure he could have reacted even if his hands and feet had been free. An unexpected punch caught him in the mouth and sent him reeling back, knocking him down toward the cold, hard floor.

He tried to brace himself as best he could, but his head still smacked violently against the concrete. He balled his fists and clenched his teeth in an effort to stifle a groan that escaped him nonetheless. There was a deep ringing inside his head, and as far as he could tell, his scalp had split just above the base of his skull. He knew right away that the fall was going to do more than just leave a bump. Chances were he had a concussion as well.

"Just in case you aren't accustomed to this sort of thing," sneered the voice that was not that of the man in front of him, "let me explain how we're going to proceed." The speaker remained hidden, but from the sound of it, he was somewhere very close by. Frank listened as the man cleared his throat, lit up a cigarette, and took a long drag on it. "I'll be the one asking the questions around here," the voice continued. "Understand? All you have to do is answer them." He took another audible puff of his cigarette and gagged as the smoke went down the wrong way, then picked up a moment later as if nothing had happened. "If you have anything else to say—*anything* at all—just shut your mouth. You're better off keeping it to yourself."

The guy that had punched him in the face started pulling his chair back into the upright position, and another man in a black uniform appeared from somewhere off to his right to assist him. He only caught a quick glimpse of the newcomer's face, but he could have sworn that he looked familiar somehow, even if it was only vaguely. "You're making a huge mistake," Frank said through clenched teeth as the "*muscle*" finished propping him up.

To his surprise, Jablonski's chair had been taken away, and a grizzled man with a crazy look in his eyes stood in its place. He was middle-aged, of average height and build, and dressed just like any other plainclothes cop might have been. He wore slate gray slacks with a plain white dress shirt, and a beige trench coat that was opened up just enough that it showed off a bit of his budding gut. Thin tendrils of cigarette smoke wafted up from his nostrils and the corners of his mouth, enveloping his face in a slowly swirling veil of white. He couldn't help but wonder how long the guy had practiced letting the smoke out that way before getting it right. It was obviously meant to impress, but he couldn't figure out why anyone would give themselves the trouble.

"The inquisitor just told you to shut up," the newly-arrived meathead snarled, "so shut the fuck up if you know what's good for you." Frank assumed that it would soon be this guy's turn to smack him around. "Walter!" the goon barked. "Quit fooling around and hold him up, already!"

Walter did exactly as he was instructed to. He circled around to the back of Frank's chair, put his hands down on his shoulders, and squeezed them firmly.

As Frank had expected, the vaguely familiar guy walked out in front of him, cracked his knuckles noisily, and wound his arm up much farther than he really needed to. There wasn't a whole lot that he could do, besides brace for the impact, but at least he knew that it was coming, this time. Part of his Starke Note training had involved abdominal contractions. Flexing the right muscles at just the right time helped absorb shock and reduced the risk of injury. He just hoped that it would be enough, and that they didn't start bashing his head in. There *really* wouldn't be much of anything he could do to protect himself then.

Mister Familiar stood there with his arm drawn back and just watched him for a second. Frank figured he was hoping to see panic in his eyes, to see him stricken with fear, but he wouldn't give him that satisfaction.

A few more seconds passed, and no doubt realizing that he wasn't going to get the reaction he wanted, the brute swung his fist out and struck him square in the midsection.

Frank had anticipated the blow and timed his contractions perfectly, but he wasn't expecting the guy to pack such a violent punch. The strength of it pummeled his insides and knocked most of the wind out of him. Grunting, he held his pain in and ground his teeth until he was red in the face.

"It looks like we've got a *tough guy* over here, Leroy," Walter laughed. "This is gonna be awfully entertaining."

"Why yes, yes it is," his partner in crime replied with a smile. "I'm going to enjoy breaking every bone in his puny, little body, the sick son of a bitch."

The inquisitor didn't seem half as enthusiastic. With his arms crossed, he stood there glowering at them in obvious disapproval. "Remember, gentlemen," he chided, "our job here is to extract information. We won't get anything out of him if you kill him."

He crossed his arms behind his back and walked up to where Frank was, then leaned to within a few inches from his face, and examined him in a way that made his skin crawl. "If you do your job properly," he lectured, clearly addressing his two henchmen, even though he was looking him straight in the eyes, "then you won't have time to *enjoy* yourselves. You can make him suffer to your sweet little heart's content, if it comes to that, but I want you to keep it effective, and I want you to be careful."

"Yes, sir," Walter mumbled dejectedly, deferring to the other man's authority despite his obvious disappointment.

"Yes, sir," Leroy mimicked in a ridiculing and snarky tone, gesticulating wildly as he did. "This is bullshit and you both know it is. If I'd'a come across this sack of shit in the streets, I'd'a had the green light to drop him to his knees and put a bullet in the back of his head, no questions asked!"

For a second, the man's violent, sweeping gestures had Frank convinced that he was going to hit him in the face with the back of his hand, but the blow never came.

"But no," Leroy further complained, "Instead, I have to tiptoe through the fucking tulips with this guy. It don't make no sense, Kay Jay. No fucking sense at all. It's not like we don't have three other schmucks just like him that we can squeeze. You look me straight in the eye and tell me that this isn't ridiculous."

Kay Jay, Frank thought. The initials certainly rang a bell. He hadn't noticed it earlier, but after taking a closer look at him, the inquisitor seemed oddly familiar, as well. Suddenly, it dawned on him. Kay Jay was short for Kyle Johnson. He was sure of it. He'd crossed paths with Kyle at least a few times in his first year out of the academy. If his memory served him correctly, he'd had a desk job of some kind back then, working in the finance department or something. He'd never gotten the chance to get to know the guy, but he did *know* him.

"This isn't ridiculous," Inquisitor Johnson replied calmly. "Listen. I know how you feel, Leroy." He set his hand down on

Leroy's shoulder then and gave it a good squeeze. "I know *exactly* how you feel," he added, his voice surprisingly compassionate for a man that dealt in pain and suffering. "I've lost just as many friends as you have to these filthy pieces of human feces." He turned his attention back to Frank then, and stared through him like he had before. "This... rat... this traitor... this poor excuse for a human being deserves much worse than just death," he uttered in a hostile tone. "He deserves just retribution. Believe me, boys, I feel it in my bones, just as much as either of you do. If it was up to me, I'd let you have your way with him. Heck, I'd even join in, and don't you forget it."

He grinned viciously then and gave Frank an openhanded smack across the face, then quickly followed up with a backhand on the return. "I know how good it feels to just let go with these sickos," he growled, the passion in his voice rising sharply. "Kind of makes you feel like you're sticking it to the bad guys, getting some well-deserved revenge for folks like Little Bill Turner and Bob Sheffield, and trust me I don't have a problem with that. All I'm asking you is to be careful not to kill him. That's all. He may lead us to more of his kind, and that should be incentive enough for the two of you, if our orders aren't."

Leroy crossed his arms and frowned in a way that reminded Frank of a pouty little girl he'd sat beside for the entire fifth grade. Pouting Patty Kruger, they'd called her, thinking they were oh so clever, and Leroy was channeling her right down to the very curve of her lips. "Do we at least get to whack him once this is over and done with?" the big man asked, almost pleading.

"No," Johnson replied with a sigh. "We have orders to turn him over to the LEA once we're done here. It doesn't matter if we're successful or not. They want him back either way. They want to follow standard protocol on this one. If you ask me, someone up top wants to be the one to flick the switch, so to speak."

"You *do* realize that I'm sitting right here, don't you?" Frank stated more than asked, indignant. "I don't know if this is how you guys *normally* operate, but aren't you at least supposed to give me the *impression* that I might have a chance of getting out of this? I don't even know how I got into this whole mess in the first fucking place, and you're already telling me that I'm a dead man. You have got to be the shittiest interrogator ever, *Inquisitor* Kyle Johnson. You should have stuck to filling out T-14 forms. It would have been a better use of government mon—"

His words were cut short as the inquisitor's fist connected with his nose. Johnson wasn't exactly a big man—in fact, he hardly even qualified as wiry—but he still packed a decent punch, for a man his size, and his nose started to bleed on impact. It hurt like a bitch, but at least it wasn't broken.

Frank knew that talking was a bad idea even before he'd opened his mouth to say something, but he couldn't help it. He was sick and tired of being treated like a piece-of-trash terrorist. Even with a throbbing nose, and the taste of blood oozing down his nasal cavity and into his mouth, he was defiant.

"We've already told you to shut up twice, now," Johnson grated. "I don't want to hear it. I don't give a damn if you're implicated or not." He took a long drag on his cigarette and blew the smoke in Frank's face. "Try me again," he threatened. "Try me just one more time and you'll see, you'll get what's coming to you." He grabbed him by the hair with his free hand then and tilted his head back in one swift motion, then crushed his cigarette out in his right eye, the one that wouldn't open to begin with.

Frank tried to stifle his scream, but it escaped through his grit teeth all the same. He'd suffered many injuries over the span of his career, some of them substantial, but having his eye burned with a cigarette was a first. Nothing could have prepared him for that kind of pain. It wasn't something he could brace for. He tried to reach up to cover his eye, but the chains jerked his hands back again. Every muscle in his body tensed, and the veins in his neck stood out as a strident pang burst from his eye to the back of his skull, then quickly travelled down his spine.

The sound of laughter echoed in his ears as a familiar rush coursed through his entire body. The world around him flashed white, and his pain seemed to give way altogether as something else flooded in and took its place: a*nger*. A blind, all-consuming rage flowed through him like a surging river, inundating his every thought and washing everything else away. The screams that he'd been fighting so hard to hold back burst free, and he bellowed out savagely at the top of his lungs.

He gripped the chair's thin armrests fiercely as the laughter continued all around him. "Not so tough now, are we?" someone jeered loudly. His concentration was shot and he couldn't tell who'd spoken, but it didn't matter. He was angry at everything and everyone. His rage knew no prejudice.

His vision returned in his good eye and he blinked repeatedly until the fuzziness left. The first thing that he saw was Johnson's big, oily grin. He didn't have much of a choice, seeing as the man was leaning in so close he could smell the hooch on his breath.

"Now," the inquisitor began in a condescending tone, "if you're all done with your interruptions, maybe I can get around to the actual interro—"

He never had a chance to finish what he was saying. Frank's hands shot up so quickly that Johnson never saw them coming. There was just enough slack in his chains to let him grab two fistfuls of his shirt, and he yanked him down to his level in one hard and unexpected jerk.

Johnson's eyes went wide with alarm as Frank sunk his teeth into his left cheek. The shrill scream that escaped the inquisitor grew even higher in pitch as he tried to back up and realized that he couldn't. Frank's grip only tightened, and his teeth sunk even deeper into his flesh.

"Hurry!" Walter barked, wrapping his hands around Frank's face in an effort to pry him off. "Help him!" Moving frantically, he pulled Frank's hair, clawed at his face and eyes, and even pushed his cheeks together, but Frank would not let go.

Leroy grabbed Johnson by the shoulders firmly and started tugging him backward. He wasn't getting anywhere fast, at first, but the resistance broke suddenly and they toppled back, Johnson screeching frantically as they went down.

Frank felt the skin tear away from the man's face as they fell. With a flap of flesh dangling from his mouth, with blood smeared across his face, and dripping off his chin, he knew that he had to look like something right out of a horror movie.

"You sick son of a bitch," Walter mouthed loudly. His shock was apparent from the tone of his voice. Meanwhile, Johnson got to his feet and hobbled away as quickly as he could, without looking back, and knocking over trays and stands as he did.

The hands smothering Frank's face from behind slid down suddenly and gripped his neck. Walter was trying to squeeze the life right out of him. Wasting no time, he looked up and spit the chunk of flesh out at his face.

The bulky SAU officer flinched reflexively, raising his hands to block the incoming projectile.

The move gave Frank a better opening than he could have hoped for, and he took it without hesitation. Stretching, he turned his head and bit Walter's hand, clamping his teeth down between his thumb and his index finger.

Walter let out a loud, piercing cry. It was a sound of surprise more than it was one of agony. "You rotten little *shit!*" he grated, balling his fist to try to yank his hand loose. "Let go of my fucking hand!" He started punching Frank in the side of the head then as he struggled to pull free. Not only did it not work, but the teeth digging into his hand clamped down even harder with each blow, and he grunted loudly every time. He continued dishing out a flurry of rabbit punches despite that, determined to get his hand back, but his delivery was slowing down, and his pain was more and more obvious with every strike.

Frank was holding on for dear life. The punches weren't exactly powerful or even well placed, but they were coming in fast and fierce. Before long, it felt like his brains were getting knocked around the inside of his skull like eggs in a mixing bowl.

All he could do to protect himself was keep his mouth shut, and he did just that. His jaws were starting to grow numb, but it was the only card that he had, his one edge on his would-be killers. He nearly panicked when he felt his top and bottom rows of teeth close together. He figured it meant that he'd somehow managed to lose his grip. Not a second later, he'd find out that he'd been right, just not in the way that the'd expected.

Walter yanked his hand back hard, and hollered as the final strips of flesh holding him back gave way. The skin between the base of his index finger and the base of his thumb was ripped clean off. In places, muscle had been chewed clear through from all the jerking motions.

He yelled out again as he stumbled back, then tripped over something noisily before going down. There was the sound of a large cart or metallic table crashing over onto its side, followed quickly by the clatter of a dozen or so small, metal instruments as they spilled out onto the concrete floor. "You dirty, rotten shit!" he screamed, infuriated.

The sound of feet clapping on the hard floor drew Frank's attention to the front again. Leroy emerged from the darkness there a second later, his fists balled at his sides and shaking with anger. "You let Old Roy handle this," he seethed, bringing his fists up to chest level to crack his knuckles. "He'll have this under control again right quick."

Frank watched intently as Leroy strode toward him. With his legs bound to the chair and almost no slack in the chains on his arms, he had no idea what to do next. He could only get away with biting people so many times before they smartened up and realized that he was completely harmless at arm's length. He was surprised that it had worked once, let alone twice. Unfortunately, it seemed like time was running out for him, and there was no escape in sight.

Leroy closed the gap between them in a matter of split seconds, and he was already winding up for a right hook when he closed to within striking distance.

Frank's keen reflexes kicked in the second Leroy took his swing at him. Anticipating the point of impact, he squeezed his good eye shut and lowered his head a notch at just the right time. Leroy's fist might as well have smashed into a brick wall. He could feel the joints in Leroy's hand pop when his fist connected squarely with his forehead. The experience was almost painless for him, but he could tell that Leroy wouldn't be using that hand so carelessly again for a while.

Leroy grunted loudly and jerked his hand back, then flapped it around rapidly as if to shake the pain out of it. "Motherfucker!" he bellowed, shaking his whole arm around for good measure. "I don't give a rat's ass *what* Johnson says. You're dead meat! *You* mark *my* words, *asshole!* Dead. Fuckin'. Meat."

"Hate to break it to you," Frank replied coldly, almost reflexively, "but if you're trying to scare me, it isn't working. Not even a little bit."

"Oh really," Leroy said, drawing a laser pistol from a holster at the back of his belt. "Is that so, tough guy? Then I guess Old Roy here's gonna have to try harder a little bit harder, ain't he?" He raised his pistol then and pressed it to Frank's forehead. "That thick skull of yours sure did a number on my hand, all right, but how do you think it's gonna hold up against this? Or do you think you can dodge it at point-fucking-blank?"

"Do it, Leroy!" Walter urged him. "Look what that scumbag did to my fucking hand! Look what he did to Johnson's *face!*" He'd pushed himself up from the floor and had hobbled over to Leroy's side. "It's not like we need him anyways, El Rey! We can get one of those other fuckers to talk."

"Indeed we can, Walter," Leroy replied. "Indeed we fucking can. Any last words, fuck face?" There was a faint clicking sound in the distance then, and all of the ceiling lights hummed to life, flooding the place with their brilliant fluorescence. Walter and Leroy threw up their hands to shield their eyes from the light. The unexpectedness of it threw them into sudden bewilderment, and they both started to pace around nervously, rolling out a steady flow of colorful expletives as they did.

Frank tried to shield his eyes as well, but was reminded once again that there were manacles securing his hands to the chair. The light burned his retina, but not as much as their last stunt with the spotlight had. His good eye readjusted relatively quickly and he was able to take stock of his surroundings.

The place they were holding him in looked like some kind of underground parking lot, except it was almost entirely bare. At a glance, he could see the spotlight that they'd blinded him with earlier, and the overturned cart that had puked its tools of torture all over the floor. Then there was the empty chair Jablonski had been strapped to. He thought that they'd taken it away earlier.

He couldn't help but wonder what they'd done with his body. They'd gotten rid of it rather quickly, but now the chair was back. That's when he noticed the smell. It was a heavy stench of urine, fecal matter and decaying flesh. The odor was so pungent that he didn't know how he could have missed it earlier.

"Hurry up and do it, Leroy," Walter pressed him. "They'll be here any second now. Go!"

Leroy raised his laser pistol and took aim, a sour expression puckering his face. "Well," he spat, "I was hoping I'd get the chance to make you cry a little, maybe even plead for your life, but it looks like we don't have time for any of that. Guess I'm'a just have to settle for putting one between your eyes."

So this is it, Frank thought. *This is really it. This is how it all ends. I get gunned down mercilessly by my own, without so much as an explanation.* A commotion from the other side of the door some distance behind his executioners drew his attention and made him look up. Staring down the barrel of Leroy's laser pistol, he decided that he wasn't going to give up just yet.

With his good eye riveted on Leroy's hand, he waited for the perfect moment to spring into action. Grimacing, he flexed the muscles in his upper body in anticipation. As soon as Leroy's index finger squeezed the trigger, he swung his arms up and shifted his weight back simultaneously, flipping his chair over.

A series of tinny blasts resounded, and a bright, red beam of concentrated light flashed just overhead as he went down. Ready for the fall, this time, he brought his head in as much as he could to avoid bashing the back of it on the floor.

At that moment, he heard the sound of a door getting smashed open, followed by the shuffle of at least a dozen heavy, booted feet. Had someone come to his rescue, he wondered. He doubted it, but a little wishful thinking couldn't hurt.

"Enough!" a commanding voice bellowed out forcefully. "Drop your weapon right now! *Immediately*, Cantelli! That's an order! *You!* Kluga! I expected better from you!"

"Yes, Staff Sergeant, sir," Walter acknowledged dejectedly. "I know, sir. I'm real sorry."

"Oh, I'm *real sorry,* sir," Leroy whimpered in a mocking tone. "With all due respect, *Sarge*, you can bite my ass. This is none of your goddamned business. Period."

"With all due respect, Corporal," the staff sergeant shot back through grit teeth, "you will relinquish your weapon *immediately!*"

"Oh, really," Leroy scoffed defiantly, clearly irritated. "And who's going to make me? You??"

The sound of a scuffle broke out almost immediately. "Just give him the gun, Leroy," Walter pleaded. "You're going to get us into serious trouble."

During the ruckus, Frank noticed two things. The first was a burning sensation in his left shoulder. It seemed to be spreading through the rest of his arm like wildfire. Second, another familiar smell had cropped up as though out of nowhere. It had somehow managed to overshadow the stench of rotting meat and human waste. It was the suffocating odor of charred flesh.

A closer examination of his arm revealed a gaping, cauterized wound just above his bicep. He'd been tagged by one of the laser blasts on his way down. The steaming hole it left was evidence enough of that. It looked like he could put two fingers inside of it, and seemed to go all the way through to the other side. It was like a chunk of flesh had been punched right out of him with a cookie cutter, he thought. The sight of it made him queasy.

He was almost certain that bone had been sectioned. If that was the case, there was a fairly good chance that his arm would just sag if he tried to move it. With an injury of this magnitude, he knew that the *real* pain would come later, and that it was only delayed pending shock. In a while, once the adrenaline had run its course, there'd be a truckload of suffering in store for him. For the time being, he was mostly just sick to his stomach.

Unable to bear the sight of it, he closed his eyes and let his head sink back. The sound of fisticuffs had picked up but was distant in his mind. Those men had come to keep him alive, he realized, but they certainly weren't on his side. That much was evident. They were probably other SAU agents that had been dispatched to bring the situation under control, to protect the information that they thought he was withholding.

With his head tilted all the way back, he took a deep breath and held it momentarily. He felt utterly helpless. He'd never once imagined that he'd one day get caught up in a mess like this one.

One second he'd been a respectable member of society, an upstanding, law-abiding citizen, a dedicated police officer, and a national hero, of sorts—or so he'd been told. But now he was being held against his will, and tortured by the very organization that he'd been hell-bent on joining as recently as a few weeks ago. He'd wanted to join them because he'd thought it the right thing to do. He'd thought that doing so would make him an even better citizen. Try as he might, he couldn't understand what it was they wanted, other than to take his life. He knew that they were after information, but he had none to offer them.

When he exhaled and opened his eyes again, the sight before him made a lump rise in his throat. Without even meaning to, he'd located the source of the foul stench, and Jablonski's body with it. The rookie's lifeless husk had been heaped onto a mound of corpses in varying stages of decay. The bodies were piled high, nearly all the way to the ceiling.

As shocked as he was by the extent of the carnage before him, he couldn't help but guess at how many corpses there were in the pile. *A hundred? he* ventured. *Two?* It looked like it might be more, but it was hard to tell. He'd never seen anything like it before. The floor surrounding the pile was covered in a thick layer of brittle debris and ash. In some places, it looked like the ash was more than a foot deep. He grimaced then as he realized what it was: poorly incinerated flesh and bone. As far as he could tell, they'd been burning the dead in this place for quite some time, and that made the death toll even more difficult to estimate.

Despite his calm nature and usual resolve, he found it hard not to panic then. If the dead were members of the Awoken, or even just suspected members, it meant that there were a lot more of them out there. He knew that the situation was bad, but he'd never imagined there'd be so many of them. And these were just the ones that had been captured. It was hard to believe that they were all terrorists.

If these really were members of the Awoken, the authorities didn't stand a chance. Judging by the intensity of the so-called "war on terror", he figured that those before him represented only a miniscule tip of the iceberg in the Awoken's army. He wasn't ready to believe that. It was too frightening a thought.

But if there weren't that many of them, if these weren't their bodies, then where did they come from? Who were they? If he had to make an educated guess based on what he'd seen so far, he'd say that Special Assignments had a pretty shoddy standard of proof, and that they used lethal force on anyone they found even remotely suspicious. He and Jablonski were evidence enough of that. He didn't know the kid that well, but he did know himself, and he knew that he had absolutely no business being there. One of them had mentioned that there were others just like him that could give them the information they needed.

Others just like me, he reflected. Had he meant other police officers? It was possible, but it didn't make any sense. Why would they do that? Why would they wrongfully target police officers? What purpose would that really serve? All of these questions and more fired off inside his head as he stared blankly at the macabre scene before him. For a brief moment, he was so focused on it that he was completely oblivious to anything else.

"Stay down, Cantelli!" The sound of Sergeant *Whatsit*'s sharp command snapped him from his almost trance-like deliberation.

"Get your hands off of me," he heard Leroy complain. "This is bullshit and you know it, Sarge! A1 quality *bullshit!*"

"Bullshit or not, you'll be spending the next few days in the brig," the sergeant replied matter-of-factly. "Take him away."

"Sir, yes sir!" another man barked out over Leroy's sustained complaints. There was a grunt, and a thud, and the sound of a struggle as he was ostensibly dragged away.

"Kluga," the sergeant continued in his no-nonsense tone, "Fall in. There's a dirty job upstairs with your name all over it. Ritter, Hauser, Sokolov: you're on me. Costanza and the rest of you: bring the prisoner to the infirmary. *Now*. No detours, no delays." He paused for a moment then before adding, "That will be all."

"Yes, Staff Sergeant, sir!" the remaining handful of men replied in near-perfect unison.

Frank listened to the shuffle of feet as most of the men filed out of the room. He could tell that they were moving quickly and efficiently, and it wasn't long before he was left alone with the sound of more cautious footsteps creeping toward him.

Befuddled, he finally forced himself to look away from the pile of flesh, but the vision haunted him yet. Moving his neck set his nerves on fire, so he just stared up at the ceiling in silence.

His throat was starting to swell and a cold sweat had broken out on his forehead. "I'm not who you think I am," he managed to say with some difficulty. His voice had weakened considerably, and much of what he said came out as little more than a labored croak. "I'm not one of them."

There was no response but the sound of approaching feet. Before long, the officers were on top of him. There were three of them surrounding him, staring down at him austerely. He read the same hatred in their eyes that he'd seen in the others.

"I hear that you're a feisty little bugger," the one standing at his feet drawled out. "We'll have to see if we can remedy that." The embroidered patch on the man's arm identified him as their ranking officer. It had two curved bands pointed skyward with a sword sticking down through the both of them. The whole of it was threaded in silver on black. SAU's hierarchy was complex compared to the LEA's, but he'd familiarized himself with their ranks and insignia when he'd developed an interest in signing up. The one doing the talking at present was a master corporal, and the others were both privates first class.

The master corporal nodded at the others then and they seemed to catch on to what he wanted without even stopping to think about it. Frank watched as the officer on his left unhooked the nightstick from his belt and took a step toward him. The man was built like a refrigerator, had a pale complexion, and a wicked grin that split his face from ear to ear. "Now, don't be alarmed," the master corporal added with mock reassurance. "This is going to be quick and *painful. I promise.*"

"You don't understand," Frank tried to say, but it was already too late. The nightstick swung down at the side of his face like a hammer, and his vision flashed white and winked out.

When he came to and opened his eyes again, he had a splitting headache. The first thing that he noticed was that he couldn't move. It was even worse than before. At least he'd had a bit of slack in the ties on his upper body when he'd been in the chair. Now the only thing that he could move was his head. It felt like an incredible amount of pressure was being exerted on every square inch of his body.

The second thing he noticed was that he'd managed to open both of his eyes with relative ease. The one that had been burned still hurt, but it was nothing compared to before. His eyes adjusted to the new lighting more rapidly than they had in the underground parking lot. There were no blinding spotlights in the dark here. There were no chains or piled-up cadavers. He was relatively sure that he was in some kind of office building.

Everything in the immediate vicinity was earthen-toned and lit by a dim glow. The area itself was about as bare as a working girl trying to score a client on a Friday night. It was dressed up just shy of naked, sporting little but the obvious office essentials. There were a few desks with chairs and numerous others without. They were all equipped with outdated monitors, and he thought he could see an old photocopier off in the distance, too. None of it seemed very noteworthy to him, but hinted that the place had been abandoned a long time ago.

As far as he could tell, he was bound to some kind of examination table. Wide metal bands secured his arms, legs and torso to the cold, hard surface. If he had to guess, he'd say that they'd been cut to spec and welded on the spot. They were tight enough that they prohibited any major movement, but they didn't make him feel crushed to the point of suffering. His breathing didn't seem to have been factored into the design, however, as the restraints on his chest kept his lungs from expanding completely. He could only breathe in short, controlled gasps.

He tried to move his fingers and toes around and found that he could, but the usefulness of this mobility was questionable at best. His arms and legs were clamped down every few inches all the way to his wrists and ankles. At least he *thought* that was the case. He was relying almost completely on physical perception. He could feel the cold bands pressing against his skin.

Something about the way that the fingers of his left hand moved felt strange to him, though he couldn't say exactly why. It just didn't feel right. He mulled it over a bit, and thought it felt like they had a little more mobility than those of his right. After a while, it didn't even seem like there was a band on his left wrist at all. The more he concentrated on it, the more it felt like the welders might have forgotten about that arm altogether.

Suddenly intrigued, he twisted his head around to the right. He'd hardly moved at all, but the exercise was difficult and painful. It revealed nothing more than what he'd expected. His right arm was clamped down by five or six u-shaped bands.

He worked his head around to the left with just as much difficulty. When he found what he was looking for—or rather *failed to* find what he was looking for—he felt overcome by a sense of sheer bewilderment. Where his arm had once been, nothing remained but a cauterized stub. It had been chopped clean off at the shoulder and burned to prevent bleeding.

It might have shocked him more if there'd been pain, but for some reason, there wasn't. Instead of panicking and screaming bloody murder, he stared at it, almost as though mesmerized. He'd seen his fair share of horrible injuries before, and he could tell that whoever had taken his arm had done this kind of thing more than once. From the look of it, the wound had been seared shut with some kind of hot press.

He was still coming to grips with the loss of his limb, and the impact it would have on the rest of his life—assuming he survived this—when a deep voice broke in from somewhere behind him. The sound of it wrenched him from his thoughts.

"You know, you're one hard nut to crack," the voice said, "and from what I hear, you're a real shit stain to get rid of, too."

"Who are you?" Frank asked, defiant and suddenly alert. "What do you want from me?"

The man at his back spoke over him, ignoring his questions altogether. "It's too bad you're one of them. We can always use people with your kind of resilience." An uneasy silence followed, but was soon broken by a horrible wail of agony that rose up from somewhere in the distance, and echoed all around them. The vastness of the place made it hard to tell where exactly it had come from.

The man started to speak again before Frank could get the chance to. "Three interrogations," he said, sounding genuinely impressed. "Most people fall apart during the first. Some hold out until the second, but not many. You've gone through two now and have given us absolutely *nothing*. Well done, Mister Fasaro. Well done. And you've accomplished this despite your previous inquisitors breaking every rule in the book just to ensure that you suffered as much as they could possibly make you. You do realize what this means, don't you?" From the sound of it, he expected the answer should be obvious. "*Don't you?*"

Frank met the man's question with silence. He knew that it would come across as less than cooperative, but he didn't care. He was too busy trying to work out a way to escape. He didn't have time for whatever mind games this guy was playing. The room began to spin then—slowly, but it was enough to make him feel dizzy. Before long, he realized that it wasn't the room that was spinning, but the table he was strapped to, which sat on a swiveling axis. The man behind him was turning it, slowly but surely.

When the table stopped, he was face to face with his new inquisitor. The man had a strong, square jaw, with pocky, umber-colored skin that had been scarred by severe childhood acne. He seemed to be in his mid-to-late thirties, with a body that had retained all of the advantages of youth. His shaved head and broad shoulders gave him a hardened look, but the semi-casual suit that he wore softened him somewhat, and made him look less threatening. The sleeves of his dress shirt were rolled up to his elbows and his top button was undone.

The inquisitor sighed deeply as he eyed Frank, arms crossed. "You don't, do you?" he asked. There was something that almost resembled genuine concern in his voice. "You might not realize it," he added in a patronizing tone, "but you're in way over your head. You might *think* that you realize it, but trust me, you have no idea. If you did, this would have been over a *long* time ago."

"Listen," Frank growled, losing his patience. "You assholes chopped my fucking arm off. I think I get it. I'm fucked, and I don't know what else to tell you. I didn't *do* anything. I'm *not* one of the Awoken. What else *can* I say? Do you want me to lie? Do you want me to tell you that I'm one of them so you can throw another corpse on the pile and move on to the next?" The questions were obviously of a rhetorical nature. "Oh, and by the way," he added with a level of snark that surprised even himself, considering his vulnerable position, "this is only the second interrogation. I don't know where you're getting your information, but it's wrong."

"No, you're mistaken. It's your third," the inquisitor replied, unfazed. He pointed to Frank's abdomen then and waited for his eyes to settle on the long, straight scar there. "You really don't remember being opened up, do you?" he asked. "I suppose you might not. Your second interrogation was by far worse the worst of the two. The boys started out with a heavy hand—a really heavy hand—and they didn't let up until your body did."

He gave him a serious look and crossed his arms again before adding, "It took a while." He looked off into the distance then, as though thinking back, and said, "You kept going on about this *Vanessa* character. Vanessa this, Vanessa that. 'Don't you dare lay a hand on Vanessa, or I swear on my life I'll kill every single one of you... right down to the last.' It was *really* scary stuff, truly. Had everyone shaking in their booties. Boo hoo, cry sob, loud screaming. Is this not ringing any bells at all? I have some recordings of the event for you, if you need me to refresh your memory."

Frank was at a loss for words. Vanessa hadn't even crossed his mind until then, and he felt consumed by guilt the second the inquisitor said her name. Now that he'd brought her up, she was all that he could think about. He didn't even know if she was safe. Maybe he *had* gone through a trauma so serious it had wiped out any memory he had of the event. He didn't have a good reason not to believe it.

The bile in the pit of his stomach was worse than any of the torture he could still remember being submitted to. He was filled with fear for her, and it was eating away at him like acid. "Where is she?" he snarled, his voice dripping with venom. "You tell me where she is *right* now, or you'll regret it." Saying the words out loud gave him a sense of déjà vu. Despite what the inquisitor had said about his ranting, it hadn't felt real to him until then.

The inquisitor chuckled lightheartedly in response. "Or I'll regret it?" he asked. "*Really?* Tell me, just what are you going to do to me, exactly? Stare me to death? You can't honestly believe that you're in a position to threaten me right now. You can't! Just look at yourself. Oh, that's right... you can't."

"Try me," Frank said through gnashed teeth. A vein stood out on the side of his head and his heart began to race. Breaking free from his bonds was a futile endeavor and he knew it, but that didn't stop him from flexing every muscle in his body in an effort to do just that.

The inquisitor started to crack up at the first sign of Frank's writhing. He tried to hold his laughter in, at first, but failed miserably. When he did start chuckling, he gave up on fighting it altogether. It wasn't a mocking laugh, but an almost hysterical one. It was the laugh of a man watching another man attempt the impossible for reasons that he couldn't even begin to fathom.

"You can't be serious," he wheezed between strained bouts of laughter. He wiped at the tears forming in his eyes and took a deep breath in an effort to calm himself. "Even if you weren't pinned to that table like an insect," he added, shaking his head in disbelief, "you still wouldn't have a glimmer of a chance."

He sighed deeply then and glanced at Frank the same way he might look at the poor idiot that didn't *get it* no matter how many times he tried to explain it to him. "You'd be like a one-winged fly spinning circles on itself in the middle of a kitchen table," he said, sounding genuinely sympathetic, "and I'd be the almighty flyswatter of justice putting you out of your misery. All it would take from me is one word—really, just the *one*—and this room would be abuzz with folks that would give just about *anything* for a chance to beat you into a puddle of red goop."

He shook his head again, obviously dumbfounded. "You've only got one arm!" he exclaimed in disbelief. "What are you going to do? Smother me with your stub? I could have Vanessa's arm cut off at the snap of a finger, need I point out, and then you could both be cripples together. It's preposterous."

"I'd only need one arm to snap *your* neck like a twig," Frank breathed through grit teeth. "Believe me. I've done more with less." The fire in his eyes burned so intensely, it looked like it might set the building ablaze.

Messing with him was one thing. Threatening his family was another. When his loved ones were at risk, it brought out the beast in him. A more primitive side surged up from the deepest, darkest recesses of his mind, and drove him to do things that were dictated by impulse more than by choice. The wave of raw emotions that washed over him was overwhelming, like a parasite taking control of its host, and he neither liked nor disliked it. It just *was*.

Boiled down to his most visceral instincts, he'd do just about anything for his mate, even if it defied logic. Breaking free from that reckless mindset went against his nature, and required all of the determination that he could muster. He would never forgive himself if his primal drive to protect her pushed her even further into the lion's mouth.

The inquisitor sighed loudly. Though somewhat amused thus far, at least from the look of it, his patience was wearing thin. "You're really not getting this," he stated coldly with a shake of his head. "If you want to get out of this—if you want *Vanessa* to get out of this—then you'll start cooperating with me *now*." He leaned in closer to Frank then, bringing them face to face, and added, "If you keep putting spokes in our wheels, I'll have to start doing some very nasty things to the both of you." He somehow managed to say that with a smile. "I don't *want* to, but this is my job, and I *will* do it the hard way if you leave me no choice."

Frank took a deep breath and swallowed his pride. Lashing out at the man in his current position was stupid and careless. "Just... who are you and what do you want from me?" he asked, trying to flip the conversation around.

"I'm your last chance," the inquisitor answered plainly. "And that's all you need to know about me." He fished through his jacket's inner pocket then, and pulled out a thin stack of what looked like press clippings. "As for what I want from you," he added dryly, "well... I think that's pretty obvious, isn't it?" He splayed the clippings out in his hand like a deck of cards and held them out to Frank before laying it out clear and simple. "I want to take out the Awoken from the top down, and I want you to be the one to help me do it."

"Oh, is that all?" Frank asked, trying his best not to sound sarcastic. "Look, if that's really what you want, then let me out and I'll gladly help hunt them down for you. That's why I wanted to join Special Assignments in the first place—to kill terrorists— even when everyone discouraged me from doing so."

The inquisitor rubbed at his temples and sighed deeply. "Boy, you almost sound like you believe yourself," he groaned, "but this charade of yours is no help at all, and it's gone on for far too long already. It needs to stop, or I'll need to start cutting fingers off, and I wouldn't assume that I'm talking about yours."

Frank scowled as he struggled to control the rage that he felt boiling up inside. "Look, I'm not the one playing games here," he retorted. "This whole thing is bullshit. With a little cooperation, I could help you bring these fuckers in."

"Now hold on, boy," the inquisitor said with a chuckle, all grins again. "I appreciate your sudden enthusiasm, but for now all I need are the locations of your masters. Grimm or Giuterrez would be a fine start, or any of the other big names that come to mind." He stroked at his chin then and gazed up pensively before looking him square in the eyes and adding, "If I'm not mistaken, a guy such as yourself could probably lead me right to the Grand Anarch himself. Isn't that right?"

"Okay," Frank snapped. "First of all, those guys are *not* my masters. I've already told you that I'm not one of the Awoken. I earn my keep working the beat, taking thugs and dealer scumbags off the streets." He saw the inquisitor open his mouth to say something then, but he cut him off promptly. "You want to go chasing after an urban legend or some fucking shit, and you expect *me* to be the one to show you where to start looking?" he asked, indignant. "Like I know where he is. Please."

"Aha!" the inquisitor exclaimed almost gleefully as he pointed an accusatory finger in Frank's direction. "So the Grand Anarch is a man. I have you now, *Awoken*. There's no point denying it, anymore. Not after that kind of slip. It's irrefutable."

"What?" Frank asked, flabbergasted. "How do you fucking figure? All I said was that he was an urban legend. And used 'he'. That's supposed to be evidence of something? Are you on drugs?"

"Where is he?" the inquisitor pressed him. The look in his eyes was that of a man that had just had the ultimate epiphany. "Tell me where he is *right now* or you'll be sorry."

"I don't know!" Frank shouted. "How many times do I have to tell you? I'm not one of the Awoken! What are you, deaf?"

"That's it!" the inquisitor grated, his temper flaring suddenly. "No more mister nice guy. No more chances." He stomped over to a covered tray that Frank hadn't noticed yet, then yanked the table cloth from it in one swift motion, revealing the arsenal of serrated instruments that lie beneath. "None of the others got you to talk," he continued angrily, a fleck of spittle flying from the corner of his mouth. "Despite their brutality, their psychological mind fucking, and even a truth serum, I hear, they got nothing. But let me tell you why it's going to be different with me. Let me show you how I'm going to succeed where they failed."

"I didn't *do* anything!" Frank shouted, though he realized that his plea would fall on deaf ears.

The inquisitor combed through the instruments on the tray, taking his time before settling on his tools of choice. He swiveled deftly then, and started pacing toward Frank with a pair of plyers in one hand, and a surgical saw in the other. Any of the sympathy that he'd seen in him earlier—fake or not—was gone now, replaced by the wild stare of a sanguinary zealot intent on letting blood. "I'll succeed because I have something that they don't," he growled through clenched teeth. "A mastery of pain unlike anything you've ever experienced or even imagined before. When I'm done with you, your very worst nightmares will seem like little more than baby smiles and butterfly kisses." And then, without further delay, he set to work, intent on proving his point.

The inquisitor had been right. Frank had never imagined that anything could hurt so much. The pain was nearly debilitating, and even when he thought that it couldn't possibly get any worse, it did. Sharp objects were hammered into the tips of his fingers and toes, just beneath his nails, and then they were pried off, slowly but surely, one by one, sometimes with a jerk and a twisting motion. Three of his toes and two of his remaining fingers were snapped through the sheer application of force before he'd lost the cognizance to keep track, and then the saw bit into the flesh of his index finger, and started to grind back and forth against bone. If he'd had the answers that the man was looking for, he'd have given them readily. He even considered serving up false information just to get him to stop, but he could hardly string two words together. His suffering twisted the bounds of reality, and before long, he felt like he was teetering on the precipice of full-blown dementia.

The inquisitor questioned him aggressively and repeatedly, administering intensifying doses of pain all the while. Before long, he felt like the man had somehow managed to slip inside his head. His invasive voice bellowed out over and over again. At times, it sounded as though the questions were ringing out from inside his skull. The same demands echoed again, and again, and made it impossible to think clearly. He tried, and when he failed to, he screamed. By that point, he wasn't even sure if his own voice was real or imagined.

At times, the pain was so intense that he fainted. He couldn't have said how often, because it was getting almost impossible to differentiate between the waking world and the nightmarish bits of dream that were starting to shroud over him more frequently. But every time that it *did* happen, the inquisitor was there to bring him back with smelling salts shoved under his nose.

In his more lucid moments, which were growing fewer and farther between, he found himself wondering why it couldn't just be over. His suffering left him with only one desire: for the pain to cease. It was a solace that he could only find in death, and he not only accepted it, but welcomed it openly.

At the end of his rope, at his wit's end, he looked down and stared at his exposed innards, which were now dangling loosely from a long gash that had been opened across his stomach. In an odd way, the sight of it comforted him. It suggested that his misery would soon be over. As the world around him began to fade, that thought made him smile. Where he was going now, the inquisitor could never follow.

CHAPTER
16

It Does What?

Edward Munro's living quarters were highly reflective of his personality. The apartment itself was plain and furnished very modestly. Intentional decorations were sparse, if they could even be found at all in the mess of reports and odd contraptions that littered the area from one end to the other. There was so much to look at, and so little of it was easily understood that most visitors found it beyond peculiar. Like Edward himself, it also managed to be warm and welcoming despite its strangeness.

It was with one of these bizarre-looking contraptions held out in front of himself that he sat ruminating on the edge of his bed. He examined it thoroughly, and fiddled around with it in a way that betrayed a certain familiarity with the device.

This odd gadget of his own invention—the *Peeping Tom,* as he'd dubbed it—looked very much like one of the "Space Man" helmets that had been immortalized in photo and put on display at the Museum of Human History. Though he was fascinated by their forefathers' exploration of the celestial vault, the design of his device was not, as some people thought, inspired by it, but merely the fruit of functionality.

He'd fashioned the helmet from thick bands of aluminum and some other, lightweight metals that had cost him a small fortune to secure. Its bulbous, tinted visor took up nearly the entire front half of it. Though few could guess at the helmet's purpose just by looking at it, most surmised that it was not meant to protect, and they were right. It was far too unwieldy and fragile for that.

Edward stood suddenly, then held the *Peeping Tom* out with both hands, and slipped it over his head. Its interior was a little on the tight side, but comfortable. It was padded with supple foam and lined with soft leatherette. As cozy as it was in there, he couldn't see a blasted thing. He brought his right hand up to the side of his head, and surprised himself when it collided against the helmet much earlier than he'd expected it to. Once again, he'd somehow managed to forget that the thing nearly doubled the size of his head.

"Confounded contraption," he muttered, fumbling around until his fingers found the dial they were looking for. He turned it clockwise until he felt it click. As it did, a fairly large, rectangular slit opened up in the center of the visor, giving him a dim, but virtually unobstructed view of the area directly in front of himself. It wasn't as bad as wearing sunglasses indoors, but he imagined it could become a strain on the eyes after prolonged use.

Squinting, he held his left hand out in front of his face and started to turn the dial in the same direction again, slowly but surely. He watched his hand very carefully as he did so. At first, it seemed as though it was enveloped in a dull, golden haze. The glow intensified as he continued to turn the dial, and before long, his fingers looked like nothing more than a grouping of concentric shapes in gradient shades of yellow and orange.

The brighter his hand glowed, the harder it was to see objects with lower heat signatures. If the *Peeping Tom's* sensitivity was set too high, the likeliness of bumping into trivial obstacles like walls or staircases rose exponentially. He knew this all too well, as he'd nearly managed to break his neck in a previous trial. Even the maximum setting had its use in key situations, and that made his creation even more versatile, but there was no denying that the tool came bundled with a steep learning curve.

He slowly scanned the entire circumference of his cubbyhole bedchamber to let his eyes adapt to his altered vision. If anyone asked, he'd shamelessly admit that he just had nothing better to do with his time. He zoomed in and out and in and out again and quickly grew tired of *marveling* at the dull glow of the ductwork.

Turning his attention to the parting wall behind his bed, he stood perfectly still and cranked the dial as far as it would go. The world turned jet black then except for those objects that emitted heat. Hot water pipes, radiators, and even his fellow scientists appeared in gradients of red, orange and yellow. Colder objects soon cropped up in varying shades of green.

In the adjoining apartment, his neighbor—Professor Swan— sat reading in front of her open television. In the unit next to hers, someone was busy doing something that made him avert his gaze immediately. When he realized exactly what all of that rhythmic fist pumping was, and perhaps more importantly *who* he'd seen doing it, he wiped his hands off on his lab coat, scrunched his face up in disgust, and promised to remind himself to avoid shaking hands with Doctor Jenkins in the future.

A few seconds later, a flame-colored biped started moving in from another area farther past the both of them. As it grew closer, he realized that it was Doctor Weissinger walking down the hall in his direction. There was really no mistaking it. He'd recognize that hurried, determined gait just about anywhere. He suspected that it would soon be time to put their plan—or rather Jerg's plan—into action.

Careful not to bump his elbows against the doorjamb on his way through, he walked out of his small bedroom and over to the front door, then waited with his arms crossed sagely behind his back. He continued watching and waiting as Jerg drew nearer, and wasn't at all surprised when the door slid open without so much as a knock. It was hard, it seemed, to teach old scientists new tricks, but he wouldn't make a fuss about it. He was much too anxious about the task at hand to bother reprimanding Jerg over his poor manners, and too excited about the possibilities that awaited them should they succeed.

Jerg, for his part, hadn't expected to find him waiting there in the entrance, and was especially startled by his bulky headgear. He was so taken aback by the sight of it that he raised his hands defensively, and nearly stumbled backward at the sight of him. After steadying himself, he caught his breath, and glared at Edward reproachfully. "You nearly scared the living daylights out of me," he growled. "What in the blazes are you doing? And that thing... what is that thing that's swallowing your head?"

Edward brought his hands up to the sides of his visor and pressed inward until he heard a very distinct clicking sound. He moved his hands away then and crossed his arms behind his back once more. First, the exterior pane of the visor closed, and then the whole thing sprung out a few millimeters and retracted up into the helmet's casing. "Oh, this?" he asked, as though he might actually have been referring to something else. "I call this little marvel the *Peeping Tom*, and I was just testing it out one last time before we hit the road."

"The Peeping Tom, is it?" Jerg asked, perplexed. "And what exactly does this Peeping Tom of yours do? Besides make you look stupid, that is. Does it see through walls?"

"No," Edward replied casually. "Not technically, at least. But it achieves more or less the same result, if what you want to see on the other side of those walls is warm enough."

"So it lets you see heat," Jerg said in an unimpressed tone. "You do know that thermal goggles do the exact same thing, don't you? You *were* aware of that, yes? Why on earth would we need a thermal *helmet* too?"

"Yes," Edward replied, stretching the word out for emphasis. "I wasn't born yesterday, you know. I know all about thermal goggles, and their capabilities *and* drawbacks. Thank you. One of said drawbacks being that they were built following outdated specifications gathered nearly half a century ago. The *Peeping Tom* puts those technological relics to shame. To shame!"

"Oh really?" Jerg asked, stretching the last word out in a way that made him sound more than just a little skeptical. "How so, exactly? Please, do tell."

"Firstly," Edward replied, using his fingertips to enumerate the reasons, "the sensitivity of my prototype far surpasses that of standard thermal goggles. It's even adjustable. *More* importantly," he added emphatically as he touched the tip of his second raised finger, "*much* more importantly, I can use it without having to remove my glasses. Put that in your logical framework and evaluate it."

Jerg sighed deeply, unimpressed. "So basically you're telling me that you've made thermal goggles but specifically for nerds." He injected a massive dose of mock enthusiasm into his next remark. "Well I'll bet you've made a lot of smarty-pants kids *very* happy with this, Edward. Now they too can dream of someday joining the force. Or use that bloated monstrosity of yours to peek into the girls' locker room. Now I see where it gets its name."

"You laugh now," Edward grumbled, "but you'll see just how useful it is when you witness its capabilities first hand, in the field. It's more than just a play on thermal goggles."

"You don't *seriously* think that you're bringing that thing with us, do you?" Jerg asked, indignant. "I strictly forbid it."

"What?" Edward stammered. "You *forbid* it? Why? And who died and made you pro tempore leader, anyway? I can't think of one good reason why I *shouldn't* bring it."

Jerg crossed his arms sternly then and gave him a look that said he should know better. "Because you look like an abject moron with that thing on your head," he snapped. "That's why! It draws the eyes like shit draws flies."

Edward opened his mouth to say something, but Jerg cut him off before he could even get a word out. "Would you please just listen to me?" he pleaded. "Just this once?"

"Fine," Edward sighed, exasperated. "Say what you must, but I'm telling you right now, it took me months to design this little wonder and work out all of its kinks. I'll be sorely disappointed if I have to abandon a fully functional prototype of its caliber. Sorely disappointed. I'll do it if I have no other choice, but I'd much rather not. And now you know."

Jerg sighed in turn, though his was one of relief. "That's fine, Edward," he answered reassuringly. "I didn't mean to say that you couldn't bring it with us at all; you just can't wear the damned thing on our mission. Not if you take it seriously. Not if you want it to succeed. Success here won't hinge on seeing the unseen, but on our ability to blend in and avoid drawing attention."

Edward nodded dejectedly and motioned for him to go on.

"For lack of a better term," Jerg said, "I managed to *corrupt* certain sentinels, and ensured that they'd be posted in the vicinity of our objective. But there will be other people along the way, no doubt... other scientists, or sentinels that I didn't approach for fear of their reaction. Most of my old men are still loyal to me, but the less people I involved in this, the less likely it was to blow up in our faces. As you can imagine, we'll want to keep a low profile until we get to where we're going, especially since we have no business being in that part of the facility. If we have to do a little bit of acting to squeeze through, then I'm ready for that, but I'd much rather we not even have to go there."

He folded his arms behind his back then, and glanced over his shoulder before adding, "It's a pretty straightforward plan. There shouldn't be any issues. But anything could happen. *Anyone* could decide to challenge us. Just because the laboratories are closed at night doesn't mean that the halls will be empty. Can you imagine the looks on their faces? The interest it would generate if they saw a giant bobblehead fumbling past? There'd be questions, Edward, and lots of them."

"Yes, I suppose you're right," Edward said. "I hadn't thought of it that way. I'm sorry if I overreacted."

"Never mind that," Jerg replied, patting him on the shoulder. "We all have our strengths, Edward, and some of us are stronger than others. You're a master of more sciences than I can shake a finger at. You're a one-man think tank. You're an inventor, a physicist, and an all-around genius. *This*," he stated, poking his index finger into the palm of his open hand repeatedly, "security, subterfuge, strategy... *this* is what *I'm* good at."

"It is indeed," Edward noted, removing the *Peeping Tom* from his head. "I'll leave the nitty-gritty of the operation to you from now on, and defer to your better judgment. No questions asked."

"Thank you, Edward," Jerg replied. "Now, how quickly can you be ready?" He pushed his sleeve up and glanced at his watch as he asked the question.

"Well," Edward said before trailing off momentarily to think it over. "I *suppose* I could be ready whenever you need me to be. I could even be ready now, if you are. I'm anxious to get this over and done with, and to get out of here as quickly as possible. The anticipation is killing me."

"You're sure?" Jerg asked, sounding skeptical. "You don't need to gather any supplies to help tide you over for the next few days? We'll have to lay low for quite some time, and I don't know when it'll be safe for us to go out for provisions again."

Edward sighed loudly and clicked his tongue in response. "I've already told you. My laboratory is well equipped and well stocked. We could hunker down in that complex for months and not have to worry about coming up for food or supplies."

"I just wanted to make sure," Jerg assured him. "Don't get your knickers in a knot. Have you had the chance to compile that little program I asked you to write? It isn't absolutely necessary, but it could slow the Commission down considerably."

Edward nodded and patted his breast pocket. "I did, and I have it right here."

"Good," Jerg said with a hint of enthusiasm. "If you're sure you don't have any loose ends to tie up, let's go." He exited the

front door then and turned right. Apparently, he knew exactly
where he was going. "And bring along that gadget of yours," he
called out to him over his shoulder, already gaining a considerable
lead on him. "I don't care how distracting it is for the first part of
our trip. We'll have it safely out of sight soon enough."

Edward, who hadn't had time to react to Jerg's drag race
takeoff, cradled his helmet under his arm, and started after him at
a jog. When he caught up to him several seconds later, he was
already short of breath and starting to sweat. He saw the other
doctor fidgeting with the buttons on his communications band, but
thought nothing of it. "Wait for me," he panted, wiping the pearls
of sweat from his brow with his coat sleeve. "Do you have to have
such an urgency to your step?"

"Well," Jerg answered, glancing over his shoulder to address
him, "yes." He led them left as they came to a junction in the hall.
A big, blue sign hanging from the ceiling read "Barracks, Infirmary,
Conference Rooms" in tall, white letters. "On the streets above,"
he explained, "the worst of the *evening* rush hour will soon be
over. If we *have* to run like there's no tomorrow, I want it to be
smooth sailing... but not *too* smooth. If we wait too long, there
won't be any traffic at all. And that wouldn't be good. We'd be
easy pickings for any pursuit. I want at least a bit of a flow for us
to lose them in, if it comes to that."

"That makes sense, I suppose," Edward conceded with a nod.
He hesitated momentarily before adding, "Listen... I know I said
I'd leave the details to you, Jerg, but could you explain exactly
what the plan is? I mean... I understand the key elements of my
role—what it is you expect of me—but I know nothing else, and I
find that somewhat disconcerting."

"Yes, of course," Jerg spluttered, mildly embarrassed. "I'll be
more than happy to elaborate on the task at hand. You'll have to
forgive me if this sounds conceited, but I've gotten used to only
sharing as much information as was needed for my operatives to
successfully achieve their objectives. Back then it was a question

of operational security," he admitted, "but this is clearly different. It *was* your idea to begin with, after all."

As they moved down the corridor, Jerg laid out the details of his plan in a hushed tone. That part of the complex was mostly deserted after working hours, and there was little actual need for discretion, but he made it perfectly clear that he wanted to take as few risks as they possibly could.

"So this Falstaff character is going to escort us all the way to the Platform," Edward recited uncertainly, "and once he's gotten us inside, I'm to inject my code into the mainframe's operating system. At that point, we're going to have to revive and stabilize Sixty-Seven as quickly as possible. Then... when we're ready to go... another sentinel will lead us to an escape vehicle?"

"Two of them will," Jerg responded correctively. "Well... two of them in addition to Captain Falstaff, that is. After regular working hours, there are always two sentinels on duty at the Platform, and both of the ones that are there right now are ready to collaborate with us on this."

"Excellent," Edward replied with a sigh. "That makes me feel a little bit safer." He hesitated a moment before adding, "I only have one more question."

"What is it?" Jerg asked. "I'm listening."

Edward furrowed his brow as he tried to find the best way to express his concern. "Isn't it going to be dangerous for the sentinels we've involved in this?" he finally asked after what felt like a very long time. "I mean... later, if they're implicated in all of this. If they're discovered. How on earth are they supposed to continue functioning here, and not get into serious trouble?"

"They aren't," Jerg answered plainly. "It would be almost impossible for them to, really."

"What?" Edward asked, flabbergasted. "We're not hanging them out to dry, are we? What's going to happen to them?"

"They're coming with us, Edward," Jerg replied matter-of-factly. "Don't get your knickers in a twist."

Edward blinked back his stunned surprise. He'd never even entertained the idea of that kind of arrangement before. He preferred working alone. The peace and quiet seemed to calm his overactive mind, and kept his thoughts from bouncing all over the place, at least long enough for him to get some actual work done.

Working in concert with Jerg was going to be taxing enough all on its own. As he saw it, he was already making substantial sacrifices just to be able to keep working on this project. He couldn't even fathom the effect that the sentinels would have on his ability to conduct his research efficiently.

Regardless, in the greater scheme of things, Sixty-Seven was much more important than any discomfort he might experience. "All three of them?" he asked, deciding to remain silent about his newfound concerns.

"All *four* of them," Jerg specified, trying not to smile too openly. "You're forgetting about the driver. He'll be waiting for us in the escape vehicle once we've wrapped everything up. Is any of this going to be a problem for you?"

"No," Edward sighed, sounding less than enthusiastic. "It's not. I just wasn't expecting to have all these extra tenants. We may have to do a bit of a spring cleaning. Still, there should be more than enough room to accommodate everyone. With a little reconfiguration, we'll have adequate living quarters, common spaces, and most importantly work areas."

"I'm glad to hear it," Jerg said, crossing his arms behind his back. "It might seem a little disenchanting right now, and I'm sure that it will require some getting used to, but this could end up being very advantageous for us."

"In exactly what way?" Edward dared ask, somehow managing to sound less doubtful than he truly felt. Just thinking about the situation made him want to groan.

"Trust me, Edward," Jerg replied, genuinely enthusiastic in his response. "The possibilities are rather interesting. These are very talented men, and I have their loyalty. Think about it. They'd make excellent lab hands, for one. Imagine never having to lift anything heavier than your stethoscope. I'm not saying they'll be full-fledged assistants, but with a little training... who knows? They *could* learn. *Besides*, even if they stick to what they do best, when has a little extra security ever hurt anyone?"

"I suppose those are good points," Edward admitted, then wrinkled his brow as a thought occurred to him. "So how did you even convince these men to sign on in the first place?" he asked. "The probability of this destroying their careers or even their *lives* is substantial, and that's putting it lightly. Why would they want to risk it all like this? I understand that you have sway with these people, but that can't be it."

"Influence was only part of it," Jerg acknowledged. "It was a big part of it, I'll admit, but it wasn't everything. The rest of it was all about presentation. I just had to make it perfectly clear how much of an opportunity this would be for them."

Edward arched his brow and turned a skeptical eye on him. "An opportunity to what? Risk their lives? Become outlaws?"

"Tsk-tsk, Edward," Jerg replied. "I didn't take you for the pessimistic type. Some of these men have real ambitions. Some of them aspire to greater things, to better jobs. For some, they are working toward a lifelong dream. For others, better paycheck is a necessity. Unfortunately, these better jobs are for the most part beyond their reach without a bit of an outside nudge."

Edward's brow rose even higher, and he stared at Jerg for three full seconds before admitting, "I still don't follow."

Jerg exhaled markedly before continuing. "Sure, we're going to see our fair share of hardship. We'll be criminals, pariahs. But once we pull this off, once we really pull everything off, show the Commission that we have a fully functional model, that we can figure everything out independently—that we did all of this for *them*—they'll be begging us to come back. We'll be the envy of our peers. When that happens, I can use my connections to reward our sentinel friends for their services."

"That's a bit farther out than I dare venture," Edward said as they walked on. "But you make a strong case for these men, at any rate." A green, wall-mounted placard with a white medical cross on it came into view on their right. They would be passing by the infirmary any minute now.

"You'll see," Jerg reassured him, "they make a strong case for themselves. I'm sure that you'll like them, if you only give them a chance and get to know them. Besides, it would do you a world of good to get out of your shell once in a while. You need to socialize. You're always locking yourself away with your work, sometimes for days on end. It's not good for you."

"Yes, of course," Edward mumbled. "You're right, I'm sure, but you can stop trying to convince me now. I already said that it would be fine." Maybe it wouldn't be as bad as he thought. He was trying to be grown-up about the situation, but was having a hard time seeing it as anything but a hostile takeover. Jerg was starting to remind him of a used car salesman, and that wasn't helping matters much, either.

"I'm just trying to alleviate any concerns you might have," Jerg said. He sounded unusually anxious. "You'll be meeting one of the men shortly. The captain—Falstaff—will be waiting for us in the hall just past the infirmary."

"That one?" Edward asked, pointing to an opening in the left side of the corridor just a short distance ahead. "I suppose this is officially *on* now, isn't it? It's actually rather exciting, now that we've come face to face with it. Despite the risks involved... despite the feeling that I might lose my lunch before this is over and done with."

"Yes, it's *on* now," Jerg said with a chuckle as they passed by the front door of the infirmary. "I'm glad to see you a little more enthusiastic about all of this. It should be a walk in the park if everything goes as planned, but low morale can have devastating effects on the outcome of any operation. If you can remain calm, we'll breeze through the rest of this, and you'll come out feeling proud of what we've accomplished here tonight. I know that you can do this, Edward. It isn't as hard as you think."

They rounded the corner to their left in silence and started down the new corridor. As expected, Falstaff was there waiting for them, exactly where Jerg said he would be. He was leaning up against a wheeled container that looked like it was big enough to house a small family of dwarves, or possibly Munros.

The sentinel was decked out in the usual white, plated attire of the Commission's elite guards. He stood just over six feet tall, was built like an athlete, and had an undeniable air of confidence about him. It was visible in his eyes, which were a dark brown flecked with amber, and in the way that he held himself. His head was kept neatly shaved, his pencil mustache trimmed thin, and the fine silver chain around his neck snug enough that it couldn't be grabbed with ease. Though his skin was only a few shades darker than their own—a tone they shamelessly referred to as *pasty white*—he was obviously of Latin origin.

"Captain Alexander Falstaff," Jerg said in an introductory fashion as he closed the distance between them. "This is Doctor Edward Munro. If it wasn't for this man, we wouldn't be standing here right now contemplating the great task ahead, and the even greater rewards that await us should we succeed."

"*When* we succeed, sir," Captain Falstaff rectified, crisping his back as he snapped a salute. He turned his head aslant then and nodded at Edward. "It's a pleasure to meet you," he stated woodenly. "The commander has said some very good things about you, Doctor Munro."

Great, Edward thought, suddenly morose. *The commander. That isn't going to go to Jerg's head at all. If I have to endure his zealots calling him that for the next few months, I'd rather we get caught right now.* Despite the loud warning signals going off inside his head, he didn't *really* believe that. He'd put up with whatever he had to so long as they pulled this off. "The pleasure is all mine, Captain," he managed to say, offering him a half-bow in return.

"Captain Falstaff here is the most reliable sentinel I've ever had the pleasure of working with," Jerg interjected. "He's devoted to his work and is a lethal weapon in his own right, but above all, he is a leader of men. He served as my second in command for six years. He started in that role shortly after arriving here at the Commission, and held it until the moment Langsarks relieved me of my duties. We aren't the only ones that have been affected by that interloper's meddling."

"I wouldn't say all that about me, sir," Falstaff objected meekly and with a brief incline of his head.

"You *wouldn't*," Jerg agreed emphatically, "and that's exactly why I have to do it for you." He raised his hand then to forestall Falstaff's further objections, looking away to get the message across that he would hear nothing of it. "You have far too much humility for your own good, young man," he chided him, "and I'm sure you'll find it's something that you and the good doctor here have in common."

He raised his other hand to silence Edward, and spoke over him, as well. "Doctor Munro is one of our brightest scientific minds, maybe even the best, but he doesn't give himself nearly enough credit. The project we'll be working on is his baby. The fact that he's allowed me to assist him in his work is a testament to his goodwill. Taking that into consideration, as well as the fact that he's not only going to be our host, but also our greatest collaborator, I want you to give him the same level of cooperation that you've always afforded me."

He'd let his hands settle at his sides, but brought them up again suddenly, just in case someone had something more to say. "He's going to be acting as my subordinate for the purpose of this operation, but this operation alone. When we're done here, when we leave this place and settle into our new compound, you might as well consider him your new CO."

"Understood, sir," Falstaff replied plainly before snapping another, more casual salute.

Edward was more than a little surprised that Jerg would make such concessions. By rights, he thought, the sentinels *should* afford him a certain level of obedience—he was going to feed and house them, after all. This *was* his project. But there was no guarantee that they'd respect his authority, and he appreciated the gesture. If they *did* try to usurp his command—to take over the project—he wasn't even sure that he'd have the nerve to say anything about it. He couldn't help but wonder if Jerg knew more about his concerns than he'd meant to express. *Am I really that easy to read?* he asked himself.

"Good!" Jerg exclaimed. "Now let's carry on before these old legs of mine take root. But first," he added, pointing briefly to the helmet under Edward's arm and then to the wheeled container, "now would be a good time to get that atrocity of yours out of sight." He reached out and took the device from Edward's upheld hands, then stowed it away inside the large container. As soon as the lid fell back into place, Falstaff started pushing the unit down the corridor, and both scientists followed after him.

Their short trip to the Platform started out smoother than Edward had expected it to. They happened upon a few familiar faces along the way, but almost everyone seemed too preoccupied with their own affairs to even bother looking in their direction.

Lieutenant Spears, on the other hand, gave them an odd look as he passed them by, and the awkward eye contact, however brief, made Edward feel anxious. The rigid-looking man was one of the few sentinels that Jerg didn't know enough about to trust, he heard him whisper. When they were much farther down the corridor—it felt like they'd been walking for a full minute since they'd crossed paths with the man, though he knew that couldn't possibly be the case—he glanced over his shoulder, trying as hard as he could to appear casual.

His eyes went wide with alarm when he saw that Spears had stopped and turned halfway toward them. The lieutenant was standing in the middle of the corridor with his arms crossed, eyeing them askance as they walked away. There was no doubt that he had his suspicions. As far down the hall as they were, he could see the stern look on the man's face, and felt his reluctance to just let them go. Despite his obvious doubts, no challenge was issued.

If he had to venture a guess, he'd say that the lieutenant was hesitant to call out a ranking officer. Questioning his actions without reasonable grounds to do so would be bad form, and so they'd have peace, maybe, at least for a little while. Still, he wouldn't be surprised if Spears turned tail and ran back to the command center the second they were out of sight.

Once he got there, he'd probably do a little snooping around. He'd do it discretely, to avoid arousing suspicions. If Jerg's orders had been followed—and he had no reason to think that they hadn't been—then Spears would do his little investigation, and find that they were delivering hardware prototypes to *the Platform*. He'd also find a note annexed to their expertly falsified orders specifying that an armed escort would be required, as well as supervision during the installation of the new hardware. It was, after all, a necessary step in the execution of the Commission's latest pilot project, which was slated to start in the morning.

Hopefully, the story that Jerg had crafted would be credible enough to dissuade any uninvited guests from challenging them. He couldn't see why it wouldn't be, but realistically, anyone with more than just a mild suspicion could start digging further past the orders themselves. If they found *anything* that conflicted, or didn't make sense, they could be in for some serious trouble. All it would take was just one nosy spoilsport bringing the matter to the wrong person's attention.

"Let's pick up the pace, gentlemen," Jerg calmly suggested. "There's no reason to panic, but I didn't like the look of that one. We can't afford to dillydally."

"Didn't much like the look of him either, sir," Falstaff added, echoing his sentiment. He started to walk faster then, and the two older men were hard-pressed to keep up with him. "I've never seen eye to eye with Spears," he confessed, never letting his eyes leave the path ahead. "Don't get me wrong," he cautioned. "I'm not saying that he's a horrible person or anything—I don't know him well enough to say something like that—but from what I've seen, it's like he's driven by ambition more than anything else. He's always looking for an opportunity to advance. Kinda seems like it's all he runs on, really. Like it doesn't matter what he has to do or who he has to step on to land his next promotion. If he thinks that he can use you to move up in the world, you'd better watch your back."

"Well isn't that a comforting thought," Edward muttered with no small degree of sarcasm. "He sounds like an absolutely charming fellow, and one that we should be concerned about."

Falstaff glanced over his shoulder and smirked. "I wouldn't be surprised if he's checking up on us right now. He's suspicious of everything and everyone. It's an attitude that's encouraged in our line of work, but he takes it to a level that borders on paranoia. A lot of the bad leads he's brought my way in the past have been nothing short of ridiculous."

"Our first stop will be coming up on our right," Jerg informed them. "Are we ready?"

"Affirmative, sir," Falstaff answered in a reassuring tone. "I asked Hildebrandt to stay close to the entrance. He'll let us in as soon as we get there."

"Good call," Jerg replied. "The longer we loiter around out here, the more attention we're going to draw."

"Have you worked out some kind of *secret* signal?" Edward asked, dead serious and visibly concerned. "How is he going to know that it's us?"

Jerg threw his head back and laughed. "Don't mind him. He doesn't know what he's saying. No offense, Edward, but you should stick to science. It's what you do best."

"There's no need for a 'secret signal'," Falstaff explained. "They'll see us on the surveillance cameras. They'll be watching our approach from the monitors in the security booth. The sentinels posted there act as gatekeepers to the Platform, controlling the flow in and out of it. They're *always* present to grant or deny access, and they'd already be scoping out anyone who wanted in, anyway."

"In other words," Jerg quipped, "he'll be waiting for us at the door. Well-devised system, isn't it?"

"Forgive my ignorance," Edward replied meekly. "I never really noticed any of that the few times I've actually gone in there." He hesitated for a moment before adding, "There's just so much going on in the Platform during the day—so much to look at, and be distracted by—that it's hard to focus on just one thing, really. What happens if someone comes in behind us?"

"Don't worry about that," Jerg answered in a reassuring tone. "No one will. Hildebrandt and Mosley have been instructed to lock the place down once we've made it inside. There aren't that many people that are authorized to enter the Platform at this time of night to begin with. But if someone with a legitimate reason to be there does show up and is denied entry, then it *will* arouse suspicion. And that's why we'll have to work quickly."

Edward rubbed at his forehead and the bridge of his nose, his mounting anxiety apparent. "What do we do if someone else is already in there when we arrive?" he mumbled.

"We work as inconspicuously as we can," Jerg answered curtly, mildly annoyed. "We still have our orders. And if that isn't enough, if something goes wrong... three out of five of us will be armed to the teeth. You do the math."

"You don't mean what I think you do, do you?" Edward asked, his voice tinged with concern.

"No," Jerg scoffed. "We won't be getting into any firefights unless we have no other choice. If our safety or the integrity of the mission is compromised, we'll do whatever we have to. What I *meant* is that we might have to subdue a few people, if it comes to that." He stalked off down the hall then, leaving Edward and Falstaff in his wake.

"Nervous?" Falstaff asked, stopping for a second to glance at him over his shoulder. From the look of it, the captain wasn't at all fazed by Jerg's little outburst.

"Yes," Edward sighed. "Most definitely."

"Well," Falstaff breathed, continuing on his way, "that's understandable, but you don't have to be. Trust me, okay? This should be a walk in the park."

"Of course," Edward groaned. "That's easy for you to say. You're still young and foolhardy, and you've had years to prepare yourself for situations like this one."

"Listen," Falstaff responded in a reassuring tone, "I'll be right next to you the entire time. If the plan goes south, you'll be in good hands. Let me do all the worrying, okay?"

"Thank you," Edward said, genuinely grateful. The thought of having the youthful giant by his side comforted him somewhat. In fact, he felt his unease start to melt away almost immediately. If he was worried now, he couldn't imagine how he'd feel once they actually got to the riskier part of their business. More than anything, he hoped that nothing would go wrong, but if things did go wrong, would he be able to keep his cool? If he was left on his own, he seriously doubted it.

"No problem," Falstaff replied with a grin. "I am, after all, still young and foolhardy, and have had years to prepare myself for situations just like this one." They walked on in silence for a moment, and he added, "I'll do my thing, and all you have to worry about is doing yours."

Farther up the corridor, Jerg had stopped and turned into an alcove in the wall. He raised his hand and waved at someone just out of their sight, did the universal index-to-thumb A-OK sign, and gestured for them to hurry up. "Get over here, you two. Quickly. There isn't any time to lose."

When Falstaff took off ahead of him, Edward thanked his lucky stars that his rickety old knees were still holding up, and followed after him. Noting the effort that the captain was putting into pushing the wheeled container, and the difficulty he was having keeping his pace, he fell in beside him to lend him a hand.

They caught up with Jerg a few seconds later, having gained far more momentum than they'd anticipated. They were moving so quickly that Jerg had to sidestep out of the way to avoid getting plowed over as they swung around the corner and into the recess in the wall.

"Move it or lose it, baldy!" Edward quipped blithely. He was relieved to see that the large double doors in the alcove had already been opened from the inside. If they'd been closed, they'd have battered right through them from the sheer force of the impact, unless they'd been locked, in which case they'd have come to a loud and potentially painful stop. Reading the calm expression on Falstaff's face, he understood that the man had expected the doors to be open the entire time.

Inside, they slowed and ground to a gradual halt twenty feet past the entrance. The Platform was a vast chamber lit only by the dull glow of its countless monitors. It felt heavy, weighed down by the pervasive thrum of electronics.

A white-plated sentinel came jogging up to them a few seconds later. He wasn't as tall as Falstaff was, but he more than made up the difference in width and girth, and he still dwarfed his own wrinkly old husk by far. His shoulders were massive. He looked like he could lift the captain over his head without even breaking a sweat. Like Falstaff, he kept his head neatly shaved and sported a well-groomed beard. His striking blue-gray eyes were the softest of his otherwise stony facial features.

"We are good to go, Captain Falstaff, sir," the colossal man stated, snapping a salute. "Ready to get down to business." The mischievous grin plastered across his face contrasted oddly with the formality of his presentation and the gravity of the situation. In a way, he reminded Edward of an overeager rottweiler.

"Cut it with the 'Captain, sir' crap, Hildebrandt," Falstaff warned, though jokingly. "One or the other will do."

A second sentinel trotted up to them then with Jerg close in tow. This one, physically average in every way, had dark brown skin, and short, curly hair that matched his grizzled beard.

At a glance, Edward would have guessed that he was in his early fifties. Or forties. Or late thirties. It was difficult to tell how old he really was. His chestnut-colored eyes were keen, and he looked like a man that had seen a lot and done it all. There was a calm assurance about him, and it gave him the impression that he was the type of person that he might want to see if he needed sage advice. Despite his otherwise unremarkable build, he moved fluidly and with the energy of youth.

"Glad that you could make it, Corporal Mosley," Falstaff said with a nod. "What's the situation at the front gate?"

"It's locked down," Mosley answered calmly. "We're ready for phase two of the operation."

"Good," Falstaff replied. "Corporal, you're on Commander Weissinger. Follow him to vat zero sixty-seven, secure the area and await my arrival. Sergeant Hildebrandt, I want you to load these supplies into the APC and set up a defensive position at the waste removal dock. Baumgartner can back you up if things get too hot, but I told him to have the escape vehicle ready the second we reach the extraction point, so try to hold out on your own if you can, if it comes to that."

He set his hand on Hildebrandt's shoulder then and looked him squarely in the eyes. "When you see us coming, we may not have very long to load our cargo into the APC. I'll need you to be ready for a quick assist."

"Yes sir, Captain, sir!" Hildebrandt exclaimed with excessive enthusiasm and a wide grin. "Ready to haul ass, and kick some, too."

"Any questions?" Falstaff asked, addressing all those present. He waited all of two seconds before nodding confidently and adding, "Good. Let's make this happen, people. Go!"

As the others scrambled off in different directions, Edward looked to the captain for guidance. He was relieved to have someone to lead the way for him. It really took a lot of the weight off of his shoulders.

"Follow me, Doctor," Falstaff urged him. "Let's show these guys how it's done." He took off at a light jog then, heading deeper into the Platform.

Edward took off after him and did everything he could to keep up. After only fifteen or twenty seconds, he had a good idea of just how hard that was going to be. He was already short of breath, and his knees—which had been miraculously *fine* up until then—were starting to feel like rusty old cogs in his worn-out machinery. It wouldn't surprise him in the least if they suddenly gave way, and he wound up facedown on the floor.

"Keep it up, Doc!" Falstaff called out over his shoulder. "We're almost there. Just keep breathing."

To Edward's dismay, the captain had picked up his pace. The sound of his own breathing was hoarse, but he persevered. His lungs felt like they were on fire, and he was rasping heavily.

As they entered the section of the Platform referred to as the Womb, he took heart in the knowledge that they were almost halfway there. Following the captain's advice, he tried to focus on his breathing. Despite the mounting pain in his chest, he did his best to take deep breaths, and diverted what little cognitive ability remained to avoid tripping and breaking his neck.

The Womb was the Platform's heart and soul. It was the heart and soul of the Commission's leading project. Row upon row upon row of metallic, cylindrical structures they called constructs rose up from the floor like so many trees in a forest of steel and neon tubing. There were thousands of them, all lined up perfectly.

Each one stood just over ten feet tall and had its own integrated keypad and multifaceted monitor. A narrow corridor of open space ran between every second row of constructs to facilitate movement between them and throughout the Womb. Travelling down them was a bit of a tight squeeze. There was barely enough room for two men to walk side by side.

At the epicenter of it all stood the Mainframe: an enormous computer that controlled and monitored just about everything that went on inside of the Platform. Its functions included but were not limited to the performance of routine maintenance checks on the Womb's integrated work instruments, the management of individual life-support systems for each of the vat-like constructs, and the tracking and storing of biotelemetric readings. The data it recorded was invaluable to the Commission.

When they finally reached *the Mainframe*, he no longer felt like his lungs were on fire. It felt like they were about to implode. He leaned against the railing at the base of the main computer and panted heavily as he struggled to catch his breath. His knees were swollen and his back ached. It was pathetic, he thought, considering how short of a distance they'd actually travelled, but he'd never been much of an athlete, even in his better days.

Still red in the face and gasping for air, he patted his pockets down and started to dig through them. His fingers fumbled around clumsily as they probed for the disk that he'd made *absolutely certain* to bring with them. He must have searched himself over about a dozen times since they'd left his quarters, just to ensure that he hadn't lost it somewhere along the way. Even though he'd managed to find it every single time, he still couldn't remember exactly where he'd put it. The disk contained strings of code that he'd compiled and was supposed to load into the system.

"Good job, Doctor Munro," Falstaff said in a way that was clearly meant to be encouraging. "Whatever you do, don't panic. Catch your breath if you need to. Relax. Take it easy. You know that you can do this." He'd gone into *sentry mode* the second they'd arrived. He stood in an offhand shooting position with his back to the main computer, his assault rifle raised to eye level as he watched and listened for anything out of the ordinary.

"Call me Edward," Munro wheezed. Finally remembering where he'd put the disk, he fished it out of his breast pocket and slid it into the appropriate slot. Wasting as little time as possible, he ran the program that he'd written and started injecting his code into the system. The patch was meant to cover their tracks, but it also served another purpose. Without it, an alarm would sound if they tried to open vat zero sixty-seven. Patching the system was a fairly simple process, and the deed was done in under a minute.

He was about to turn to Falstaff then to let him know that he was done, but stopped and hesitated a moment, thinking back to his secondary objectives. Jerg had asked him to do whatever he could to hamper the Commission's progress. By wiping certain areas of *the Mainframe*'s memory, he could further mire any investigation into what had happened here. If he wanted to go a step beyond that, he could seriously cripple their research.

If he did go that route, the Commission scientists would have to fall back on collective memory and older data they might have stored elsewhere. This would definitely give them an edge in the race to bring their research to fruition.

Jerg had also talked about the possibility of tampering with the life-support systems in order to achieve similar results. The suggested modifications would leave the test subjects intact, at least *technically*, while reducing them to little more than catatonic vegetables. Even if Jerg had seemed insistent about it, the thought of it didn't sit well with him. It seemed unethical, inhumane.

Decided, he ejected the disk, tucked it away in his lab coat, and prepared to erase those pockets of data that he could easily recognize. The request to alter the life-support systems would be ignored altogether. At least he *preferred* to think of it as a request, even if it had sounded a lot more like an order.

He was about ready to start carrying out the deed when he was struck by another case of conscience. He didn't want to feel like a cheater for the rest of his life. Though their actions were unlawful, all they were doing was taking back what was rightfully theirs. These extra steps Jerg wanted him to take were downright underhanded. There was no need to turn the blade in the wound and further provoke the Commission's fury.

Decided—*truly* decided this time—he started tapping at the keyboard at a furious pace. The data wipe would ensure that no record was kept of vat zero sixty-seven being opened that night. If this played out the way he intended it to, the Commission would only be able to pick up on what they'd done here through visual confirmation, and that could take them a while. It would happen, eventually, but it should buy them some time.

He covered their tracks and he covered them well, but he drew the line there. There would be no erased corporate data, no mindless vegetables. After a final keystroke, he stepped back from the console, and exhaled cathartically.

"We ready to go?" Falstaff asked him, still scanning the area for possible threats.

"If we can *walk*," Edward specified, somewhat embarrassed. "Otherwise, I still need to catch my breath. I can hardly breathe as it is and my joints are killing me."

Falstaff motioned for him to be silent then. His eyes were riveted on *something* he couldn't make out himself, somewhere off in the distance. His own eyes just couldn't see that far.

"Did you hear that?" Falstaff whispered, a look of concern wrinkling the corners of his eyes.

"Hear what?" Edward asked, perplexed.

"We have to get out of here *now*," Falstaff urged him. "They're trying to ram through the front doors."

Edward mumbled something under his breath and wiped at the sweat trickling down his wrinkly forehead. "What do we... what are we going to do?" he managed to say, his tongue tripping up over the urgency of the situation.

"You sure you can't run?" Falstaff asked, slinging his assault rifle over his shoulder.

"Positive," Edward responded dejectedly.

"Then get over here and hop on my back," the captain said, kneeling to a crouch. "I know that getting carried around like a sack of potatoes isn't appealing, but we don't really have a choice.

We have to move ASAP. They'll be through those doors any second now. There isn't any time to lose."

"If we must," Edward conceded, too anxious to care how ridiculous he'd look when they met up with the others. He was somewhat afraid that he'd hurt Falstaff back, and consequently, he was extremely careful as he climbed on. He narrowed his eyes and cringed as he wrapped his arms around the other man' neck.

His concerns were dispelled the second Falstaff stood up. The strapping young man grabbed the undersides of his knees to better support his weight, and he suddenly felt as light as a feather, like he was no burden at all. He might as well have been a backpack carrying some lightweight supplies or the captain's lunch. *A salad, perhaps,* he thought, *with crackers and cheese.*

"Hold on tight, Doctor," Falstaff more than just suggested. "This is going to be a bumpy ride." He rounded *the Mainframe* then and darted off in the direction they'd originally been heading in, seemingly unencumbered by the extra weight. He turned right at the first opening between the constructs, and narrowly avoided a pipe that was protruding from the corner of one of the vats.

As soon as they started down the new aisle, a loud explosion rocked *the Platform.* It sounded like it had come from the front gates. Edward cramped up reflexively, tightening his stranglehold on Falstaff's neck. At the back of his mind, he was worried that he might choke the life right out of him, but on the other hand, he wouldn't loosen his grip if he was asked to.

The captain continued without flinching, unfazed by the loud detonation or the scrawny but tensed arms squeezing his Adam's apple toward the back of his throat. "Breaching charge," he stated simply, as though he'd expected it. "We're almost there."

"We're almost there," Edward repeated at a mumble, almost as though to reassure himself. They turned down the second aisle on their left and he was relieved to see that they were, in fact, *almost* there. Mosley stood in an offhand shooting position up ahead of them, his rifle aimed dangerously in their direction—or rather into the distance behind them, he noted. The man signaled to them briefly before returning his hand to his gun.

Jerg stood beside him, tapping his foot nervously as he glared at his watch with an air of perplexity. He looked up at them as they approached. "I was about to open the vat," he snapped, visibly miffed, "with or without you."

Edward grunted as he slid down from Falstaff's back. "Then I'm glad we got here when we did," he said, smoothing out his wrinkled lab coat. "Proceeding without me would have been a horrible, horrible mistake."

"I'd ask what took you so long," Jerg retorted defensively, "but if we don't hurry, this is going to be horrible for *all* of us."

"If you'd opened it on your own," Edward growled, "all of this would have been for nothing!" Maybe it was the stress getting to him, but he felt like his well of patience had dried up. His reaction was even more visceral than he'd expected it to be.

He stalked over to vat zero sixty-seven's keypad, grumbling incoherently all the way. "You can't just yank the wires and pull the plug! We have to do this *carefully, gradually.*"

Jerg opened his mouth to say something, but Edward cut him off just as quickly, furiously tapping away at the keypad all the while. "No offense, Doctor Weissinger, but you should stick to security. It's what you do best." He felt a twinge of remorse the second the words left his mouth, but there were more pressing issues to worry about.

Jerg furrowed his brow and crossed his arms. He clearly hadn't appreciated that last comment, but was making an apparent effort to ignore it. "All I'm saying is that we're running out of time," he breathed. "The sentinels must have botched their first breaching attempt. If they hadn't, they'd almost be here right now, and I seriously doubt it's going to take them more than a second try."

"You know, he's right," Mosley added, still peering down his sights. "The gate's pretty solid, but even an idiot could blast through it with a second charge."

"Look," Edward sighed, glancing over his shoulder at Jerg. "This whole thing's got me off my rocker. I'm nervous, I'm scared, and *I'm sorry*. Now come over here and help me with this, will you? I can't do it on my own."

"What do you need me to do?" Jerg asked, his flared temper just as quickly forgotten.

"Watch," Edward mumbled, pausing briefly as he squinted at the monitor in front of him, "learn, and be ready to do exactly as I say." What they were about to attempt would be complicated and risky, but *he* was in command now, and he meant to take every necessary precaution. There was too much riding on this to mess it up now.

CHAPTER
17

A Bad Time to Take a Nap

Daniel stirred from his sleep, woken by a noise that hadn't fully registered with him. He didn't know *what* the sound had been, exactly, but he knew that it couldn't be good. *He just knew it.* Confused, and more scared than he'd care to admit, he gathered his velvety blankets around himself, and pulled them up over his head, so that just his eyes and nose peeped out.

Now fully aware, he stared out into the surrounding darkness apprehensively. Frozen with fear, all he could do was wait and listen for the sound of the approaching zombie, or whatever other horrible creature it was that was lurking just beyond the bounds of his tiny, twin-sized bed.

He waited and listened, and waited and listened some more, unblinking, his imagination running wild. The more he thought of the noise, the more it frightened him. The more it frightened him, the more he thought of the noise, and it drove him further and further into a vicious cycle of dread and inertia.

Before long, his fear had become a self-sufficient entity. It had taken on a life of its own, and grew stronger with every passing second. Just like his imagination, it seemed to know no bounds.

He started to tremble, and when he heard his teeth clattering, he snapped his mouth shut to avoid alerting any unwelcome visitors to his presence, even if he was certain that whatever was out there already knew exactly where he was.

Some light from an unknown source filtered in through the curtains on his window then, and the wide shaft that it cast lit up half the bedroom with a dim glow. Was the dark silhouette over in the corner of his room just a shadow, he wondered, or was it something else? He couldn't say for sure, but his money—all ten of the talers that he'd stored away in his *Mister Happy-Pants* piggy bank—was on *"something else"*.

The misshapen diamond of light morphed, and shrunk, and winked out almost as quickly as it had appeared, and plunged the room into complete darkness once more. He could no longer see the "something else". He couldn't see anything at all. The thing was probably blacker than night, he imagined, and lurking around on the floor, waiting for him to get out of bed. If he did get out of bed, it would pounce on him like a rabid alley wolf. It was evil, and twisted, and had a taste for tender human flesh, especially that of terrified children. He could feel it in his bones.

Suddenly, he heard the noise that had woken him once again, and it was both reassuring and disconcerting all at once. It was reassuring because he knew that it hadn't been the sound of the living dead, or the strident cry of some terrifying, nocturnal beast, or even just a mysterious bump in the night.

It was nothing more than the sound of his father's voice travelling down the hall, and through his open bedroom door. By the time it reached his ears, he could hardly understand a word of it. It was muffled, distant, and what he *could* hear of it sounded only like so much nonsense. As far as he could tell, it was little more than emotional, at times livid gibbering. And that bothered him.

As glad as he was that he wouldn't end up as an appetizer for some famished ghoul, he couldn't help but wonder what had troubled his father so. The desperation in his voice was palpable.

He'd never heard him so downtrodden before. His father was sad, and that made him sad. Sad, and a little scared, too.

He leaned over the side of his mattress then to take a quick peek under his bed, just in case he'd been wrong about everything, and there really *was* something lurking around there lying in ambush, waiting to grab his ankle the second his foot hit the floor. Satisfied that the coast was clear, he hopped out of bed and scurried across the floor toward the open doorway.

When he reached it, he stopped and hesitated for a moment before crossing the threshold. He did want to know what was going on, but was it really worth getting caught out of bed after *lights out*? When he heard his father's violent sobbing once more, he decided that it was.

Something odd happened then. For the very first time, Frank realized that he was having one of his recurring "Danny dreams" as it was unfolding. It wasn't that he hadn't had a lucid dream before. He had, and the ability to call down lightning, or leap over tall buildings, or summon pretty much anything his heart desired was always entertaining. But this was something else entirely.

The "Danny dreams" almost always played out in the first person. They were oddly linear, and so vivid that they managed to fool him into thinking they were real every single time. When he was dreaming, he thought what Daniel thought, felt what Daniel felt. He saw the dreams through the child's eyes, lived them through his body—or through someone else's, on occasion. They were so lifelike that he was sometimes confused and disoriented for a few minutes after waking from them.

This wasn't exactly a lucid dream, but it did break from tradition. Most notably because he was completely aware of the fact that it was a dream, and that somewhere back in the real world, there was a good chance he was about to die. And then things got even stranger. One second he was Daniel MacBride, and the next he was completely separated from him, left hanging in the air nearby like some kind of strange, ethereal presence.

Despite this "splitting", he had no influence over the dream itself. It was like watching a three-dimensional movie that was playing out inside the confines of his own mind.

"Wake up!" he called out. There was a frantic urgency in his voice, but he knew that it produced no sound except in his thoughts. He wasn't sure when he'd fallen asleep, but he was all too aware of the fact that his innards had become "outers" at the hands of some psychopathic inquisitor.

There wasn't much that he could do to escape his fate, and he knew it, but he didn't want to go out like this. Not in his sleep. As long as he was awake, there was a chance—albeit a small one—that he'd live to see another day. Even if that opportunity never materialized, at least he'd be able to go down with a little dignity. He wanted to be defiant until the bitter end. He didn't know why, exactly. He just did.

Instead, he had to watch this cryptic, rerun dream-garbage while bleeding out like a stuck pig. "Wake up!" he shouted again, but still there was no sound from his disembodied consciousness. For the briefest of moments, he could have sworn that Daniel had seen him somehow, or heard him, but he soon realized that he was looking *through* him, toward his parents' bedroom, toward the source of his father's weeping.

Determined to wake up, he concentrated as best he could on opening his eyes. When that failed, he tried crossing them. The trick had worked rather well for him as a child, when he'd wanted to wake from particularly terrifying nightmares. Even though he had no physical representation in the dream, he could still *feel* himself, somehow. Nothing could deter or sever that link between his conscience and his body—nothing short of death, at least.

He tried over and over again without result, and meanwhile, Daniel stood in the doorway, staring down the hall, deliberating on whether or not to step out into it. Maybe he was frozen on the spot for fear of the spanking he'd get if he was caught out of bed, or maybe it was something else. He couldn't say for sure.

He could no longer tell what was going on inside of the little boy's head except from memory. There were so many different "Danny dreams", some of them seemingly pointless and similar to each other, that it was hard to tell them apart. With the small matter of imminent death hanging over his head, he couldn't recall what had happened in this one specifically.

He soon realized that if the torture being inflicted on him wasn't enough to keep him awake, then any discomfort he caused himself by crossing his eyes would be utterly futile. Maybe he was just doomed to die in his sleep. Maybe it was just the way things were meant to be. In his final moments, he was trapped inside a bloody dream, and it wasn't even one that he could enjoy.

He could have dreamt of the things he'd always wanted to do but had never gotten around to doing. He could have dreamt of magically clean air, of verdant mountain ranges drowned in blue skies. He could have seen his life flash before his eyes. Heck, he could even have dreamt of Vanessa's ample breasts, and of the way they felt when the warm flesh of them pressed up against his back. Instead, he was saddled with yet another pointless and downright irritating dream of the recurring variety.

Maybe these dreams of his were nothing special after all. Maybe everyone had them but kept quiet about it because they were afraid of being labeled *batshit crazy*. Maybe he never had a chance of understanding what any of it meant to begin with, if it even meant anything to begin with. There were a lot of maybes.

The boy's father growled viscerally then, so loudly that even through the closed door to the master bedroom, it snapped him back to attention immediately. At that precise moment, he knew that he was having a brand new dream. He was sure of it. As distracted as he was, he would have remembered something as animalistic and uncharacteristic of him as that.

"I'll kill them all," Harrold growled further, seething with an anger that was barely kept in check. "I'll kill every single one of them, Elizabeth, right down to the last! You mark my words!"

"Harrold!" Elizabeth cried out in a way that conveyed much. Just one word, spoken with such emotion, replaced many. The grief that Frank heard in it rivaled her husband's own, but lacked any of the hatred that was currently consuming him. *This is killing me too*, it said. *I know that you're angry, but we have a sleeping child in the other room. Please, try to control yourself.*

He'd experienced the dreams so often now that he knew every character by heart, from their personalities to their mannerisms. She probably would have put it some other way, had she been less stricken with grief, but Elizabeth's message was clear. He knew what she'd meant, what her intentions were. She was trying to be the voice of reason. She was trying to keep her husband from doing something rash, something that might traumatize their child.

"No, Elizabeth!" Harrold snapped. He was so quick about it that she couldn't have said more if she'd wanted to. Apparently, he'd understood her too, but wasn't in the mood to be reasonable. "They've gone too far, this time, and you know it," he barked. His voice was hoarse and broken from the violent fits of sobbing that were still wrenching free from deep within his chest. "I'm going to hunt them down, and when I find them, they're going to rue the day that they did this to me... to us. It's the only way. Do you understand me, Elizabeth? The only way! They're going to regret it. They're going to regret ever being born."

"The only way to *what*, Harrold?" Elizabeth asked in shocked disbelief. "It isn't going to bring Frank back! It isn't going to make you feel any better about any of this."

"They took him away from us!" Harrold shouted, furious. "They took him away, Elizabeth! We'll never see him again— ever! Do you realize that? Do you? They had no right to take him away from us... no right whatsoever!"

"That still doesn't make it right to—"

"Yes it does, Elizabeth," Harrold groaned. "Yes, it does." He was still obviously distraught, but seemed to be fighting hard to put down the storm raging on inside of himself. "No one has the right to cause so much pain and suffering. No one has the right to take a life the way that they did and not face any consequences. To do what they did... to take the life of a child..."

Frank saw a contradiction there, but he couldn't fault him for it. Obviously, something both terrible and tragic had happened to this child, to this other Frank. He'd always thought that Hopper, as they also called him, had run away. That's what he'd gathered from his other dreams, at least, but apparently, that wasn't the case. No, something more sinister had transpired. He'd probably lose it too, if he had a child taken from him that way. He couldn't even imagine what that would feel like.

"How many more need to suffer?" Harrold asked, pressing on adamantly. "How many more need to die? This *will* happen again, Elizabeth. I know it will. And it'll keep happening until someone does something about it."

"It was an accident, Harrold!" Elizabeth wailed in agony. Despite the frustration in her voice, she didn't sound angry, but like she was at her wit's end. "It was a malfunction of some kind—a factory defect—and Frank was just at the wrong place at the wrong time."

"Even if that was true," Harrold snapped, not at all deterred by his wife's objections, "they refuse to acknowledge that it even happened! He was murdered, Elizabeth! Murdered! There were witnesses—witnesses that *I* trust—and that isn't something you can just brush under the carpet. It *isn't*!"

"And what if the police just don't know about it?" Elizabeth asked heatedly. "Have you ever considered that?"

"Have I ever considered *it*?" Harrold shot back indignantly. "If we ignore the fact that close to a dozen people saw the entire thing go down, you mean? Or that those *machines* of theirs are rigged with recording equipment that transfers everything they see, hear or do right back to their precinct headquarters? Yeah, I've considered it, and it's not fucking likely. They saw it all firsthand, as it was happening. There's no two ways about it."

Elizabeth failed to respond at first. Frank could imagine her sitting on the edge of her bed, speechless, her head hung low. She probably knew that he was right, but didn't want to believe it.

Farther up the hall, Daniel had started creeping toward him, toward the master bedroom. As far as he could tell, the little boy hadn't understood a word of his parents' argument. Maybe he'd been too far away, or maybe he'd heard everything, but none of it had registered. Whatever the reason, it was probably for the best. If he'd understood correctly, and he was pretty sure that he had, the boy's brother had been murdered, or at least killed in a violent manner, and he probably wasn't even aware of it.

Even if it was just a dream, the thought of the kid finding out about his brother's death that way troubled him deeply. If he could have, he'd have warned the boy, told him to turn around and go back to bed. If he could have, he'd have covered his ears to spare him from his father's emotional raving. He'd have done everything in his power to keep him from that grief. But it was hard to do anything at all when you were nothing more than a disembodied nonentity without a voice.

"What about Daniel?" Elizabeth asked dejectedly, breaking the uneasy silence that had settled in. "What about your other son? Have you thought about him in all of this? Have you thought about how all of this is going to affect him?"

Yes, Harrold, Frank added disapprovingly, though only in his mind. *What kind of role model are you going to be for your son when you turn to a life of crime?* He felt utterly helpless. There wasn't a thing that he could do to intervene; point that was driven even further home as Daniel stepped *through* him, or rather through the spot that he'd be standing in if he even had a body.

"He'll be fine," Harrold answered gruffly. "He's not going to know about it." The madness was gone from his voice, and his words were like music to Frank's ears. If he could just change the subject now, Daniel might be able to continue living a normal, carefree childhood—at least for a while.

Frank felt his stomach wrench violently then, and for a brief moment, he was convinced that the inquisitor was busy ripping his intestines out back in the *"waking world"*. *This is it*, he thought, but death never came for him. His stomach was a ball of agony and he felt nauseous, but he was still there, still alive.

He started to sag forward then, and everything went dark. When his vision returned, he was looking down at his hands. Apparently, the dream had decided to give him his very own set, replete with arms, a torso, and when he looked down, he saw, even legs and feet. He felt like he was going to fall, so he turned and reached for something to lean on. As he did, he realized that Daniel was no longer there. He'd vanished without a trace, along with all of the mural decorations in the hall. Even the doors were gone. He was alone in an empty hall that seemed to stretch out infinitely in both directions.

Before he knew it, he was assailed by another gut-twisting jolt of pain, this one nearly overwhelming, and the world around him started to waver. He felt like his knees had turned to water, and he was hard-pressed to maintain his balance. If he'd had all of his concentration, he'd have thought nothing of it, but the pains he'd been suffering were starting to take their toll, even in the dream, and it was a struggle just to remain on his feet.

He leaned against the wall to keep from falling over, and his eyes went wide with surprise as he fell right through it. It wasn't a wall at all, he realized, but another figment of his imagination, and it too was now gone. Everything was gone, yet he remained. His knees still felt like jelly, and that feeling had spread to the rest of his body, but he knew that he couldn't possibly be falling, so he took a deep breath to calm himself, and floated freely in the vast emptiness that he found himself stranded in.

There was a great sense of quietude pervading the void, and he couldn't help but take a moment to reflect on his life. His best moments, his worst moments, his successes, his shortcomings, the people he loved and would be leaving behind, and everything else that mattered. If his life wasn't going to flash before his eyes all on its own, he was going to have to help it out a bit. There wasn't much else he could do, anyway.

He regretted the way that his last conversation with his father had ended. Deep down, he knew that everything that he'd done had been done with his best interest in mind. Gordon *was* his real father. Being adopted changed nothing. He loved him just the same, and he hoped that his father knew it. He didn't care who his biological parents were anymore. He never really had. It had been nothing more than a fleeting preoccupation.

More than anything, he worried about Vanessa, and regretted getting her involved in this whole mess, which would surely be the end of him. He'd never asked for any of it to happen, but he could find no one to blame but himself. If she didn't make it, if she died because of this—because of him—then he'd just as soon never wake up anyway.

He hoped beyond hope that they did let her go, that they realized the futility of their actions, and set her free. She had nothing to do with any of this. Then again, neither did he, but that wasn't going to stop them from putting an end to him—any second now, as far as he knew.

He heard a low, continuous rumble off in the distance then, and the sound of it made the hairs stand up on the back of his neck. He didn't know what it was, but it was growing closer, louder. Within seconds, it had gotten so loud that his ears were throbbing. It was like the roar of an earthquake over radio static blasted through a battery of megaphones.

The sound seemed to come from everywhere and nowhere all at once. Its vibrations pressed hard against his flesh and covered him with their smothering ripples. He felt like a fly trapped on the inside of a blasting speaker. He tried to cover his ears, but soon realized that it was a pointless effort. Just when he thought that he could take no more, that anything louder would make his eardrums explode, he was proven wrong.

"Can't you work any faster?" an unfamiliar voice boomed out from the void. He'd never heard anything so loud in his entire life. Like the static rumbling, the voice didn't seem to have any one point of origin, but came from all around him. The words were heavy, weighted, like they were actual, physical things, and they sent fresh shockwaves throughout his entire body. He knew that it was impossible, but it felt like they could crush him. All that he could do was cringe under the pressure and hope for it to pass, but he'd have no such luck.

"They've breached the gate!" the voice exploded again. There was an urgency to it that was pressing but not panicked.

The empty space before him started to shift and distort, and he was instantly reminded of something he'd once seen, but since forgotten. Translucent, shimmering pockets of *nothing* fluctuated in and out of existence, then drew together and started to take shape. The semblance of a face emerged, and he knew right away that he'd seen it before. The same phenomenon had occurred the day that he'd been beaten to within an inch of his life, just before he'd passed out and woken in the hospital.

He'd been farther away from it the first time, and everything had seemed less clear to him then, but he knew that they were one and the same. They were almost face to face now, and he could make out distinct features that he hadn't noticed previously. It was still a bit of a blur, but concrete enough that it gave him an idea of what he was looking at. It was the face of an old man, with great tufts of curly, white hair jutting out from the sides of his head.

"I'm going as fast as I can," the face said in a voice that boomed just as loudly as its peer's. He felt like his head was going to cave in, and he had to remind himself that it was just a dream, even if the pain seemed real.

"He's almost through!" the voice resounded with a tinge of both anticipation and concern that was mirrored perfectly by the shifting features of the disembodied, floating face. "Be ready to help me catch him!"

Slowly but surely, more shapes emerged and came together in the void surrounding him. They were no longer only translucent. Color bled into them, and helped complete what was starting to look like a living, comprehensible picture. The process reminded him of the way that coated paper bubbled up and blackened before bursting into flame.

He flinched as a series of loud, rat-a-tatting blasts went off like multiple rifles firing. The face—not yet fully materialized—shot a glance off to the side with alarm, but turned back to him again almost immediately. Another frantic barrage detonated all around them, but the *face* took no heed of the noise this time.

All of a sudden, what blank spaces remained in the void seemed to melt away, completing the otherwise abstract scene before him. It gave it all a certain sense. It was almost possible to understand what he was looking at now that he saw the entire picture, but the complex machinery surrounding him on all sides was like nothing he'd ever seen before.

His eardrums were still sore, but the auditory assault on them had quieted significantly. It no longer seemed like everything was being amplified beyond normal decibel levels. On the downside, he was starting to feel dizzy and his stomach was roiling. Every square inch of his body was in its own special kind of agony, every second a fight to remain in control, to avoid panicking.

At first, he was sure that he'd simply woken from his dream. The difference in feeling between the "Danny dreams" and this was too marked. The realism of what he was seeing and feeling—of what he'd *woken into*—was just too pronounced for it to be a dream. The scraggly old men that were holding him up by the armpits felt real. The wateriness of his legs felt real. His complete lack of energy, and the certitude that he couldn't stand on his own two feet if he wanted to also felt very real.

On the other hand, there were certain inaccuracies that he just couldn't ignore, certain details suggesting that he'd woken from one dream right into another. Firstly, this wasn't the last place that he remembered being when he'd passed out. He certainly wasn't on the inquisitor's cutting board, or even in an abandoned office building. It was, again, like nothing he'd ever seen before, and he imagined he'd never see anything like it again. The setting was unfamiliar, the men keeping him from falling flat on his face were unfamiliar, but most of all, *he himself* was unfamiliar.

One thing in particular stood out to him like a sore thumb, one detail so major that it practically convinced him all on its own that he *must* still be sleeping. That *detail* was his arm, which he clearly remembered being amputated, but now, apparently, was back and completely intact. It had been sliced clear off—he'd seen the stump that remained with his own two eyes—and yet there it was: feeble, sore, perhaps a little more skeletal than he remembered it being, but very much there and attached to the rest of his body. There were no visible sutures to suggest that it had been grafted on again, either.

As disconcerting as that was, it soon became the least of his concerns. In the thirty or so seconds that had passed since he'd woken, he hadn't taken a single breath, and he only realized this when he felt something like an invisible hand tightening its grip around his lungs. He tried to gasp but no air came. Soon, panic set in and his chest began to heave violently.

"He's going to choke if we don't liberate his airways," one of the old men stammered. "His body might do it all on its own, but I'm not going to sit here and wait to find out." Then, before he could react—he wasn't sure he'd have had the strength to do anything, regardless—they pushed his shoulders forward and lowered him to his knees. The cold concrete beneath him made him aware of his complete lack of clothing. He was stark naked, and covered from head to toe in some slimy, transparent goop.

His vision was starting to blur and become interlaced with bright specks of light when one of them clasped their hands around him from behind and squeezed violently, just below his chest cavity. There was a sharp pain in his ribs as they strained under the pressure, but there was nothing he could do about it, and they repeated the process over and over again.

On the fourth or fifth try—he couldn't tell which, because his head had started to swim after the second crushing thrust—he felt his insides buck. His chest heaved, and a geyser of pinkish liquid sprayed out from his mouth, showering the floor beneath him. The warm liquid splashed against his hands and knees, but he didn't care how disgusting it was. He was just happy for the short gasps of air he was able to suck in between bouts of retching. After his trachea had been cleared and his stomach emptied, he started to black out and almost fell forward, but the old men caught him and he snapped to.

He wasn't sure exactly what he'd just thrown up, but it was very similar in texture to the gunk that he was already covered in. All of a sudden, he was hit by a distinct, physical memory of being completely submerged in warm, viscous liquid. He remembered the weight of the thick, oily gunk pressing against him from all sides. The memory was strangely comforting.

The old men helped him to his feet, and he was so tired that all he could do was sag against them. His eyelids felt like they were weighted with lead. He fought to keep them open, but it was a losing battle, and they closed despite his efforts. Even though he wasn't able to open them again, he was far from sleep.

Surrounded by darkness, he waited and listened and tried to keep his feet moving in tandem with the others. When his eyes did flutter open briefly, he saw that his feet weren't even really moving. They were just dragging along the floor like dead weight. Any movement of his legs was solely the work of his imagination.

"He weighs a ton," one of the old men complained loudly. He could hear them grunting and groaning as they labored, and for a second, he thought they might drop him on the floor.

"Don't give up, Jerg," the other man's voice beseeched him. "Whatever you do, don't give up. Maybe one of your men can give us a hand."

Another series of loud blasts sounded and Frank's eyes shot wide open. In front of him, two rows of tall, cylindrical machines stretched out farther than the eye could see. The glow from their monitors and the flickering guide lights embedded in the floor made it seem like he was moving down some kind of psychedelic techno-tunnel. It was impressive, almost bewildering, but what he saw next made it pale in comparison and seem insignificant.

The third machine ahead and to their right looked noticeably different from the others, and it gave him at least a bit of an idea what they were used for. If what he was seeing was real, if it wasn't just his mind playing tricks on him, some kind of stress-induced hallucination, then the greater part of the machinery's outer layer was nothing more than a protective casing. Beneath it, something else was housed—something bizarre, and inexplicable, and bordering on madness.

The machine that he was staring at contained a large, glass vat that was filled with a rose-hued liquid. In its center floated an inanimate human being. He—it looked like a man, but he wasn't entirely sure—literally looked like he'd been pickled. The flesh covering his or *its* skeletal body was pasty and bloated, like that of a drowning victim that had been pulled from the lake.

The sight of it made his skin crawl, but that wasn't the worst of it. If he looked carefully—and looking carefully was all that he could do at present—it almost seemed like the thing was alive. And then he was certain that it was. The signs weren't all that obvious, at first glance. The rise and fall of its chest was slow and so faint that it could easily be missed, but it was there, and constant. Its pale eyes remained open, staring blindly into nothing, and that was about as lifeless as anything could get, he thought. But then it started to blink spasmodically, if only for a second.

There was another exchange of what he now realized was actual gunfire, but his eyes were so heavy that they closed all on their own. He tried to open them again, but to no avail. He was already asleep, and dreaming another dream.

This one made even less sense than the last one had. The colorful scene in the distance far beneath him reminded him of an abstract painting he'd once seen. The version he was looking at now was an aerial view of the plaza sector, but he had a feeling that no one but himself would know that just by looking at it.

Everything was fragmented and grouped into approximate shapes. Even his physical manifestation in the dream looked like it had been painted with loose strokes. It was made up of solid but distinctly separate blobs that barely fit together. His skin was a bright shade of pink, almost as though the artist hadn't had the right colors to blend a proper flesh tone, or was a child that didn't know any better or just didn't care.

There was no perceivable logic to the dream. It had neither rhyme nor reason. Crude and oftentimes deformed images floated past him and each other on this mad painter's acid trip canvas. Some of the images looked familiar, others not so much, but he doubted that any of it really meant anything.

Somewhere in the distance, thunder rolled. At least that's what he thought it was, at first. The rumbling grew in intensity, died out completely, and was back again in full force within seconds. The louder it got, the less it sounded like thunder. After listening to it attentively, he decided it was closer to the sound of automatic weapons discharging in long, drawn-out bursts, like assault rifles firing in slow motion.

All of a sudden, he heard a man scream, and it tore him from his current setting. He was back in the *techno-tunnel* with the two old men. He heard the scream again and winced. The person doing the yelling wasn't very far behind them, and was in serious pain, from the sound of it. He let out another shrill, bloodcurdling cry of anguish, and didn't hold back in the least.

"Pick up the pace, Edward," one of the old men was saying. "If you don't want to end up dead or worse, move faster!"

Frank let his head sag to the left and glimpsed at him from the corner of his eye. This one kept his head shaved almost immaculately, right down to the scalp. There was something oddly familiar about his gaunt face and the grim set to his mouth. It sent a chill up his spine, though he couldn't say exactly why. Even his voice—nasal, drawn-out, and ardent in its emphasis— had a haunting effect on him.

"It wasn't supposed to be like this," the other old man— Edward—complained loudly, overcome with emotion. "You said that there would be no bloodshed."

Limply, sluggishly, Frank swung his head around to the right, toward the sound of his voice. The normally simple exercise turned out to be an extremely laborious one. His neck ached and burned from the exertion, but there was something reassuring about that voice, even in all of its anguish, and it made the effort he'd put in seem worthwhile, somehow.

When his eyes settled on him, he found that this *Edward* character looked equally familiar, perhaps more so. Unlike his counterpart, he evoked warmth, kindness. His white tufts of thick and curly hair, his bushy mustache and soda bottle glasses made him seem completely harmless. Even his distraught complaints were oddly comforting. They made him appear more human, more humane. At present, he was upset; that much was obvious from the tears welling in his eyes. He looked like he was carrying the weight of the world on his shoulders.

"I know that you don't want to hear this right now," the bald one grunted laboriously, "but you can't make an omelet without breaking a few eggs." He struggled momentarily as he sought better purchase on Frank's arm, and continued trudging along without missing a beat.

"Yes, I've heard that one before, Jerg," Edward muttered angrily, "and it doesn't make any of this any better, does it?" He was absolutely livid, fact evidenced by the deep red spots that were blooming in his cheeks. "These are people I've known and worked with for years. They're not just eggs that you can break. I don't even understand how you could say something like that."

He sighed heavily then and let his shoulders sag, always careful not to loosen his grip on Frank. "Killing wasn't part of the plan."

"Sometimes even the best laid plans go awry," Jerg stated solemnly. "We should consider ourselves lucky. We're almost out of here, and we're still in one piece, at least for the time being. I couldn't ask for more."

"Don't you have any compassion at all?" Edward growled indignantly. "These were *your* men. They looked up to you!"

"Oh, for the love of *Pete*!" Jerg exclaimed, visibly annoyed. "They're kitted up for crowd control."

"What do you mean?" Edward asked after another deafening burst of gunfire. There was a perplexed expression on his face, and it was obvious that he didn't know what Jerg had meant or how he was supposed to react to it, if at all.

"Their rifles are loaded with rubber bullets," Jerg harrumphed exasperatedly. "Falstaff, Hildebrandt, Mosley—every single one of them—they're using nonlethal ammunition. Sure, the rounds hurt like the dickens on impact, but nothing barring a freak accident of the worst possible kind would actually kill someone. And these men *are* qualified marksmen, might I add."

Edward stopped suddenly and loosened his grip on Frank. "What?" he howled, his eyes going wide with disbelief. "Well why didn't you just say that in the first place?" The crimson in his cheeks started to spread to the rest of his face. "I can't believe that you let me go on like that, you... you ignoramus!"

"If you must know," Jerg sighed, "you walk a lot faster when you're in a huff. Unfortunately," he grunted, straining under the extra weight that Edward had left him with, "you also become a whiney, insufferable little prick."

From that moment on, everything started to blur for Frank. He opened his eyes periodically to find that he was staring at the floor or the ceiling, but these moments of semiconsciousness were growing fewer and farther between. The minutes dragged on and seemed more like hours.

For a time, his eyes were open, but he saw nothing. When his vision returned, he was lying on the bed of what looked like an armored personnel carrier. The holding area was cast in a dull red glow from the LED lamps overhead. Three of the vehicle's walls were lined with a U-shaped bench that was filled near to capacity. About half a dozen uniformed men were sitting all around him.

Their plated white body armor looked pristine and somewhat surreal to him, like a clash of modern tactical gear and something right out of a history book. To him, they looked like some kind of elite honor guard, a select few men of higher caliber chosen from amongst their peers to provide guardianship over some sacred relic or mysterious artifact. He found it all very *science-fictiony*.

Three of them wore the same light but sturdy-looking armor. The other two—the old men that had carried him along that seemingly infinite corridor of bizarre machinery—wore long, white coats that dangled just beneath their knees. While their clothing seemed to lack any protective attributes, they appeared to match fairly well all the same. *Maybe they're officers*, he mused. It was a possibility, all things considered.

Most of them were busy talking amongst themselves, but about what, he couldn't say. His head was fuzzy, his ears were pulsing, and it was just too much to try to follow. It sounded like everyone was talking over each other, their voices melding into one incoherent mess of confused gobbledygook. It was nearly impossible to distinguish between the different speakers. For all he knew, they were speaking another language. Try as he might, he couldn't understand a word of it.

They seemed particularly enthusiastic about *something*. At least that much was clear. Some of them even looked like they were about ready to start celebrating. All of them except for those two elderly men, again.

At first glance, the bald one seemed placid, without emotion. Looking at his eyes, however, it was easy to see that he was alert and at the ready, like he was expecting the unexpected.

In contrast, the one with the wild tufts of hair that looked like they were locked in mortal combat with each other—Edward—was a pack of nerves. He kept glancing over his shoulder, through a thin slot that communicated with the cockpit. "Are we almost there yet?" he finally asked, clearly on edge. For some reason, even though he spoke much more mildly than the others in his raucous group, he could actually make out what he was saying. "Lieutenant Corporal Baumgartner?"

"Yes, Doctor Munro," a man replied from the cockpit with an extensive, intentionally exaggerated sigh.

Frank realized suddenly that he could hear more than just this Edward character. The conversations were starting to make more sense. The haze in his mind was slowly dissipating.

"Estimated time of arrival is five minutes," that voice from the cockpit spoke again. "Don't worry. It should be a smooth ride from here on out."

"Don't jinx it," one of the younger men called out in a grave tone. "We're not out of the woods yet." He paused dramatically then before adding, "We still need to go pick up some burgers on our way there." There were a few chuckles at that. The driver—Baumgartner—was laughing too, if he wasn't mistaken. Even *old, bald and silent* looked like he had a smirk tugging at the corners of his tight-lipped mouth.

Must be an inside joke, Frank thought, because he didn't see how any of this was funny. He felt like he was dying, like he'd already died and been resuscitated just so he could die again.

"Come on, Hildebrandt," the tallest of them replied, grinning despite a disapproving shake of his head. "You're scaring Doctor Munro for no good reason. That's enough. Seriously."

"Yes sir, Captain Falstaff, sir!" Hildebrandt barked jokingly. He followed up by snapping a brisk, exaggeratedly formal salute.

The captain shook his head again and looked up, holding his hands out in a *do-you-see-what-I-have-to-put-up-with* kind of way. "Don't mind Sergeant Hildebrandt," he told Edward. "He's a nice guy and all, completely harmless, but he just isn't right in the head." He grinned at Hildebrandt then, probably to let him know that he was kidding. "Some of us may be feeling a little skittish right now, but we shouldn't. Despite Lieutenant Spears being a pest, despite our plan going haywire midcourse, we still managed to pull through. We're almost in the clear."

Edward nodded repeatedly, slowly, obviously not convinced that it was over. "I keep expecting to hear sirens," he admitted in a dejected tone. "Sirens, gunfire, and the sound of our tires blowing out before the lab wagon screeches to a violent halt." He frowned and rubbed at his brow, then paused to think for a moment before adding, "It's probably nothing, to be sure. It's probably just a silly concern, and not really worth mentioning, but I find the possibility unsettling all the same."

"You have nothing to worry about, Edward," the old bald one said in a way that was more dismissive than it was reassuring. "We've shaken the Commission's pursuit."

"What about the police?" Edward asked, sounding skeptical.

Jerg furrowed his brow and looked at him gravely. "Have you breathed in too many exhaust fumes?" he asked, incredulous. "*You* more than anyone should understand that the nature of the Commission's work makes it reluctant to seek outside help—even from the police, even for something like this. Their very existence is a secret. They wouldn't jeopardize that, or risk compromising the integrity of their many highly classified programs."

He shook his head then, looking down at the palms of his open hands. He appeared annoyed, but in some bizarre manner, genuinely sympathetic to Edward's plight. "We've lost our tail for now," he added, "so we should have some peace of mind, at least for a while. Realistically, Langsarks will use a team of in-house investigators to try and track us down. I concede there's a chance he might try to involve the big hand of the law in this, eventually, if he has to. But if your facilities are *off the grid*, as you put it, and absent from any official maps or registries, then I don't see why we'd need to worry about them in the first place. They wouldn't even know where to start looking for us."

Edward ruffled his curly tufts of gray hair, frowning. "Thank you," he said with a sigh. "Sometimes, I'm too stubborn to get my mind around the obvious, even when I *know* the answers to my own questions."

"You don't have to feel bad about it, Edward," Jerg assured him, eyeing Frank's subtle movements openly without really heeding them. "Stress can do things to the mind, especially in high-pressure situations like this one. We've undergone rigorous training for this kind of scenario. You haven't."

Edward followed Jerg's gaze, and for the first time, he really noticed Frank's movements. "Sixty-Seven!" he gasped, his eyes shooting wide-open like he'd just taken a hit of the *Fair Lady*. "He's moving!" There was a certain degree of urgency in his voice, mixed in with one part wonder and another part concern.

"What?" Jerg asked him, caught off guard. "That isn't normal? His squirming around like that, I mean."

"No," Edward answered curtly, dropping to his knees beside Frank. "Not like this. Not so quickly. A little reflexive movement on waking is to be expected, but he should be near catatonic right now. He's trying to *talk*, for the love of Pete! He's going to burn himself right out!"

"Is there anything we can do to help?" Captain Falstaff asked, his voice tinged with concern.

"You need us to hold him down or something?" the one that was built like a refrigerator half suggested, half asked him almost just as quickly.

"No, Hildebrandt! Absolutely not!" Edward warned, staving both of them off with an upheld hand. He looked up at the giants that he'd just stopped in their tracks, then all around him. Jerg was still in his seat, but looked somewhat fidgety. Mosley—a puzzled expression etched upon his face—had started to push himself up from the bench, but was now frozen in an awkward-looking squat. From their reactions, he might have told them that he'd just stepped on a landmine.

He sighed deeply then and waved them back to their seats. "Thank you, gentlemen," he said, "but if you really want to help, the best thing that you can do is sit down and be quiet." Quirking his brow, he leaned in for a closer inspection.

"He's already agitated enough as it is," he added in a hushed tone, almost as though to himself. "He's tired, exhausted. The *last* thing that he needs right now is for the lot of you to kick up a ruckus. As silly as it may sound, I want you to pretend like he's a newborn baby... a newborn baby that's currently taking its nap. And I'm its mother. If you make too much noise, I *will* box your ears off." He offered them a stern look then to show them that he meant business. He wouldn't be putting up with any shenanigans from anybody. If any of them interrupted baby's quiet time, he wouldn't hesitate to back up his claim, not even for a second.

Sergeant Hildebrandt was already struggling visibly with a sudden urge to laugh. His face was turning beet red and he looked like he was on the verge of breaking up, but Falstaff's well-placed elbow to his ribs helped calm him right down.

After laying his hand on Frank's shoulder, Edward tilted his head slightly and lowered it to within inches of his face. Looking him straight in the eyes, he spoke softly, reassuringly. "I know there's too much going on right now for you to really understand this," he whispered, "but you're safe now. It's a long and dark road that lies ahead of us, but you *are* safe."

Frank couldn't have said why, but the panicky feeling he felt eating away at him dissipated almost instantly. The older man's voice—so familiar, so peaceful—had a comforting effect on him. His eyes grew heavy once more, and it wasn't long before he'd closed them and fallen asleep again. It was a long, deep, and more importantly *dreamless* sleep.

CHAPTER
18

Nice Digs

When Frank came to, he was splayed out on a soft mattress, with warm, fuzzy blankets heaped around his feet and drawn up all the way to his chin. At first, all he could think of was how comfortable he was, and how he'd like nothing more than to fall asleep again, but then he realized that he wasn't in his own bed, and his eyes went wide with alarm. He tried to sit up suddenly, but hardly managed to move a muscle.

Getting out of bed would be out of the question, it seemed. He was exhausted. Every square inch of his body ached. He felt worse off than he had the time he'd wrecked his bike and gone skipping along the pavement for about half a city block. And that had been pretty bad. For the time being, all he could do was lie there and try to figure out what was going on.

His recollection of the previous night was shoddy at best. One second he was getting tortured by SAU's inquisitors, then he somehow managed to fall asleep, *of all things,* and finally, he'd been hauled down a corridor lined with bizarre machinery and heaped into the back of an APC. He still wasn't sure where the dreams had begun and reality ended. And if that hadn't been trippy enough, he'd just woken in a strange bed. He didn't know where he was or how he'd gotten there. He didn't know what these people had in store for him. He didn't even know who they were, and that worried him more than anything else.

Were they members of the regular police forces, come to spring him from captivity and certain death? He didn't recognize their uniforms, but who was to say that they hadn't donned new ones to maintain team recognition while avoiding identification. White seemed like a very poor choice for that sort of thing, and the idea that other officers would put their careers on the line for him seemed far-fetched, but he couldn't rule out the possibility. Whoever they were, they were working outside the scope of the law. That much was clear.

Were they members of the Awoken, planning to use him for their own vile designs? Were they mob associates, holding him for ransom despite the likelihood that SAU was just going to kill him off anyway? Whatever the case may be, they were doing a poor job of keeping an eye on him, and his accommodations seemed a little too cozy for anything like that. The place was certainly no Fitzgibbons, but it was a far cry from the beat-up storm cellar he imagined that kind of thing would normally take place in.

It was a large room, but every every square inch of its ceiling was visible due to its height. There were no surveillance cameras that he could see, and if he could trust his hearing, there weren't any guards in there with him, either. They might have someone posted outside the door, but even then, that left him the freedom to do whatever he wanted to inside the confines of these walls.

He could hardly move his head, but he could see all kinds of expensive-looking equipment just lying around on the edge of the room. If he'd kidnapped someone, he wouldn't have given them access to things they might use to escape. Then again, he was less mobile than a paraplegic, and they probably knew it all too well.

He broke off from his train of thought as he heard the sound of steel bolts grinding on metal, followed by a faint whir and oiled bearings sliding on metal tracks. A mechanized door was opening somewhere beyond the foot of the bed, he knew, but he couldn't look to see who was coming. Crisping his arms and legs, he tried to defy his crippled body and sit, but failed miserably. He hadn't risen an inch from the mattress. He was utterly helpless and there was nothing that he could do to change that, but if he was lucky, he might be able to get answers to at least some of his questions.

"I'm glad to see that you're awake," an old man said in a voice that was both warm and gentle.

Frank knew that he'd heard that voice before. It belonged to the smallish doctor with the great mess of wavy, nimbus-like hair, he thought, but not for the life of him could he remember what his name was supposed to be.

"I'm Doctor Edward Munro," the old man announced, as if to answer his unasked question. "You may not remember me, but we've spoken before. Or I've spoken to you, at least—quite a bit over the past few weeks, in fact."

Afterward, he walked over to the side of the bed, took out the small leather kit that was tucked away under his arm, and set it down on the nightstand with great care. Frank could barely make out his face from that angle, but the crazy wisps of gray, almost white hair were unmistakable.

"Though you *have* been able to communicate some simple messages," Edward droned out absentmindedly, engrossed by whatever task he was busy with, "your vocal chords are still far from functional. In any case, there's a good chance you won't remember this conversation this time tomorrow."

"Why?" Frank tried to ask, but all that came out was an unintelligible croak. He couldn't even understand his own voice, but the doctor seemed to get exactly what he meant. Maybe it was the confused look in his eyes, or maybe he'd just read his lips. Maybe it was just obvious.

"You've been in a coma-like state for a very long time," Edward explained. "Your body has been dormant, so to speak, and consequently, your muscles have atrophied from lack of use. Your chemoreception comes and goes, as do most of your basic senses, but they're getting better... stabilizing, if you will. It's taxing I'm sure, but we'll get you there."

He pulled out a long syringe from one of the sleeves in his medical kit and held it up to the light, giving it a quick once over. It was filled with a yellowish liquid that glinted briefly as the light shone through it. "To top it off," he continued, still heavily focused on his preparations, "the medicine we've been giving you to help speed up your rehabilitation is strong enough to knock out a horse and keep it down for the night. That probably isn't helping."

He squeezed some liquid from the syringe then and flicked the end of the needle with the tip of his finger, which shook a few droplets free. "What I mean by that," he said, "is that even though it's helping you heal... even though it helps you get the rest that you need, I think it might be contributing to the short-term memory loss you've been experiencing. It's as disappointing for you as it is for me, but there's no getting around it."

Frank's inability to communicate was starting to piss him off. He wanted to object to their cramming him full of tranquilizers, but he couldn't. Hell, he couldn't even furrow his brow. No matter how *gentle* Edward seemed, his story didn't hold the road, and he wasn't buying it, not even for a second. He wanted to say that "a few weeks" wasn't a long time at all. Not long enough to cause his muscles to atrophy, anyway. Even with his head all jumbled up as it was, he knew that it didn't make any sense at all.

Edward leaned over him then and examined both his right and left arm in turn, palping around for a good vein. "It's a pity we didn't coerce one of the nurses into joining us," he murmured, half to himself, half to no one at all. He raised his tone a little for Frank's sake as he added, "You're probably going to feel a little bit of a sting, but it won't last long."

Something dawned on him then as the doctor held his left arm up, the tip of his needle pressed firmly to the area between his bicep and his forearm. His arm, he quickly realized, was very much still *there* and attached to the rest of him. It was somewhat skeletal in appearance—just like the rest of his body, for that matter—but it was there.

He remembered there being nothing left of that arm but a messy stump cut off at the shoulder. He recalled it *quite clearly*. It hadn't been a dream, of that he was sure. And yet there it was, boggling his mind to the point that it made him question his sanity. A brief flash of Doctor Munro and some other man helping him down a brightly-lit corridor reminded him that this wasn't the first time he'd noticed the anomaly, and that did even less for his confidence. Was he losing his mind? It felt like he was.

He wanted answers. He *needed* answers, but it was already too late. The tip of the needle punctured his skin and sunk in. His eyes rolled to the top of his head as Doctor Munro squeezed the so-called "medicine" into his vein. Personally, he wouldn't have called the pain "a little bit of a sting".

His arm felt like it was rigged to some kind of high-pressure hose that was filling it past capacity with a mildly corrosive acid. There was so much tension exerting against the inside of his forearm that he thought it might explode. Luckily, Edward had at least been right about the brevity of the pain. It was intense, but short-lived. Within seconds his suffering was but a memory.

He soon learned that Edward had been right on other accounts, as well. Almost as soon as the pain in his arm subsided, the rest of his body became heavy, starting with his eyes. The world *around him* felt heavy, warm. He felt like a baby that had been wrapped up tightly in its blankie. There was little he could do to stave off his imminent slumber. His body demanded sleep.

"Good night, Sixty-Seven," he heard the doctor call out as though from a distance, which was a little odd considering he was standing right next to him. "I'll see you again in the morning."

Sixty-Seven, as the doctor had called him, was fast asleep before Edward could gather his things and exit the room. He had another dreamless night ahead of him. Another stretch of much needed, recuperative sleep. In the world of the waking, twelve hours had passed, but when he woke again and opened his eyes, it was like he'd never gone to sleep at all. He might have blinked and it would have been the same to him.

Doctor Munro came by again that morning, just as he'd promised he would. Frank wasn't even sure if it *was* morning. It was hard to tell without any natural daylight entering the room, but he assumed that it was. Much to Edward's surprise, Frank greeted him with a wave and a hoarse croak that sounded vaguely like, "Hello," even in his own ears. *Did you even leave?* he wanted to ask him, but his throat was sore and he decided against it.

He remembered their last exchange fairly well, and Edward verified as much by administering a pop quiz with the aid of a pen and a pad of paper. The peculiar little man helped him as much as he could without outright scribbling the words down for him or feeding him the answers. There was a look of unbridled amazement in his eyes the entire time. When it seemed like Edward had wrapped things up with his mundane questions, Frank scrawled out "Vanessa" with some difficulty. His hand felt cramped, but he added three question marks for emphasis.

Edward scratched his head, squinted at Frank's note for a few seconds, and shrugged. No doubt satisfied with the results of his tests, he scooped the pen and paper up and slipped them into one of his lab coat pockets. "This is all rather extraordinary," he chirped, barely able to contain his excitement. "This is exactly what we were hoping for. *Exactly.*"

Frank hadn't the slightest idea what he was going on about, but he wasn't sure it was worth the effort it would take him to find out. Communicating was a hassle, and in any case, he now firmly believed that whatever the doctor's intentions were, they weren't to bring harm to himself or to Vanessa.

The mystery surrounding his miraculously present arm still boggled his mind, but he wasn't going to bother inquiring about it just yet. As perplexing as it was, his head needed a rest. For all he knew, the thing had been surgically reattached. He hadn't noticed any stitches or scars, but with the right tools in a capable doctor's hands, that meant next to nothing.

Efficiency had been a trademark of Innerstadt's healthcare system as far back as collective memory went. The government poured obscene amounts of money into scientific and medical research, most probably due to their isolation and the constant threat of extinction lurking just around the corner. Their doctors could cure just about anything, except for a few terminal illnesses they couldn't seem to wrap their heads around.

"You seem to have recovered most of your memories," Edward said. "It's usually a slow and fragmented process." He rubbed his hands together then like a kid in a candy store. Smiling widely, he added, "You're recuperating about twice as fast as I'd expected you to—twice as fast as you *should* be according to the guidelines, if you will. I find that fascinating." He followed up by launching into a lengthy yet energetic discourse on a few of his theories, scientific progress in general and the amazing success they were experiencing thus far.

Frank couldn't understand half of what he was saying, but Edward was so into it that he managed to keep his attention, at least for a little while. Before long, however, the man's extensive rambling became so technical that it was nearly impossible to follow. There was one overarching theme that he did understand, though, and it might be the only one that really mattered. He was getting better, and quickly. With a bit of luck, he'd soon be able to speak again. Then he could start figuring out what had happened to him and what exactly was going on now.

Over the course of the next week, Frank endured multiple acupuncture and physiotherapy sessions, purportedly to stimulate his atrophied muscles and promote tissue development to within reasonable levels. It was the tall, bald doctor that administered the acupuncture treatment. Weissinger, he thought his name was. The physiotherapy sessions were handled by who he could only assume were security personnel. Though they removed it for the sake of practicality, they always arrived wearing that white, plated armor of theirs. It didn't look like that of any official force he knew of, and for the love of him, he couldn't figure out what else they might be. Whoever they were, they took turns moving him around every which way to limber him up, and exercise muscles that seemed to have forgotten how to function properly. At times, he felt like a rag doll. It was difficult, at first, but ended up paying dividends.

Gaunt-faced Weissinger was almost always silent when he worked, and something about the way that he moved made him look like a mechanical brute, but his big hands and long fingers were precise. He was extremely patient and went to great lengths to ensure that he performed his work flawlessly. From time to time, he'd turn to the clipboard that he kept with him to jot down notes, feverishly and in one of those indecipherable doctor scripts that looked like little more than blots and scribbles.

Frank had caught a glimpse of his notes once, ever so briefly, but hadn't been able to make heads or tails of it. Even if the man's handwriting had been legible, he had a feeling that he wouldn't have been able to understand it. Chances were it was medical mumbo jumbo, and beyond his ability to comprehend.

The guards or security personnel were a blatant contrast to the creepily quiet Weissinger. They put every effort into making him feel at home, or at least that was the impression they gave him. Though contributing to conversation in any meaningful way was still beyond him, they were fairly talkative, for the most part.

His own attitude surprised him somewhat. He couldn't understand how he could be enjoying himself at all in his current predicament, but he was, at times, at least to a certain extent. Every day he found himself a little more convinced that these people, whoever they *really* were, meant well. They'd rescued him from the prongs of Special Assignments, and they'd probably rescued Vanessa, as well—if she'd even been taken into custody in the first place. He didn't know if she had, and being bedridden for hours on end thinking about it was gnawing away at him.

With so much downtime to deal with, it was only natural that he'd long for some kind of company, and the guards provided that with funny anecdotes and generally pointless banter. In time, he started to learn a little about each of them. Despite his inability to speak, he still managed to show an actual interest in what they had to say, and that helped them open up a bit. Or at least he liked to think that it did.

Captain Alexander Falstaff was a tall, broad-shouldered and athletic man with a healthy tan and a neatly shaved head. He reminded him a lot of his cousin Carlos, the way he'd been back in the days before he'd gotten tangled up with drugs. Falstaff was the most forthcoming of the lot, and the most likely to open up and discuss serious matters. He spent a significant amount of their time together talking about his personal life and convictions.

It wasn't that he didn't have a good sense of humor. He just didn't fall back on it quite as frequently as some of the others did. Alexander Falstaff was a man with few secrets. He was essentially an open book. He went on and on about his wife, Nuria, and their children, Maria and Alex Junior. He talked about his own childhood, his reasons for choosing his profession, his wacky belief system and other such topics. Most of the time, he just talked about home. It was obvious that he missed his family.

Frank found the fact that he had two children astounding. He looked no older than he did. Mid-twenties at most, he thought. Taking his children's ages into account, he figured he must have been barely old enough to work when he'd fathered his first one, which begged the question of where he'd gotten the money for the permits. Rich parents, maybe? It wasn't really his business, but he still couldn't help but wonder. Personally, he'd have a hard time making ends meet if he sprung for just the one, and that was taking his and Vanessa's combined incomes into account. Children were expensive little beasts even before they were born.

He didn't understand why—Alexander hadn't explained it, and he wasn't exactly in a position to ask—but the man hadn't been home in years. The captain talked about everything and nothing and none of it ever seemed out of place or like too much information. He had a natural charisma about him that drew people in, and an ease with words that left his audience wanting more. It was easy to see how he'd earned his rank, assuming the title meant the same thing in whatever organization they were a part of as it did to the rest of the law enforcement community. He was willing to wager that it did.

Sergeant J.J. Hildebrandt was a behemoth of a man, and it was no doubt the first thing that anyone noticed about him. There wasn't a shadow of a doubt about that, as far as he was concerned. It wasn't that he was particularly tall, either. He stood a respectable 5'9" or 5'10", at most. But he had shoulders wider than any he'd ever seen before. He was an imposing mass of muscle and sinew that was set on a frame that looked like it had been built to withstand whatever the world might throw at it.

He kept his head neatly shaven, very much like the captain did. His eyes were a chill blue-gray that reminded him of the sky on a clear day. They were cold, and strikingly so, but there was a certain warmth to them as well, lying just beneath the surface. Whenever they turned on him, Frank was under the impression that they could bore holes all the way to the back of his head. They were eyes that he'd have a hard time lying to, even if he wasn't such a horrible liar to begin with. He supposed they might not soften him at all if it wasn't for his hard face, which looked like it had been chiseled from a block of stone. On anyone else, those eyes would be nothing short of intimidating.

Despite his gruff appearance, the sergeant was arguably the friendliest of them all. His mouth seemed to fear silence, and was a seemingly endless stream of witty commentary. Frank thought he was an absolute laugh riot, and while he didn't have anything to reproach him personally, he could easily see how some people could grow tired of his company after a time. As for himself, he appreciated his colorful, spirited monologues. Bedridden as he was, he wasn't in much of a position to complain anyway.

Lieutenant Corporal Baumgartner and Corporal Mosley were both very reserved individuals, but their reasons for being that way were as obvious as the differences in their appearance. He'd be hard-pressed to find any similarities between the two men.

Mosley was a rugged-looking man somewhere north of forty, with dark brown skin, and eyes and teeth that were so white they were almost blinding. His black hair and beard were kept short and were peppered with gray. He was of average height and build, but there was a quiet confidence about him, and a fluidity in his step that betrayed a superior control of mind and body. He was a man that was very focused in his thoughts and actions.

He seemed disciplined, determined, like a dedicated career enforcer. He may have been a veteran, but there was nothing tired about him. He seemed inexhaustible, relentless. He was a man of few words, but there was nothing cold about him. From what he'd observed, he just spent more time thinking about what it was he was supposed to be doing than he did chitchatting about trivial matters. He did do some talking at times, when he had a mind to, but it was mostly out of courtesy and usually brief.

Baumgartner was the day to Mosley's night. The lieutenant corporal was about Frank's age. He had a sinewy build, stringy hair that hung limply around his shoulders and emerald green eyes that had a permanent look of mischief about them. At times, he remained silent for the duration of their sessions. Other times, like Hildebrandt, he liked to laugh, and laugh a lot, but the two subscribed to entirely different brands of humor. The sergeant was witty and spontaneous. Baumgartner's jokes—if they could really be called that—seemed rehearsed, like the unfortunate product of a cheesy joke book he'd found in a bargain bin sale. Some of his puns drew a grin and a shake of the head, but most of his one-liners fell flat, and his repertoire was limited at best.

When the puns ran dry, he repeated old material or fell awkwardly silent, but not before making drum and cymbal noises with his mouth and adding an emphatic, "Thank you. Thank you," at the end. Though far from hostile, at times he didn't seem to know what to say to fill the void. Frank didn't have any issues with that as some of his colleagues in the force had been quiet and withdrawn. It was the man's lack of consistence that sometimes made him feel uncomfortable. At times, it was like the lieutenant corporal was in a trance, and on other occasions, it was like he needed more than anything to be the life of the party.

Occasionally, he'd roll what looked like a *hobo smoke*, which was a cigarette rolled from leftover tobacco crushed out of butts found on the street, but he suspected they might be laced with some kind of recreational narcotic. The symptoms varied and ranged from near-hysterical fits of laughter to long bouts of antsy, nervous silence that reeked of paranoia. He felt a bit awkward whenever Baumgartner lit up, and this was due only in part to his being a man of the law. Nothing he did was over the top, per se, so it was something he could deal with. He just found it bizarre.

Weissinger was another matter altogether. He found him a little bit creepier every time he came by to prick him with his acupuncture needles. It wasn't necessarily anything the doctor did. He'd already accepted the fact that he wasn't the chattiest guy in the world, and was also perhaps a bit of a natural weirdo. But he had a gnawing and inexplicable feeling that he'd seen the man before. He couldn't put a finger on it, but he was familiar, there was no question about that. Something about him just didn't feel right.

By the end of the first month of his stay, he was back on his feet for at least an hour a day. His physiotherapy sessions had progressed from massages and assisted flexions to actual self-propelled movement, and while the exercise proved difficult at first, it wasn't nearly as much of a pain in the ass as his vocal rehabilitation was.

His muscles, Edward had confided, were convalescing and developing to within acceptable levels for the execution of basic every day movements. His vocal chords were an entirely different story. He'd made *some* progress, which he supposed was better than none at all, but he was still embarrassed to open his mouth because he had difficulty pronouncing more than a single syllable, and even those were tongue twisters. In his own ears, he sounded mentally retarded, which wasn't very encouraging, but he knew that he had to keep at it if he ever wanted to speak normally again, so he persevered.

After a time, he was able to start piecing basic sentences together. It was a difficult process, and his voice still sounded slow and alien to him, but it was a step in the right direction. Soon, he was able to participate actively in conversations with Munro and the sentinels in at least a minimal way. He didn't even bother when it came to Weissinger. The man seemed stranger to him by the minute, and he wouldn't really feel like talking to him even if he had the capability to do so with confidence.

Sometime during the fifth week, his overall progress started to skyrocket. By the end of the sixth, he was in good enough shape to participate in team activities with the sentinels. He didn't feel up to par with his old self yet, but he was doing well enough to give them all a serious run for their money. It was almost as though something unseen had kicked in once his healing had reached a certain threshold, and now he was advancing in leaps and bounds every day.

It wasn't long before he was seeing the same kind of results with his vocal rehabilitation. By the end of month two, he was speaking almost fluently again. The pronunciation of certain words still presented a challenge, but aside from the occasional blunder that was barely noticeable to anyone but himself, he was speaking almost as well as he used to.

By that time, his body was back to the way that it used to be, and he was ready to start dishing out smackdowns on most of the sentinels. Every other day, there were friendly competitions in a wide variety of skills tests and team sports. Falstaff still had the upper hand on him in certain situations, Hildebrandt had him beat in others, and Mosley was a toss-up in just about everything they did. His hand-eye coordination still needed some tuning, he'd tell Falstaff jokingly any time he'd beat him, though his words might be closer to the truth than he'd care to admit.

Trying to overpower J.J. Hildebrandt was like trying to wrestle an alley wolf with his arms tied behind his back. He'd never really tried anything like that, but he imagined it would be just as hard. The only person he could think of that was even remotely as strong was a lieutenant by the name of Moose Johnson that he'd worked with when he'd first started as a cop. At one time, they'd sparred frequently, and he'd gotten used to having his ass handed to him on a regular basis. Moose had been a beast, but he wasn't even sure if he would have measured up to Hildebrandt.

Regardless, he felt as good as he ever thought he would, and couldn't help but wonder why they were still holding him. Though they had treated him rather decently, he wasn't allowed to roam freely. He wasn't allowed to leave their facility. Every evening after mess, they'd lock him inside what he'd come to think of as his living quarters. In all practical senses, he figured, he was their captive. It was something he planned on bringing up with Edward the next time he came to check on him, and he wouldn't have to wait very long, as Edward came to see him that very night.

"Are you a hostage?" Edward asked, flabbergasted. "Heavens no!" A look of worry creased his brow and he combed his fingers nervously through his fluffy, mostly-white hair.

"Then what am I?" Frank demanded. His voice was firm but lacked any trace of hostility. He might have acted differently had he been speaking with someone else, but there was something so likeable about the old man—something so kind, and gentle and caring, that he'd rarely seen in anyone else—that he would've had a hard time being any more firm than he already was. Plus, there was that gnawing familiarity about him, like he'd known him his entire life. Oddly, it seemed to be a mutual feeling.

There was a moment of hesitation in Edward's response, like he wanted to say something, but decided against it. "Why, you're a guest here, Sixty-Seven," he breathed, visibly hoping that his answer would be enough.

It was not. "If I'm a guest here," Frank said, "then why can't I leave the compound?" He sat straight up in his bed then and held his left forearm out to Edward. The doctor was holding a large needle in his hand but seemed to have forgotten about it. It was just a mild sedative, he knew, and its purpose was to ensure that he got a good night's rest.

He motioned for him to go ahead with the injection, to put him at ease and reassure him that he wasn't going to start getting stubborn with him. He'd already noticed that Edward was a little fidgety all on his own, and that was when he didn't have anything to worry about. Concentrating on the task at hand seemed to calm him somewhat.

"It's for your own security," Edward sighed, holding Frank's arm up with a steady hand. "When we brought you here," he added, furrowing his brow as he looked for a vein and quickly found one, "you were in horrible condition, just horrible." He pressed the tip of the needle to Frank's forearm then and hesitated a moment before finally injecting the sedative. The exercise was a quick and painless one. He'd gotten rather good at it after a month and a half's worth of at least daily dosages. "Or have you already forgotten?" he asked, still a little absentminded after his moment of intense concentration.

"No, I haven't forgotten," Frank answered. "I don't know why you rescued me, or how things got as bad as they did, but I am grateful for you getting me out of there, and for the care that you've provided so far."

Edward nodded a wordless "you're welcome" and set the needle down in the kit that he brought with him on these routine visits of his. Clearly, he was hoping that would be the end of the conversation, but if he knew anything at all about Frank William Fasaro, he'd know that he didn't give up easily. Especially now that he'd found the ability to speak again.

Frank exhaled pointedly. "Listen, Doc, I know I was in really bad shape when I got here, but I'm doing a lot better now." He felt a little like a child trying to negotiate a later bedtime with his father. "Would slacking off with the security measures and letting me go outside once in a while be so bad? I'm not going to run, if that's what's got you worried."

"If you did run, I'd be extremely worried about your well-being," Edward stated calmly, "but that's not really what I'm concerned about. I know you enough to trust that you'll keep your word when you give it." He ruffled his hair again, looking a little uncertain, but finally added, "More than you can imagine or even understand right now."

"Then what's the problem?" Frank urged him, mildly annoyed. "I know how to keep a low profile."

"That's not it, either," Edward said, shaking his head from side to side vigorously, "but the fact that the police are looking for us doesn't help things." He took a moment to gather himself, clearly looking for an easier way to explain, then shook his head and threw up his hands. "It's complicated," he muttered, giving up. "Your mind just isn't ready for this."

Frank remained silent for what seemed like an extremely long time. He shook his head lightly, disappointed but not at all surprised. "You're not going to tell me anything, are you?" he asked dejectedly. He had no idea what Edward had meant when he'd said that his mind wasn't "ready".

Edward held his hands out at his sides—the standard "I don't know what to tell you" pose—and shook his head once, looking genuinely apologetic.

"Can you at least tell me what's going on with Vanessa?" Frank asked, nearly begging. "Or is that too complicated too?"

Edward repeated his previous gesture, adding, "I'm sorry, Sixty-Seven." Without further notice, he turned and walked toward the exit. He stopped in the doorway and glanced over his shoulder. "I'll answer all of your questions in time. *All of them,*" he said, trying to sound reassuring but accomplishing no such thing. He walked out then and disappeared from sight, leaving him alone and with more questions than answers, as usual.

The door closed behind Edward and he heard the grinding sound of the heavy, metal bolt sliding into place. Baumgartner would be on duty just outside if he felt like talking to someone through the door, but the sedatives flowing in his bloodstream were already starting to kick in hard, and all he wanted to do was sleep. As expected, the bedroom lights went out, just as they did after every lockdown.

After resting his head on his pillow, he joined his hands behind it and let his thoughts drift to Vanessa. It had been about two months since he'd last seen her. Two long months that had dragged on, seemingly forever. He was worried about her. He was worried about her and he missed her. He missed her more than words could say.

Even before his vocal chords had healed enough for him to utter a few words, he'd found ways to inquire about her. Though he'd learned nothing of consequence, he'd observed Edward's reactions every time. He was generally good at reading peoples' body language, but was even more so with the good doctor, and from what he could tell, she wasn't dead. He was hiding *something* from him, but it wasn't that. He'd be able to tell if it was.

With the pitiful state that he was in, and all of the work that he had to do to get on his feet again, he'd have thought it would take his mind off of her, but it hadn't. Not completely. There was nothing he could do for her anyway, so maybe it was best that he not dwell on it. His therapies kept him focused on other things, but she was always present somehow, whether she was lurking at the back of his mind, or taking up residence at the forefront of his thoughts. It was at night that he thought of her most often, when he was faced with the dismal solitude of those final minutes before the sedatives kicked in.

He couldn't help but feel nostalgic every now and then. He missed her smile, her laugh, the feel of her skin against his own. At the very least, he wanted to see her in his dreams. He *longed* to see her in his dreams. It seemed like a reasonable enough thing to hope for, and a plausible balm for his aching heart, but something had happened to him after he'd been rescued. He couldn't tell what it was or why it was happening, but he couldn't remember any of his dreams anymore, not a single one.

He imagined he *must* be having them, otherwise, he'd literally go insane, but he had no memory of them. Not remembering his dreams was more than mildly disappointing, but by the same token, he was glad that his sleep wasn't tainted by those nagging, recurring ones. It was a lot easier to get actual rest without them. If it hadn't been for the drugs, he might have lain there for quite some time, just thinking about Vanessa. Before he really knew what hit him, he'd fallen fast asleep.

CHAPTER
19

Procrastination

"I don't know," Edward repeated for the third time in the last minute, his voice filled with uncertainty. "Are you *absolutely* sure that he's ready for this? I have a hard time believing that he is." He shifted in his chair and looked down, askance, at the ceiling—anywhere but at Jerg's eyes.

The cafeteria was small but well laid out. If not for the efficient use of space, it could scarcely have serviced more than a dozen people at once, but in its current configuration, there was enough room to seat twenty-four. Since he and Jerg were the only ones in there, it made avoiding his gaze all the more difficult. To make matters worse, the large, white tiles on the floor and walls were so clean that they shone like mirrors. Seeing his own reflection in the ceramic made him realize just how horrible he was at hiding his emotions, and that made everything even more awkward.

"Edward," Jerg replied in a firm tone, pausing deliberately for emphasis. "There's no doubt in my mind that he's ready for this. This really isn't the time to snivel and procrastinate. You know, I expected you'd get cold feet like this, and I think I've been pretty good about it, so far. Listen, I don't want to alienate you or make you feel any more uncomfortable than you already clearly are, and that's why I went to great pains to produce a full and well-thought-out rationale for this. I wouldn't have given myself the trouble if I didn't think that we were ready to take this to the next level. I wouldn't have."

"How confident are you that he's ready for this?" Edward asked. "Are you unequivocally certain?" He was already skeptical when he wasn't being a worrywart of the worst possible sort, but he wasn't completely without reason. He could be stubborn when he wanted to be, but he was never completely close-minded. Not unless he was being asked to do something unethical.

"The procedural manuals are clear," Jerg stated matter-of-factly. "This is an important step in the process. If we don't do it, we won't know if our years of effort have had the effects we were aiming for. If we don't do it, we can't continue our research in a scientifically measurable way. What's the point of doing research if it isn't scientific? That *is* what we came here for, isn't it? To continue the research? To finish this project on our own?" He had many questions, but never slowed to give Edward time to answer them. "If it isn't, then I'm not sure why we've thrown our careers away, or put our lives in jeopardy."

Edward sighed. He knew that he came across as a bit of a mother hen sometimes. "It is what we came here for, Jerg. You're absolutely right." He drummed the fingers of his right hand on the table, slowly and rhythmically, while using his other hand to fiddle around with the handle of his coffee mug. When he was nervous, it showed in more than just his face.

"I just can't bear the thought of us coming this far, Sixty-Seven included, just to have everything blow up in our faces because we acted hastily." He set his palms down on the table then and turned a serious eye on Jerg. "I don't want to push him past his limits."

"Edward," Jerg sighed, choosing his next words carefully, "I'm going to go by the books on this one. You know me. You *know* I will." He hesitated briefly, as though weighing his options. "I'm going to be completely frank with you, Edward," he finally added. "If he can't handle the next phase of the program, then we've already failed here."

Edward's reaction was immediate and visceral. He saw his own reflection in the polished finish of the table then, and almost surprised himself with how crazy he looked. "I can't believe that you would even say such a thing," he growled, flustered. "You do realize that this is a person we're talking about, don't you? You do realize that if we push him too hard it might kill him?"

"That's always been the biggest difference between the two of us, Edward," Jerg replied calmly. "You're too invested in your work, and it isn't for the right reasons, either. You get far, far too attached for your own good. Far too attached."

Edward opened his mouth to protest, but Jerg cut him off before he could even get a word out. "All I'm saying is that you let your feelings cloud your judgment, Edward. Sometimes you let your emotions get the better of you, and it could be a liability."

Edward furrowed his brow. If Doctor Weissinger thought that he was winning him over, he was sorely mistaken, and had another thing coming to him. He was *dying* to get a word in, but again, Jerg stifled him before he had a chance to speak.

"I said that I'd go by the books on this," Jerg stated pointedly, "that I'd follow the rules to the letter, and that's exactly what I'm going to do. He couldn't be in more capable hands than my own, and there's a damned good reason for that. Do you want to know what that reason is?" Edward couldn't have answered if he'd wanted to, as Jerg did that for him almost immediately. "There isn't a single person that knows the procedures better than I do, *Doctor*, and that's because I wrote most of them myself."

The anger flushed from Edward's face and was replaced by an expression of shocked consternation. "You... did?" he asked, struggling to piece both words together. "I didn't know that," he finally managed to say. "Why have you never told me this before?"

"Because I was asked not to," Jerg answered plainly. "My involvement in that respect was on a need-to-know basis only. Just because you have top secret security clearance doesn't mean you're privy to everything that goes on at the Commission. I trust that you understand this. I don't mean to sound like an arrogant prick, but even the basest of simpletons should."

"Yes, I realize that," Edward replied, clearly unaffected. "I'm just surprised, that's all." Finding the right words seemed like a challenging and strenuous task, and he knew that it was obvious. "I don't mean to insult you," he added after some hesitation, "but I'd never even considered it a possibility—you having that kind of role in the program, I mean. I thought you'd always just headed up security. To be completely honest with you, I'm having a hard time connecting all the dots."

"You know, I don't hold it against you," Jerg replied. "but that just reinforces what I've always said about the Commission's apparent lack of appreciation for my scientific contributions. I must admit that it's soured my mood on more than one occasion. Though few knew the full story behind my discontent, most everyone was aware of it. I couldn't be more positive about that, because they actively contributed to it.

"Like any other social environment, the Commission has its share of bullies, of pathetic malcontents that try to boost their own piss-poor self-esteem by deriding anyone they see as an easy mark. Many of our peers never missed an opportunity to take a jab at me over my position in the security detail. That aggravated my dissatisfaction, and in the end, I felt ostracized from them and from the scientific community at large. In a way, I really had been.

"If you really want to know," he sighed, "the Commissioner wanted me to work on the procedures because I had relevant experience. While most of our colleagues saw me as a laughing stock because of my previous career in law enforcement, for once, the skills and knowledge that I'd acquired there were not only considered pertinent, but crucial."

"Oh, I do want to know," Edward confessed, though he was still clearly confused. "I'm embarrassed to say it, but I still don't see how all of this fits together... how your time with the police made you the ideal candidate."

"Well, it's fairly simple," Jerg replied, "but you're not the first to have missed the obvious." He loosened his collar then and leaned back in his chair. "First of all," he stated woodenly, "I've written more procedures than you can shake a finger at. Even excluding the manuals that I wrote for the academy—most of which are still in use to this day, might I add—writing procedures was a major component of all my postings with the LEA. By this point, it's almost second nature to me."

He folded his arms behind his back then and glanced off as though into the distance. More precisely, he looked to the far end of the cafeteria, which wasn't very far at all. This was his usual lecturing pose, Edward knew, and he assumed it every time he got into any serious elaboration. If there'd been more people around to listen to him, chances were he'd have gotten up and started pacing around the table.

"The other major point in my favor at the time," Jerg droned out almost mechanically, "was my profound understanding of the human body, of its capabilities and its limitations." He looked down at Edward momentarily, perhaps to ensure that he was still listening or even still there, and satisfied that his words weren't falling on deaf ears, he looked off into the "distance" again and picked up where he'd left off.

"More specifically," he continued in his best PA system voice, "I have an in-depth understanding of the government's expectations, especially in the area of combat-capable personnel." His voice was so monotonous, he might as well have been telling the occupants of floors six through twelve to please vacate the premises as part of their emergency evacuation drill. "Physical aptitudes, psychological profiles... *pain thresholds*." He lingered on those last words like they explained everything.

"Yes, I see," Edward mumbled, his brow still creased with worry, "and I'm not sure why I hadn't thought about all of that before." He'd interlocked his fingers and was busy staring at his thumbs as he twiddled them around repetitively. He was almost always fidgety when he was nervous, and he was almost always nervous, except when he was heavily concentrated on his work. Sitting completely still wasn't something that he did very often.

He sat there almost motionless for a while as he mulled it over. "I'm not going to try to stop you or get in your way," he finally sighed. "If you think that he's ready, I'll take your word for it."

By all appearances, Jerg was having a hard time containing his smile. Obviously, those were the exact words that he'd been hoping to hear. He looked like the cat that ate the canary.

It was exciting stuff for any scientist, Edward realized, but even more so for someone with Doctor Weissinger's professional background. This was his chance to see exactly what the next wave of law enforcement had to offer. More than a few would have envied him the opportunity.

Jerg's reaction confirmed it. He was grinning from ear to ear now, and with little to no restraint. "You won't regret this, Edward," he exclaimed gleefully.

"I do have *one* thing to ask of you," Edward added pointedly, "one thing for you to keep in mind, if you will."

"What is it?" Jerg asked, arching his brow.

"I just want you to remember that we're here today because Sixty-Seven is different," Edward said in a very serious tone. "He might just be the best candidate the program has ever produced, and that's because he doesn't fit the mold." He met Jerg's gaze then and held it. "I ask only that you be mindful of that. He isn't like the other candidates. His body... his mind... they might not go by the books, so to speak. His reaction to your procedures might not be what you'd expect. If we push him too hard..."

Jerg rubbed his chin pensively, considering his words. "I understand your concerns full well," he finally replied, "and to be honest, I don't think very much of them. Decreasing the intensity of the experiments just because the subject might not be tough enough to handle them? It sounds like we'd be taking the easy path, the coward's path. To top it off, it would mean going back to the drawing board to ensure that all of the data we collected remained scientifically measurable. Still, you do have a legitimate point behind your scattering of emotionally-driven arguments.

"All of the risks that we've taken so far would be for nothing if Sixty-Seven died on the operating table. I may be a bit of a zealot at times, but I don't want to ruin everything. That much is obvious, I hope." He paused then and looked away, grimacing as he thought it over. "I'll be careful," he finally conceded. "However spineless it feels, I'll exercise extreme caution. If the trials are too much for him, I'll change the game plan accordingly. It'll be an absolute headache, but I will."

"Good," Edward sighed, visibly relieved. "Thank you." For the first time since the beginning of the conversation, he eased up a little, but there was still something on his mind. Someone that knew him *really* well might have noticed it, but most would probably mistake it for his usual anxiety. The nuance was slight, but it was there. His fidgeting was a little more intense, his gaze a little blanker, more distant than it would be for a set of equations that he had a hard time wrapping his head around.

"What is it?" Jerg asked him, clueing in on all of the subtle indicators. "You don't seem very satisfied with my concession. Is it not enough?"

"It's not that," Edward assured him, even more nervous now that the other cat was coming out of the bag. And there was no doubt that it was coming out. He knew that he couldn't keep it to himself even if he tried. "I mean your concession, as you call it," he specified in a hurried way. "It *is* enough. It's just that... it's just that," he started to say, but couldn't seem to finish.

"It's just that *what*?" Jerg asked pressingly, clearly annoyed. "Come on, now. Out with it, man!"

Edward exhaled markedly and took in a deep breath. He knew that even to the untrained eye, he probably looked like he was getting ready to churn out one of his patented, longwinded replies. All he was really trying to do was work up the courage to say what needed saying. It took him a few seconds too long for comfort, but when he found his words, he *did* unleash them in one constant, relentless flow.

"It's just that he's starting to ask a lot of questions," he breathed, "a lot of questions that I don't have answers for. Or can't respond to because I'm not entirely convinced that he's ready for that... for the truth. He deserves it, though. The truth. To have his questions answered. Remaining silent is eating me up inside. Don't you think that it's time we told him? Don't you think that it's time we at least explained what's going on? Wouldn't you expect the same if you were in his place?

"He spends his days cooped up in his room, or undergoing examinations of one kind or the other. We never even let him go outside, for the love of Pete. I think you'd be asking yourself a lot of questions too, if you were in his shoes. *I* know I'd be going batty. Well... actually, no I wouldn't, because I'm used to being caged in, but anyone else would, I'm sure. Anyone normal." He was starting to run out of wind from speaking so quickly. He wanted to say more, but he was getting red in the face and had to stop to catch his breath.

Jerg must have realized that he was about to launch into the second part of his long-drawn ramble, as he threw his hands up in the universal "stop right now" sign. "Doctor Munro," he uttered in a commanding tone.

Edward opened his mouth to start anyway, but Jerg cut him off promptly. "*Doctor,*" he repeated with a severity that would bring the most panicky of worrywarts to heel. "That's enough! Calm yourself! I get it. I understand. Really, I do. And I think you're right. He *does* deserve to hear the truth... but not yet, not now. He couldn't *handle* the truth right now."

"How can you be so sure?" Edward asked. Jerg's intervention had calmed him somewhat, but his concerns were serious, and they wouldn't be so easily dismissed.

"The first series of tests will be particularly demanding on him," Jerg answered pointedly. "He'll have enough to deal with already without us taxing him further." He waited a moment, most likely to ensure that he was listening, and not simply waiting for an opportunity to cut in and break into a new panic. Satisfied, he continued. "Can you imagine what his reaction might be to something like that?" he asked, though he had no intention of letting him answer. "It would demolish him, psychologically speaking. Any kind of morale that he did have would go straight through the floor... *because* he's different."

He took a deep breath then and looked him straight in the eye. "Look... these procedures are going to be trying enough as it is, both physically and mentally. Put simply, telling him the truth now would be doing him a great disservice. It would be the drop that made the vase overflow."

"Then why don't we delay the tests?" Edward asked, hopeful and ready to take the idea to the bank. "He really *needs* to know," he added. "*I* need him to know."

"That's out of the question," Jerg objected brashly. "I know that this project is your baby, but if you think about it for two seconds, you'll understand." He gave him exactly that—two seconds—and after getting nothing but a confused look in return, he exhaled sharply. "If we tell him now, there's no knowing how long we're going to have to delay the tests," he snapped. "First of all, there's a chance he'd be depressed for *months*, and secondly, I doubt he'd make it any easier on us afterwards." He planted his fists on his hips then and shook his head adamantly, his face puckering up as though the words had left an awful taste in his mouth. "I really don't expect him to cooperate as it is," he spat, "but you can bloody well be sure that he's going to resist us to the *bitter end* if you open your piehole now."

Edward let his shoulders sag suddenly, defeated. He was very passionate about all of this, but not completely beyond reason. He'd mulled everything over in his head, and accepting Jerg's perspective as sensible, he sighed extensively. "You're right," he muttered. "I don't like it, but you are. Again." He removed his glasses then and rubbed at the bridge of his nose. He felt another of his notorious headaches coming on, and if his cringing was any indicator of its intensity, it was going to be a real humdinger.

"Listen," Jerg said, his voice transformed by this newfound empathy thing he'd been trying his hand at, "you shouldn't fret over this half as much as you do. It's not good for you. It worries me." He sounded awkward and unpracticed, but his sincerity shone through. "I know that it's hard to do," he added, retaining his sympathetic tone with some difficulty, "but you should just sit back and let me handle all of this. Just trust me, okay? Let go. I'll take good care of your *baby* for you. I won't overdo it."

"You're right," Edward conceded, still massaging the bridge of his nose. "I know that you are." He was in too much pain to continue any serious dialogue.

"You should go get some rest," Jerg suggested. "I'll see if Falstaff or one of the others can bring some hot tea up to your quarters. It's three packets of sweetener, yes?"

"Yes, Jerg... thank you," Edward answered, sincerely grateful despite the slight delay in his response. "I *could* use a bit of a nap right now." With that he rose, then walked toward the doorway. When he reached it, he stopped and looked over his shoulder. He hesitated a moment before asking, "When will you be starting with all of this?"

"Tomorrow," Jerg answered plainly.

Edward nodded weakly and mumbled a faint, "Tomorrow," before turning around and exiting the hall.

Jerg waited until the door had closed behind him to raise his clenched fist in triumph. He did feel bad for Edward. The man had turned pale as a ghost before he'd shambled off. For the most part, their colleagues at the Commission had probably been right in thinking that *Jerk* Weissinger was a coldhearted asshole, but he wasn't *completely* devoid of emotion. He just didn't feel the need to be nice to everyone, especially not to self-righteous snobs and haughty dander muffins. Edward was one of the few people that he actually concerned himself over, one of the few that he actually *felt* like being nice to, when he could afford to be. He still failed to understand why he took everything to heart the way that he did, but despite his obvious weakness, he was the closest thing that he had to a friend.

He did worry about him, but the prospect of poking holes in Sixty-Seven took precedence. The thought of it was exhilarating. He felt like getting up and breaking into one of those hippity-hop dances, like the ones he sometimes saw in commercials. This was something he'd wanted to do for a very long time. He'd never been taken seriously at the Commission. Not seriously enough to be given domain over a project of this magnitude.

He let out a long sigh of relief then and joined his hands behind his head. During their conversation, he'd worried that he was being too blunt with Edward, too honest. *Mostly honest*, he thought. He had fudged a few things, but nothing he'd said had been an outright lie. As far as he was concerned, it was crucial that Doctor Munro be left out of the testing phase altogether. The poor man just didn't have the stomach for that sort of thing. He'd have gotten in his way and delayed the whole process.

He was still surprised that he'd managed to convince him the way that he had. He'd have said or done just about anything to get his way, if it had come to that, but if he'd pushed too hard, Edward might not have bowed out so peacefully. He wasn't one to gloat, but there was a certain satisfaction in victory.

Not only would he be testing out Sixty-Seven's capabilities firsthand, but he was going to be the lead on the exercise, as well. Despite the fact that he'd be leading a team of just *one*—himself, namely—it was nothing to smirk at. The sentinels didn't really count as team members, per se, no matter how useful they might be. Not a single one of them had relevant experience or even a mild scientific bent. It limited the ways in which he could use them. He'd share his vast wealth of knowledge with anyone that wanted to learn, if it could help advance his own cause. But that would require a lot of time and a lot effort, and at present, he didn't have much of either of those to spare.

CHAPTER 20

In the Drink

A loud buzz at the door to his quarters wrenched Frank from his thoughts and he bolted upright reflexively. He'd been awake for nearly a half hour, which had given him plenty of time to make his bed, relieve himself in the small, portable toilet he'd been provided with for his convenience, and then lie down on his tidied-up covers to do some thinking. Whether he wanted to or not, he'd been doing an awful lot of that, lately—*thinking*—and most of it had been about Vanessa.

He could be doing far more productive things with his time, he realized, but whenever he asked about his girlfriend's location, he was met with more than a little reluctance, and that irked him. It seemed like everyone was stonewalling him, and he was starting to fear that the worst had happened.

He'd put off worrying about her as best he could for as long as he could, because quite frankly, he couldn't allow it to get to him. But he was failing miserably at it. *If anything has happened to her,* he mused, *anything at all...* He didn't even want to finish the thought. There was a plethora of bad things that could have happened to her, and each one made his stomach roil.

When he'd first woken in this place, he'd assumed that his liberators had also rescued and taken good care of her. Maybe, he'd once thought, they'd allow them to reunite once they'd both fully recovered, but he was even less sure of that now. Maybe she hadn't even needed rescuing in the first place, but if that was the case, he didn't understand why they couldn't just tell him as much.

He'd been treated fairly and with relative kindness by most. Ultimately, they'd saved him from a certain death. It was only natural that he'd afford them some degree of trust. But despite all of that, he was starting to feel like a prisoner, and that feeling was growing with every passing day.

The jarring noise of the door's heavy steel bolts grinding on metal as they unlocked severed any lingering thoughts that he had of Vanessa. He was a little surprised that anyone was coming to see him so early in the morning. As far as he remembered, he didn't have anything scheduled until his physical rehabilitation session in the early afternoon.

There was a whir and the sound of metal sliding on metal as the heavy mechanized door slid open. A second later, Doctor Weissinger walked in, his arms folded neatly behind his back. His lab coat was as pristine and brilliantly white as usual. Lieutenant Corporal Baumgartner and Sergeant Hildebrandt filed in behind him, and stood at his sides as the procession came to a halt.

"Good morning," Weissinger droned out, sounding as cold and as lifeless as he always did. "I'm glad to see that you're already awake. You'll need to be alert for the next series of experiments we're about to conduct. Trust me."

As always, his monotony made his skin crawl. Whether it was intentional or not remained a mystery. Baumgartner wore the same blank expression that he put on whenever he didn't have much to say. It was impossible to tell what was going on inside of that ragged head of his, if he was even thinking at all.

Hildebrandt, on the other hand, was easy to read, and not just because he knew him better than he did the others. He was expressive by nature, and what he was expressing at present left him perturbed. At first glance, it looked like he'd swallowed a poisonous cocktail of guilt, regret and disappointment.

J.J. was, without the shadow of a doubt, the most intense person he'd met in the facility, perhaps in his entire life. He always seemed to work and play harder than everyone else. It was as though he was fueled by some inner zeal, a fervent passion that he rarely saw in others. This intensity mirrored every aspect of his personality, including his emotional temperament.

Since the sergeant was almost always in contagiously good spirits, he had a hard time taking his current disposition as anything but a bad omen. He tried to make eye contact with him, but Hildebrandt averted his gaze the second he saw him looking. *Yes,* he thought, *there has to be something wrong here.* He didn't know exactly *what* that something was, but there wasn't much that he could do about it anyway.

"I don't want to push you this morning," Weissinger added in a sarcastic tone, "but we *are* pressed for time." He looked at his watch then and grimaced. "Please," he beckoned, "follow me." He turned then and left the room just as quickly as he'd entered it. "We have much to do," he called back to him as he stepped past the threshold and turned right down the hall beyond.

Frank was reluctant to follow, but he didn't have much of a choice. Hildebrandt and Baumgartner remained behind, and only started moving again once he'd left his quarters, trailing him like sheepdogs driving a lamb to its pen. They trod down the narrow corridor in awkward silence until they reached the open doorway Weissinger had disappeared through only seconds earlier.

Frank stopped and hesitated for a moment before stepping through. Peering into the chamber sent a shiver down his spine. Everything about the place felt wrong, dead wrong, but he wasn't sure why. The room itself was tall enough that it took up a whole other story, like someone had simply knocked the ceiling out to join the two levels together. It was practically bare, except for a set of consoles in one of the far corners, and a tall cylinder made of glass or some kind of thermoplastic compound standing in its centre. The strange tube was enormous, and reached about half of the way up to the chamber's high ceiling.

He glanced back at the sentinels as he heard them come up behind him. Baumgartner motioned for him to step inside, and all Hildebrandt offered him was a blank stare. It was almost like the sergeant was looking through him, like he refused to see him. On closer inspection, he thought he might be ashamed of himself.

"Right this way," Baumgartner casually suggested, gesturing toward the open door once more. His attitude contrasted sharply with Hildebrandt's. While the sergeant looked ridden with guilt, Baumgartner didn't seem to be very worried about anything at all. He looked like he just didn't give a damn, but that wasn't very surprising, all things considered.

Obliging them, Frank drew a sharp breath and stepped inside. He headed straight to the spot where Weissinger stood waiting for them, by the large consoles. The two sentinels never left his heels.

"A word before we get started," Weissinger droned out with his usual lack of emotion. "Doctor Munro's been unduly worried about your well-being of late. He's asked me to keep you informed about the procedures that we'll be performing over the next few weeks. As I can, of course, and where it isn't problematic."

"Procedures," Frank half said, half asked, sounding more than just a little suspicious. "What kind of procedures are we talking about here? What do you plan on doing to me, exactly?"

"Now now," Weissinger cooed in obvious mock reassurance, "there's no need to worry about specifics." He punched in a few keys at the central panel then, almost idly.

Frank peered at the screens briefly, and wasn't at all surprised to find that he couldn't make sense of the technical gobbledygook displayed there. "If you're not going to tell me what's going on," he muttered, "then what the hell *can* you tell me? And why, pray tell, has Doctor Munro been worried about my *well-being?*"

"*Unduly* worried about your well-being," Weissinger corrected him. "I said that I was asked to inform you as I could, and where possible. It would be useless, even counter-productive to go into too much detail here, right now." He tapped away at the panel more furiously then, and for a while, it almost seemed like he'd forgotten about him altogether.

"To answer your other question," he finally breathed about ten seconds later, "Doctor Munro's been worried about your well-being because these procedures are going to be very unpleasant, at times venturing into the outright painful, and that's a best-case scenario. They won't be *fun*, but they're low-risk. What can I say? He's got a weak stomach when it comes to this sort of thing."

"Well aren't you a warm blanket on a cold winter night," Frank grumbled, visibly unsettled by the promise of pain. "Thanks for that. Really. Appreciate it."

"My my, aren't we testy this morning," Weissinger retorted mockingly. He turned away from the consoles then to offer him his full attention. "I'm not here to reassure you. I'll tell you what you need to know and *only* what you need to know. Ultimately, I want you to remember two things, just two. Do you think you can remember them, or is that too much to ask?"

"Just say what you have to say, already," Frank muttered under his breath. He preferred the monotonous Weissinger that was completely devoid of emotion. This one made him want to punch him square in the teeth.

"First," Weissinger stated, obliging him, "these tests are a necessary step in your development. We wouldn't be doing them if they weren't crucial. Secondly, you don't really have a choice in the matter, so please do make this easy on all of us and cooperate, won't you? That would be marvelous."

"Well, I'd already gathered that I didn't have a choice in this," Frank said, glaring back at Hildebrandt momentarily, "but I wouldn't mind if you explained *how* this is supposed to be necessary to my... 'development'." He pronounced that last word with a certain grand vagueness, and coupled it with the universal finger-hook gesture for quotation marks. "Please excuse my ignorance, but I don't see how I could '*develop*' any further. I feel about as good now as I ever have."

"Well, you're going to have to trust me on this," Weissinger stated curtly. "There's plenty of room for development. We've only just begun to scratch at the surface of your full potential."

"Do you even *know* how to give a straight answer," Frank barked. "My full potential for what? Why is this necessary for my development? Why is my so-called *development* even necessary in the first place? I feel *fine!*" He was usually good at controlling his anger, but his fists were currently clenched at his sides.

"Tut-tut-tut," Weissinger cooed, slowly shaking his head from side to side. "These are just a few of the things that I can't tell you, Sixty-Seven. It's essential, and that should be enough."

"Well maybe it *should* be, but it's not," Frank muttered.

"Well that's just too bad for you then, isn't it?" Weissinger snapped. He was starting to sound a little edgy. "You'll get no more on the matter than I've already given you and that's that, so let's get over it, shall we, and move on."

"Is there at least *one* useful thing that you *can* tell me?" Frank asked, barely able to keep a rein on what was starting to border on outright animosity.

"Are you having a stroke in the left side of your brain?" Weissinger blurted out. "I don't have to tell you *anything*, so you should be more than satisfied with the basics, which are as follows: we'll be conducting some experiments over the next few weeks because you *need* us to. Some of them will hurt so damned much that you'll wish you were dead. But never, ever, not even for a second will you be at risk of dying." Their eyes locked for a moment then, and he added, "You have my word."

If Weissinger hadn't decided to tack that last bit on, Frank might have let his arrogance slip, but if the man expected him to trust him blindly just because he asked him to, he had another thing coming to him. "With all due respect," he said, "your word isn't worth a sack of shit to me, *Doctor*."

He glanced over his shoulder at Hildebrandt then, and added, "And neither is yours." What he *really* felt like hurling at him was something along the lines of, "I thought we were friends," but he realized how silly and juvenile it would sound, and that it would resolve absolutely nothing. It didn't matter that it felt like a knife had been plunged firmly between his shoulder blades.

Though the growing feeling that he was nothing more than a prisoner in this place prevented him from considering anyone a *real* friend, he *had* gotten closer to Hildebrandt, as well as Mosley, Falstaff and Doctor Munro, and it was equally hard to consider them anything but. He'd never truly gotten along with Lieutenant Corporal Baumgartner, and he trusted him about as much as he trusted Weissinger, which was next to not at all.

For a second, Weissinger looked like he was going to explode with rage. He grit his teeth, held his fist up like he was going to shake it, and opened his mouth to lash out, but didn't. Sighing, he took off his glasses, wiped the lenses down with his coat sleeve and then slipped them back into place.

"Why would I deceive you?" he asked, leaving him no time to respond. "What reasons other than the one provided could I possibly have to do something like that? Think things through logically. We saved you from a horrible fate. We've been nursing you back to health for weeks now at our own expense. We can't even leave this founder-forsaken place without looking over our shoulders because we're wanted by the police for helping *you*. What interest could I *really* have in killing you now? What point would there be in doing such a thing?"

"I don't know," Frank mumbled then trailed off. He was at a loss for words. Weissinger made some good points. Was he being a big baby about all of this? Suddenly, he couldn't help but feel that he was. He didn't even know what they planned on doing to him yet, but he was already acting like a rebellious teenager.

"None," Weissinger answered for him, a little bluntly. "None whatsoever. Now if you're done sniveling," he added with a point of contempt, walking over to the cylindrical tank in the center of the room, "I'd appreciate your cooperation."

Feeling slightly ashamed of himself, Frank bowed his head and conceded. "What do you want me to do?" he asked gruffly. He joined the doctor by the giant upturned test tube and eyed it warily. It stood well over ten feet tall, and was about four feet wide, maybe a bit more. He didn't know what they had in store for him, but he was willing to wager that he'd be on the inside of that thing before they broke for breakfast.

"Simple," Weissinger answered, much more calmly now that things were going his way. "First of all, I want you to put this on," he said, fishing a small object out of his pocket. He laid it out in the palm of his hand and showed it to him. Once it had been unraveled, the thing looked like some kind of supple finger brace. The bottom half of it was lined with stretchy nylon fasteners. At its top was a thimble-like receptacle with two prongs on the inside of it.

The small prongs were about half a centimeter in length, and felt like little more than a bee sting when the doctor pressed them into the tip of his index finger. They went in like a knife through warm butter. He gasped as they pierced his skin, but his reaction was one of surprise more than anything. Before he knew it, the straps had been tightened and secured for him, and he wasn't even sure that he could remove the brace if he wanted to.

"Whatever you do," Weissinger warned him pointedly, "make sure this stays on. I couldn't be more serious right now, so listen. For your own safety, it *must* remain in place."

Frank nodded idly, eyeing his finger as he flexed it in and out, testing the brace's adhesion. It wasn't going to come off without a lot of help. "What now?" he asked. He was puzzled beyond belief, and sure that he looked and sounded it, as well.

"Next, I want you to step inside this vat, here," Weissinger instructed. He pointed toward the tank with both hands in a pose that reminded Frank of an assistant presenting the wares on the Home Shopping Network.

"And how do you propose I do that?" Frank asked, genuinely confused. The vat seemed to be completely without seam. There was no door or even mechanism that hinted at the possibility that there might be one hidden somewhere.

Weissinger motioned to Baumgartner, who was standing by the entrance. He twirled his index finger upward and called out, "Bring her up!"

The lieutenant corporal walked over to a large lever on the other side of the doorway and pushed it all the way up. At first glance, nothing changed, but then the top of the tank started to rise as its base slowly extended from the floor. Before long, an opening became visible in that part of the glass that was still rising. This noiseless extraction continued until the opening was about five and a half feet tall, then stopped with a low clunk.

Wasting no time, Frank ducked his head and stepped inside. "What now?" he asked, shrugging at Doctor Weissinger.

On Weissinger's cue, Baumgartner brought the lever down, and the entire tank started to slide back into the floor, just as slowly as it had risen. "Watch your toes," the doctor warned, pointing down at Frank's feet.

There was a circular channel cut into the floor for the glass to slide through, and Frank stepped back from it immediately. He didn't want to get his toes cut off by the opening's top edge as it retracted back into the floor. The inside of the tube was so tight it was almost suffocating, but he was still able to get a good look at it. High above him, at the cylinder's topmost extremity, dozens of small holes had been drilled. Beneath him, at floor level, a thick, rubber lip lined the inside of the tank. As he watched the opening sink into the floor, he recognized the feel of grating beneath his feet, and a sudden realization made him shudder.

"This may not seem very scientific," Weissinger called to him through the glass, the sound of his voice somewhat muffled by the thickness of it, "but keep in mind that we're breaking new ground here. Or should I say treading new water? Regardless, try to keep an open mind about it."

"I don't know if that's supposed to make me feel any better," Frank shot back, "but it doesn't!" The doctor had already turned his back, and he was almost positive that he hadn't heard a single word he'd said.

Weissinger spun around then and raised the tip of his index finger, as though to signal that he'd just remembered something. "I almost forgot," he shouted, drawing close to the glass. A low thrumming noise had started up, and it nearly drowned out the sound of his voice. "Do *not* struggle," he continued. That would only make it worse. Trust me, it would be pointless. The glass is too thick. You'll crack before it does. Just do as I say and you'll be fine. Stay calm and ensure that the oxygen monitor remains on your finger at all times!"

With that, he scurried back to his consoles at the far end of the room. When he reached the central panel, he began tapping away at its keys at a furious pace, like a man possessed. Once again on his queue, Baumgartner turned an enormous blue valve just to the right of the lever that he'd previously used.

Frank watched helplessly from the confines of his glass prison, trying his best not to focus on what would happen next. He wasn't entirely sure what was going on, but he'd understood the gist of it, and he knew that it wouldn't be good. As determined as he was to remain calm, doing so was no easy task. A sudden, wet chill between his toes made him gasp sharply then as water started to flow up through the grating in the floor.

The water was freezing cold and was filling the tank rapidly. Within mere seconds, he was almost completely submerged, but he managed to arch his head back to take one final breath before it was engulfed completely. As the water washed over his eyes and mouth, the intense cold struck him like a slap in the face. His lungs felt like they were being crushed by a blanket of ice.

He floated higher and higher as the water rose, and didn't stop rising until his head butted against the top of the tank. The water pressing against him and gushing past overflowed through the holes that had been drilled there. The flow from the pump was so powerful that it had to be cut off promptly once the tank was filled to capacity. Failing to do so quickly enough would result in a shattered tank, no doubt, but the small vents at its height would buy them a few more seconds to get that done.

He pressed his hands against the inside of the tank to steady himself, and tried to hold his breath as best he could. The glacial water battered him into uncomfortable positions and pried at his lips, and it turned the simple task of keeping his mouth shut into a complicated one. Despite the initial shock, Frank somehow found it in himself to retain at least a measure of calm. He tried to focus on the others, watching them intently as they set to work.

Squinting, he saw Weissinger motion wildly at Baumgartner from behind his console. It looked like he was yelling something, but with all the water jetting up around him, it was impossible to make out any of the words. He could tell that he was irritated, though; that much was clear. He was irritated, and perhaps even a little worried.

The display below did little to quiet his nerves. When the water stopped splashing down around the base of the vat a few seconds later, he realized that this was what the squabbling had been about. Now that the pump had been turned off, he slowly sank to the bottom. When his feet touched down, he closed his eyes, hoping that it would help him focus on his task.

Even the effort to concentrate helped him maintain his calm. Still, he couldn't help but wonder how much longer they were going to keep him in there for, or if they were even going to let him out at all. Had he been deceived? Would this giant test tube become his watery grave? He tried to remind himself that they had nothing to gain from disposing of him, that the idea itself was illogical. He tried to and managed, though just barely.

His instinct for self-preservation was strong, and it made him question his surroundings almost perpetually, even in situations that others might consider mundane. At present, his mind was shifting into overdrive. Without even realizing it, he reached out with both hands to test the surface of the glass. Would it really contain him if he tried to break through it, he wondered. How much pressure could it withstand before it gave way? Was it as resilient as Doctor Weissinger had let on?

He recalled having briefly gauged the thickness of the glass as he'd entered the tank, and he imagined that it was. It would be hard enough to break through without factoring in water resistance slowing down his movement. Still, the tank was narrow enough that he could brace himself against one side with his back, which would give him significant push.

Reverberating taps on the glass shook him from his thoughts, and his eyes shot open instantly. On the other side of the glass, Weissinger stood facing him. The man looked genuinely pleased with himself as he grinned from ear to ear. "Three minutes!" he cried out, pointing at his watch before holding up three fingers. His words were muffled and distorted, but reading his lips and following his gestures made them easier to understand.

He imagined the last thing the doctor had said was, "Keep it up," as it was followed by two thumbs up, but he wasn't entirely sure. He felt like telling him that he'd kept it up long enough, but that would have been impossible. Weissinger had already trotted off again, so he couldn't even signal to him.

If anything, the doctor's brief intervention reminded him that they weren't out to get him. He closed his eyes again and tried to regain some semblance of serenity. The task wasn't as easy this time around, because the lack of oxygen was really starting to get to him. Still, he waited, and tried to remain as calm as he possibly could. Despite his efforts, he eventually started to wonder how long it had been since he'd last taken a breath, and then it was all he could think about. If he'd had a watch or a timer with him, his eyes would have been riveted to it nonstop. It would probably have driven him mad.

It seemed like he'd been waiting an eternity when his body finally started to twitch and jerk violently. It was just one isolated instance, at first, but the spasms soon multiplied and came at him more frequently. He tried to stop the jolting, but it was all reflex, and impossible to control.

It felt like his lungs were contracting, gasping for oxygen that just wasn't there. "Do *not* struggle," Weissinger had told him. "That would only make it worse." But try as he might to resist, there was a growing sense of urgency inside of him, and it was taking over. He knew that no amount of resolve would spare him from the imminent freefall into outright panic that was sure to follow. He'd try to breathe eventually, whether he wanted to or not.

Weissinger's instructions be damned, he thought. He was *not* going to just float there and wait until he drowned. He felt his mouth just itching to open up and breathe in a deadly dose of the drink. Without hesitating further, he wedged himself into a sitting position, with his back pressed up against one side of the tank, and his feet pressed up against the other. All of a sudden, a violent convulsion racked his entire body as his lungs made another grab for air. His eyes shot wide open with frenzy, but as soon as his spasms had passed, he started kicking against the glass with the plants of his feet.

A flash of movement from his left drew his attention, and when he glanced over, he saw that Hildebrandt had moved right up to the glass. The giant of a man looked about as panic-stricken as he felt. He stood there shouting something loud and largely incomprehensible over his shoulder.

Frank never stopped to analyze any of it as time seemed to be running out for him, and at a breakneck pace. Every little scrap of concentration that he could muster went into pummeling the walls of his glass coffin. Anything else became little more than a faint background noise.

He didn't know if the glass was letting up, but he couldn't think rationally by that point anyway, as he was acting solely on instinct. He kicked against it again and again, losing momentum with every thrust. The next convulsion forced him into a ball of cramped muscle and taut sinew.

The moment he came out of it, he pushed off from the grate at the base of the tank and launched himself straight up, like a fish trying to break surface. Instead of surfacing, he smashed his face against the top of the tank. He rammed right into it at full speed, and the only thing that kept him from blacking out immediately was the burst of adrenaline that was coursing through his veins.

He floated there, listless and without motion, slowly sinking toward the bottom again. His arms and legs were splayed out limply like those of a rag doll. Barely conscious, the scene below him registered like a hazy dream. Hildebrandt was still standing at the base of the tank, but now he was smashing against it with the butt of an assault rifle, and from the look of it, he was putting all of his weight into it.

The change was subtle, at first, but everything was starting to take on a pinkish hue. Through the cloudy water, he saw a pink Baumgartner come up from behind the now-pink Hildebrandt and try to wrestle his pink assault rifle away from him. The pink giant shrugged the smaller pink man off with ease, and continued to whale against the glass with great clanking thrusts.

The world around him grew darker and darker yet, and pink soon turned to red as the wound on his forehead bled ever more profusely into the water. Weissinger suddenly entered the bizarre *picture show* that was playing out for his eyes only, and then exited the stage just as quickly. He ran by the struggling men with such haste that he looked like little more than a reddish blur.

The seconds dragged on, and the fog of blood engulfing him darkened so much that he couldn't see a thing. A suffocating queasiness wrenched through him then, and it felt like his life was being squeezed right out of him.

The hand of death was gripping him tightly, he was sure, but contrary to what Weissinger had told him back in his room, he didn't feel like dying. He just wanted to breathe again. He just wanted to take one more breath. He'd do anything at all to take one more breath. It was all he wanted, all he needed. No longer thinking, he opened his mouth and took that breath, and then the darkness overtook him.

CHAPTER
21

Guinea Pig

Frank bolted upright and thrashed around at his covers for a few seconds before realizing that he was back in his quarters. Just moments ago, he'd been drowning, or so it seemed. But now here he was, not at all dead, but dry, warm, and breathing in deep breaths of sweet, sweet air that he'd never take for granted ever again. He let out a long, deep sigh of relief, and fell back on his pillow with a satisfying thud.

The low buzz of a droning snore drew his attention then, and it didn't take him very long to locate the source of it. Near the foot of his bed, Hildebrandt sat sleeping in a rickety folding chair, his head and shoulders slumping precariously forward and off to one side. His setup looked like it was less than comfortable, but he seemed to be managing just fine despite that. In fact, the sleeping giant was slumbering so deeply that he looked like he might fall over at any given moment.

The thought of stomping his foot on the floor to startle him out of his chair crossed his mind briefly, but he remembered how Hildebrandt had tried to break him free from what could have been his waterlogged coffin, and just the thought of it quelled his momentary scorn almost instantly. Though he *had* helped put him there in the first place, he couldn't exactly fault him for following his superior's orders, could he?

He might not like it, but even he'd bought into Weissinger's pitch about the importance of the test. He couldn't really blame Hildebrandt for buying it too. The more he thought about it, the harder it was to stay angry with him, especially after the show he'd put on when he'd tried to smash him out of that glass tank. He couldn't recall how he'd gotten out of that mess, but he did remember Hildebrandt's frantic hammering against the glass with the butt of his rifle, and the way that he'd wrestled Baumgartner off when he'd tried to stop him.

He doubted Weissinger had been very pleased about that. If he'd gauged the doctor's person well, and he was fairly certain that he had, there was a good chance that the sergeant had been chastised for his "ill conduct". The fact that he was sitting at the foot of his bed now—watching over him, it would seem—was both touching and mildly disconcerting all at once, which wasn't to say he didn't understand why he was doing it. It just felt awkward to him. He wasn't used to getting that kind of attention, and he probably never would be.

Just as he began to lose his balance, Hildebrandt stirred in his sleep and snapped upright. He blinked repeatedly and rubbed at his eyes with the palms of his hands. "What time is it?" he asked with a yawn, addressing no one in particular. He glanced over at Frank then with sleepy eyes. There was a guilty look of accidental sleep about him, like that of a guard that had just been caught snoozing on his watch.

There was no doubt in Frank's mind that Hildebrandt felt bad about what had happened, but for exactly what reason, he wasn't entirely sure. Maybe he felt responsible for getting him into that mess, somehow. Maybe the "procedure" had been a lot worse than he'd expected it to be, or the outcome of it, at least. Maybe it was a bit of both. The only sure thing was that it was a burden for him. That much was about as clear as day. Compared to usual, he looked like he was carrying the weight of the entire world on his shoulders. He wasn't used to seeing him so somber.

"You know, I don't blame you for what happened," he said, thinking aloud. "I may have given you a dirty look or two this morning, but I was just taken off guard by everything. I was angry. The heat of the moment and all that."

"This *morning*?" Hildebrandt asked in disbelief. "You're not being serious right now, are you? Listen, Frank... I'm glad you're not pissed off at me and everything, but you've been out cold for a day and a half now." He looked at his watch for confirmation then and nodded. "A little bit more than that, actually."

"I never would have guessed it," Frank replied, genuinely surprised. "It feels like it was only seconds ago that I was..." He was going to say, "thrashing around in a fish tank, fighting for my life," but trailed off instead. He didn't want to guilt-trip the guy more than he needed to with a poor choice of words. "Undergoing the... uh... procedure," he added after a brief hesitation.

"I guess you were pretty burned out by that whole thing," Hildebrandt noted. "Your body basically shut down before we could even get you out of the tube. I'd never seen anything like it before." He mulled it over for a few seconds before adding, "Not in a controlled environment as part of some *test*, at least." His last words were tinged with disgust.

"So... what exactly happened after I blacked out?" Frank asked, suddenly curious. "From the sound of it, it's like I had to be revived or something."

"*Revive* might be too big of a word for it," Hildebrandt admitted gruffly. "You never really came 'out of it' until just now. Anyway, I guess I kind of panicked when you started flailing around like a madman in there," he recounted. "It seemed like I was the only one that was really worried about it, at first." He was starting to get flustered as he went on, and deep spots of crimson were blooming in his cheeks.

"Now that I think about it," he breathed, "no one seemed to give a flying fuck until you stopped responding altogether. I'd never seen Weissinger run like that before. Surprisingly, all we had to do once he flushed the tank was get the water out of your lungs and you were good to go."

He didn't seem to realize it, but he was fidgeting around in his seat quite visibly. "Good to go into some kind of coma," he added with a growl. "I'm no doctor, but I think we almost lost you back there, and I think Commander Weissinger knows it, too."

"Wow," Frank breathed, at a loss for words. He sat up at that and took a moment to let it all sink in. "That's pretty messed up," he finally managed to say, leaning in toward the sergeant. "But honestly, though, I've never felt better. It's like nothing even happened to me. Nothing at all."

"Well I'm glad to hear it," Hildebrandt stated gruffly, "but that doesn't make it any better." He managed to keep his anger in check, but still looked like a bee had stung him in the ass.

"Why not?" Frank asked, eyeing him quizzically. "I thought these *tests* were supposed to be 'important', 'necessary'."

"Don't get me wrong," Hildebrandt warned, "I trust Doctor Weissinger. He's been my commanding officer for a really long time." He stopped then and took a deep breath, either to calm himself or to herald a long-winded rant. It was hard to tell which one it was going to be.

"If he says it's important, then it's important," he spluttered out hastily. "That much I know. It's just that none of it seems very scientific. Not even just a bit, to be honest. Now, I'm no man of science, but what did we learn from all this? That you can hold your breath for about seven minutes before almost dying? Oh, I'm sure that's pretty good and everything, but seriously now, whoop-de-friggin'-doo. I don't get what the point of any of that was. I don't. Really. Like at all."

"And that's exactly how it should be," Weissinger stated from the open doorway, a little snarkier than usual. "I really don't have time to explain everything in terms that a layman might understand, and I shouldn't have to, either." He waltzed inside then just as abruptly as he'd made his presence known, with his hands clenched firmly behind his back and his retinue of the day following close behind him.

It wasn't a big surprise to see Baumgartner there. He followed Weissinger around pretty much everywhere he went. Corporal Mosley had come along as well, this time. Both men stood behind and to either side of him, their shoulders squared, their faces without expression. The scene was all too familiar.

"Sir," Hildebrandt said, firing off an awkward salute as he got up from his chair. "I understand that, sir, but I can't be expected to like it." He furrowed his brow then and looked down before adding, "Not one bit."

"And that's exactly the reason why I've precluded you from participating in similar exercises in the future," Weissinger replied coolly. "While I appreciate your concern, I don't have time to waste with questions about my motives or my methods. I have even less time to spend repairing valuable equipment after it's been damaged by panicky assistants with weak stomachs."

"I understand, sir," Hildebrandt answered mechanically. He didn't sound like he understood much of anything, but seemed resigned to accept the situation without further questioning. "It's probably for the best."

"You don't say," Weissinger commented sarcastically. "Of course it's for the best, but this is neither the time nor the place. I have a very tight schedule to respect and more experiments to conduct before the day is over."

"Already?" Hildebrandt asked, both shocked and obviously displeased. As much as he tried to mask it, it was apparent for all to see. "He hasn't even had time to get back on his feet yet. Don't you think he should at least be given the chance to recuperate from your last botched experiment before you make him suffer through another?"

"Botched experiment?" Weissinger huffed, his eyes widening with disbelief. "Sergeant, I want you out of this room and out of my sight. Immediately. Leave or I'll have you forcefully ejected." He turned askance then and pointed toward the open doorway. "Now. Go. Don't make me repeat myself."

The doctor's reaction angered Hildebrandt visibly. Clearly, he hadn't expected that strong of a response. Fuming, he balled his fists at his sides and glared at him for what felt like a really long time, but was probably no more than three seconds. He looked like he was going to say something more, but stopped himself. "Fine," he finally breathed through clenched teeth, then marched out of the room without looking back.

Mosley and Baumgartner exchanged puzzled glances, mildly confused by what had just transpired. Frank was a little surprised by Hildebrandt's defiance, but not at all fazed by it. It was actually nice to see someone looking out for him for a change, even if it *felt* a bit strange. That last experiment had probably been the closest call in his growing list of near-death experiences, but he felt like he was in top shape now, and wasn't nearly as troubled by all of this as the sergeant seemed to be.

He'd do what they asked of him. He'd told them that he would, that he'd trust them, and that was that. "He means well," he said, fully aware that his opinion meant next to nothing in Weissinger's eyes. The doctor confirmed as much by ignoring him outright and launching into a diatribe that he could have seen coming from a mile away.

"I don't think that I need to remind you of the importance of these trials," the doctor droned out in that monotonous tone of his. "I expect that you already understand the value of my time, and the importance of not wasting it. Similarly, I don't think that I need to underline how your cooperation would only be in all of our best interests."

The stern look that he gave him then would have intimidated someone of weaker character, but he'd had plenty of experience dealing with Captain Leonard Boston, so this was nothing. "Your unruly behavior during the last experiment nearly got you killed," Weissinger added matter-of-factly. "It almost cost us equipment that we can scarcely afford to repair, let alone replace."

"I *tried* to follow your instructions as well as I could," Frank responded, more than a mite defensively.

"Well you obviously didn't try hard enough," Jerg replied in a scolding tone. "We were just about done when you had to start panicking and thrashing around like a frightened little girl."

"I'm not sure if you're aware of this," Frank said, arching his brow, "but drowning *calmly* isn't exactly easy."

The doctor continued speaking as though he hadn't even heard him. "I'm going to need your *full* cooperation from now on," he stated, "and that means making at least a *semblance* of an effort. I'll have no more of this half-assed participation on your part. Frankly, you should be embarrassed."

"You have my *full* cooperation," Frank groaned. He pushed himself out of bed and got to his feet. Maybe the doctor would at least acknowledge him if they were looking eye to eye. "I screwed up," he admitted. "I tried to keep my cool and I failed. Now can we just forget about this and get on with it?"

"Yes, of course we can," Weissinger replied, much to Frank's surprise. "As long as you understand how important it is that you cooperate fully from now on, there's no point wasting any more of our time with futile words."

"Good," Frank breathed. "So tell me, what do you have in store for me today?"

"Follow me," Weissinger answered curtly. He clicked his heels as he turned, then left the room. His 'procession' waited for Frank to catch up to him before falling in behind them.

Straight to business, no formalities, this was the Weissinger he was used to. He followed him down winding corridors for what seemed like a very long time, completely oblivious to what they had in store for him. As casual as he pretended to be about all of it, remaining entirely calm was impossible. Still, he thought that he was doing all right, considering the fact that the last "test" had nearly killed him. *It can't be that bad every time, can it,* he asked himself, though he wasn't entirely sure he wanted an answer to that question. In his experience, tests started out easy enough, and got progressively harder.

Weissinger stopped in front of a plain-looking door a short distance ahead of them. When they caught up to him, he opened it and ushered them all inside.

Compared to the room they'd done the last experiment in, this one looked like little more than a storage closet. It was small and crowded with everyone inside. With all of these warm bodies in such a confined space, he knew that it wouldn't be long before the temperature started to rise.

There was no fancy machinery here, no high-tech console. With one quick glance, he'd seen just about everything that there was to see. One sparsely littered desk, a visitor's chair by the door, an examination table with a thin sheet of paper spread across it, and an oversized storage cabinet that was most likely filled to the brim with medical supplies. That was it.

The place looked no different from any of the triage booths they had in the Plaza district emergency room. He'd seen more than his fair share of those, and though the hospital was far from his favorite place to be, he felt a sudden wave of nostalgia wash over him then as he realized that this was the first familiar-looking thing he'd seen in a while.

"Take off your clothes and lie down," Weissinger uttered coolly. "Face up." He opened up the supply cabinet and scanned its contents while Frank followed his instructions, quickly and without hesitation.

In the short time that it took him to disrobe and lie down on the examination table, Weissinger had found everything he was looking for and closed the cabinet doors. He was so focused on what the doctor was doing that he was taken completely off guard when Baumgartner and Mosley sidled up to him and pulled straps out from the underside of the table. They slipped the loops at the ends of them over his hands and feet and tightened them in a combined effort. There was one strap for his arms and another for his legs. Pulling on the ends of them beneath the table tightened the loops around his wrists and ankles even more, and stretched his limbs out into the shape of an x.

"Make sure they're nice and tight, gentlemen," Weissinger more than just suggested. "He shouldn't be able to move at all."

"Yes sir," Mosley responded gruffly, then gave him a nod once he was satisfied that the bonds were secure.

That's when Frank finally noticed what the doctor had fished out of the supply cabinet. In one hand he held a scalpel, and in the other he had some kind of firm-looking rubber baton.

"Now, don't worry," Weissinger reassured him, managing to sound *almost* sympathetic. "This is probably going to sting pretty badly after a while, but the cuts won't be very deep."

"The cuts?" Frank asked, suddenly nervous. "What cuts?"

"No more questions," Weissinger retorted. "Here, take this," he added, lodging the rubber stick into Frank's gaping maw. "Bite down on it... *hard*. It should help keep your mind off the pain."

Frank obeyed willingly, chomping down on it so hard that he felt his teeth dig in. He wasn't sure what the doctor was up to, but he was fairly certain that whatever it was would be excruciating. He clenched his fists, took a deep breath—as deep as he could with a mouth full of rubber—and watched the scalpel intently as the doctor's hand hovered over him.

The first cut sent a jolt through his arm, but his reaction was mostly one of surprise. He'd seen the blade coming down toward the backside of his wrist, and imagined what it would feel like, but imagining it and actually feeling it bite into his flesh and slash all the way across were two entirely different things. The pain was little more than a sting, and nothing he couldn't handle, but it was persistent and extremely uncomfortable.

No time was wasted between the first and second incisions. Weissinger's hand moved about an inch up Frank's arm and the scalpel slashed across it again, and again, moving up at an almost equal distance each time. By the time he reached his shoulder, what was first a tingly, stinging sensation started to feel more like a burn throughout his entire arm.

His teeth dug into the rubber a little harder with each cut, but he managed to stay calm the entire time, even when Weissinger moved on to his other arm. The man hadn't lied: the cuts weren't very deep, but he wasn't exactly being careful about them, either.

He felt like he'd managed relatively well for his legs, too, but when the serrated blade sliced all the way across his abdomen, the burning sensation intensified. He felt like a slab of raw meat that had been thrown onto a hot grill, his tender flesh sizzling as the dancing flames licked and lapped at him. His one consolation was the great speed at which Weissinger worked, and the growing likelihood that it would soon be over.

He'd hoped that the doctor would stop at his neck, but he didn't. Instead of slashing across it, he made vertical incisions, with a little more care than he had before then. He imagined this was to avoid slitting his jugular or puncturing his windpipe.

Frank's eyes rolled as the tip of the scalpel's blade bit into his flesh and sliced through it like butter. His teeth clamped down on the rubber stick so hard that he could taste his gums bleeding. He'd noticed the cuts on the rest of his body were only oozing out a trickle before, but now he could feel his warm blood squishing through his fingers and into his tightly clenched fists. He wanted to scream, but he held it in. If he tensed his neck or moved his head around in the least, the doctor's blade might go awry and cause some real damage.

It wasn't long before Weissinger had finished up there and moved on to his head. These cuts were surprisingly less painful, and much to Frank's relief, they were done and over with faster than he could say "Victor van der Vossen."

He felt a wave of relief wash over him then as Weissinger set his scalpel down on the metal tray beside him and stepped back to stretch his arms. *Finally*, he thought, sure that his silent suffering was over and done with, at least for the time being. This wasn't nearly as bad as the drowning had been, he thought, though after a while, his skin had become increasingly sensitive to pain, and the constant, burning sting had become almost unbearable.

Weissinger cracked his knuckles then, and much to Frank's dismay, he took up his scalpel once more. He waved it around at Mosley and Baumgartner in a small, circular motion. "Well?" he barked, eyeing them impatiently. "What are you waiting for? Flip him over onto his stomach. We haven't got all day."

The sentinels wasted no time carrying out the doctor's orders. Working quickly and in seemingly perfect unison, they untied the straps at his wrists and ankles and flipped him over onto his stomach. They made sure to keep a good, strong grip on him as they did, just in case he started to flail around or tried to escape. It was unceremonious and quickly over with, and Frank thumped down on the table a little harder than he'd expected to. The baton popped out of his mouth as he did and rolled off the table.

He might have been able to give them a hard time if he'd wanted to. His arms and legs were slick with blood and slippery, and he could have used that to help wriggle free from their grasp, but he knew that it wouldn't have been in his best interest to do so anyway. Even if he had managed to break free, it would have helped him in nothing. There was nowhere to go and nowhere to hide. He didn't even know how to get out of their compound. In any case, he'd all but promised that he'd be a *good little boy*.

He wasn't perfect—not by a long shot—but he *was* honest. He was honest and he kept his word. Sometimes his honesty was detrimental to his own well-being. He realized this full well, but it was still important that his word have at least some meaning. If he told them he'd stay then he'd stay, at least as long as he could, until he felt like his life was in serious jeopardy.

The sentinels fastened his restraints and secured him to the examination table once more. He took one last, deep breath and ground his teeth as he waited for the scalpel to puncture his flesh. No one had thought to put the stick back in his mouth, but he wasn't about to ask for it, either.

He was already growing accustomed to the sharp pain that the blade produced. It was the burning, stinging sensation that bothered him most, and it had only gotten worse when they'd flipped him over onto his stomach. The weight of his own body pressing down on his fresh wounds was more than just a little uncomfortable. *Maybe one pain will take my mind off of the other*, he thought grimly. When Weissinger finally got started, he was fairly certain that it wouldn't.

The doctor sliced his back up like he was in a race against time. It took him half the time that it had taken him to score his front side. Still, this did very little to soothe him.

As much as he'd wanted to deal with the pain like a man, he was already on the verge of screaming when Weissinger reached the halfway point of that segment of his little "operation". His stifled grunts through clenched teeth only harried the doctor and further precipitated his work. Weissinger was usually meticulous, precise. What he was doing now was just sloppy. The difference was remarkable. Despite his better judgment, he couldn't help but wonder who'd pissed in the doctor's oatmeal that morning.

The obvious reason for Weissinger's haste was to put an end to his suffering as quickly as possible, but the abruptness of his strokes only caused more pain. Consequently, Frank's grunting and groaning grew louder. But instead of slowing down to make his incisions with greater care, Weissinger seemed even more determined to get everything over and done with as fast as he possibly could.

When he finally laid his scalpel down several minutes later, Frank didn't have to see his back to know what a bloody mess it had become. He could easily imagine it. About halfway through the test, if he'd stopped and concentrated hard enough, he could almost have counted how many cuts there were by *feel*, but now his entire body felt like it had been tenderized.

"All done," Weissinger stated plainly. "You gentlemen can take it from here." With that, he threw the towel that he'd been wiping his hands on into an empty bin, and stalked off without giving further instruction.

"Please tell me I don't have to walk back to my room like this," Frank moaned, only half serious. He didn't really think that they'd expect him to. There was a certain obscure humor to his complaint. It wasn't ha-ha funny, but a sign that he'd remained in relatively good spirits despite his condition.

"Don't you worry, Frank," Mosley reassured him, smiling faintly as he leaned closer. "You won't have to move a muscle."

The man was obviously trying to be sympathetic to his plight, that much was clear, but the sentiment didn't reflect in his eyes. Those were difficult to read at best. He was looking at him with what could almost be described as a blind stare, though that wasn't exactly it, either. He was looking in his *direction*, but it was like he couldn't see him, or refused to see him. *Like he doesn't want to see me,* Frank pondered. *Or even be here, maybe.* He'd gotten the same kind of feeling from Hildebrandt.

Mosley knelt and reached down suddenly, and there was a loud clicking noise as he tugged at what must have been the release mechanism for the table's brakes. "I'll wheel you back to your room," he said. After straightening himself, he turned to Baumgartner and added, "Get the door, lanky legs."

Almost as soon as they passed through the open doorway, Frank was hit by a sudden and overwhelming fatigue. With heavy eyes, he wavered in and out of consciousness as Mosley rolled him along the empty corridor. In one of his fleeting moments of lucidity, he arched his neck to look back at him, and was finally able to see what that look in his eyes was. It was horror. Maybe he was having a hard time stomaching what he'd just witnessed, or what he was looking at right now. Maybe he was trying to find a way to rationalize it. Whatever it was *exactly*, he was doing a fairly good job of covering it up.

He blacked out for a moment, and came to again back in his quarters, just as Mosley and Baumgartner had finished lowering him onto his bed.

"Looks like you're going to be out of action for a while," Mosley breathed, drawing a blanket over his naked, mutilated body. His cuts had been left unwashed and untreated, and scabs were already starting to form all over him. "You'll want to sit tight and rest while you can." With that, he straightened his legs and headed for the door.

"No meds?" Frank managed to ask just as Mosley was about to leave the room. Lieutenant Corporal Baumgartner had already slipped away unnoticed, probably the second his head had hit the pillow. He could hear the distant commotion of the medical table being wheeled away somewhere in the distance.

"Sorry, Frank," Mosley replied in a grim tone, shaking his head from side to side as he leaned against the frame of the gaping doorway. "Doctor's orders. You need anything else?"

"No," Frank answered reflexively, sighing. He was about to thank him regardless when it dawned on him that he didn't even know what his name was. He didn't know many of the sentinels by first name, for that matter.

Captain Falstaff was Alexander. He'd found that out rather quickly. Sergeant Hildebrandt was "J.J.", but he didn't know what that stood for, and the sergeant didn't seem too keen on sharing that information. Mosley and Baumgartner remained question marks. Most of the men that he'd worked with in the past had been in the habit of addressing each other by surname, by rank, or by a combination of both. First names were oftentimes reserved for friends. That was just how things worked.

He wouldn't say that Mosley was his friend, but he seemed like an okay guy, and he'd lost count of how many weeks they'd spent cooped up together in this place. The man was quiet to the extreme, bordering on outright secretive, so he didn't know all that much about him, but calling him Mosley just didn't feel right anymore. He figured he should at least know that one, small detail about him. "Actually," Frank said, trailing off momentarily as he broke what had just become an awkward silence, "there is *one* thing you can do for me."

"Sure," Mosley replied with a grin that didn't touch his eyes. There was still a bit of that strange look of horror left in them from the ordeal he'd just witnessed. "What is it?"

"Tell me what the guys call you when you're not on the clock," Frank answered, wincing as his facial muscles tensed and pulled at his fresh cuts. "I assume your parents gave you a name, or are you just plain old Mosley?"

Mosley chuckled at that. "*'Plain old Mosley'* Mosley, at your service," he jested. "For a second, I thought you wanted me to write your last will and testament. You'd have to see yourself right now to understand, but I guess you're feeling it good enough to get the gist of it." He crossed his arms then and took a deep breath before continuing, looking at least a little relieved. "You're right about the *'plain old'* part," he said. "The name's Fred."

"Hey," Frank cautioned, "one diminutive to another, there's nothing wrong with Fred. Fred sounds very... uh... *neighborly.* Yeah. Something like that."

"Neighborly, huh?" Mosley guffawed. "How do you figure?"

"Well," Frank said, then paused briefly as he tried to find something to follow that up with. "Fred isn't very abrasive, for one. Fred sounds like he keeps his nose out of other peoples' business, but still invites them over for beer and barbecued khesh every once in a while. I'm not sure how else to put it, but everyone loves a Fred. When's the last time anyone complained about you?"

"Man, we do *not* have the same neighbors," Mosley chortled. "I could have sworn the commander said 'no meds', but you've clearly gotten into something already."

"I guess I just laugh in the face of pain," Frank said with mock pride, "or maybe this is just less embarrassing than crying about my 'boo-boos'."

"Your boo-boos," Mosley repeated as he shook his head from side to side, clearly amused. "You're certifiable, Frank. Decent, but certifiable, that's for sure."

"Now there's a bad name," Frank observed. "*Frank*. Franky! Sounds like a filthy old plumber smuggling fifty kilos of crack in the backseat of his pants."

"Dear lord, boy," Mosley said with a cackle. "That joke was horrible the first time I heard it, twenty years ago. It hasn't aged very well. No, sir."

The comment was made in jest and Frank took it that way. It made him laugh, and laugh hard, but laughing hurt, and that showed. The pain was bad enough that it made him forget what he'd found funny in the first place, but he kept laughing all the same. He was exhausted. He felt like he'd been awake for two days straight, and smoked something illicit to boot.

He hadn't done anything stupid like that since he and Andy had joined the academy. Andy, his partner both in crime and in justice. They had gotten into their fair share of trouble in their younger years, and that was *exactly* what this felt like: the last time they'd "lit up", sometime in their later teen years. It felt like that if he ignored the cuts and the burning sensation all over his body, that was. He was starting to feel extremely lightheaded.

The details of the event were foggy at best. Memories of the effects produced by the drug were not. For some reason, he found everything funny. He wondered where his friend was and what he was doing just then and even *that* made him giggle on the inside. The better part of his judgment told him that these warm and fuzzy feelings were probably a side effect of blood loss.

"I should probably let you get some rest," Mosley said in a serious tone, clearly concerned. "You look like you could use it." Leaving Frank no time to protest, he flashed him a quick salute and stepped through the gaping doorway. "Take it easy, Frank," he said before disappearing down the hall.

Left on his own, it wasn't long before exhaustion took over. He spent his last lucid moments trying not to giggle over nothing in particular. He couldn't help but wonder if his lightheadedness was really the result of blood loss, or if he was just going insane. Had some defense mechanism kicked in and had that triggered his uncontrollable laughter, he wondered. Whatever the reason was, he didn't have very long to think about it. Within seconds, he was fast asleep and dreaming a series of unsettling, acid-trippy dreams.

CHAPTER
22

Brains

Images of familiar faces and memories of places and events both recent and long past danced and comingled before his inner eye. Founder's Day fireworks in the Plaza district. Vanessa. The apartment they shared. Andy. The images filed by in a disturbing show of light and color, blending into each other as more and more of them joined the fray. His twisted trip down memory lane seemed more like drug-induced psychosis in a frenetic nightclub.

The first time he'd ever had to kill someone. Captain Leonard Boston. A diner his parents used to bring him to when he was a kid. The jar his grandfather kept the cookies in and the shoebox that concealed his old service pistol. They came in faster and faster, and flowed into the constantly spiraling mess of memories that was starting to take shape into some sort of all-consuming vortex.

Vanessa... again. Jablonski, before he'd been butchered by SAU agents. Jablonski, dead and rotting after they'd overdosed him and beaten him to a pulp. Vanessa, Vanessa, Vanessa. The first time they'd met. The first time they'd kissed. Making love to her. Proposing. Everything was swirling by so quickly now that he could hardly make heads or tails of it, but he didn't need to see very much of each memory to know what they were. Just a flash was sufficient. They were already engraved in his mind.

His first crush. His mother. His father. That swirling vortex of memories was all that he could see now. It was everywhere and all around him. One image slowed and stood out above the rest. It was a portrait of his younger self in a cadet's uniform, sporting the enthusiastic grin of a rookie fresh out of the academy.

His younger self smiled back at him with the oily smile of a boy that was too naive and too foolish to realize that he couldn't change the world overnight. After a while, the image bubbled and darkened and burst into flames like an old photograph tossed into a fire. He watched his own face melt and slide away as the rest of the living memory started to combust.

The flames fanned out through the rest of the vortex and it too caught fire. The orange and red wisps danced and leapt as they spread from one edge of the mass to its centre and then out again, darting across the horizon as though everything had been drenched in kerosene. Before long, the entire web of memories was engulfed in flames, and he found himself trapped in the center of that blazing inferno.

When the fire died down and the ashes settled, he found himself standing in a crowded marketplace in the Plaza district. He could see Vanessa a short distance ahead of him. She was busy cutting a path through the milling droves of people. They seemed to shy away from her as soon as she approached them, opening a gap for her wherever she went.

He tried to catch up to her, but soon found that it would be no simple task. While the busy crowd squeezed in on itself almost instinctively to make way for her, everyone seemed completely oblivious to his presence. "Vanessa!" he cried out, but he could hardly hear the sound of his own voice over the hubbub of the bustling market. "Vanessa! Wait!"

Vanessa kept on without offering the slightest sign that she'd heard him, as ignorant to his presence as the swarm of people that was now closing in on him from all sides. He tried to squeeze past as best he could, and apologized periodically as his shoulder or elbow grazed someone that he just couldn't avoid.

"Vanessa!" he cried out again, louder. Putting one foot in front of the other became more and more difficult as he trudged on. He'd thought the marketplace crowded before, but now the situation was deteriorating. It seemed like more and more people were flooding into the square without any of them ever leaving it. Getting anywhere at all without grinding up against at least a few people was becoming nigh on impossible.

Soon, he had no choice but to shove people out of the way just to get past them. He'd have felt bad about it, but they were doing it to each other as well. Each and every one of them, without exception, though in a seemingly unconscious manner. They walked around aimlessly, by all appearances blind to the world around them, and they didn't seem to care when someone bumped into them, made them fall over, or even walked over them. It was starting to look a lot like mayhem, but he was the only one that was even remotely worried by any of it.

He lost sight of his quarry altogether when she rounded a bend almost a full city block ahead of him. In that moment, he felt his heart sink. He *had* to see her, even if it was just this one last time, even if all of this was just a dream, albeit a horrible one. Deep down, he knew that it was, that it *had* to be, but it didn't matter. He longed to see her more than he'd ever longed for anything else in his entire life. He yearned for her so badly that his chest hurt. She was his oxygen, his air, and he was gasping for her like she was his last breath.

Even though he couldn't see her anymore, a short trail of emptiness had been left in her wake where the mob had parted ways for her. That gap was closing rapidly, but it gave him an indication of her whereabouts, and at least some hope that not all was lost. If he hurried, he might be able to catch up to it before he lost her trail forever.

He redoubled his efforts to make his way through the dense crowd. In the meantime, more people continued to file into the marketplace and the boisterous folly intensified. Soon, he too was walking over the fallen. There were more and more of them now, sometimes piled several high. It was like they'd fallen and tripped over each other, and resigned themselves to just lie there helplessly.

When he neared the corner that she'd gone around, he realized how bad the situation was. Every step landed on a gut, a back, a face. It was increasingly difficult to maintain his balance on this uneven, living, breathing terrain. He could hardly see the large shop windows over the heads of those pressing against him. It gave him a horrifying idea of just how deep the layer of wriggling flesh and bone beneath him went. It had to be a few feet thick, from the look of it, and it was only getting worse.

Where the fuck are these people coming from, he wondered. He couldn't even venture a guess, but he didn't have time to ponder the question more thoroughly. He had to press on, and press on frantically, no longer just to catch up to Vanessa—though that did remain at the forefront of his thoughts—but to keep from sinking under this rising tide of mindless automatons.

He yelled her name out at the top of his lungs, but as he rounded the corner, he knew that it had been in vain. A swarming mass of unfamiliar faces lie spread out before him, more careless zombies struggling halfheartedly, more to keep moving than to stay on top, but there was no sign of her anywhere.

There were more of them than he could ever count. Though obstructed by distant buildings, he somehow *knew* that the sea of souls stretched farther than the eye could see, even beyond them. She could be anywhere in that tangled mess. Regardless, he knew that he had to keep going if he wanted to see her again.

Any previous inhibition he'd had about stepping on people was gone. With complete disregard for anything but Vanessa, he dug his heels in and pressed on, using others to propel himself forward, tackling anyone that got in his way. There were fewer people standing on top now, and he was able to pick up his pace to a light jog. Maintaining his balance was even harder than it had been before. His footing was never certain, and he almost spilled over on several occasions, but he felt like he was moving at lightning-quick speed compared to earlier.

The change of pace was invigorating, however perplexing, and he continued on his way as quickly as he could. If anything got in his way, he plowed right through it, only avoiding obstacles if the maneuver presented no risk to his own person.

He was moving almost as quickly as he would have down in the streets, he realized, and was actually making decent time. He glanced down alleys and side streets as he passed them by, but not one of them was a fruitful lead. Suddenly, he spotted her just a short distance ahead of himself, or he *thought* that he had, at least. It was hard to tell in this mad jumble, as there was nothing to look at but the back of her head. But he wanted it to be her. He *needed* it to be her.

He needed it to be her so very much that he failed to notice the abrupt dip in the wriggling landscape beneath him. His next step landed in thin air, and he plummeted down the steep slope at a tumble. The experience was a less than pleasant one. It was like falling down a rocky hillside that flailed and let off the occasional grunt or groan. He continued hurtling down over what felt like a distance of fifty feet, and when he reached the bottom, he rolled a few feet more, and came to a staggering halt as his ribs butted up against a head that was sticking out almost entirely past the rest of the suffocating mass.

He thought he heard something snap gruesomely, and he was almost certain that the *something* was the sound of someone's neck breaking. His fall had more than likely killed someone, but under the current circumstances, he found it difficult to care or even think about it as anything more than just an afterthought.

His side hurt and most of the wind had been knocked out of him, but he knew that he could keep going. He knew that he *had* to keep going. He grit his teeth as he tried to push himself up and off of his back, but a small rift opened up in the crowd beneath him and he started to sink in.

Suddenly, he felt like he'd fallen into quicksand. The more he struggled to free himself, the farther down he sank. He was getting dragged toward the bottom by the horde of careless drones that sought not to free themselves, but only to continue writhing for as long as they possibly could. Within seconds, he'd sunk so deep that the light of the sky was almost completely blotted out, blocked by a multitude of thrashing limbs, reduced to that which could pass through the gaping hole above him. Before long, that gaping hole began to shrink and close in on itself.

Soon, the struggling crowd had tightened around him so much that he was left in complete darkness. Bodies pressed into him on all sides, and he grunted loudly as elbows, knees and other, unidentified appendages poked and ground into him.

He was starting to feel short of breath when his face became someone else's stool. He had no idea how deep he'd travelled, but he continued his forced journey downward, completely helpless. It looked like it was going to be the end for him, whether he liked it or not. Moments later, his entire body was pulverized as he was trapped between a bevy of feet and a hard place. That hard place was concrete, he soon realized, and it scraped against the side of his face like sandpaper.

Just as he felt that his body was going to let up, just as he'd accepted that this was probably going to be the end for him, the sea of writhing flesh vanished in an instant and he was left alone, lying battered and broken on the marketplace floor. There was a great flash of white light somewhere in the distance, like the blast of a nuclear warhead going off. It extended up and outward 'til it drowned everything in its blinding brilliance. The silent explosion lasted mere seconds. When it passed, he found himself floating suspended in a great white void. Everything was blank now. There wasn't a sight to see or a sound to hear.

It was oddly familiar. He didn't have to think very far back to recall that it wasn't the first time he'd been stranded in such a void. It had happened in his recurring dreams, back when he was still having them. No matter how real everything felt, at least a part of his subconscious realized that it was nothing more than a dream. The one obvious difference he noticed in this place was its tone. The void had always been black before, but now it was white.

While it was easy to imagine dark or wicked things lurking in the infinite shadows of the black void, this white one seemed only desolate and lonely. He could clearly see that he was alone in this place. But soon a small speck appeared somewhere in the distance straight ahead of him. It was hard to gauge distance in this great, big nothing devoid of depth and relief. It could have been miles away or right in front of his eyes.

The speck grew bigger and bigger and started to take shape. It was getting closer, and fairly rapidly. When it got close enough, he could tell that it was a person, a female from its silhouette. Guessing how far out it was became child's play. Even before she was close enough to be able to distinguish her facial features, he knew who she was.

He gasped for air and felt his heart stop as she grew closer. It was *her*. It was Vanessa. He felt like crying, but no tears came. He wanted to call out to her, but when he spoke, no sound escaped him. No matter how hard he'd tried to expel her from this thoughts after his rescue from SAU—an effort that he'd deemed necessary for the preservation of his sanity—he'd always missed her, but never as much as he did in that precise moment. He wanted to hold her tightly in his arms. He wanted to kiss her. He wanted to tell her that everything was going to be okay. He wanted to more than anything else, but he couldn't.

All he could do was wait and watch as she drew near. An overwhelming sense of nostalgia was growing inside of him by the second, and it was quickly taking over every single one of his thoughts. When he saw the white of her eyes, he was so wracked with emotion that he wasn't sure he could take any more of it. As she closed the final gap, he opened his arms and reached out to her in anticipation.

Her eyes were without expression, not quite blank, but still and distant, as though she was staring past or even through him into the great emptiness of the void. Even though he stood no more than a dozen steps in front of her, Vanessa seemed to ignore his presence once more. She never stopped or slowed down, but drifted toward him at that constant, unwavering pace, almost as though she was being carried by some invisible force.

She was moving in so fast that he worried she might hurt herself in what was starting to look like an inevitable collision. When she was within arm's reach, he threw up his hands and tried to grab her by the shoulders in a reflexive attempt to soften the blow. He tried to clutch onto them, but to his surprise, his hands passed right through her. His fingers closed in on his palms like she wasn't even really there.

There would be no contact, let alone collision. She could have tackled him to the ground and broken three of his ribs in the process if it meant that he'd get to touch her one last time. But instead, she went right through him, like a ghost or an illusion, a cruel trick of smoke and mirrors. He was almost too shocked to be disappointed; a *lmost*, but not quite.

He'd have turned his head to watch her go, but he couldn't move an inch. He was suspended in the great big nothing like a wet sock hung out to dry. Somehow, he knew that he'd never see her again. It went against everything he'd hoped for, but he felt it in his bones. He felt like it was game over, like it had all been for nothing, completely pointless. The thought of living without her made him feel turbid and morose.

He started to think of the life that they'd built together, of the happiness they'd shared, the difficulties they'd overcome, but the mental images flashed and were over in the blink of an eye. Any second now, he felt that his heart would stop beating, but it did not. It drummed faster and faster by the second. His insides were churning at the onset of what he imagined was a panic attack.

In the waking world, he snapped from his sleep, leaned over the side of his bed, and emptied the contents of his stomach all over the floor. When his chest's heaving stopped, he let his head sink back onto his pillow, and fell asleep again almost as quickly as he'd woken. He'd drifted off so quickly that he hadn't even had time to piece a single coherent thought together.

The rest of his sleep was light and dreamless and interrupted frequently. The world was a hazy blur each time he woke, but at least the nightmares had stopped. More often than not, he found himself alone with his inner voice, that familiar commentator that accompanied him in his daily activities and gave narrative to his thoughts, whatever those thoughts might be.

In this uneasy place between sleeping and awake, his inner voice riddled him with questions that for the most part remained unanswered. *Where's Vanessa? Has something happened to her? Who are these people? What's happening to me? Where am I? Who am I? What am I?*

At some point, he heard the shuffle of feet and the sound of two voices that had become very familiar to him. Doctors Munro and Weissinger were at each other's throats again in another one of their "old couple spats". He was almost completely certain that the exchange was real, that the two of them were standing nearby, arguing, but he was too tired to even open his eyes.

"Do you know what you've just done?" he heard Weissinger growl. "Do you have any idea at all? Even the faintest?"

"Of course I do!" Edward snapped. There was more emotion in those four words than in anything Frank had ever heard him say before. Doctor Munro was always so calm and reserved, even when he argued. It wasn't like him to be so loud or firm.

"I did what any other human being with even an iota of compassion *would* do," Edward continued furiously, then added, "you bloodthirsty *barbarian!*"

"Oh, poppycock," Weissinger retorted, incredulous. "What you've done is put a proverbial stick in my wheels. What you've done is completely sabotage my research. You've bungled up the results of my latest trial is what you've done, you old rube!"

"Nonsense," Edward grated. "Your so-called *trial* isn't even scientific, so how could I bungle up its results?"

"It... isn't even scientific?" Weissinger stammered. "*It isn't even scientific?* Of *course* it isn't scientific! This has never been done before, you loon. There's no established way of measuring any of this, but that doesn't change the fact that it needs to be done, or that you're interfering directly in my work."

"*Your* work?" Edward stated pointedly more than asked. "Do I really need to remind you whose *project* this was in the first place? You're not alone in this, I'll have you know!"

"Don't get your panties in a bunch," Weissinger sneered derisively. "That isn't what I meant and you know it. Of course I'm not alone in this. Of course I'm not. I know that this is your project just as much as it is mine, but you told me that I could take the lead on this phase of the operation."

"I did," Edward acknowledged, somewhat vehemently, "but you also agreed not to go too hard on him."

"And I haven't!" Weissinger snapped.

Both men's tempers had flared to new heights. It sounded like they were on the verge of breaking into fisticuffs. Frank tried to open his eyes again and managed, but just barely, and not for long.

"Oh, hogwash," Edward howled. "Are you completely blind or do you take me for a fool? You've absolutely butchered him. Look at him. *Look* at him! He looks like he's been put through a meat grinder. What were you going to do with him next? Chop him into bite-sized pieces and stew him in boiling water? Skewer him with a shower curtain and roast him over a fire?"

"This is completely ridiculous," Weissinger sighed loudly. "Do you even hear yourself right now? Do you? This obviously looks worse than it really is."

"Oh, really," Edward harrumphed, at a loss for words.

"Yes, really," Weissinger echoed mockingly. "Besides, how else do you expect me to gauge his body's regenerative abilities?"

"I don't know," Edward conceded, "but there has to be a better way than this, you savage."

"Oh, for the love of Pete," Weissinger sighed. "You're being a drama queen about all of this, Edward. Any damage inflicted has been controlled and superficial."

"That's a load of rubbish if I've ever heard one," Edward stated in disbelief. "*Controlled. Superficial.* Pshaw! All of our work is pointless if you kill the subject, Jerg."

"What are you getting at?" Weissinger asked in a whiny, high-pitched tone. "Are you calling me a liar?"

"Well, why don't you tell me," Edward blurted out in a huff. "Does almost drowning the poor boy qualify as 'controlled and superficial damage'? Are you so completely full of yourself that you actually believe that bullsh—"

"Enough!" Weissinger shouted, cutting him off abruptly. "The subject's life was *never* in danger. You can't chastise me for doing what had to be done, what you basically agreed to when you gave me the lead on this."

"What had to be done?" Edward growled. "That's not what I heard about all of this."

"Well you heard wrong," Weissinger spat.

"I seriously doubt that," Edward shot back.

"And who is it exactly that brought this exaggerated piece of news to your attention, might I ask?" Weissinger inquired. "Was it Hildebrandt? I should have expected he'd come crying to you after I relieved him of his duties."

"It doesn't matter *who* told me," Edward sighed loudly. "*All* versions of the events support each other. Frankly, the fact that I heard anything at all is cause for concern." Weissinger started to say something, but it was his turn to get cut off, and he let out a bewildered groan instead.

"Face it," Edward continued, "these are grown men we're talking about here, full-blown veterans that have seen their share of violence. If they think there's something's wrong with the way that you operate, then I can't help but think that they have a point." There was a certain austere finality to the way that he crossed his arms when he finished speaking.

"I'm not sure what you're talking about," Weissinger lied. His dishonesty was evident just from the sound of his voice.

"First, you almost drown the man," Edward barked, "and then you slice him up like a slab of meat. Fiddlesticks, Jerg! *Like hell* you're not sure what I'm talking about."

"That little incident during the lung capacity testing was accidental," Weissinger groaned.

"Accidental?" Edward scoffed. "I thought you said you had everything under control. And you couldn't have just used a peak flow meter or something, could you." He rolled his eyes at those last words and shook his head disapprovingly.

"I did have everything under control," Weissinger stated defensively. "I *do*. And no, I couldn't have just used a flow meter. This isn't a conventional patient we're talking about here. These aren't conventional tests that require conventional tools. I had to see how he'd perform under stress. I had to see how he'd perform in a real-world situation. It's textbook procedure." He hesitated briefly, and added, "Like I told you already, Edward, his life was never really in danger. I intervened in good time. There was never anything to worry about."

"He had to be reanimated for pity's sake!" Edward trumpeted loudly. "I'd say that that counts as his life being in danger. Wouldn't you? And what about your handiwork with the scalpel? Is there a reason why one incision wasn't enough? Did you really have to score the man from head to toe?"

"There is a reason," Weissinger answered plainly, "but you don't sound like you're in the mood to hear reason. Your mind was made up long before we even started this conversation."

"So you're not going to explain yourself?" Edward said more than asked, sounding not at all surprised.

"No," Weissinger breathed through grit teeth. "I've wasted enough time on this silly nonsense already."

There was the sound of shoes smacking against the cold, hard floor then as someone stalked off in a hurry.

"I'll be watching you closely from now on," Edward called out. "You *are* going to respect your promise, Jerg." There was no answer to his warning except for the sound of Weissinger's furious footsteps, which grew quieter and quieter as he moved farther and farther away from them. After five or six seconds, Frank couldn't hear them at all.

He'd have watched the entire scene if he'd been able to, but his eyes were heavy, and no matter how hard he willed them to open all the way, the best he could manage was an occasional peek. He was lucid enough to know that he wasn't dreaming anymore, at least, though he couldn't have pinpointed exactly when his dreams had ended and when reality had kicked in.

He'd been drugged, that much he knew, and with a fairly potent sedative, from the feel of it. When Mosley had left him there earlier, he'd been in agony, but the pain was mostly gone at present. Now he just felt sluggish and tired from oversleeping. Despite his obvious lack of energy, staying put was the last thing he wanted to do, but he couldn't bring himself to *do* much of anything besides lie there and wait till he fell asleep again.

The next time he managed to crack his eyes open, Edward was looming over him, busying his hands with something he couldn't quite see. They were too close to his neck, just out of his line of sight. At some point, he saw him bring out bandages and sutures, and he dismissed all of it as routine stitching. It hadn't really worried him. He trusted the doctor.

There was a peculiar sense of familiarity about the withering old man, a feeling that he knew him from somewhere, from some time just beyond his ability to recall. He had no memory of him at all prior to his unexplained rescue from SAU, but that feeling persisted for reasons that eluded him yet.

There was something warm about him, something comforting. He managed to be nurturing even while pricking him with needles, but it went well beyond just being a good caregiver. At times, he seemed to act almost like a father to him, or at the very least like he was protecting a child that couldn't defend itself. It was an odd thought, he knew, and it should have been disconcerting to him, but for some reason it wasn't.

While he didn't exactly appreciate being coddled like a baby, there was something so earnest, so sincere about Edward's nature that Frank found it endearing. As bizarre as he knew it was, he appreciated the man's overprotective behavior and *felt* like being a part of that pseudopaternal bond, at least to a certain extent. If he looked past the inherent weirdness of it all, it was good to know that someone had his best interests at heart.

He thought on it for a while longer, but could make very little sense of it. He was so comfortable, so relaxed, that his squinting eyes had closed all the way again despite his efforts to keep them open. It wasn't long before sleep started to overtake him again. As he was drifting off, he told himself that the drugs were to blame. He wouldn't just fall asleep while someone was busy patching him up—not with cuts like the ones he had. Not even if he trusted the person doing the patching.

CHAPTER
23

Breather

When Frank opened his eyes again, Weissinger's face was hovering only inches above his own. It startled him so much that he nearly jolted upright, but he managed to stop himself at the last second, and narrowly avoided an involuntary head-butt.

It wasn't that there was anything outright *frightening* about the man. There was something strange about him, that much was undeniable, but that wasn't it. It wasn't that he'd put him through more than his fair share of hardship, either, though he had. His face just wasn't something that he wanted or expected to wake up to. Not by a long shot. To make matters worse, the gaping smile that split the doctor's face from ear to ear was enough to give just about anyone the heebie-jeebies. It made him look completely insane.

"Incredible," Weissinger whispered in astonishment, staring at him with that patented look of his that made him feel like an inanimate curio. He straightened himself and folded his arms behind his back, the look of wonder that had animated his eyes fading somewhat. "I must say," he added, almost as though he was addressing an imaginary audience, "*that* is scientific progress if I ever have seen it."

The shock from Frank's rude awakening dissipated almost instantly. He wrinkled his brow and squinted as he tried to work out exactly what Weissinger was going on about. "What do you mean, 'scientific progress'?" he finally asked, too groggy to work it out for himself.

"Why, just look at yourself," Weissinger blurted out, his voice brimming over with excitement, his eyes lighting up again. He looked like he was on the verge of laughter. "It's amazing, simply amazing. *You're* amazing!"

"Now hold on a just a second, Doc," Frank warned him defensively, shrinking as far back from him as possible, which wasn't very. His head sunk into his pillow and he held his sheets up to his chest with a death grip. "I'm flattered—really, I am—but I just don't swing that way."

"You imbecile," Weissinger retorted in a scolding tone as he drew his head back and rolled his eyes in disbelief. "Your arms, your legs... look at them." He waited for him to do so before adding, "The cuts. Where are they?"

Frank opened his mouth to say something, but arched his brow as he found himself at a loss for words. "That *is* amazing," is what he might have said had he been able to. Despite his speechlessness, his thoughts were easy to read. There was a look of dumbstruck surprise plastered across his face, and he knew it.

"It's something, isn't it?" Weissinger said more than asked, lending his voice to Frank's unspoken astonishment. "Oh yes it is indeed," he added, drawing the words out for emphasis. "Now tell me, where do you think all those incisions went?"

"They're gone," Frank finally managed to say. "Vanished. Like they were never even there." There were no scabs, or scars, or any other indications that he'd been cut repeatedly. For some reason, he was having a harder time digesting that than he'd had realizing that his arm hadn't been amputated when he'd clearly seen the messy results of it with his own two eyes. He still wasn't sure what had happened there, and he meant to press Doctor

Munro about it in the near future, even if Doctor Munro hadn't been very forthcoming in the answers department so far.

Somehow, this business with the incisions felt more *real* to him. Maybe it was just fresher in his mind, he supposed. His concepts of time and reality had gotten much better than they had been when he'd first woken in this place. Anything would have been less confusing than that. He couldn't help but wonder how the two miraculous recoveries were related, if they even were.

"Oh, come now. They haven't *vanished*," Weissinger assured him, and rather convincingly, at that. "That's just crazy talk, a preposterous idea at best."

"Okay, so where have they gone?" Frank asked, feeling more than a little foolish. It seemed like it was his excuse for everything lately, but maybe he was tired. He'd just woken, after all.

"Well, I really shouldn't have to explain all of this to you," Weissinger warned, "but just think about it for two seconds and you'll have your answer." He looked like he'd gotten over any excitement he'd previously felt and sunk into a curmudgeonly mood, which probably explained his sudden unwillingness to share. *This* was the Weissinger that he was used to. It wasn't much, but it was the closest he'd been to gaining any real insight into his situation since his rescue.

"They've healed?" Frank asked tentatively, feeling even more foolish than he already had. It was the most obvious answer, but it made absolutely no sense to him. Healing that fast and that well was impossible. It didn't take a genius to figure that out. "You can't be serious," he added, probing up and down the length of his arm with his hand.

Crossing his arms, Weissinger met his inquisitiveness with silence, a scowl, and a stubborn gaze. Obviously, he thought he'd said enough already, and wouldn't open up again if his life depended on it.

"Fine," Frank groaned. "Be that way. I think I've figured it out anyway, sort of... not *really*." For a brief moment, he thought they might be using him to research better and quicker medical techniques, but after thinking it through again, that too seemed borderline ridiculous. It didn't really explain or warrant any of the sadistic experimentation they'd done on him.

He was pretty sure there were better ways of carrying out that kind of experiment. The methods they employed were excessive, to say the least, and by "they" he really meant Weissinger. Even though he had some help doing the dirty work, he was clearly the one pulling the strings.

At first, he'd put up with anything they'd thrown his way without question. At the time, he'd felt that he owed them that. At the time, he'd hoped that his full and unwavering cooperation would expedite his reunion with Vanessa. His blind obedience had seemed justified then, but it was getting harder to see this as anything but torture. Every passing day saw his hopes of ever seeing her again dwindle.

He was grateful for the help they'd provided him so far, but he didn't know how much more punishment his body could take, or if he really owed them enough that he should continue serving as their guinea pig. He'd already endured more than one man should ever have to, and they hadn't even answered one of his questions yet. Not one that mattered, at least. For all he knew, they had no idea *where* Vanessa was, and didn't care either. He'd never been allowed to walk the halls of the complex on his own, but he'd seen enough of it to know that there weren't many places they could be hiding her, if she was even there at all.

His situation made his future seem bleak and limited to a life of medical servitude, most probably a short one. Sometimes, he got the impression that they were nursing him back to health just to ensure that he lived through the next experiment, just so they could advance their agenda, whatever that agenda was.

The only indication to the contrary was the seemingly good nature of the better part of the personnel. Even taking that into consideration, it begged a question. *Am I going to let them dissect me just because they're being nice about it?* As sincere as some of them seemed, they might just be trying to pacify him, to keep him from breaking down, so they could force their tests down his throat for as long as they possibly could.

Weissinger coughed into his fist then and cleared his throat in a noisy fashion. "Anyway," he said, sounding only moderately bitter, "you'll have lots of time to think about it. I'm leaving you to your own devices for the rest of the day."

Frank was dumbfounded. It wasn't like Weissinger to hand out freebies. He couldn't help but wonder what he was trying to play at, and how this fit into his broader agenda. Reticent or not, he wouldn't say no to a "day off". He really needed one.

CHAPTER
24

Popcorn

Frank lie thinking quietly in his neatly made bed. More than two weeks had passed since Doctor Weissinger had shred him near to ribbons. Many things had changed in the past month, some of them good, some of them bad, but ultimately the trade-offs seemed to balance each other out. For one, the experiments they were conducting on him weren't nearly as agonizing as they had been. Weissinger had shifted to a more targeted approach, as opposed to one of blanket mistreatment.

To his surprise, the doctor had continued giving him the occasional "day off". Sadly, he needed them now more than he ever had before. The experiments weren't as excruciatingly long as they used to be, and they no longer put him out of commission for extended periods of time, but the frequency of them had increased significantly. Sometimes, he underwent three or four procedures in the very same day, and even though they weren't nearly as bad as they used to be, they were for the most part severely unpleasant and extremely taxing.

Lucky for him, painkillers were now administered as needed. Maybe not so luckily, the painkillers were so powerful that they left him feeling loopy for hours on end. His concept of time in this place without even a semblance of daylight was shoddy at best, so he'd taken up the habit of scratching a line on the wall before receiving the nightly shot that Doctor Munro gave him. If he hadn't started doing that, he'd have had no way of knowing how much time had gone by since the latest change of regimen. The sound of approaching footsteps wrenched him from his almost trance-like contemplation.

"Oh good, you're up," Weissinger stated coldly as he entered his quarters unannounced. "The first trial of the day is going to be... well, let's just say it's going to be a little different. We really don't have much time to dawdle, so if you could please be ready to go as soon as possible, that would be appreciated."

"Hey, I'm ready when you are," Frank said, but Weissinger didn't seem to hear him as he was too busy checking things off on that big clipboard of his that he carried around with him almost everywhere he went.

Baumgartner appeared in the doorway then like an awful rash or a severe allergic reaction. Frank couldn't think of anyone he wanted to see less. The guy had gotten progressively stranger over the past few weeks. He'd always been a bit odd, a little off-kilter, but now he almost managed to make Weissinger seem friendly. His mere presence fouled his mood instantly.

"Excellent," Weissinger said as he noticed him, sounding all too pleased. "As usual, your timing is impeccable."

Baumgartner stood in the doorway for a couple seconds saying nothing. He was too busy staring at him with those crazy eyes of his that reminded him of a rabid wolf about to pounce on a cornered rat. "Wouldn't want to be late for this," he finally said, his eyes never leaving Frank. "Been looking forward to it."

"Good," Weissinger replied after the briefest of hesitations. For once, even *he* seemed disconcerted by Baumgartner's peculiar behavior. Ordinarily, the two of them went hand in hand. Doctor Weissinger was the mad scientist of ill repute, and Baumgartner was the avid henchman with little in the way of scruples. He was the Igor to Weissinger's Victor Frankenstein.

He'd never seen them at odds before, but it seemed like there *was* such a thing as overenthusiasm in Weissinger's unwritten code of conduct. In that moment, at least, the doctor found him almost as creepy as he did, he could tell.

Despite the blatant awkwardness that Baumgartner had just generated, Weissinger drew no further attention to it. Frowning as he was, he almost looked like he was going to say something for a moment. Instead, he rubbed at his eyebrows nervously and skipped ahead to the next item on his agenda. "Has the dielectric chamber been prepped?" he asked him plainly.

"Yes it has," Baumgartner confirmed with a quick bob of his head. "To your exact specifications."

Frank hadn't noticed it until just then, but Baumgartner's pupils were constricted to pinpoints and he could smell the reek of vinegar and old man's cologne on him from halfway across the room. Someone had clearly gone to town with the opioids before reporting for duty. The lieutenant corporal had probably dipped into the pharmacy's reserve of Cilephtine seconds before coming over. It wouldn't have surprised him one bit.

Baumgartner was almost always high on something, as far as he could tell, and since no one was allowed to leave the complex, it only stood to reason that his own stash had dwindled away a long time ago. From what he'd gathered so far, the crew had very little luggage with them when they'd first arrived and set up shop. He'd overheard bits and pieces of conversations that led him to believe that his rescuers had previously been stationed at the very location that SAU had been holding him at. If the brief flashes he'd had of their great escape could be trusted, the vehicle they'd used to rescue him had been almost empty.

Just as he had dozens of times before, he couldn't help but ask himself who exactly his rescuers were. It seemed obvious enough at first glance, but things weren't always as they seemed.

As far as he was concerned, the most likely answer was that they were renegade Special Assignments officers. Maybe they'd gone rogue because they were fed up with the inhuman treatment of innocent suspects. Maybe they had completely different reasons. He couldn't say. Another possibility, this one less appealing, was that they were unsatisfied with the mediocre results of SAU's barbaric interrogation techniques, and were determined to master them, but on their own terms.

That last hypothesis didn't seem very likely to him. Sure, what they were doing here was tantamount to torture, but there was, apparently, a purpose to all of it, and questioning him was not it. Whether he agreed with that purpose or not was beside the point, as he was kept in the dark on just about everything, and for all he knew they could be lying, but they'd never once pumped him for information, and that changed just about everything.

As bad as all of that seemed, it wasn't what concerned him most at the moment. It was the dielectric in "dielectric chamber" that had him worried. He couldn't remember exactly what that meant, but he was fairly certain that whatever it was wouldn't be pleasant, and that made him nervous. Truth be told, he'd bet a week's worth of painkillers that it wouldn't be, but the only one that would want to get in on that action was Baumgartner.

"Let's get on with it then," Weissinger stated plainly, putting an end to the awkward silence that was permeating the room like a thick fog. "This morning's procedure should be a fairly brief one, but that's no reason to lollygag."

"No reason at all," Baumgartner added, his voice brimming over with enthusiasm. He walked over to Frank's bed and raised the safety rails in short order. After flicking the brakes off with the tip of his foot, he took up position at the head of the bed.

Frank felt a knot form and grow in the pit of his stomach as Baumgartner wheeled him out of his quarters. Hildebrandt and Mosley were posted just beyond his door. They sat there in their folding metal chairs, their arms crossed, staring straight ahead as though refusing to see anything at all. He only caught a quick glimpse of them, but their displeasure was apparent at first glance. It would have been difficult to miss.

They'd have looked like two oversized, brooding children if not for their uniforms and the rifles slung over their shoulders. He was under the very distinct impression that their sulking might have something to do with whatever was about to transpire, and that did little to comfort him.

Frank looked straight up and watched the ceiling lights file by as his bed got rolled down the hall to their left. At first, the long, horizontally-disposed fluorescent tubes passing by reminded him of the lights of a scanner or a photocopier, and he almost felt like a document sitting on the glass, getting copied over and over again. *Maybe they'll shred the original once they've finished duplicating it*, he couldn't help but muse.

The longer he watched, the quicker they seemed to pass by, and the harder it was to focus. After a while, all of it was such a blur that the white bars started to remind him of end credits. Was this how everything would end, he wondered. Would these be the closing moments to the movie that was his life? Was it the end of the line for him, or maybe worse, just another stop on a very long commute that would lead him to the exact same place? He would soon find out whether he wanted to or not.

His bed on wheels swiveled hard to the right and he butted his arm against the railing on his left, which kept him from rolling over. He instinctively looked up at the man that was carting him along, and felt almost queasy as he noted that he was still sporting that demented smile of his.

When he'd first met Baumgartner, he'd thought him a little unusual. At first, he'd attributed most of the lieutenant corporal's bizarre behavior to drug abuse, but now he wasn't so sure it was just that. He'd processed a lot of junkies in his time, a lot of addicts under the influence of a lot of different substances, but this guy was twisted even by their standards.

Maybe it *was* a contributing factor, but it probably wasn't the root problem. Maybe Baumgartner was plain sick in the head, and needed help. Maybe the drugs had triggered some kind of psychosis. He wondered why it had taken him so long to see it, and if he was the only one that did. He'd had his own problems to deal with, though, and he doubted anyone would have listened to him if he'd talked to them about it anyway.

It wasn't like they could have done much for him in the first place, unless they wanted to watch him around the clock to make sure he didn't pillage the pharmacy. They could restrict his access to drugs, but laying him down on a sofa to talk about his feelings probably wouldn't help him much. Sadly, he'd just have to deal with it. They both would. These *experiments* or *tests* or whatever it was they wanted to call them were bad enough on their own. The last thing he needed was a stark raving lunatic at his side while they were taking place.

Before long they turned again, this time to the left. They kept on for about half a minute before the wheels on his bed ground to a sudden, rough halt.

"Get up," Baumgartner ordered mechanically. After lowering the safety rail on his left, he glared at him and repeated the words again, more aggressively, then poked him in the ribs with the butt end of his assault rifle. "It's time to rise and fry, Sunshine."

Frank groaned and sat up slowly. Baumgartner's prodding had caused more discomfort than it had actual pain. He clearly wanted to remind him that he was the one carrying the gun in these parts. The intimidation was unneeded and uncalled for as he had every intention of cooperating, but he wasn't about to start arguing with him.

Baumgartner hit him in the ribs again, this time hard enough to make him flinch and grind his teeth. "Come on," he urged him. "We haven't got all day, old buddy old pal."

"Will you stop antagonizing the test subject," Weissinger more than just suggested. There was reproach in his voice, but it was mild and halfhearted at best. "There's no need to agitate him any more than he already is."

Weissinger looking out for me, Frank mused, unable to hold back a smirk at the irony of it. *How rich.*

"No, I suppose there isn't," Baumgartner conceded with an emphatic sigh, then looked over at Frank and flashed him an oily grin. "This little 'experiment' will be traumatizing enough all on its own, am I right? And I just want to watch the show."

"For the love of Pete!" Weissinger barked. "Are you daft?" His patience had visibly worn thin. He'd been busy fiddling with a control panel by the door to the so-called dielectric chamber, but he spun around to square off with Baumgartner then, his face beet red, his index finger pointing threateningly in his direction. "I don't know what's gotten into you, Lieutenant Corporal, but that's enough! Just get him into the dielectric chamber without a fuss." He shook his head disapprovingly then as he returned his attention to the control panel, muttering, "Some people, I tell you," as he did, more to himself than for anyone else.

Frank pushed himself out of bed and made his way to the chamber door without further prompting. He wasn't going to give Baumgartner any reasons to "assist" him. A quick look inside the room revealed that there wasn't much to it. It was about eight feet by eight and almost completely bare. Its walls, floor and ceiling looked like they were made of polished aluminum or some other glossy metal. There was a strong light shining down from a recess in the middle of the ceiling, and perforated slits all around it that looked like they might be some kind of ventilation grid.

"In you go," Weissinger said, glancing over at him briefly as he did. "Oh, and please remove all articles of clothing and any other items you may have on your person before you do."

Frank quirked his brow as he looked over Weissinger's shoulder to the control panel on the wall. It seemed fairly simple. The font on the buttons was large and easy to read. Most of them bore single digit numbers, but there was also a "start" key as well as a "stop". Some of the buttons were impossible to make out as they were partially hidden. Just above all of that there was a small screen with a digital readout that reminded him of the one on his alarm clock, or...

"No fucking way," he breathed, suddenly realizing what this place was, and what it was they planned on doing to him. What he was looking at was the equivalent of a microwave oven—an industrial-sized microwave oven. He wouldn't be surprised to see a button with his name on it, right beside a few others labeled "popcorn", "poultry", and "frozen dinner". The lock mechanism on the door pretty much clinched it for him. It was a sliding bar that closed from the outside. "I am not going in there," he added, stepping back from the door. "Forget it. I'm out."

"What's that?" Baumgartner sneered at him even though he'd clearly heard him. The assault rifle trained at his chest was proof enough of that.

"I am *not* going in there," Frank reasserted firmly, his eyes wild and charged with sheer revulsion.

"You don't exactly have the benefit of choice," Weissinger stated calmly. He shot him a disapproving look before returning his attention to the control panel once more. "Now please disrobe and step inside the chamber."

Frank clenched his fists and glared at Weissinger's back with eyes that had become like daggers. "Yes, I do have a choice," he growled through grit teeth.

"What?" Weissinger grated, hunching his shoulders. He looked like he was about to lose it again.

"I've put up with way too much of this bullshit already," Frank fulminated. "I've put up with more than I can even remember right now. Maybe I owed you, maybe I still do, but enough is enough. You've nearly drowned me. You've broken my bones. You've skinned parts of me just to see how long it would take for it to grow back. You've had me run circles 'til I blacked the fuck out. You've cut me up like a side of roast pork... and now you want to nuke me like a TV frigging dinner?" There was no one word to describe the flood of emotions he felt coursing through him, but there was something close to rage or maybe even loathing in his voice. "I don't think so, Doc."

"You'll do as you're told or I'll discharge a burst of hot lead into your belly," Baumgartner sneered, sounding like he meant every word of it.

"Like hell you will!" Weissinger barked as he rounded on Baumgartner. "If you kill him, this will all have been for nothing, you abject imbecile!"

"What is this?" Frank demanded. "If you're not SAU, then who are you? You treat your prisoners just as badly as they do, but at least *they* have the decency to kill theirs off once they're done with them. They don't torture theirs for months on end."

"*Doc,*" Baumgartner pleaded, incredulous, "you're kidding me, right? You know as well as I do that he'd survive it anyway, right? Don't you? I mean, that's the whole point of all this, isn't it? It would be for science and stuff. Fuck."

"Enough!" Weissinger bellowed, glaring at Baumgartner with eyes that looked like they could bore holes through his skull. It was a look that said, "Try me," and it shut the lieutenant corporal right up. "Is that what you think we're doing?" he asked, turning his attention to Frank. "Torturing you for sport?"

"What else do you expect me to think?" Frank stated more than asked. "This hasn't exactly been a pleasant experience."

"I can't imagine it has been," Weissinger responded plainly, "but every single thing that we've done here has been for you... for your own good."

"Is that so?" Frank asked, his voice dripping with sarcasm. "I guess this is what they call hard love then, isn't it?"

A flash of movement from the corner of his eye caught his attention then and he lurched back, just in time to avoid the butt end of an assault rifle that had been thrust at the side of his head. It whooshed past his face and missed him by less than an inch.

Baumgartner had sneaked around and tried to flank him while he was distracted, and he'd almost succeeded.

Almost wasn't good enough. Baumgartner stumbled past him and came to an unceremonious, squeaking halt a few feet farther. Frank squared off with him and waited for him to recover his balance. It didn't take the lieutenant corporal more than a second and a half to do just that. Though he'd just passed up a golden opportunity to get the drop on him, Frank noted the ease and speed with which he regained control and swung about to face him. He was obviously no stranger to combat.

Standing at ease, he observed Baumgartner carefully as he moved in on him. He made his approach cautiously, positioned and ready to swing his rifle at him like it was a club. As he closed the final gap, he flipped it around to the way it was supposed to be held, and didn't stop moving until its muzzle pressed lightly against Frank's cheek.

"You get the fuck inside that room right fucking now," Baumgartner growled, his index finger hovering dangerously over the trigger, ready to squeeze it at any moment, "or you'll get what's coming to you."

What came next happened so quickly it was almost too fast for the eye to register, from the time Frank decided on a course of action, to the moment he executed his plan. What seemed like a single fluid motion was actually a series of well-coordinated ones. Arching his neck to the right, he simultaneously lunged forward with his right arm, then hooked the rifle with his open hand, and pushed it away to the left.

A single shot rang out, and the bullet flew over his shoulder and ricocheted dangerously off the wall. The quick push made Baumgartner lose hold of his weapon, and the grip was already out of his hand and swinging away from him when the shot went off. All Frank had to do then was step in, grab hold of the grip, and turn the gun on him. All of this had gone down in about a second's time, if that.

Shock hadn't fully registered on Baumgartner's face when it was replaced by a sudden expression of pain. The plant of Frank's foot connected solidly with his gut in a straight, forward kick that he'd never seen coming, let alone braced for. The force of it knocked the wind out of him and sent him reeling back 'til he stumbled through the gaping doorway to the dielectric chamber. He reached for something to hold onto but tripped on his own feet and fell. On his way down, he tried to swing around to stop his fall with his arms, but ended up smacking the side of his face on the cold, hard floor instead.

Before Baumgartner could so much as grunt, Frank swooped in and closed the door, then slid the bar across, locking him in from the outside. Wasting no time, he turned a stern eye and his newly acquired rifle on Weissinger. The man looked surprised, but not terrified. His hands went up almost instinctively, but there was no sense of urgency in his movement. He'd been in similar situations before, Frank surmised. "Show me the way out of here *now*," he growled. "I've had enough of this bullshit."

"I can't do that," Weissinger replied calmly. "At least not yet." His eyes turned toward the end of the hall, toward the sound of boots slapping on the hard floor. From the sound of it, two people were running toward them, maybe three.

"Then take me to Munro," Frank barked. "Right now!" He'd managed to remain relatively calm about everything else that had transpired since the rescue. He'd rationalized all of it, even when it made little sense to him and went against his better judgment. But now that he'd passed the breaking point, all of his pent-up frustration was boiling over.

"Give me one good reason to," Weissinger replied, a little too cheekily for someone in his position. "Help will be here any second now, and you'll be outmanned and outgunned—"

His threats were cut short by the crack of Frank's assault rifle going off. He fired three shots around the man's feet in rapid succession, the bullets kicking up sparks and letting off audible zings as they ricocheted down the hall. "Next one's going in your head," he warned in a dead serious tone, raising the gun again.

Weissinger's arrogant airs melted away instantly and all the blood seemed to drain from his face. "This way," he managed to say with some difficulty, turning on his heels before taking off at a fast walk. "Just don't shoot me."

"Shut up and keep moving," Frank growled, following after him. He kept a vigilant eye on their six as they advanced. Just as they were about to round the corner, Falstaff sprung into view at the other end of the hall, far behind them. He was moving at a sprint, with Mosley and Hildebrandt following close in tow.

"Frank!" Falstaff called out to him urgently. "Frank... stop!"

"No, you stop!" Frank shouted back at him. For the briefest of moments, he considered the consequences of surrendering. He doubted there'd be any formal discipline. There'd be no point in punishing him or locking him away. If he could trust even half of what these people had told him, he was far too important to their work. He doubted they'd want to hold up their program just to get a point across. They'd likely reinforce their security measures, and the "tests" would continue as scheduled.

Either way, he was counting on Munro having his back on this one, especially after what had happened. If he knew Falstaff and his men at all, they'd have no part in punishment on principle alone. They may have been Weissinger's eager little lapdogs at the start of all this, but he'd seen their loyalties slip and even shift over time. The commander, as they called him, had lost his men's willingness to participate a little more each time they had to bear witness to his inhumane behavior.

They might drug him up real nice and try to keep him that way, though. He realized it was only natural that they'd want to pacify him, but he couldn't let them do that. If he did, there'd be no keeping Weissinger and his faithful lackey Baumgartner from doing whatever the hell they wanted, and he wasn't entirely sure that they weren't completely out of their minds.

They might look for a chance to get even, to put him in his place; maybe by doubling down on their mistreatment of him, or by increasing the frequency of their little "tests". Both seemed like plausible outcomes. No, there'd be no stopping for him, no giving up. It was too late for any of that now. The wheel had been set in motion. He'd had enough and he was getting out.

"We're almost there," Weissinger panted. His voice was shaky and tinged with fear, and even though they'd only travelled a short distance, he was short of breath and struggling for air.

"Don't you stop until we get there," Frank ordered gruffly. He'd never seen the man in such a pitiful state before, but after everything he'd put him through, he didn't feel sorry for him in the least. It almost felt good being the one telling someone else what to do for a change.

CHAPTER
25

Revolución

Edward Munro stood hunched over a large worktable on the
bottom level of the area they referred to simply as "the atrium".
The second floor, which consisted of little more than a walkway
lining the four walls of the large, open space, was dotted with doors
that led to supply rooms, offices, and other areas he hadn't quite
figured out yet. In the center of each of the four walls was a large
recess that gave onto the facility's main arteries. Every story above
it was identical to the last, and there were six of them in all, though
the building itself was much taller.

The place seemed startlingly vast, especially to such a small
speck of a man, standing at the bottom of it as he was, but in all
fairness, it wasn't nearly as big as it looked. It had a sterile feel to
it, an almost immaculate sheen despite its unfinished state, and
that seemed to open it up and make it look even more enormous
than it actually was.

There were no decorations to speak of, just steel beams set
against steel walls that looked like they were thick enough to stop
a cannon ball, or an artillery strike, or maybe even an atom bomb.
The atrium could easily have served as a grand operating theater,

with onlookers gazing down from the catwalks to the sunken area below, where Munro presently stood, looking up, starting to feel queasy. Pretending there was a logical reason to have half the city in attendance, of course, and assuming they brought binoculars.

He raised his glasses and rubbed at the bridge of his nose, then returned his gaze to the worktable in front of him. If there had been observers, the current object of his attention would have looked like little more than a mess of wires and scrap metal from that far up. They wouldn't see how the wires interconnected, or how they linked together pieces that were vaguely reminiscent of human bones, but larger and cast from a particularly bright alloy. They might be able to tell that it was an advanced, humanoid robot. Its thick segments lay strewn out in approximately the position they'd be in once he finished assembling them.

Squinting through the monocle-like magnifying lens that was suspended over his left eye, he furrowed his brow and reached to the tray behind him to grab what looked like a long, flatheaded screwdriver. He swooshed it around in the jar of rubbing alcohol sitting on the worktable in front of him, wiped it off on the sleeve of his lab coat, and carefully inserted the tip of it into a narrow gap in one of the machine's elbow joints. After a few seconds of careful fiddling, the hand connected to that arm twitched and contracted its fingers in one swift motion.

"Remarkable," Munro whispered, even though he realized that it was anything but. Getting this pile of junk to move around a bit might impress a few science teachers and their students, but he'd already known that it would work even before he'd tried it.

The truly amazing stuff was still a work in progress. He said pretty much the same thing about everything he put his hand to, but this was his life's work. That *Peeping Tom* gadget of his, to name but one project, and various other doodads of questionably limited use were *all* his life's work. They'd also been put on the back burner the second they'd bored him, or after he'd worked on them so much that he saw no point in further perfecting them.

But Zero Sixty-Seven was different. It went without saying, considering he'd spent the better part of two decades working on him without losing the slightest bit of interest. This was different, too. His "robot". He hadn't found a name for it yet, but that was what it was, at least for the time being.

By the time he finished working on it, it would be much, much more than just that. He couldn't take all the credit for it, of course, and he wouldn't even dream of trying to. Then again, he doubted his creation would ever be recognized publicly, let alone hit the mainstream, even if he did decide to share it. It wasn't exactly intended for the open market.

At best, it might see limited, very specialized use in law enforcement, and that was if he managed to clear his name and reintegrate society at some point in the future. For the time being, he was an outlaw. He wouldn't share his location, let alone his creations. The fact that his prototype was built from "borrowed" government hardware made that even less likely.

The pieces on the table in front of him had come from a mechanized unit the Commission had designed for the purpose of law enforcement. There was nothing inherently wrong with its design, but it had been dropped in favor of larger, more resilient models like the Infiltrator series.

Simply put, they just weren't as effective in the field as the big boys were. An almost life-sized, humanlike mech wasn't as scary as a towering steel giant was. Oh, they were impressive enough in their own right, but their fear factor—the psychological impact that they had on the enemy—just couldn't compare.

It also didn't help that they were prone to being tipped over. An unexpected body check or a few well-placed rounds could throw it right off of its feet. Unlike the larger models, this one could actually *get up* when that happened. But in a high-risk situation, falling down meant precious seconds lost. For an officer in need of immediate support, a few seconds without it could mean the difference between life and death.

Despite these limiting drawbacks, they did have some merit. Though less than appropriate for grunt police work, their superior mobility and reaction time were notable. They could have been useful for reconnaissance or even bunker breaching missions, but the powers that be had decided to stick with the human option for those tasks, at least for the foreseeable future.

All questions of money aside—cost-effectiveness was *always* a consideration—the rationale was that they couldn't compete with a human's wits. He planned on changing that. He'd be the very first to combine two groundbreaking technologies, one that he'd had no part in developing, but that he could easily modify at his whim, and another that he'd practically perfected all on his own. Together, they would make the perfect... he wasn't sure exactly what he could call it.

A simple "robot" didn't do it justice. "Mechanized Support Unit" fell short. It was too generic, too confusing. Most mech units fit that bill. *Perhaps a Mobile Mechanized Support Unit*, he considered. *Or a Multipurpose Mechanized Support Unit.* Though a bit on the boring side, he supposed the name would be sufficiently *relevant*, but in truth, his creation would be so much more.

He looked up suddenly as a set of double doors on the second floor kicked open violently. His eyes shot wide open as Jerg stumbled into the atrium with his hands on the back of his head, Sixty-Seven following close behind him, an assault rifle in hand and trained at his colleague's back. "Jerg?" he stuttered, clearly confused by this unexpected interruption. "Sixty-Seven? What in the vortical flow is the meaning of this?"

"What does it look like?" Jerg called down to him snidely. "Your baby is having a temper tantrum."

"I'll do the talking from now on," Frank growled, pressing the tip of his barrel to the back of Jerg's neck as though to remind him that he was still the one holding the rifle.

"Sixty-Seven," Edward implored. "Frank. Please, tell me what's going on here."

"He has me at gunpoint," Jerg complained loudly, sounding as though he was explaining the obvious to a complete imbecile. "What in the blazes do you *think* is going on?"

"I said shut it," Frank snarled, then gave Jerg a light nudge to the back of the leg that made him drop to his knees.

"Sixty-Seven!" Edward called out to him pleadingly. "Please! Whatever's wrong, we can work it out. Why are you doing this?"

"I'm doing this because I'm tired of being this sicko's guinea pig," Frank answered bluntly as he glared at Doctor Weissinger's back. "I'm tired of getting poked and prodded and pulled apart. Your friend here was just about to run me through the microwave to see how long it would take for me to explode."

Edward furrowed his brow and frowned with concern. "Is this true?" he asked Jerg, turning a dubious eye on him. Receiving no immediate answer, he arched his head back and sighed deeply. "Yes," he breathed, "I suppose it would be, wouldn't it? You've never been one to tell a lie, have you, Sixty-Seven?" His concern quickly changed to anger and he glared at Weissinger sternly. "We can't say the same thing about you, can we," he snapped. "I told you to go easy on him, you coldhearted jackal." He hadn't gotten this angry in a long time.

He closed his eyes momentarily and took a deep breath to steady his nerves and calm his shaking hands. "You know, you basically begged for this to happen," he called up to him in a pointed tone. "Sixty-Seven has never been like the others, and that's exactly why we're all here, if you'll recall. I can't even imagine why you thought that he'd just comply with everything you put him through, no questions asked."

Turning his gaze on Frank, he added, "If it's any consolation, you would have been fine. It would have hurt like the dickens, and you'd have been in recovery for a considerable length of time, but you would have been just fine in the end, I assure you."

"It isn't a consolation," Frank muttered in discontent, "but thanks for trying anyway, I guess." He stared at Edward for what seemed like a really long time, then looked down, perplexed, and continued. "Look. I'm getting out of here, but there's something I want to know, first. Why do you keep talking like you've known me forever? And why are you so damned familiar? Even the first time I saw you here, I felt like I knew you somehow, or like I was *supposed* to know you. It's the sound of your voice, I think, or at least that's part of it. I know that I've heard it before. You can deny it all you want if that's your prerogative, but I know that it's not just a coincidence."

Edward froze upon hearing those words, dumbstruck. A few seconds later, he blinked repeatedly and closed his gaping mouth. "So... so you're telling me that you recognized me?" he asked, his voice no more than a whisper. The wheels in his genius mind started turning then, and he pondered Frank's words for some time before finally snapping out of it, his face a contracted web of wrinkles after his sudden, discomforting realization. "I'm sorry, Sixty-Seven," he sighed, apologetic, "but I can't answer you."

"Can't or *won't?*" Frank asked, furrowing his brow.

"Can't," Edward responded hastily. "I mean... technically I *could*, I suppose, but you don't want to open that can of worms right now. Trust me."

Frank exhaled extensively in response. He'd always been patient with him, but it looked like that patience was starting to wear thin. "Why?" he asked him bluntly. "Why wouldn't I want to know the truth?"

"Because you couldn't handle the truth," Edward answered him plainly. "Not like this. Not all at once. Not now."

"I think *I'll* be the judge of that," Frank snapped. He looked down at Jerg then, frowning, and poked the back of his shoulder with the butt end of his rifle. "You," he groaned. "Jerk. Quit your whining and tell me."

"Politely, respectfully... no," Jerg stated in a tone of voice that was neither polite nor respectful. "I don't have to answer any of your questions, you brute."

"Listen," Frank sighed, glancing down at Edward, "Doctor... I appreciate all the kindness that you've shown me, but this has been a bum friggin' ride. I've had enough. I'm sick and tired of all these bullshit experiments, and I'm getting out of here whether you like it or not." He waited for a few seconds to let that sink in, and added, "So you can tell me now—and I mean *everything*—or I can walk away and try to figure it out all on my own. If what you're really concerned about is my well-being, then how would you rather this play out?"

Edward hunched his shoulders and sighed deeply. He opened his mouth to respond, but the large doors swung open again with a loud bang, and Falstaff burst through them at the ready, his own rifle aimed loosely at Frank's back.

"Drop your weapon, Frank," Falstaff ordered gruffly. There wasn't a trace of anger in his voice, but it was firm enough to show that it wasn't just a suggestion. "We have you surrounded." Just then, Mosley and Hildebrandt came through opposing arches one level up, and rushed over to the balustrades, their weapons poised and ready in much the same way.

"What in the blazes took you so damned long getting here?" Jerg complained furiously. He glared at the captain over his shoulder then and started to get to his feet.

Frank had held onto his rifle despite the captain's warning, and he reminded Jerg of this by slamming the butt end of it squarely in his back.

The doctor yelped loudly as he lurched forward and stumbled to his knees once more. No one said anything or even lifted a finger to intervene. They just stood there with their weapons aimed in Frank's direction.

Falstaff's brow was creased and he looked haggard. "Frank," he repeated unyieldingly. "Drop your weapon, buddy." His voice seemed heavier somehow, his words a burden. "Baumgartner," he breathed, then trailed off momentarily. "He's... dead." The announcement was met with stunned silence. "We tried to get him out of there—out of that... room—but by the time we got in, it was already too late. It was already operational. We weren't able to shut it down in time."

"Then what are you waiting for!" Jerg whined. "Take him down *now, you fools!*"

"No," Falstaff answered sharply, frustration creeping into his voice. "This is your fault. *All* of this is your fault."

Edward arched his brow, surprised by the captain's response to his commanding officer. He glanced over at Hildebrandt and Mosley briefly, and his surprise grew even greater. They weren't aiming their rifles at Frank, he noted. They were aiming them at Doctor Weissinger.

Jerg's eyes shot wide open upon hearing the captain's words, and his face went beet red as he took in the turn of the situation. "What is this insubordination, Captain?" he shouted angrily. "A mutiny? You're disobeying a direct order! Now you put an end to this little revolt of yours and take him down *now. Immediately!*"

"You're the only one that we'll be taking down," the captain responded in a firm tone, without flinching. "Down to the brig, that is. I think you need some quiet time to calm down and straighten out your thoughts."

Jerg's eyes were ablaze with feverish intensity, his face twisted by an all-consuming rage. He looked to the others, maybe to guilt them, maybe expecting to find some kind of support there. It was hard to tell exactly what was going on inside of the man's head. He reminded Edward of a bewildered beast, like a fierce bird of prey with a snagged wing, currently encircled by a group of alley wolves or sand schakals.

"It's unanimous, sir," Hildebrandt stated plainly, reinforcing his captain's position. Mosley only nodded once—crisply—and stared, typically without emotion.

As he watched the scene play out, Edward was almost as confused as he imagined Jerg felt. Everything was happening so quickly, he could hardly tell what to make of it.

"Frank," Falstaff urged him again. "Stand down. Hand over your weapon. I've got this. *We've* got this. We won't try to stop you, but no one else has to get hurt over this. Please, just trust me," he added. "I need you to hand it over."

Frank grimaced as he stared at the assault rifle in his hands, obviously perplexed. He stood there motionless for what seemed like an eternity. "Fine," he finally sighed, then took one last, deep breath before holding the rifle out so the captain could take it.

"Thank you," Falstaff breathed, visibly relieved. He took Frank's rifle by the strap, slung it over his shoulder and waved the others over. "Mosley, Hildebrandt," he called out to them as they approached. "Bring the commander to his new 'quarters'. I'll catch up with you in a minute."

"Sir, yes sir," Sergeant Hildebrandt called back, almost a little too eagerly under the current circumstances. "Koo-friggin'-da!" He added that last part with a smile and a wink for Weissinger's benefit. The sergeant might be a wisecracker, but he was a real trouper. Relieving a commanding officer of his duties was serious business, but it was clear for all to see that the CO had tested his loyalty once too often. The respect that he'd once had for the man—a respect that had been shared by all under his command—had all but evaporated.

Less than a minute later, Mosley and Hildebrandt arrived on their floor, and Frank stood silently as he watched them help Doctor Weissinger to his feet despite his wriggling protests. When they managed to get him up, they each grabbed him by an arm with both hands, just above the elbow, and led him away, his feet dragging on the floor behind them as he refused to walk.

Edward was still trying to figure out what to make of the situation. He was relieved for Frank, relieved that the situation had been dealt with, but disappointed that things had gone so far, disappointed that he'd *let* them get so bad to begin with. Giving Jerg free rein had been a bad idea from the start, and he'd been a real pushover when the man had abused of his authority. He felt guilty for it. He was angry at Jerg, too, and disappointed in him. Knowing him, this would be a major blow to his ego. He'd surely find it unbearably humiliating.

"I trust you'll be fine on your own from here on in," Falstaff half-asked, half-stated, addressing Edward. Accepting the doctor's flurry of casual nods as confirmation, he started to turn, but then stopped himself and leaned over the balustrade. "One last thing," he added. "This man deserves answers. A lot of them. We all do. This *isn't* what we signed up for." And then he turned and walked away, presumably to rejoin the others.

There was no reproach in the captain's words, just certainty. He must have known that his intentions were good, and if blame was to be pinned on anyone for what had gone awry, it would be on Commander Weissinger and his seemingly morbid obsession with pain. Still, there was a certain authority in his voice that made it clear he meant business.

"Yes," Edward mumbled, staring down at his feet. "Yes, I suppose you're right." When he looked up to the doorway again, the captain was already gone. Sighing deeply, he turned his eyes to Frank. "I'll tell you everything I know. You won't like it, but I will." He motioned for him to come closer then. "Well?" he asked. "What are you waiting for? Come down from there and follow me. I have things to show you."

CHAPTER
26

Revelations

Wasting little time, Frank hurried down the rickety flight of metal stairs, and followed Edward into the small room that was nestled behind them. The place looked like any of the closed offices he'd seen over at plaza precinct headquarters, except for the piles of not-so-neatly-stacked documents that were strewn out from Edward's desk, to the tops of his filing cabinets, to the corners of the tiled black floor. The two large blackboards on the wall to his left were covered in a chaotic mess of white chalk smears and complex algorithms that were far beyond his ability to comprehend.

"What is this place?" he asked him. Squinting, he leaned in toward the blackboards and looked the calculations over briefly before giving up on them altogether. "Your study?"

"I suppose you could call it that," Edward answered simply, nodding once. "It's where I do most of my more serious thinking, which explains the notes and research lying around all over the place." He smiled weakly at that. "I know that you noticed. I'm a little messy, I won't deny it, but I know how to find what I'm looking for this way. Tidy is completely overrated. You could almost call this place my study slash storage room. I have a lot of keepsakes here from past projects, as well as other trinkets of a sentimental yet scientific nature."

"I have a feeling you're going to show me some of them," Frank stated plainly, mostly to himself.

"In a manner of speaking, yes," Edward answered. "These are your own belongings, actually." He took a seat behind his desk and slid the bottom drawer open. "I've been holding onto them for you for around twenty years, now. You can have them back now if you want them."

Frank arched his brow, intrigued but skeptical. "For twenty years?" he asked. "How is that even possible?"

"In your current mind-set, I suppose it isn't, is it?" Edward said more than asked, depositing what looked like an oversized shoebox on his desk. "But it is. I did tell you that you weren't ready for the truth. I *know* that you're not going to believe it, but you insisted, so you're going to get it."

Frank watched with hesitant anticipation as Edward removed the lid and set it down on the table, then lifted the items out of the box and laid them out one by one, handling them with great care, like they were fragile or very precious to him. The seemingly random objects sparked little interest, at first. There were several articles of clothing, some tiny shoes, a small comforter, a rubber ball. The items had obviously belonged to a young boy, but they were as generic to him as the box they'd been stored in.

When the last item was lifted from its resting place, however, it captured his attention fully. His breath caught the second he set eyes on it, and he felt like his heart would soon follow suit. It was a small book with gold leaf lettering gilded across its black cover, and it was more than just a little familiar.

It was a birthday present from a father to a son, given in the recurring dream that he'd been having for months before waking in this place. For a moment, he felt like all the air had gone from his lungs, like it had been squeezed right out of him. His concept of reality shattered like a dropped glass.

"I see that you recognize this," Edward mumbled. He tried to slip the book into Frank's open hand, and quickly realizing that he was too stunned to grasp it of his own volition, he curled his fingers around the edges of it for him. "You should probably sit down right now," he added, somewhat worried from the look of it, but not at all surprised.

Frank obeyed without hesitation, dropping into the doctor's guest chair like a sack of potatoes. He raised the book and stared at it blankly for what seemed like an eternity, utterly silent, then set it down on the desk and averted his eyes as though suddenly repulsed by the sight of it.

He couldn't understand what was going on. His mind was racing. He felt queasy. "W-what... what is this?" he finally asked in a voice that was as broken as it was distraught. "This can't be real." *This* was something from a dream, albeit a dream so bloody persistent that it had once made him doubt certain aspects of his past and parentage.

Granted, those doubts had proven to be well founded, though his father's account of things had done nothing to lend credence to the idea that his dreams were actual memories. Hadn't Gordon insinuated that he'd been left at the orphanage by paupers or maybe junkies? Maybe he'd only inferred that himself.

Or maybe his father had lied to him. Again. He'd done it for years. None of this would bother him as much as it did if the sole purpose of it was to shed light on the identities of his biological parents—he'd done his own searches in that regard—but he knew that Edward hadn't brought him to his inner sanctum to discuss family history. There was something else waiting to be unearthed here, something much bigger that would change his life forever. He could feel it. His mind was trying to tell him something, but he refused to hear it. Just thinking about it made his stomach churn, and for a moment he thought he was going to heave.

The doctor slowly waved his hand in front of his eyes then. He hadn't realized it until then, but he'd been staring at the lamp on the man's desk for quite some time, almost as though he was in some kind of trance.

"I've thought long and hard on how to best break this to you," Edward confided. "To be completely honest with you, I've drawn little more than a blank in that regard, even though I've had years to mull it over." A frown tugged at the corners of his mouth as he looked at his weathered old hands, momentarily lost in thought. "I never thought for even a second that I'd *really* be the one to tell you all of this. But I had thought about it."

"In a way," he said, "I've always been the ideal candidate for the task. In a way, it always should have been my responsibility. Should have, but that's just not how things work. It was never planned out that way, wasn't my role in the greater scheme of things. It wasn't even a consideration. I should be thankful for the opportunity, I suppose. I'd always imagined that I would be, if it ever came to this. But now that I'm here, facing you, I'd almost prefer that the opportunity be left to someone else."

"This isn't helping me very much, Doc," Frank managed to say with some difficulty.

"Please, let me finish," Edward humbly requested. "Believe me... this is about as hard for me as it is for you. I think the best way to do this would be to tell you everything, raw and uncut, however brutal that may seem."

Frank nodded and listened. *Just rip the bandage off.*

"Everything you know," Edward stated plainly, "everyone you thought you knew... none of it is true, none of them are real. You've been living a lie, Sixty-Seven, though I hate to say it that way. You've been living a lie almost your entire life. Your name isn't Frank, it's Daniel MacBride, and everything you know and remember has been nothing more than a perpetually sustained dream. A dream that was chosen for you. Chosen for you and controlled from the outside. An induced, remote-controlled coma, if you will. Your earliest memories were prefabricated, false. I know this because I designed most of them myself."

He looked at his hands then and took a deep breath before continuing. "I chose the name that you go by, can you imagine. It was well-known to me that your brother Frank had been slain in a freak accident involving a defective mech unit. Giving you his name was my trivial way of honoring his memory. My colleagues have always considered me a little... sentimental, I suppose, but I like to think that I have a deeper respect for human life, especially when it comes to children. It's a sentiment that too few of them seem capable of understanding."

Frank wanted to say something, to cut him off and dismiss everything he'd said as ridiculous, but he couldn't. He was frozen up, his tongue stilled by that name. Daniel MacBride. How could he have even known about that? As incredibly far-fetched as the doctor's explanations had been so far, all he managed to ask him was, "Why?" Even that took his best effort. Hearing the name spoken out loud was disconcerting, to be sure, but the rest of his story sounded at best like a tale of the tallest order. He couldn't even begin to believe it.

"Crime," Edward answered plainly. "Or terrorism to be more precise. Our city's been plagued by it for as long as anyone can remember, and it's only gotten worse in recent years."

"The Awoken?" Frank asked, though he already knew that he was right. He didn't understand how any of it tied together, but he'd grasp at anything that he *did* know for certain like it was a buoy that might keep him from sinking into a panic. *Where did he hear that name?* he asked himself insistently.

"Indeed," Edward answered sullenly, nodding once. "The Awoken, or the Enlightened, or whatever other moniker they go by, these days. Sometimes they use different names, but they're all the same, rabble-rousing band of murderers."

"Agreed," Frank noted casually. "They all claim that there's an entire world thriving outside our walls, civilizations other than our own. They want to travel out into the wastelands, lead us on an exodus from the city, and they pressure the government into letting them do so by attacking it openly. I suppose the plan is to make the cost of keeping them here greater than it would be to simply let them go. It doesn't matter to them that civilians get caught in the crossfire. They even put them there on purpose." He frowned at the thought of it. "If you ask me, we should just let them have their way. Let them go and be rid of them."

"You'd think that, wouldn't you," Edward said with a touch of sarcasm, "but the rules that keep us here were created for a reason. Not that there's any love lost on them on my part, but we'd be sending them to a certain death, and one that we could never prove happened without risking the lives of our own men. And that's just not going to happen. We have a shortage of law enforcement officers as it stands. Sending out our own men after them to investigate would be a monumental waste of resources. Or of human lives, as I prefer to call them."

"I was just saying," Frank retorted, somewhat defensively.

"That you were," Edward acknowledged, "and I don't hold it against you. The real problem here is that there'll always be more fools ready to jump on the bandwagon. If we let these terrorists leave and—surprise, surprise—they never come back, people will think it's because they found something better somewhere else. They'll think that the terrorists were right all along. Then we'll have a new batch of *Awoken* on our hands, even more extreme, more driven, more determined to leave than their predecessors ever were. Then we'd have a real exodus on our hands, droves of people marching to their deaths. If we let the Awoken go, this city will wither away until there's nothing left. That's why we need to keep fighting them, just as we have been all along."

"I don't want to interrupt you," Frank said, doing just that, "but when do we get to the part where this starts to make sense?" To be fair, most of what the doctor had just said did make sense. To a police officer or a government official it was just common *sense*. But it didn't explain why his entire life was a *lie*, how his memories were prefabricated, as Edward had put it.

"I'm afraid it's only going to get worse for you from here on," Edward answered with something that sounded like sympathy, "but try to keep an open mind."

He gave his head a quick scratch and leaned forward intently before continuing. "We need to keep fighting them," he repeated for emphasis, "but *better*. We've been fighting a losing war and our odds have only been getting worse. They're starting to look insurmountable. Law enforcers are dying almost every single day now, did you know?"

The crease in Frank's brow deepened as he leaned forward to rest his chin on his clasped hands. It sounded like a rhetorical question, but *yes*, he knew. If anything, he thought the doctor was understating the situation, and he resisted the sudden urge to ask him what rock he'd been living under. As bad as things had gotten, high fatality rates were nothing new for the agency.

The academy—or the factory, as some now begrudgingly called it—pumped out new recruits on an almost daily basis, and they didn't really have a choice in the matter, either. They had to just to sustain the agency's reliably dwindling numbers. It hadn't always been that way, granted, but sometime after his own promotion, which felt like ages ago to him now, things had taken a turn for the worse. They'd gotten so bad, in fact, that rookies no longer graduated in classes. Instead, they were pushed into service the second they'd earned enough credits to.

Accelerated courses were no longer optional; they were the norm, and there were plenty of bonus programs in place to help hasten the process. Personally, he thought that might be part of the problem. New recruits were so green they'd be lucky to get through their first APB without getting themselves or someone else killed. It kept the force bogged down in a vicious cycle.

"Twenty-something odd years ago," Edward continued, "the powers that be mandated the Commission of Higher Sciences with finding a long-term solution to this terrorist problem of ours. According to the system's records and my sometimes-faltering memory, you are one of the oldest remaining subjects from our original pilot program."

"The Commission of Higher Sciences?" Frank half said, half asked. "Never heard of it."

"You wouldn't have," Edward confirmed, "for more than just one reason. Suffice it to say that we're... or rather *'they're'*," he quickly corrected himself, "a secret government department comprising the scientific community's greatest minds. We'll leave it at that for now."

Frank nodded and motioned for him to go on.

"For a while," Edward murmured, "we were given free rein to research options as we would, but once the president found an idea that he *really* liked, he latched onto it like a baby suckling at its mother's teat, and it soon became our primary focus. Without mincing words, we were tasked with initiating a... a rehabilitation program, in a manner of speaking. Its sole purpose would be to recycle the refuse of society into perfect, government-controlled killing machines. Our *volunteers* would include, but would not be limited to captured enemies... criminals of the worst kind."

"This is starting to sound a little far-fetched," Frank said, though it had already hit that point some time ago.

"The gap with what you'd deem credible can only grow," Edward assured him, "but it's the truth, I promise you."

"Help me out a bit then," Frank stated plainly, doing his best to keep his skepticism in check. "When you say *'rehabilitation program'*, what you're really talking about is brainwashing, right?"

"That would be part of it, yes," Edward responded promptly. "First, we'd wipe the slate clean, so to speak, and afterward we'd replace those suppressed memories with ones more conducive to successful rehabilitation: a good childhood, good parents, proper motivation... that sort of thing."

"Why even bother?" Frank asked, genuinely confused. "Why go to the trouble of creating such elaborate backstories for your future 'killing machines'? I don't get it."

"We did it that way because we had to," Edward sighed. "We *did* try to cut some corners in the beginning—by implanting memories that were closer to the final desired result—but it was a complete waste of time, and more importantly of resources. Most of the candidates rehabilitated in this fashion were utter failures. They just weren't very good, or very well adapted, for that matter. Almost an entire panel was lost, can you imagine. If only we'd realized then that remembering something doesn't automatically make you good at it, then we'd really have saved ourselves a lot of trouble. An actual learning process was required, you see. We had to ensure that our future police officers had a strong desire to learn, to excel, and we had to provide them with an environment in which they could do that."

Frank thought about his own family history for a moment. His father had been in the force and so had his grandfather. Had that been *conducive* to his becoming a police officer? He supposed that it had. Was it just a coincidence? *Probably.* He rubbed his head as he considered the doctor's words. A few of his points just weren't sitting well with him. "First things first," he said. "If this program was designed for criminals, then what was a child doing in it? You said it yourself, I'm one of the '*oldest*', and this program was started twenty-something years ago."

"You're something of an exception," Edward sighed. "I don't know how to break this to you, Frank, but your father was a terrorist. Both he and your mother died when he attacked the team that had been sent to bring him in. I never once agreed with it, but it was decided that you'd be brought to the Commission for insertion into the program."

Frank narrowed his eyes and wrinkled his lips. He wasn't sure if he should laugh or be angry. It all sounded like a crock of shit to him, and since it was only getting worse, he decided it wasn't worth getting into a huff over. "You'd put a child in a fast-track program to becoming a killing machine?" he asked, a little more snidely than he'd intended. "You surprise me, Doctor."

"I was firmly against it," Edward retorted defensively, "but the governing bodies decided it would be in your best interest. They said that it would be your only chance at leading a 'normal' life, that living life as an orphan in a city like ours—a city that was being ripped apart at the seams by criminals and terrorists—wasn't really a life at all. My protests fell on deaf ears, of course, and without any decisional power, all I could do was comply, and try to keep a watchful eye on you... help you survive the learning process, if you will. When strictly necessary, and when I could do so without drawing any attention to myself."

"What kind of learning process are we talking about here, exactly?" Frank demanded. "Did everyone at the academy go through this 'program' of yours?"

"I just want to point out that the learning process began much later for you," Edward said, still somewhat defensive. "We didn't just throw you into the mix. No, that wouldn't have been good at all. When you were a child, you were subjected to a prolonged period of mental conditioning. It was something of an advantage you had on everyone else, but it was a curse as well as a blessing. Putting you through the actual training at such a young age would have been pointless, not to mention completely immoral. As for your question concerning the *'academy'*," he added, then trailed off momentarily as he struggled to find an answer. "I'm afraid it just isn't as simple as that."

"What do you mean, Munro?" Frank asked. "It was a pretty straightforward question, and you didn't answer it."

Edward closed his eyes and rubbed at the bridge of his nose as though trying to soothe a sudden ache, his glasses bobbing up and down in time with his fingers as he did. A few seconds later, he repositioned his glasses, exhaled slowly, and shook his head from side to side. "No, I suppose I didn't. The academy, the Law Enforcement Agency, virtually everything you remember," he whispered, loudly and somewhat disjointedly, "none of it was real. None of it *is* real. Your family, those you called friends, the places you liked to go... they were all *fabricated*. I wasn't speaking metaphorically when I told you that your entire life was a lie." He stopped then and hesitated briefly before continuing.

"Let me try this again. When you were five or six years old," he added, meeting Frank's gaze and holding it, "you were placed inside a stasis chamber that would maintain your health as well as your link to the rehabilitation program. Most of us referred to it simply as the rehab or *the common dream*. It's a virtual world, a pale reflection of our own that lives in the minds of its candidates. Its consistency across those minds is maintained by the miracles of science and technology."

Frank remained silent for what seemed like an extremely long time, completely motionless, frozen like some frightened animal caught in the headlights of an incoming vehicle. And then he burst into a laughter so sudden and so sharp that it gave Edward a start. "Oh, man," he wheezed out between shorts gasps for air. "You really had me going for a minute." He wiped at the tears that had formed in the corners of his eyes with the back of his hand, then glanced around the room as though searching for something. "Where are they?" he asked, still out of breath. "The cameras. Come on, you can tell me now, Doctor. The jig is up."

"This isn't some cruel practical joke," Edward sighed, "but yours isn't the worst reaction I'd imagined, so I suppose I should be grateful for that. The last twenty or so years of your life have been lived out in a VR simulation shared by thousands of men and women who—just like you—were being prepared to provide a tangible solution to this *real* world's *real* problems."

Frank had calmed down considerably and caught his breath, but his lips were still stretched tight across his teeth, and he felt like he might start laughing again if he wasn't careful. "Answer me this," he breathed. "If everything you say is true, then why am I here? Why me when there are thousands of others?"

"To be completely honest," Edward answered plainly, "I've always had a deep interest in your well-being. You were my first subject, after all, and a child, at that. How could I not look out for you? I watched over you to the best of my ability for all those years, even cheated for you on occasion to ensure your safety, but this time I didn't have a choice. I couldn't cheat. I *had* to break you out or you would have died. I couldn't let that happen."

"Wait a minute," Frank interjected, skeptical. "Didn't you just say that the entire thing was a VR simulation?"

"I did," Edward confirmed, nodding curtly, "but as virtual as all of it is, the effects of injury and even death are very real in the common dream. It may seem harsh—it most definitely *is* harsh—but that's exactly how the Commission intended it to be. It's how they weed out the 'weak links'."

"Okay, so explain how my life was in danger specifically," Frank demanded while trying his best to remain polite. "Why did you have to break me out?"

"I won't delve too deeply into the technical aspects of it," Edward explained, "but the system was coded in such a way that injury perceived in the dream would be translated directly to the bodies of the candidates in the real—"

"No," Frank groaned, effectively cutting him off. "That's not what I meant. I'd already assumed that much. What I want to know is what happened that you absolutely *had* to break me out this time. Why couldn't you have just 'cheated' for me again, as you put it?"

"Normally, I might have been able to," Edward sighed, "but this time you were scheduled for termination."

"Come again?" Frank muttered.

"Putting it as plainly as I possibly can," Edward responded, "every now and then a candidate tries to *wake* from the common dream. We're not entirely sure why it happens, to be honest, but the most widely accepted hypothesis is as follows: if for some reason a candidate begins to doubt their perceived reality, the veracity of the virtual world around them, their subconscious tries to warn them, to wake them up. The chances of something like that happening without any outside intervention are relatively slim, mind you, but these subconscious reactions spill over into the common dream. When that happens, a candidate's behavior starts to get erratic. They'll act out, begin to question their reality. To test it. This can spread and trigger the effect in others, and if the ripple effect is great enough, it can compromise the system's homeostasis. It can create a serious imbalance in the training environment. One that's difficult to recover from. This is where scheduled termination comes into play."

"And what exactly would that entail?" Frank asked, his curiosity genuinely piqued.

"Well, it's rather simple, really," Edward answered. "When a candidate is scheduled for termination, agents of the Commission intervene directly via the Interface. Think of the Interface as a sort of control panel for the common dream. It allows agents to access the dream, or communicate with it, if you will. By using it, they can add all kinds of incriminating evidence, or even replicate a candidate's likeness to place them at the scene of a crime. They could even modify AI routines if they wanted to, though that's a messier business. Essentially, what they do is think up crafty ways of eliminating specific targets from the program without arousing too much suspicion in the other candidates. Essentially, it's just a question of killing them off without making the other candidates further question the credibility of the world they live in."

"So I was going to wake up," Frank half asked, half stated.

"In all honesty, I don't think so," Edward confided. "In fact, before all of this happened, I thought that you might be the key to solving this whole 'awakening issue'. I... we tried to convince our colleagues and superiors of this, but no one would listen. No one that mattered, at least. The decision to terminate you had already been made. It was too late."

"I don't follow," Frank said. "Care to explain?"

"Of course," Edward answered, somewhat apologetically. "After years of fine-tuning, the system has become sophisticated enough that it can detect symptoms of a candidate's awakening as soon as familiar patterns begin to emerge in their cerebral activity reports. Usually, it catches them even in their earliest stages. *Your* symptoms had been there for years, but were never picked up, which is... well, it was extremely odd. It usually takes no longer than a few weeks from the time that the patterns first emerge for the candidate in question to go full-out 'code red'. But the pattern in your case was subtle, different. That's why I thought you might hold the solution to the problem. Where others rejected their environment, and spiraled out of control, you refused to doubt the veracity of your surroundings, even though your subconscious was trying to force you to."

As insane as all of it sounded to Frank, he couldn't help but appreciate the level of detail that Edward had wrought into his obvious work of fiction. There was no way that any of it could be true. The doctor's knowledge of Daniel MacBride was strange, to be sure, but after the initial shock of hearing him say that name out loud had passed, he was convinced he could find a perfectly reasonable explanation for it. He was kind of dry on ideas for the moment, but he'd find something.

"So you thought you'd found a way of fixing the program, of improving its stability, but they'd have nothing of it, huh," he said, spurring Edward's story along. A tall tale such as this one had obviously taken him a lot of time and effort to prepare, but the way he saw it, the longer he kept the doctor talking, the more likely he was to slip up.

"They might have at least heard us out if it hadn't been for that meddling grumblebum *Langsarks*," Edward said, scrunching his face up as the name left his lips.

"Langsarks?" Frank asked. "Who's that?"

"An agent from the Ministry of Inner Workings," Edward complained angrily. "Apparently, he noticed the anomalies in your cerebral activity reports at about the same time as I did, and almost immediately after arriving at the Commission, to boot. I didn't even know that the Ministry had sent an official until I found out that you'd been scheduled for termination. As far as I can tell, he's the one that convinced the Commissioner that your termination was necessary."

Frank questioned Edward on the subject until he felt like he'd exhausted every avenue worth exploring, and till all of it sounded like a mess of names, and committees, and hierarchical structures he could barely understand. All he'd wanted was answers, but now that he'd gotten them, he felt none the wiser for it. Though he'd tested the doctor at length, Edward hadn't slipped up once, and he was almost convinced that he was telling the truth, or at least what he *thought* was the truth.

No one could have pulled a story like that one out of their hat without at least a few inconsistencies cropping up. He was sure of it, and he knew a thing or two about interrogations. He'd conducted more than a few in his time. Besides, the one thing he'd always appreciated about Edward had been his sincerity. Though he'd had fleeting doubts about the man, he knew that he was no liar. He was, however, beginning to wonder if he was delusional, or just very easily duped.

He was now certain that if he wanted the truth, he was going to have to look for it elsewhere, but there was one final thing that he had to ask, one burning question that he had to squelch. It was one that had tormented him ever since he'd woken in this place, his world turned upside down.

"Where's Vanessa?" he asked. Though his voice remained firm, the mere mention of her name brought on a stir of emotion, and he felt a sudden rise of pressure in his chest. His heart felt like it was being clutched in a vice. Previously, when it had become obvious that he'd get no answers concerning her whereabouts, he'd tried to not think about her too much. He'd tried and failed miserably, but at least he'd kept from mentioning her at every turn. Now that Edward's books were open, he wouldn't pass up the opportunity to ask again. He missed her more than he'd ever missed anyone or anything before. He missed her and he worried. At times, the worrying had been almost unbearable.

"Sixty-Seven," Edward breathed before falling dramatically silent. The look of dismay on his face made it evident that he had no idea what to say next. Finally, he exhaled extensively, his eyes downcast. "There is no Vanessa," he whispered. "At least... not outside of your memories, there isn't."

"What?" Frank asked, furrowing his brow into an angry-looking crease. He didn't believe the rest of Edward's far-fetched story, so why should this bother him? He wasn't exactly sure, but it did. "How can you say something like that," he added through tightly stretched lips.

"No matter how vivid your recollections of her," Edward cautioned, "no matter how strong your feelings, *Vanessa* is not real. She's nothing more than a series of very sophisticated, coded strings. She's an accessory to the common dream, a virtual actor endowed with an artificial intelligence, just like everyone else you *knew* that wasn't a serviceperson. She was decoration, Frank... a prop on the set of the movie that was your life, your training. I know that this must be hard for you to hear, but she isn't *real*."

"You want to know what's hard for me?" Frank asked, bolting upright. "Having to sit here and listen to you go on and on, and all the while pretend like I don't think you're batshit crazy. This whole thing is a steaming pile of shit."

"This '*steaming pile of shit*' as you put it is the truth, Daniel," Edward retorted. "What do I have to do to make you see that?"

"Don't call me that," Frank snapped. "That isn't my name and you know it." As his anger rose, he felt a familiar rush of adrenaline pumping through his veins. He felt volatile, like he could put his fist through a wall. Edward wasn't necessarily to blame, either. The man was delusional or gullible or maybe both, and he probably needed medication.

"Well, thanks for 'filling me in', Doctor Munro," he stated coldly, "but I think I've heard enough." Deciding that he should leave at once, before things got out of hand and he did something brash, he turned quickly and stalked off toward the office door, knocking his chair over in the process.

"Wait," Edward called out after him. "Frank! There's so much I haven't told you, so much more that you need to know. Don't you want to know what Weissinger's tests were about?"

"Nope," Frank replied, "can't say that I do." He stopped in the atrium and gave the place a quick once over, trying to get his bearings. "I don't really care anymore," he added, turning back toward Edward, who'd followed him out. "All I care about right now is getting the fuck out of here as quickly as I possibly can." If they weren't going to tell him where Vanessa was, he was going to have to go looking for her himself.

"But you really should know these things," Edward protested with about as much authority as a fuzzy little kitten. "They *are* going to have an impact on just about everything you—"

"Just show me the way out, Doc," Frank urged him, cutting him off. "I seriously couldn't care any less right now."

"I can show you to the surface, Frank," Captain Falstaff interjected. He was leaning against the staircase that led to the upper level of the atrium.

"Could you please?" Edward asked with a dejected sigh.

Falstaff nodded, grabbed the assault rifle that was propped up against the staircase beside him, slung it over his shoulder, and started to climb the stairs at a jog. "Follow me," he said, glancing back over his shoulder.

Frank started after him immediately. When they reached the top, he followed him through an archway on their left.

"Frank!" Edward called out from below. "Be careful, please!"

Frank heard him, but didn't respond. Even if he'd felt like answering him, he was too busy trying to keep up with Falstaff to bother. The captain was fast, even when he wasn't trying to be. He was a very athletic man, and his long legs covered a lot of ground even at a light jog.

He followed him down a winding corridor that branched out twice before finally stopping by a heavyset steel door. Crossing his arms, he watched as Falstaff punched a code into the keypad on the wall beside it. Once the code was entered, there was a low buzzing sound and the door slid open.

"Right this way," Falstaff said, motioning for Frank to take the lead and go in first.

Frank stepped through the open doorway into what looked like some kind of maintenance room. The concrete floor here was damp and dirty, like an army of feet had tracked mud all over it. There were a couple racks mounted against the wall on the left side of the room and, at a glance, they seemed to be lined with a variety of tools and cleaning products. The only thing that really drew his attention was the freight elevator that was set against the back wall. The door was already open, so they both got in.

Falstaff produced a key from his shirt pocket, slid it into a slot beneath the floor selection panel, and turned it clockwise. An "In Service" sign blinked on and the door slid closed. He hit the button marked "P2" and let himself slump heavily against the back wall of the elevator.

The seconds ticked by as the elevator grumbled and groaned and slowly made its ascent. "So how much of that conversation did you actually hear?" Frank asked him, breaking a silence that had quickly started to border on awkward.

"Oh, I don't know," Falstaff replied, offering him a brief side-glance. "All of it?"

"What do you say to something like that?" Frank asked him, completely befuddled. "I mean... seriously. 'Your whole life has been a VR simulation.' Okay, I guess?"

"Something tells me I'd be better off just keeping my trap shut," Falstaff breathed. "I don't think you want to hear what I have to say about any of this right now."

"If you think that shit's true, then you're probably right," Frank conceded. He wasn't in the mood for more crazy talk. Not from Alexander. He was the closest thing that he had to a friend in this place, and he didn't want to be pissed off at him, too. "So just how far down are we, anyway?" he asked, changing the subject. The only buttons on the panel were "S" and "P2", but it seemed to be taking forever just to go up one floor.

"Honestly, I'd have to guess around ten stories," Falstaff ventured. "Ours is the only floor accessible by elevator. There are other levels above and below ours, but we can only get to them via maintenance hatch or stairwell. Those that are still intact and aren't blocked off by rubble. The other floors ran on a separate elevator system, but those shafts are all condemned. They broke down a long time ago, looks like."

"Huh," Frank said, his curiosity appeased. He wasn't really that interested in the first place. He just didn't know what to do with himself short of twiddling his thumbs. Heck, they couldn't even talk about the weather. He hadn't been outside or even seen the sky for longer than he could remember. He didn't even know how long he'd been underground. It was easy to lose track of time in a place like this. As gray and overcast as the sky always was, he couldn't wait to see it again; in all of its dull and mundane glory.

"You know," Alexander said, staving off the silence once more, before it had a chance to settle in, "you might not see it this way, but Doctor Munro is probably the best friend that you have right now. He's really been looking out for you."

"If you say so," Frank noted sullenly, his voice devoid of any real emotion. The door slid open then, and one after the other, they stepped out into another room that looked like a large utility closet. It was almost identical to the one they'd just come from, except for the broken top shelf on one of the storage racks, which lie bent and slanted against the one beneath it. Most of the bottles and cans it had once held lie scattered loosely on the floor.

"I know you don't want to hear it right now," Alexander sighed, leading him through a plain door to what seemed like an abandoned underground parking lot, "but he's sacrificed a lot for you; more than you could ever imagine." Still leading the way, he skirted around a few rusty vehicles that looked like they'd been stripped of anything of value, including their tires. A few more seconds of awkward silence passed before he finally added, "All I'm saying is that if you ever need anything—anything at all—or if you get into some kind of trouble, you'll always be welcomed back here, with him. With us."

"Thanks, but I think I've had my fill of this place for now," Frank responded gruffly. When he didn't know what to say, he could always fall back on the truth, even if the truth was blunt. They reached a ramp leading up, and the light filtering down it suggested that they were getting awfully close to the surface.

"I'm just saying, is all," Alexander stated. "Don't forget that we're here, okay?"

"Okay," Frank sighed, following him up the ramp. "I won't."

The higher level was completely empty except for a curiously overturned dumpster in its center. It was much easier to see up here, as the light of day was streaming in through the level's only entrance, and casting everything in a dim but sufficient glow.

What little trash had been left scattered around the mouth of the dumpster looked dry and dusty, like it had been lying there undisturbed for a very long time. He stopped and picked up an empty soda can at random as they walked past. "Cuda Cola?" he mumbled as he read the label. "Sounds fishy." Its colors were faded, but it was otherwise intact. The cartoonish barracuda that was printed on it grinned at him stupidly while pointing its fins down at the lettering beneath it. "Taste the ocean," it read, and in an even smaller print beneath that was a small block of text. "*Produced using only soft water fish and artificial flavoring. Does not contain actual barracuda. Prepared by Nussenbaum Foods Inc. Packaged by Schwarzwald Canning Co." Neither of those company names looked familiar to him.

"So what are you going to do with Doctor Jerkface?" he asked, tossing the bizarre-looking can back into the heap.

"We'll let him out, I guess," Alexander answered, shrugging. "After he cools off for a while and comes to his senses, that is. We can't keep him locked up forever."

"What a surprise," Frank groaned, falling back in stride with the captain. They were getting closer and closer to the entrance. In his mind's eye, he could already see the cool, gray sky, heavily aswirl with low-hanging clouds and dense with steam-like smog.

"I know that you're not going to put much stock in this," Alexander stated plainly, "but I've known the commander for a very long time, and he's not crazy. He gets kind of overzealous about things, and this time he went way too far, but believe it or not, he actually means well."

They stopped just past the entrance and looked out to survey the scene before them. The earth surrounding the decrepit-looking building of granite, brick and sandstone was gray and cracked, like a thick mud that had dried up until it had become hard and brittle and baked by the sun. This barren landscape stretched out a few hundred feet in front of them, 'til it reached a tall fence that had curled up and rusted over the years.

Though twelve feet tall in some places, some sections of the fence hung over so low that someone could easily have stepped right onto it and walked across it. Farther in the distance, great, windowless buildings that were larger than they were high stood against the blurred horizon like a mob of angry, smoking giants. Most of these architectural eyesores had one or more smokestacks that belched out a constant flow of thick, foul-looking smoke in colors that ranged from white to yellow to outright black.

"Lovely piece of real estate you have here," Frank noted sarcastically. "South End Industrial sector?" The sky here looked even more sickly than he was used to seeing it. It was almost completely blotted out by yellowish, light brown smog, but he was happy to see it all the same. Any other day of the week, it was tantamount to sickness and a slow death by asphyxiation. On this day, however, it meant freedom.

"On its southernmost outskirts," Alexander stated, smirking. "Place used to belong to Janssen & Janssen. At least that's what I've gathered from my numerous forays onto the other levels."

"Huh," Frank said. "Janssen & Janssen like the detergent? I wonder what happened. Those guys were huge."

"Janssen & Janssen like the facial cream," Alexander replied, grinning, "the laxative, the painkiller, the morphine, the canned khesh, the mouthwash, and yes, even the detergent. I don't know exactly what happened, but I do know that the city shut it down, condemned the place. Mustn't have been up to code for their type of operation. Company had to get rid of it and move to another building. Looks like it fell into disrepair ages ago."

"And somewhere in all that," Frank said, nodding slowly, "Doctor Munro must have managed to pick it up at a bargain. I guess officiously. Probably still cost an arm and a leg, which kind of makes me wonder." He looked off into the distance then and another awkward silence set in. Finally, he turned to Alexander and offered him his hand. "I suppose this is goodbye then."

"I can come with you, if you want," Alexander suggested, gripping Frank's hand firmly. "At least until you get to wherever it is you're going."

"Thanks," Frank responded plainly, "but I think I can make it back okay all on my own." He gave Alexander's hand one good shake, then let go and started to turn away from him.

"Hold on a second," Alexander blurted out in a hurry, like he'd just remembered something. He lifted a flap at the hip of his uniform and fished his wallet out of the pocket there, then pulled out a stack of bills and handed it to Frank. "Here, take this," he insisted. "It's not much, really, but it should get you a cab across town and a few days' worth of food."

Frank wasn't big on charity—not on receiving it, at least—but the regrettable truth was that he had nothing but the clothes on his back. Those talers would at least save him a few hours getting downtown. "Thanks," he said, then shook his hand again.

He took the bills, folded them in two and slid them down his shirt pocket. There was actually enough there for a few cab fares and a weeklong supply of food for a small family. He didn't know what the big deal was. He had money stashed away at home and could just grab more from the bank, if his account hadn't been frozen. But he wasn't in the mood to argue. "I won't forget this," he added with a nod, then turned and walked away.

Alexander stood there and watched him go, and as he did, he couldn't help but wonder if everything they'd done had been for nothing. As disturbing as the thought was, it wasn't his place to interfere. Besides, he had a job to do, and it was probably just as dangerous for him out there as it was for Frank, if not more so.

He was almost sure that the police would have a positive ID on him by now, and even if they didn't, it wouldn't be very long before they did. All he could do was wait and see what happened. "Be careful," he called out, though he wasn't even sure if Frank was within earshot. He certainly gave no sign of hearing him.

"Unsettling, isn't it," Edward said softly as he walked up from behind him and took a place at his side. "Watching him go off like that on his own, I mean."

"It is," Alexander replied, nodding once. "He'll be virtually defenseless out there." He furrowed his brow at the thought of it. "He won't even know what hit him."

"Sixty-Seven may be many things," Edward argued, "but by no means is he defenseless. Still, I worry. I worry about how he'll take it when he finally sees the truth with his own two eyes."

"I offered to go with him," Alexander said. "He refused."

Edward shook his head disapprovingly and planted his fists on his hips. "I know," he groaned. "I heard. And it didn't really surprise me. He's always been rather pigheaded." He started to dig through the various pockets in his lab coat then, both inner and outer. When he finally found what he was looking for, but clipped to his belt, he pulled it free and rubbed it down with his sleeve. "Captain," he breathed, "I've a favor to ask of you."

"A favor?" Alexander asked, quirking his brow. "What is it?"

"I'd very much appreciate it if you could keep an eye on him," Edward confessed, then handed him the sleek, black object that he'd pulled from his belt. The device had a monitor built into its front side. On it, the locations of several nearby factories were displayed, as well as a lone, wandering blip conveniently labeled "Sixty-Seven" that was slowly moving away from them.

"Is this a tracking device of some sort?" Alexander asked. "Very sneaky, Doctor, but why is he even showing up on this? How'd you do it?"

"Simple," Edward answered, grinning weakly. "We grafted a geolocation chip under his skin when we first brought him here." He fell silent then as he looked down at his hands, his feelings of guilt apparent. "Will you do this for me?" he asked. "Follow him? At least until he gets to safety. I only want to ensure that he doesn't get himself into more trouble than he can handle."

"Yeah, sure," Alexander replied without hesitation, nodding vigorously. "Of course I will."

"Good man," Edward said, giving the captain's arm a light slap and a shake. "Just remember to keep the tracking device safe. We don't want it falling into the wrong hands."

CHAPTER
27

Home Sweet Home

Frank looked up at the towering mass of mixed skyscrapers in the distance, and for a fleeting moment, he was awed by the dark majesty of it. He'd been around the city more times than he could remember, but never before had he seen it from such an angle.

In all but a few places, the buildings were so tightly packed together that they kept any natural light from shining through. Looking up at it from within the city proper, the sky appeared small, distant, impossibly far away—if it could even be seen at all through the mess of skywalks and the near perpetual haze. But from the southernmost reaches of the industrial sector, it looked vast, and the downtown core was like one great spire, jutting skyward in a vain but valiant effort to touch the firmament. It loomed over the outlying sectors like a sheer mountain of steel, glass, and concrete, drowning them all in its expansive shadow. But despite its magnificence, it somehow managed to look small and isolated, like a lone castaway figure lost in a never-ending sky, surrounded by a largely desolate landscape.

He couldn't remember the last time he'd been so far from the city center, or if he ever had. Only rarely did he work outside of his own jurisdiction, and when he did, it was in his neighboring sectors. There was no other reason for him to visit the outskirts. He couldn't imagine why *anyone* would want to unless it was for work. There was the view, of course, and it really was something, but now that he'd seen it, it just made him want to go home even more than he already did.

A rush of wind blew in from the east then, and he turned into it with a raised arm to shelter his eyes from the sand blowing past. When the wind finally subsided, he wiped the dust from his brow, brushed his fingers through his hair, and glanced at the high city wall less than a quarter mile away. There was nothing specifically remarkable about it, per se. It was one of those things he'd always taken for granted. Even as close to it as he was, which was closer than he'd ever been, he could just barely make out the shapes of the guards patrolling the length of its parapet. He'd never stopped to think about all the work that had gone into erecting something so tall and so thick around the *entire* city. But now he did, and the immensity of the task was difficult to fathom.

Most of the roads this deep inside the industrial sector were worn and cracked from years of neglect, and the one currently underfoot was no exception. It could hardly even be called a road at all, with the large chunks of it that had gone missing, and what remained fragmented and largely blanketed with sand. The city's administration, it would seem, had other priorities, more pressing issues to attend to. Without the proper funding and maintenance, streets and structures alike had given way to the erosive passage of time. He continued walking for another fifteen minutes before he saw a single vehicle roll past, and it took another half hour before there was a light but seemingly steady flow of traffic.

It was much quieter here than he was used to. Anything was quiet compared to the daily cacophony of the busy city streets, but this was as close to tranquil as he'd ever been outside. The quasi silence seemed to clear up his mind, and made it easier to mull his thoughts over in peace.

They were thoughts of Vanessa, for the most part. As he continued on his way, he could almost feel the distance between them shrinking, and it made his spirits soar. Just being free was an elation all its own. After being cooped up in a pseudo prison camp for so many months that he'd lost track of time, each and every step that he took felt like the first in a new life. Liberty had never felt so good. The feeling was almost overwhelming.

He still couldn't wrap his head around everything that had transpired, or how he'd gotten involved in the whole mess in the first place. Doctor Munro's cockamamie explanation wasn't really an explanation at all, as far as he was concerned.

Despite his confusion, Vanessa remained at the forefront of his thoughts. She overshadowed *everything* without exception. He hadn't seen her in so long that he was like a wolf with two tails at the mere thought of holding her in his arms again.

If I ever get to hold her in my arms again, he thought, furrowing his brow as his mood soured. He couldn't allow himself to think that way. He *had* to see her again. He *would* see her again. He'd do anything and everything that he could to ensure that he did. But he also had to entertain the possibility that she'd been taken into custody, just as he had. *If SAU took her, if they interrogated and tortured her,* he thought, grimacing before cutting away from that train of thought. He didn't want to go there. If he did, he feared he might dwell on it overly. He needed to remain focused, and just thinking about it angered him.

If they did have her, he'd deal with it accordingly, but he didn't want to get worked up over nothing. He didn't want to build up his hopes just to break himself down, either. She might not be at home waiting for him when he got there. Chances were she was at work, and that's exactly where he asked the driver to bring him once he finally managed to hail a cab.

Before long, traffic had picked up and the cityscape grew and began to unfurl before him. Circulation was fluid and they reached the library in good time. According to the clock over the taxi's counter, exactly twenty-seven minutes had gone by, but as far as he was concerned, it was the longest ride he'd ever taken. The seconds had seemed to stretch out into minutes as they'd approached their destination. The anticipation reminded him vaguely of those final minutes of the last day of school, as he'd looked up at the clock, unflinching, waiting for the bell to ring.

The library was housed in a five-story, castle-like building of granite slab that was topped with a gabled copper roof that had greened with oxidation. When the taxi pulled up to it, he was so excited that he jumped out immediately and nearly forgot to pay his fare. After a confused shout from the driver, he doubled back and reached through the open passenger-side window to hand him what was probably way too much money. "Thank you," he blurted out in a rush, then spun around again and ran toward the wide stone steps leading up to the library as fast as he could. When he reached them, he sprinted up them in leaps and bounds. At the top, he threw open the heavy double doors like a man on his way to interrupt his sweetheart's forced wedding.

The librarian behind the reception desk was a frail, wrinkly old thing with overly-big glasses and silvery gray hair that was tightly drawn into an unforgiving bun. The screaming purple vest that she had on was by far the most colorful thing on the entire, almost-palatial first floor, as well as all visible parts of the atrium, which reached all the way up to a large glass dome that was set in the center of the ceiling. Her shoulders crisped as the doors swung shut behind him with a thud, and she pursed her lips and glared at him with eyes that invited him to spontaneously burst into flames.

He couldn't put a name to her, but he didn't dwell on it. Most of the resident librarians were eerily similar in appearance, and he found it difficult to differentiate between them. Vanessa was an exception. This woman was not.

"Excuse me," he said quietly as he approached the desk, the librarian's scornful eyes following him closely all the while. They narrowed to sharp slits as he set his hands down on the smooth melamine surface. "Sorry," he added. "Do you know if Vanessa is here right now?"

She crossed her arms in response and glared at him even harder, something Frank hadn't even thought possible. "What do I look like to you," she asked in a whisper so loud that it hardly qualified as one. "An information booth, maybe?"

He wanted to say that yes, she did, but thought better of it. Instead, he shrugged, took a step back, and glanced around the library. The place looked relatively devoid of foot traffic. Seeing Vanessa nowhere, he suspected she might not be there. If she had been, Old Lady Fashion Disaster could have just told him as much without being so brazen. There was no way she could be around without this old shrew knowing about it. It was already well past midday, and it would be nigh on impossible for them to miss each other for more than fifteen or twenty minutes at most.

He pulled away from the desk without notice, and decided to comb through the rows of bookshelves anyway, just in case he was wrong. After a quick walk-through of all five levels, he'd seen absolutely no sign of her. He'd peered down every single aisle at least once, sometimes affording them a second glance on his way back. She just wasn't there. Dejected, he followed the escalators down to the first floor, then walked toward the entrance, his eyes downcast, his shoulders slumped.

When he pushed through the double doors and looked up again, he felt his heart swell with joy. "Vanessa?" he whispered quietly, his voice failing him. There she was, walking down the final steps that led to the street. He couldn't see her face as she had her back to him, but he could tell that it was her. Her hair looked exactly as it had the last time he'd seen her. Her clothes looked like something he'd seen her wear before. Even the way she walked seemed familiar. "Vanessa," he called out again as he trailed down the stairs behind her, his voice restored. As he closed in on her, he reached out to touch her arm, but she recoiled at the contact and swiveled around on him, bewildered.

She wasn't Vanessa at all, he realized, both surprised and disappointed. They looked nothing alike, now that he'd gotten a better look at her. She was pretty enough in her own way, but she wasn't *her*. She was just some random girl on her way home from the library—a random girl that he'd nearly scared to death. "I am *so* sorry," he said with a measure of regret, shaking his head from side to side. "I thought that you were... I just thought that you were someone else. My mistake."

"Yeah, um... no problem," the woman replied nervously as she backed away. Then, without any further lingering, she turned on her heels, and scurried off at a noticeably quicker pace than the one she'd been travelling at previously.

"Am I really that scary?" Frank found himself asking. The people of the inner city weren't exactly known for their warmth, especially not when meeting absolute strangers in the street, and he understood why. Muggers, murderers, rapists and generally bad people could be found lurking around just about any corner. Still, he hadn't expected *that* reaction.

He supposed his clothes might have something to do with it. He was wearing a pair of the short-sleeved, front-zipping, faded orange coveralls that the doctor had outfitted him with. And they looked like prison pajamas. He hadn't given it much thought until then, but after giving himself a quick once over, he could see it. He looked like an escaped convict or psych ward patient. He'd have to put on something less glaring once he got back to his apartment. Conveniently, that was his next stop.

That was where Vanessa would most likely be, if she wasn't out window shopping or visiting her parents. If she wasn't around when he got there, at least he'd have somewhere to wait for her without feeling overly awkward or drawing too much attention.

He had to consider the possibility that SAU was looking for him. Walking the streets in plain sight made him feel nervous. Fortunately, he didn't have very far to travel out in the open. Their apartment was only a few blocks away.

As he made his way home, he tried to remain vigilant without giving into outright paranoia. Every now and then, someone would turn and give him an odd look, but for the most part, no one even seemed to notice him at all. Even the officer that drove past him in his bullet-riddled squad car afforded him no more than a brief, disinterested glance.

An odd and unsettling feeling started to seep in as he took in his surroundings. Everything seemed very familiar to him, as well it should. He had lived in the area for some time, after all. The buildings. The streets. The vehicles rolling by. Even the dull, gray cast of the sky. All of it was familiar, and yet different somehow. Try as he might, he couldn't figure out why that was. He didn't recognize any of the names of the stores and restaurants lining the streets, but staying afloat in a competitive market such as this one had always been a complicated and risky undertaking, especially for small businesses, so he dismissed that thought immediately.

He *was* disappointed to see that Delaney's was no longer in business. It had been his and Andy's regular, after-work watering hole for years. Now it was a noodle shop: Mister Oodle's Noodles, according to the tall, white and yellow sign centered on the wall above it. Most of its letters were made to look like bloated bunches of steaming noodles, except for the oes, which were eggs replete with whites and bright yellow yolks. They looked like eyes, and with the curved peppers beneath each set of them—one green and one red—they formed cartoonish smiley faces. As stated in small white letters printed across the face of the storefront window, they used only *real* egg flavoring in their noodles. They also boasted selling a wide variety of fresh-*tasting* bubble teas.

At least it's a fancy noodle shop, Frank thought with a note of sarcasm. *Real flavoring and fresh-tasting... how could anyone go wrong with that?* The taste was probably the only "fresh" thing about it. If anyone believed that they used anything other than dehydrated, factory-produced, synthetic junk, even for a second, he had a whole crate of sunscreen lotion to sell them. The menu posted on the door was far too affordable. There was no way they could sell real food at that price and still turn a profit.

As he neared their apartment building, he swept the area with his eyes for any evidence of a surveillance detail. Doctor Munro and company had seemed relatively confident that he shouldn't have to worry about the law, at least not yet, purportedly because this so-called "Commission" of theirs couldn't risk compromising the secrecy of its work.

He didn't know very much about the Commission of Higher Sciences, but he did know a fair deal about SAU, and if they were still involved in this and looking for him, he'd have to exercise extreme caution. There was no way he was going to let them get their prongs in him again. Not unless they had Vanessa and it was the only way of getting her back. Even just questioning whether or not something might happen seemed pointless. He didn't care what Munro thought; it was too easy. Anyone in their right mind would have the place staked out, or at the very least tapped. He had to assume that was the case. Regardless, he couldn't let that stop him. He had to go in.

Spotting nothing out of the ordinary, he entered the building through the back door and headed straight for the elevators. After stepping into the first one that arrived, he pressed the button for the twenty-fourth floor, watched the door slide shut and waited. It seemed to take a virtual eternity for the cab to set in motion, but it eventually did, with a rattle, a groan, and a clank. It took much longer for it to actually reach its destination. In one day, he had experienced both his longest taxi *and* elevator rides, or so it felt. At moments, it had seemed like time itself had slowed down. When he felt that familiar wave of anxiety wash over him, there was no question as to why that was.

Deep down, he knew that he was setting himself up for more disappointment, but he couldn't help it. He hadn't seen her in so long that it hurt. All he could think about was holding her in his arms again. All he wanted to do was look into her eyes and kiss her, so much so that he could almost taste her peach-flavored lip balm, the one she usually wore. He was excited, and nervous, and letting the anticipation of seeing her get the better of him.

When the elevator door slid open, he stepped out into the hall, hesitated a moment and started the long walk toward his front door. It felt like he was moving in slow motion, or walking through deep water, just like in a dream. When he finally reached the door to their apartment, he stood facing it for a few seconds, breathing deeply. He was almost as afraid of opening the door as he was of not going in. As silly as he knew that was, he didn't want to find that she wasn't there.

Gathering himself, he exhaled extensively, raised his balled fist to the door and knocked three times. It wasn't long before he heard a scuffle of feet coming from the other side, and once again he was filled near to bursting with hope. There was a familiar sound of locks and bolts sliding, and the door cracked partway open. The joy that he'd felt welling up inside of himself subsided immediately, and gave way to confusion.

"Hello?" the middle-aged woman peeking cautiously through the crack in the door addressed him in a suspicious tone. "What do you want? Who are you?" Her face was gaunt, her eyes sunken. She looked tired and underfed. Her straight, black hair was thin and heavily-laced with gray. It looked greasy, like it hadn't been washed in weeks, just like her clothing, which was neglected, and smelled of mildew, but was otherwise unremarkable in every way.

"What are you doing here?" Frank asked, clearly confused.

"What am I doing here?" the woman shot back, incredulous. "I live here! What are *you* doing here?"

"Where's Vanessa?" Frank demanded, ignoring her question.

"Listen," the woman responded in an annoyed tone. "There ain't no Vanessa here. Got the wrong place. Now if you'll excuse me, I got better things to do right now."

She started to close the door, but Frank put his foot forward to block it, and forced his way into the entrance. "Where... is...

Vanessa?" he asked her again, vehemently. "What have you done with her?" He wasn't sure what he was doing or even what to think. This lady didn't look like she had anything to do with SAU, but that didn't preclude her from being involved in whatever it was that was going on here.

He had absolutely no idea what was going on, but this *was* his home. He wasn't about to believe that someone else had moved in during his absence. He hadn't been gone that long. Or maybe he had. It was hard to tell. Either way, he wasn't going to leave until he knew for certain that Vanessa wasn't there. "Vanessa!" he called out loudly. "Vanessa! Are you there?"

"Get out of here now or I'm calling the police!" the woman shrieked, one part angry, one part frightened.

"Go right ahead," Frank snarled, brushing past her. "I *am* the police!" He thought about what Munro had told him again and reminded himself that he didn't care. He *was* an officer of the law. Nothing that had happened in his absence could change that.

The light contact sent the woman scurrying to the farthest reaches of the living room in a panic. "Chuck!" she screamed at the top of her lungs, frantic. She was shaking uncontrollably and looked like she was on the verge of having a meltdown. "Chuck! Where are you? Get out here!"

Frank spared only a quick glance around the open areas as he made his way to the bedroom. When he reached the open doorway, he walked right in. Seeing nothing blatantly out of the ordinary, he proceeded to the back end of the room, where he opened the door to the walk-in closet, half-expecting to see her there. Again, he found nothing. The only truly surprising thing about that was that it wasn't a walk-in at all. It was just a regular closet of about three feet by two, and jam-packed with nightshirts, jackets, and other articles of clothing that belonged to neither of them.

"Vanessa?" he called out, shoving clothes and hangers aside and onto the floor to bang his fists against the back wall. *Maybe they've walled her in*, he thought in a moment of panic. He knew that it didn't make much sense, but none of this really did. He hammered at the wall until he heard a hollow thud, then stopped, wound his right arm up and rammed his fist right through to the other side. There was nothing waiting for him there except for some electrical wiring, a thick pad of insulation, and the sharp edge of a junction box that he managed to scrape his hand against.

He pulled his hand back to inspect the deep gouge running along the left side of his index finger, and felt more than a little foolish for it. "What am I doing?" he asked himself aloud. Maybe Vanessa's moving away in the time since he'd been taken wasn't likely. Maybe new tenants coming in and renovating everything was doubtful. But it *was* possible. For all he knew, Vanessa had moved on from this place... moved on with her life, from him. He didn't like the idea, but for all he knew, Vanessa could be SAU's prisoner. For all he knew, she could be chained up in a dark cell, cold and hungry, beaten and mutilated, or even worse: dead. Just thinking about it was difficult, but he knew that it might be true.

He didn't *want* to think about it. "These people must think I'm crazy," he whispered, backing away from the closet. "Maybe I *am* crazy." He'd rarely felt so ashamed of himself. It was time to leave, and leave quickly. He'd done enough damage here already, and he still had one more lead to explore.

He doubled back toward the doorway in a hurry. As he passed through it, he glimpsed a flash of movement from the corner of his eye and recoiled backward, narrowly avoiding the tip of the baseball bat that was swinging straight at his face. It whooshed past his nose and smashed into the framing to his left, snapping the thin plank with a loud and tinny sound.

"Brain-dead fuckin' junkies," his assailant, presumably Chuck, growled angrily, moving in to block the doorway, his aluminum bat raised like a sword. "How many times," he huffed, smashing a hole in the wall. "Do I have to tell you," he continued, swinging again and hitting nothing but air. "You want a hit, you pay." He took yet another wild swing, and this one missed by even more than the last, but managed to knock every single item off the nearby dresser. *"You rip me off, I kick your ass."* With that, he raised the bat over his head with both hands and lunged toward him.

Thinking only to protect himself, Frank raised his left arm to parry the anticipated blow. When his attacker came closer, he took one step toward him, and thrust his open right hand into his chest to halt his advance. The result was not at all what he'd expected. He'd only meant to stop him. Instead, Chuck's feet left the floor, and he was flung backward through the air with great force. He flew straight through the doorway like a rag doll, and crashed down with a loud thud eight feet farther, in the kitchen.

Frank stared down at his upturned hand with eyes that had gone wide with consternation. There were fine rivulets of blood running from the cut on his finger into his open palm, and trickling down and around his thumb and wrist, but that wasn't what concerned him. What concerned him was that he'd hardly even touched the guy. He'd just wanted to hold him off, to throw him off his guard—not knock him clear into the next room. He lifted his eyes slowly and glanced toward Chuck, who was sprawled out spread-eagled in the hall—unconscious by all appearances—and then looked down at his hand again, dumbfounded.

It defied physics, gravity. He could have stood there all day, befuddled by what had just transpired, but the sound of screaming brought him back to the reality that he had to get out of there, and quickly. He hurried out of the bedroom as quickly as he could, and headed straight for the front door, sidestepping past the fallen man as he did.

The raggedy-looking woman stood screaming wildly between the kitchen island and the L-shaped counter that ran the entire length of the back wall. The butcher knife she had pointed up at him vacillated from side to side, and shook with the rest of her. She might have looked threatening if not for the obvious difficulty she was having just trying to keep the knife steady. She looked like she might drop it on her own feet at any second.

As he closed the final distance between himself and the door, he couldn't help but notice two things about her. First, she had the windpipe of an opera singer. He could easily picture glasses shattering in the cupboards as they succumbed to her shrill, high-pitched wailing. Second, he couldn't remember the last time he'd seen someone so frightened.

Her eyes were stretched wide open and bulging with horror, her orbits so large she almost looked like she'd put her finger in an electrical socket. And why wouldn't she? A strange man in prison pajamas had forced his way into her home and thrown her friend, or husband, or whatever he was to her halfway across the room, and with very little effort. He couldn't blame her for being frightened. It was a frightening situation—a situation he'd created. He had no business being there.

He rushed out into the hall and sprinted toward the elevator, not out of fear—he seriously doubted a dealer would call the cops over something like this—but out of a sense of urgency. He *had* to find Vanessa, and fast. He was running out of options, which had to mean that he'd be with her again soon. Or so he hoped. The elevator cab was waiting for him when he got there, and if that wasn't convenient enough, the door was already open, too. He ducked inside and hit the button for the ground floor.

The door slid closed with a low rumble and a clack, and the cab jolted before starting its slow descent. It wasn't long before he'd wished he'd taken the stairs. He hadn't noticed it on his way up, but there was a faint, downtempo jazz piece playing in the background. In the song—if it could even really be called that—a man with a warm, bass-baritone voice was crooning a series of seemingly random doos, dees and das over a track that sounded like it had been composed for the sole purpose of driving him mad.

The cab stopped on the fourteenth floor, the door opened, and a frail old woman with a curved cane got on. She was wearing a baggy, short-sleeved muumuu with a flower motif: lemon peel yellow against a swirling backdrop of white and bright blue. Her oversized granny sunglasses had elongated edges that curled at the top and pointed up and outward. Scraggly tufts of white hair hung out from the sides of her wide-brimmed visor cap. A pudgy-looking dog poked its head out from her purse and glared up at him intently. "Seymour," the old woman chided him lovingly. "You know it isn't polite to stare. Where are your manners?"

The background music came to a sudden end as the elevator door closed again. "That, gentlefolk," an irritatingly eager voice announced, and he realized they were listening to the radio, "was Johnny Bellows singing his number one hit single, *Doo-dee-dah-dee-doos.* If you're in the mood for more groovy listening, just stay tuned to 106.4, *The Elevator*—all elevator music, all day long—but first, this message from our sponsor."

A cymbal crashed and trumpets blared. "Tired of that same old, generic, supermarket sody pop?" a man with a deep, gooey voice bellowed out overenthusiastically. It seemed to be the only tone his vocal chords could emit. "Bored of that bland taste and the way it leaves your mouth feeling dry, dry, dry? Then pick up a can of Cuda Cola today and *taste* the ocean!"

"It's made with one hundred percent *real* fish enzymes," a female voice whispered loudly and in a way that suggested that this was somehow supposed to make it better.

"What the fuck," Frank mouthed silently. Was any of this for real? He felt like he'd just stepped into an episode of the *Midnight Whispers.* Luckily for him, the elevator had descended all the way to ground level without stopping again. The door opened and he got out just as "Doo-dee-dah-dee-doos" started airing again for a second time in a row.

He wasted little time as he exited the building. The thought that he might soon be with Vanessa again pressed his step. The strip mall across the street had a payphone in its parking lot, and he started walking toward it as soon as the street was clear.

He didn't remember the strip mall being there before. As a matter of fact, he remembered there being four or five different stores set up in that exact same location. Off the top of his head, there had been a Jolter juice bar, a Taig's Tools, a Hedwig's Pawn Shop, a moneylender's office, as well as a butcher shop with a big, red sign out front that simply read "MEAT" in bold, white letters, that sold nothing but prewrapped meat that was processed and particularly suspect. Above them had been several levels of low-income housing, but all of that was gone now, replaced. The new unit was joined, and its stores were spread out over multiple levels. Just like the changed businesses he'd spotted on his way home, he dismissed it as the result of a competitive economy.

As he walked up to the payphone, he fished around in his shirt pocket, and pulled out what remained of the money Falstaff had given him. He unfolded the small stack and flipped through it until he found the smallest denomination, one taler. He folded the rest of the cash again and tucked it back into his pocket, then picked up the receiver with his left hand. With his right, he introduced the edge of the bill to a slot on the front of the payphone.

About a second later, there was a low whirring sound and the payphone sucked the bill in like a vacuum cleaner. "One hundred pfennigs credited," a prerecorded female voice announced in a mechanical way. "Please dial your number." His hundred pfennigs appeared on the digital display that covered the top half of the payphone, just beside the time of day, the date, and the message, "Thank you for using Innercom networks. Have a nice day!"

He punched in the number for Vanessa's parents' house and waited. The ringback tone buzzed a few times but no one picked up. Instead, he was transferred over to a voice messaging system. "You've reached the answering machine of Larry, Darryl and Darryl," a tired-sounding voice drawled out slowly. Maybe it was just his imagination, but Larry, or Darryl, or the other Darryl, really sounded like he'd gone to town with the liquor cabinet. "We're not home right now," the voice further explained, "so leave us a message and we'll get back to you in a jiffy." A loud beep signaled the end of the recording.

"Now that's just bizarre," Frank breathed, more than a little confused. He checked the number on the display to ensure that he'd dialed the right one, and found that he had. He didn't know why they would, but maybe they'd changed their number.

He held the phone to his shoulder and pressed down on the switchhook to cut the line. "Seventy-five pfennigs remaining," the prerecorded voice droned out.

"Directory," he uttered, clearly and slowly, pronouncing each syllable distinctly. The display changed suddenly to a simple, green on black, alphabetical listing. He navigated through the familiar touch screen index and scrolled down, but couldn't find Vanessa *or* her parents anywhere. Puzzled, he looked up his own parents, but came up with nothing. Even his own name was absent from the directory listing.

After a moment of hesitation, he decided to look up the Law Enforcement Agency. Normally, he'd contact dispatch with his communications band, but he was currently without one. He was so used to relying on it that he couldn't even remember what the phone number for headquarters was. When the results came back, he scrolled through them until he found the entry for the Plaza district precinct. Maybe Andy could tell him what was going on. He wasn't sure why he would know any more about any of this than he did, but he didn't know who else to call. Maybe they'd been erased from the system, he considered. But why? The more he thought of it, the more it worried him.

He tried to put the thought out of his mind and pressed the tip of his finger to the entry for his precinct. He left it there until another screen popped up. This one displayed the precinct's address. He pressed the telephone icon in the top-right corner of the new screen, and to his surprise, the line connected almost instantly.

"Innerstadt Law Enforcement Agency," a gruff-sounding man yawned. "Plaza district."

"Hey," Frank breathed. "Could you please patch me through to Andrew Gilroy?"

"Andrew *who?*" the operator asked, evidently confused.

"Gilroy," Frank repeated, *almost* as slowly as he had for the payphone's automated voice response system.

"Yeah, that's what I thought you said," the operator responded matter-of-factly, "but there ain't no Andrew Gilroy here. Not in this precinct, anyway. Sorry, pal."

Frank furrowed his brow and remained silent for a moment. "Well, could you check the global directory?" he asked, fighting hard to keep any anxiety from his voice. *Maybe he's been deployed elsewhere*, he thought. *Or maybe this guy's new and doesn't know what he's talking about.* He couldn't say that he recognized his voice.

The operator sighed loudly and the line went silent for about ten seconds. "G-I-L-R-O-Y?" he asked, sounding mildly annoyed as he spelled it out.

"Yeah," Frank answered plainly. There was a brief spurt of typing on the other end of the line, followed by a painfully loud clack of the return key.

"Let's see," the operator mumbled. "We've got a Barnabas Gilroy in the Barrios, and a Terrence Gilroy up in Portsmuth. But no Andrew. Sorry." He didn't sound very apologetic.

Frank felt a knot forming in the pit of his stomach. Despite his best efforts to remain calm, his voice was shaky as he asked, "Could I speak with Captain Leonard Boston then?" The guy had essentially sold him down the river, but he couldn't have known about all that other shit that would happen afterward, could he? It wasn't likely. Letting him know that he was still alive probably wasn't the best idea he'd ever had, but good ideas were in short supply, and he wasn't sure what else he could do.

"Listen here, buddy," the operator barked. "I don't know what your problem is, but I've got better things to do than sit here and take prank calls from douchebags like you." There was a brief silence then, followed by the sound of muttered profanity, and something else Frank couldn't quite make out. "Leonard Boston," the man added at a grumble. "Doesn't even sound like a real name."

And then there was an audible clack, and the line went dead as the operator hung up on him.

Frank returned the phone to the hook and let his shoulders sag. "Twenty-five pfennigs remaining," the payphone reminded him. He furrowed his brow and glared at the display fixedly, and not just because it cost twice as much to call the police as it did to make any other call. He just didn't know what to think.

He navigated back to the main directory and tried looking up some of his colleagues, his relatives, anyone that he could think of, but found nothing. He'd been standing there in dazed silence for almost a full minute when a flash from one of his old, recurring dreams came to him. "Tom Tamlin," he whispered cautiously, almost afraid to say the name out loud.

Thomas Tamlin was one of the supporting cast members in his recurring dreams. He was one of Daniel's friends, or rather one of Daniel's brother's friends. If his memory served, he was also one of the only characters that hadn't been cut from the miniseries in his mind by way of a horribly gruesome death. He couldn't believe he was actually considering looking him up. He didn't even want to think about the implications that finding him would have.

He stood there staring blankly at the phone until it reminded him of his twenty-five remaining pfennigs for about the fifteenth time. "Fuck it," he finally muttered, then scrolled through to the names that started with tee. A sense of dread seized him as he stopped on a listing for "Tamlin, Thomas".

He hesitated for what seemed like an eternity, then finally brought the phone up to his ear. Licking his lips nervously, he pressed the green telephone icon beside Tom's name and waited, breathless. There was a brief series of bleeps and bloops as the payphone dialed the number for him, followed by an audible buzz that signaled that the phone at the other end of the line was ringing. The ringback tone went off at least a dozen times—it was hard to keep track over the sound of his heart beating in his ears. He was about to hang up when someone finally answered.

"Hello?" a man answered with a yawn.

Frank remained silent for a few seconds, unsure what to say.

"Hello?" the man repeated, annoyed. "Who is this?"

Frank took a deep breath, gripping the phone tightly. "Daniel MacBride," he finally whispered, uttering the first thing that came to mind. He didn't mean to speak so softly, but his words seemed to lose all strength upon leaving his mouth.

His whisper was met with an intense moment of glaring silence, until the man broke it, and with more than just a hint of animosity in his voice. "What did you just say?"

Frank was almost certain that the guy had understood him, but he repeated himself nonetheless, reflexively. "Daniel MacBride," he said, his voice quavering halfway through. Saying that name out loud felt wrong. All of this felt wrong. He couldn't even begin to describe the feelings of anguish weighing down on him.

"Where did you get my phone number?" the voice at the other end of the line demanded. If the man had been sleepy earlier, he certainly wasn't now. He was indisputably livid. "I said, 'How did you get this number,' fuck nuts?"

Daniel MacBride had been taken into custody and enrolled in some kind of secret government program when he was still just a child, Frank remembered Doctor Munro telling him. As far as anyone who'd known him was concerned, he'd died and had been buried a long time ago. The more he thought of Daniel as an actual person, the more he thought of *himself* as Daniel, and the more disoriented it made him feel.

The man at the other end of the line—*Tom*, Frank struggled to accept—was outright screaming something now, but he wasn't really listening to his words anymore. A rush of overwhelming emotion had washed over him like a tidal wave, and everything else seemed drowned out, distant. None of it had been real. His father. His mother. The academy. They were all just figments of his imagination, or "elements of the common dream", as Doctor Munro might have put it.

He let the phone fall from his hand and dropped to his knees. The phone twirled slowly as it dangled on its cord before him. His entire world had just come crashing down. He tried to rise to his feet, but couldn't find the strength or the motivation to. His friends, his dreams, his aspirations, his family, Vanessa; they were gone— all of them. Even worse, they'd never *been*.

"Vanessa," he groaned achingly, his eyes welling with tears that would not fall. If any of it could be real, if he could choose just one thing out of all the others, it would be her. There wasn't a shadow of a doubt in his mind about that. But he *couldn't* choose and she'd *never* been real.

I'll never see her again, he thought, though deep down, he knew that he'd never even seen her to begin with. How could he have seen what wasn't there? But she *was* there. In his heart and in his mind she was, at least. There, she was always present, and as real as anything. He imagined this was what being a schizophrenic with prevalent visual hallucinations might feel like.

He set his palms down on the sidewalk to steady himself, and brace against the imminent meltdown, but still, his tears would not come. His entire body heaved as he stifled a sudden urge to cry out in agony. He felt like he was on the verge of bawling. The more he fought it, the higher the pressure rose in his chest, and the more spasmodically his body reacted.

There were people all around him. Most of them ignored his presence, or pretended not to see him, but a few actually stopped for a second to sneak a curious glance at him before continuing on their way. He knew what it must look like to them, but he'd stopped caring the second he'd lost control. He'd lost control the second he'd lost her.

He'd never been the suicidal sort—in fact, he'd always had an excellent survival instinct—but in that moment, he felt like dying. Without Vanessa, he felt like the empty shell of a man, like all the joy had been sucked out of life. It was a gray and dull landscape devoid of light that he'd woken to, and ending it all now seemed like the logical conclusion to everything that had transpired. But he wouldn't go down that path. He *couldn't* go down that path.

He couldn't understand why he'd even want to cling to this meaningless existence, but he did, and he *knew* that he would. He had to. He searched the depths of his soul for a reason why, and came up empty-handed, but it changed nothing. It was like there was something hardwired inside of him, a natural drive that kept him from just giving up on life altogether.

Somewhere in all of his deep reflections, he'd regained control. Finally finding the resolve to push himself to his feet, he stood, and took a contemplative look around himself. *The 'real world'*, he thought. He wished he'd never woken to it. He wished he'd never woken from the dream that had been his life. He could have kept dreaming that dream, happily and until the day he died.

As he was brushing himself off, a flyer peeled off from the wall of a nearby building, and carried by a small gust of wind, it came to rest at his feet. He peered down at it with only partial interest, then took another quick look around, and noticed there were similar posters plastered sparsely all the way up the street, and as far as the eye could see.

He knelt and picked the flyer up. Though he'd lost almost all interest in the world around him, what he found on it still managed to intrigue him.

The word "CAUTION" was written across the top portion of the flyer in large, bold lettering. In a smaller font beneath that was the message, "The following individuals have been identified as members of the 'Awoken' group of terrorists. If sighted, please contact law enforcement immediately. All suspects are considered armed and dangerous, and are to be avoided at all costs. Aiding and abetting criminals is punishable by law."

Beneath that were photos of some very familiar faces along with captions of their names. Edward Munro, Jerg Weissinger, Alexander Falstaff—the whole "gang" was there. So much for the Commission of Higher Sciences not getting the police involved.

He finally understood why Hildebrandt went by "J.J.", and refused to give out the meaning of those initials. "James *Jalbert*," he said aloud as he read it. He might have laughed had the situation been less serious, but all he could muster was moderate disbelief. What kind of parents would name their son Jalbert, he wondered.

When he looked up again, he noticed someone walking in his direction. It was a tall man with an impressive build. He wore a loose hoodie that was drawn partway across his face, and was looking down at the sidewalk so intently, it was a wonder he could even tell where he was going.

"You look like shit," the hooded figure said, stopping directly in front of him. He pulled his hood back to reveal his face, then let it settle back into its drooping position. It was Alexander. "Are you okay?" he asked, his voice tinged with concern.

"Alex," Frank breathed in surprise. He hadn't expected to see him so soon, or even at all, really. "Did you see all that?" he asked him, mildly embarrassed. He was, of course, referring to the display that he'd just put on—alongside a fairly busy street, and in broad daylight, no less. His eyes were bloodshot and weary, and he knew it all too well. They tingled uncomfortably.

"I did," Alexander answered plainly, "but don't worry about it. It's a lot to take in, I know. I can't fault you for being shocked, but that kind of thing draws a crowd." He stopped and looked around then, and noted that more than just a few stragglers were openly ogling them. "I wanted to get to you faster," he added, glancing at the poster in Frank's hand, "but as you've probably guessed, it's kind of hard for me to get around right now."

"What's up with this bullshit, anyway?" Frank asked, both anxious about the implications of such a thing, and relieved by the quick change of topic.

"Not so loud," Alexander warned, then snatched the poster up and tucked it away in the front pouch of his hoodie. "We can talk about this elsewhere. I *really* can't be seen right now." He turned around then and started walking back the way he'd come.

Frank hesitated briefly and followed after him. They travelled almost two full blocks up the street before Alexander crossed it and got into the driver's side seat of a plain-looking gray van. For the first time since "waking", he noticed that all the vehicles he'd seen so far had *wheels*. All of them without exception.

He didn't make a case of it, but instead got into the passenger side of the van and waited wordlessly. It *was* strange, though. He hadn't seen a single hovercraft in this "real world" yet, and he was used to seeing them everywhere, every day. He supposed it was just one more thing he was going to have to get used to in a seemingly interminable list of oddities he'd noticed so far.

Alexander pulled the slightly crumpled flyer out of his front pouch, snapped it out at its edges to straighten it, and looked it over. "I was just as surprised as you were when I heard them say my name and 'terrorist' in the same sentence on the radio," he said, then shook his head and tapped at his photo with his index finger. "Bastards got that from my ID badge at the Commission."

"Shit," Frank breathed, furrowing his brow. "So you don't know what any of this is about either."

"Oh, I'm pretty sure I do," Alexander answered, "but I never thought something like this could happen to me—or to anyone, really. It's got me questioning all kinds of things, all kinds of things I thought I knew about our government. I've been reassessing everything. And it's got me worried, Frank, worried about my family. I've never been this worried before."

"You think the government did this to get to you?" Frank asked, glancing over at him as he did.

"I *know* that the government did this to get to me," Alexander answered. "And to Munro, and to Weissinger, and to everyone else on that poster. That's obvious. But it's not us they want. It's you they're after. They want to use us to get to you." He set his hands down on the top of the steering wheel then and stared at the back of his hands. "The Commission couldn't have gone to the police just because you went missing. The rehabilitation program is top secret. No one's supposed to know about it except for the president himself, certain MIW officials, and authorized personnel at the Commission. I mean... most of the police force wouldn't even be cleared to know about the Commission itself." He pushed off from the steering wheel then, and sagged back against his seat. "No, I'm almost sure someone over at MIW pulled some strings to have us put on the terror watch list. That way, if the police pick us up, we wind up right back at the Commission."

"You wind up right back at the Commission?" Frank asked, clearly not following.

"Yeah," Alexander answered, "that's where terrorists end up, along with all sorts of other scum, just like Doctor Munro told you. They get shipped to the Commission for insertion into the common dream, to get recycled. If they managed to get us back there, they could interrogate us, and eventually find out where you are. At least I think that's the idea, and it would probably work, if we didn't all die in the process. Cops aren't too lenient with terrorist dirt bags, but odds are at least one of us would survive, and that's all they'd need: just one. They've got ways of making people talk."

"Why go to all that trouble?" Frank asked, baffled.

"You mean aside from the fact that the Commission's very existence is a well-guarded secret?" Alexander stated more than asked. "I guess they have something to hide."

"Well that's specific," Frank remarked with a smirk.

"Look at it this way," Alexander said after a brief moment of hesitation. "If the Commission's cover is blown, and everyone finds out that they've been brainwashing criminals, and recycling them into officers of the law, there might be repercussions for the president, sure, but he'd probably bounce right back from that. I think it's pretty fair to assume that most people dislike thieves, murderers and rapists. Excluding the most hardcore human rights activists, I think that the general population might actually come to appreciate an idea like that one. If, however, the people found out that *children* had been used in this project, they'd probably break out the torches and pitchforks."

"All this over little old me," Frank noted idly. He found that idea really hard to swallow.

"All this over little old you?" Alexander asked pointedly. "Frank, listen. You got a bum deal—a really bum deal—and if you ask me, that's enough to shake the hornet's nest all on its own. But this is about much more than just you now... much, much more. Believe me."

"What do you mean?" Frank asked, arching his brow. "I'm not the only one this happened to? I thought my insertion was supposed to be borderline accidental... an act of 'pity'."

"It *was*, Frank," Alexander responded calmly, "but did you really think that you were the only one? I've seen the records. They did this to all kinds of kids in the beginning. There was a lot of so-called 'collateral damage', as they put it... a lot of accidents, and a lot of freebie test subjects in need of their so-called pity. Your friend Andrew?" he asked precipitously. "He's the *Eighty-Four* to your *Sixty-Seven*, and it wasn't just the two of you. No way. Sometimes I can't help but wonder if they were *targeting* children on purpose. This happened to *hundreds* of kids after you, Frank, maybe even thousands. The First Gen, I've heard some people call them."

Frank's thoughts went to Andrew then. Somehow, he'd almost managed to forget about his friend in all of this. He'd been so caught up with everything else, he'd spent so much time and energy worrying about Vanessa, that there was little room left to worry about anything else. But she wasn't *real*. He had to keep reminding himself of that. He hated admitting it, even just to himself. He didn't know how he was going to cope with that, or if he ever could, but she was gone now, or rather *never was*. Andrew, on the other hand, was very real, very tangible, and floating in stasis in a vat somewhere, dreaming his life away, locked up in a secret government research facility.

Even though his own waking had been a bitter one, the idea of his friend rotting away like that revolted him. Would Andrew be just as jolted by the truth as he had? He assumed that he would. Though he didn't feel the decision was his to make, he couldn't bear the thought of his friend being terminated in his sleep, either. "How hard would it be to break into the Commission's compound?" he asked, breaking from a spell of deep contemplation. "What kind of security does it have?"

"I know what you're thinking," Alexander responded, "and I can't say I blame you, but you can forget about it right now. I hate to be the one to break it to you, but it's impossible. Even if we forget about the small army of elite sentinels, we're wanted by the police. We're their top priority. I'm not saying we won't try *ever*, but we need to keep a low profile right now. Besides, the Commission will be on full alert now and expecting it."

"That reminds me," Frank breathed, trailing off momentarily. "How did you even find me? More importantly, why didn't you turn back when you found out that you were wanted by the police? Why take that risk? I appreciate it and everything—really, I do— but are you stupid? They know what your face looks like, Alex."

"I didn't have to find you," Alexander answered, grinning weakly. "I've been watching you ever since you left, but let's just say that I have my ways and leave it at that for now, okay?" He scratched the side of his head then and made an uneasy-looking face as he struggled to find his words. "As for my reasons why," he finally added, trailing off again, though only for a moment, "well, I couldn't have left you alone right now. Not with a clear conscience. I knew that it was going to hit you hard, once the anger passed and reality sunk in."

Frank opened his mouth to say something, but soon realized that he didn't have anything to say. Instead, he remained silent and listened carefully.

"Frank, I'm not even going to pretend that I understand what you're going through right now," Alexander admitted, "but just thinking about it, just imagining the same thing happening to me, it makes me feel sick to my stomach. To just wake up one day and realize that my wife and my kids are gone, that they were never there, that they were nothing but a dream... I don't even want to think about it. I mean... just before I got to you, you looked like you were about to jump headlong into traffic."

"Oh, I'd thought about it," Frank confided, "and now that you bring it up again..." Noticing the captain's concern, he set to putting him at ease. "I'm not going to do that," he added. "I couldn't if I wanted to."

"Well, there's a really good chance you would have come out okay even if you'd tried," Alexander noted, "but I'm glad you didn't. You have friends, Frank. Even if you feel alone, you do—friends that want to help you. *I* want to help you, and that's why I'm here. You left real fast earlier this morning, but we owe you more answers than we've given you. There are things you should know about yourself... about what was done to you. If you come back with me now, I can promise you I'll keep an eye on Doctor Weissinger. He won't ever hurt you again. Not on my watch."

"Oh, you owe me answers all right," Frank stated. He was thinking back to the incident in the apartment building. There was something extremely unnatural about what had happened there, something awesome, and exhilarating, and terrifying all at once. He needed to know what they'd done to him, and what other surprises he might expect. He needed answers, but those answers would have to wait. Going back now was completely out of the question.

"Listen," he added, "I'd love to know what the Commission did to me, but I'm going to have to take a rain check on that for now. I can't come back with you."

"But Frank," Alexander protested emphatically. "It's crucial that you speak with Munro, even if it's only for a few minutes."

"Don't take this the wrong way," Frank forewarned. "I appreciate you looking out for me. Really, I do. But how would I be any safer with you? You said it yourself: the Commission is using you to get to me. As far as I know, no one even knows what I look like. But you, on the other hand... your faces are probably posted all over the city by now. There are warnings about you on the radio. Forgive my caution, but I don't see how going with you could be a good idea right now. I just can't do it. Not under the current circumstances, I can't."

"You're right," Alexander sighed. "I guess. At least in part, you are. Being seen together in public couldn't be good for you. It's actually pretty dangerous. But you need to keep two things in mind. First, Doctor Munro's laboratories are off the grid. They don't know where it is. His compound is one of the safest places you could be right now. Second, the police might not know what you look like yet, but if you're not careful, you *will* end up drawing their attention. You need to understand yourself if you want to have a chance at surviving, if you want to avoid bringing the entire government down on your head."

"I get it," Frank responded plainly, "but there's no way I'm going back with you. Nothing you could say right now would change my mind. I see what you're getting at. Really, I do. But if going my own way is a risk, it's a risk I'm going to have to take. I've got more important things to do right now."

"What could be more important than this?" Alexander asked. He didn't sound like he expected an answer.

"Figuring out who I am, for one," Frank answered. "If that's even possible at this point."

"Okay," Alexander sighed. "All right. I get it. I won't bring it up again. But I want you to call me if you need anything, okay? Anything at all."

"Thanks," Frank replied, putting his hand on the door handle. "I guess this is goodbye then, or see you later."

"At least let me drop you off somewhere?" Alexander pleaded. He didn't look like he was going to take no for an answer. "I mean... you're on foot, man. Where you headed?"

"I'm going to visit an old 'family friend'," Frank responded plainly. "You can drop me off nearby if you want." If he was ever going to understand who he was, he was going to have to piece his past together bit by bit. He didn't have very many leads, but Tom Tamlin was as good of a place to start as any. He just hoped that he wasn't as hostile in person as he was over the phone.

The End
of the First Book of
Apokalypse

ACKNOWLEDGMENT

I'd like to take this opportunity to thank Julie Bergeron for being the first to read this book, and for helping me to change Vanessa into more of a girlfriend and less of a raging bitch.

I'd also like to thank Nick Wise, Eric Lauzon, Johanne Coucke, Janice Young, Kevin Kit, Sylvie Portelance, and all of my other beta readers for their feedback, and for the constructive criticism that they provided when I felt I needed it most. Your opinions, suggestions and questions were truly appreciated. I can't say that enough. From the bottom of my heart: thank you.

Last but not least, I'd like to thank Javier Carrera Gomez for his amazing chapter icons, Phu Thieu for the incredible art on this book's cover, and Maria "Renflowergrapx" Gandolfo for her beautiful map of Innerstadt.

GLOSSARY

Academy, The: The police training school all cadets must attend and graduate from before being drafted into the Law Enforcement Agency. It offers an array of specializations that may help secure starting positions at a higher rank or in expert branches such as SWAT, but mastering the base curriculum remains the minimum requirement for graduation. Many of the tactical and combat textbooks used by the academy were written by ex-Commander Jerg Weissinger, and though he has long left the force, he is still revered by many as a sort of demigod on campus.

Awoken, The: According to the government, a group of violent terrorists hell-bent on bringing the current regime to its knees. They claim that, contrary to government doctrine, life beyond the city walls is viable, that the people of Innerstadt have been imprisoned in order to better control them. As the media put it, they fancy themselves liberators and will stop at nothing in their pursuit of freedom, often putting the lives of innocents in harm's way as they spread their destructive message of salvation. Their successful attacks and a high cost in both police and civilian lives have made their eradication the government's top priority.

Baumgartner: Lieutenant Corporal and sentinel at the Commission of Higher Sciences. Following his once commander Weissinger, he helped liberate subject Zero Sixty-Seven. A rampant addict, he'll use whatever he can get his hands on, be it illicit or a powerful pharmaceutical.

Barringer Mark II: Semiautomatic .44 caliber pistol. Though considered outdated by most servicemen, it's a well-balanced sidearm with respect to range and precision, and is still manufactured specifically for the Law Enforcement Agency in limited quantities.

Bedford, Roger: Law Enforcement Agency sergeant serving under Captain Leonard Boston. Participated in the takedown that brought Frank William Fasaro into police custody.

Bertha: The name that Salomon Grundy gave to the old combustion engine motorcycle he repaired for Frank when Special Assignments trashed his hoverbike. Dating back to the old world, it truly is ancient, but it runs extremely well for an antique. It has a flame paint job, and the words "Blitz Racing" printed on it hint at its make and model.

Caldwell, James: Commissioner of the Law Enforcement Agency.

Caldwell, Oliver: Law Enforcement Agency Lieutenant serving under Captain Leonard Boston. Participated as a spotter in the takedown that brought Frank William Fasaro into police custody. No known relation to Commissioner Caldwell.

Cantelli, Leroy: Corporal in the Special Assignments Unit.

Chez Joignon: Ritzy French restaurant just off the Red Light district. It caters to the city's crème de la crème.

Circle of Aspirants: Collaborators and potential recruits of the Awoken terrorist organization. They carry out a multitude of tasks handed down to them in hopes of currying sufficient favor to be promoted to full-fledged members. The jobs they do are often of the dirty variety. No assistance is provided by the Awoken should things should go south.

Commission of Higher Sciences: Top secret ministry mandated with the research and development of tools, technology and arms intended for government use.

Dubuc (Dybuk), Jean-Pierre: Headwaiter at Chez Joignon. Recruit aspirant of the Awoken terrorist organization.

Falstaff, Alexander: Captain and sentinel at the Commission of Higher Sciences. He reported directly to Jerg Weissinger until

Commissioner Richardson had the commander transferred out of his position. Convinced by his old commander, he decided to go rogue and helped spring subject Zero Sixty-Seven free.

Fasaro, Gordon: Adoptive father of Frank William Fasaro. He was a police officer in his youth, like his father before him.

Fasaro, Magda: Adoptive mother of Frank William Fasaro.

Fasaro, William Bernhardt: Frank William Fasaro's grandfather and his namesake. He served the Law Enforcement Agency loyally his entire adult life. His sidearm, a Barringer Mark II, has been handed down as a sort of family heirloom.

Gilroy, Andrew: Childhood friend of Frank William Fasaro. They grew up together, went to the academy together, and served together in the Law Enforcement Agency's Plaza district precinct.

Giuterrez, Jimeno: A Master in the Awoken terrorist organization.

Grimm, John (Havoc): A Master in the Awoken terrorist organization.

Griswold Thurman High School: One of the oldest schools in Innerstadt. Located in Langdon, it was named after President Griswold Thurman one year after his death, nearly two-hundred years ago. The president had held his tenure for nearly thirty years.

Grundy, Salomon: Mechanic in the Law Enforcement Agency's Mechanic Corps. He managed to get an old combustion engine motorcycle running for Frank when Special Assignments borrowed his hoverbike and returned it completely destroyed.

Hawthorne, Bors: Right-wing populist president of the United Americas. Purportedly responsible for the nuclear war that ravaged the earth several hundred years before the events of this book.

Hildebrandt, James Jalbert ("J.J."): Sergeant and sentinel reporting to Captain Falstaff at the Commission of Higher Sciences. Assisted in the liberation of subject Zero Sixty-Seven.

Inquisitor: Special Assignments Unit officers tasked with the interrogation of prisoners and the extraction of.

Janssen, Hiro: Former Starke Note Meister of the Law Enforcement Agency. He was banned from practice for refusing to come out of retirement at the employer's request.

Johnson, Kevin (Kay Jay): Special Assignments Unit Inquisitor. Calm, cruel and usually effective, he uses his mastery of pain to extract information from suspected Awoken.

Gostobalis, Tom: Law Enforcement Agency officer serving under the command of Captain Leonard Boston. He's a friend and colleague of Frank William Fasaro.

Grand Anarch, The: Fabled leader of the Awoken terrorist organization. Though few are those who claim to have actually seen him, it's rumored he's the one pulling all the strings and calling all the shots.

Kight, David: Lead on psionics at the Commission of Higher Sciences. He's a sharp scientist that catches on quickly. Sometimes he seems to get lost in thought rather easily, but his colleagues know that this usually means he's cooking up some genius idea.

Kluga, Walter: Special Assignments Unit officer.

Langsarks, Emril: Emissary of the Ministry of Inner Workings dispatched to the Commission of Higher Sciences. Though few know his intentions or the extent of his plans for the Commission, his first order of business upon arrival was the termination of subject Zero Sixty-Seven. His jet black within black eyes and the wiring visible just beneath the skin on both sides of his head suggest heavily of cybernetic augmentation.

Law Enforcement Agency (LEA, "Leah"): Innerstadt's police force. They fight crime and keep the civilian population safe. With a low tolerance for criminality and flexible discretionary powers, the LEA acts as both judge and executioner.

MacBride, Daniel: True identity of Frank William Fasaro.

MacBride, Elizabeth: Mother of Daniel MacBride. Not much is known about her, but dreams suggest she died running from the Law Enforcement Agency's Mech Units in an attempt to save her son's life.

MacBride, Harrold: Father of Daniel MacBride. Not much is known about him, but dreams suggest he went on resource gathering expeditions outside the city walls, and that he died holding off the Law Enforcement Agency's Mech Units while his wife and son tried to escape.

Masters, The: Top brass of the Awoken terrorist organization.

Mechanic Corps: Branch of the Law Enforcement Agency tasked primarily with repairing vehicles in the police fleet, and to a certain extent, with maintaining, repairing or improving other equipment utilized by the force.

Mech Unit: Vaguely humanoid androids used by the Law Enforcement Agency in their fight against crime.

Ministry of Inner Workings (MIW, "Miew"): The Ministry is a central agency, and a liaison between all government agencies and departments. Providing departments with direction in order to optimize governmental efficiency, and reporting directly to the president of Innerstadt himself, in a certain sense, they hold the reins of power. They have the authority to set policy, reallocate budgets and realign departmental priorities.

Mosley, Fred: Corporal and sentinel at the Commission of Higher Sciences. Following his once commander Weissinger, he helped liberate subject Zero Sixty-Seven.

Munro, Edward: Scientist at the Commission of Higher Sciences. Edward worked on the Commission's Rehabilitation Program for over twenty years, ever since its inception. He has a keen interest in Sixty-Seven, his first subject, and will do everything in his power to ensure his safety.

Plattz, Ludovic: Lead on cellular engineering research at the Commission of Higher Sciences. A brilliant man with a keen eye for observation. He often spaces out or goes off on wild tangents that are completely irrelevant to the matter being discussed.

Richardson, Stephanie: Commissioner of Higher sciences. Though many of her underlings see her as little more than an empty suit, Commissioner Richardson is an astute businesswoman and seasoned professional with statesmanlike qualities. Though firm, she is also fair. She continuously strives to achieve the Commission's mandates while juggling to keep the eccentric band of scientists under her command motivated.

Special Assignments Unit (SAU, "Saw"): Historically, an elite branch of the Law Enforcement Agency utilized in missions involving greater than usual risk, such as high-profile kidnappings, bank robberies and terrorism. In recent decades, SAU has acted more as a military organization than a police force. Traditional SWAT teams have taken over these responsibilities. SAU's ranks are broken into groupuscules that operate together or alone toward the ultimate goal of taking down The Awoken. While no longer an official branch of the Law Enforcement Agency, they still operate under the same banner, and their mandate gives them the authority to handpick their recruits from the LEA's roster, and requisition whatever equipment they may need. Prime qualities of a SAU officer are resilience, loyalty and aggression. A full-fledged agent must be willing to follow orders without a second thought, no matter what those orders are.

Starke Note: Martial arts fighting style employed by the Law Enforcement Agency. Starke Note's techniques were developed around the principle of manipulating an opponent's strength against itself, destabilizing it before striking hard, if it cannot be dispatched immediately. Practitioners of the art aim to kill or neutralize an opponent as quickly as possible, while factoring in and reducing risk to their person. It uses a ranking system graded in Machts. New practitioners start as Novitiates at Macht 1, and only the most accomplished fighters attain Paramount at Macht 18. The expert and grand teacher of the discipline is referred to as the Meister.

Street Sentinel: Mech Unit widely used by the Law Enforcement Agency. Heavily armed and armored, these hulking behemoths patrol the city's streets regularly. Though formidable tools in combat, their fear factor alone acts as a powerful deterrent.

Urban Infiltrator: Mech Unit that has seen limited use by the Law Enforcement Agency. Though much smaller and less heavily armored than the Street Sentinels used for regular street patrols, the Infiltrator remains a force to be reckoned with. It is more mobile than its heavier counterparts, and can more easily access tighter areas.

Van der Veen, Sigur: The president of Innerstadt.

Watchers, The: High ranking members of the Awoken terror group. They serve the Masters directly as their eyes and ears, bodyguards and assassins. They are ruthless and kill without remorse. Other members of the Awoken fear them, and harming them is forbidden, even for the Masters. Only the Grand Anarch himself may take the life of a Watcher without retribution. Anyone else who dares raise their hand against them is put down swiftly.

Weissinger, Jerg: Chief of security at the Commission of Higher sciences. His earlier career in law enforcement saw him advance from the rank of Investigator to that of Head of Tactical Operations, culminating his years of service as Head of Criminal Psychology. He wrote several volumes on combat tactics, and many of them are still used as part of the Academy's current curriculum.

ABOUT THE AUTHOR

Michel Provost was born in 1980 in Woodstock, New-Brunswick. His family migrated to western Quebec when he was four and he still lives there with his son, Lugh, in an old shack in the woods. About halfway through high school, he decided to tack "Logue" onto his surname as he didn't think it was fair that his mother's maiden name should be forgotten to time.

Having benefited from an entirely French education, he developed his English reading and writing skills through careful observation. He started writing *THE REHAB* in 1999, when he was just nineteen years old, though the book was called *FRANKY THE ANGEL* back then, and was written in a quicker pace. Life happened and the book was put on the back burner until a couple years ago, when he decided there'd never be a better time to finish what he'd started—during his long daily commutes on the city bus. Among other things, he enjoys playing hockey, spending time goofing around with his son or just whittling the hours away with a good video game. He hopes that you enjoyed reading this book as much as he enjoyed writing it, as he plans on adding a slew of installments to the *APOKALYPSE* series.

He also hates editing with a passion, and after poring over this book more times than he can remember, has a newfound respect for anyone with the patience to do so professionally. Props, guys and gals of the editing world. I'll probably get one of you to help me with this, next time.

www.ingramcontent.com/pod-product-compliance
Lightning Source LLC
Chambersburg PA
CBHW020606040726
47498CB00003B/658